PENGUIN

THE SPOILS OF POYNTON

Henry James was born in 1843 in Washington Place, New York, of Scottish and Irish ancestry. His father was a prominent theologian and philosopher, and his elder brother, William, was also famous as a philosopher. He attended schools in New York and later in London, Paris and Geneva, entering the Law School at Harvard in 1862. In 1865 he began to contribute reviews and short stories to American journals. In 1875, after two prior visits to Europe, he settled for a year in Paris, where he met Flaubert, Turgenev and other literary figures. However, the next year he moved to London, where he became such an inveterate diner-out that in the winter of 1878–9 he confessed to accepting 140 invitations. In 1898 he left London and went to live at Lamb House, Rye, Sussex. Henry James became naturalized in 1915, was awarded the O.M., and died in 1916.

In addition to many short stories, plays, books of criticism, autobiography and travel he wrote some twenty novels, the first published being *Roderick Hudson* (1875). They include *The Europeans, Washington Square, The Portrait of a Lady, The Bostonians, The Princess Casamassima, The Tragic Muse, The Spoils of Poynton, The Awkward Age, The Wings of the Dove, The Ambassadors* and *The Golden Bowl*.

David Lodge is Honorary Professor of Modern English Literature at the University of Birmingham, where he taught from 1960 to 1987. In 1964–5 he held a Harkness Commonwealth Fellowship to the United States and in 1969 he was Visiting Associate Professor at the University of California. He has lectured and addressed conferences in many other countries. David Lodge is married with three children. His novels include *The Picturegoers, Ginger, You're Barmy, The British Museum Is Falling Down, Out of the Shelter* and *How Far Can You Go?*, which won the Whitbread Book of the Year Award for 1980, and *Small World*, the sequel to *Changing Places*, which was shortlisted for the Booker Prize in 1984. He has also written four books of literary criticism, *Language of Fiction* (1966), *The Novelist at the Crossroads* (1971), *The Modes of Modern Writing* (1977) and *Working with Structuralism* (1981) and a collection of occasional essays, *Write On* (1986).

Patricia Crick, one-time Scholar of Girton College, Cambridge, is currently Head of Modern Languages at Long Road Sixth Form College, Cambridge.

General Editor for the works of Henry James in the Penguin Classics: Geoffrey Moore.

HENRY JAMES

❊

THE
SPOILS OF POYNTON

❧❧❧❧❧❧❧❧❧❧❧❧❧❧❧❧❧❧

EDITED WITH AN INTRODUCTION
BY DAVID LODGE
AND NOTES BY PATRICIA CRICK

PENGUIN BOOKS

PENGUIN BOOKS

Published by the Penguin Group
27 Wrights Lane, London W8 5TZ, England
Viking Penguin Inc., 40 West 23rd Street, New York, New York 10010, USA
Penguin Books Australia Ltd, Ringwood, Victoria, Australia
Penguin Books Canada Ltd, 2801 John Street, Markham, Ontario, Canada L3R 1B4
Penguin Books (NZ) Ltd, 182–190 Wairau Road, Auckland 10, New Zealand

Penguin Books Ltd, Registered Offices: Harmondsworth, Middlesex, England

First published 1897
New York Edition published 1908
Published in Penguin Books 1963
Reprinted in Penguin Classics 1987
3 5 7 9 10 8 6 4

Introduction copyright © David Lodge, 1987
Notes copyright © Patricia Crick, 1987
Extracts from *The Notebooks of Henry James* copyright 1947 by Oxford University Press
All rights reserved

Filmset in Linotron 202 Bembo

Typeset, printed and bound in Great Britain by
BPCC Hazell Books
Aylesbury, Bucks, England
Member of BPCC Ltd.

CONTENTS

❀

INTRODUCTION

꙰

The Spoils of Poynton, first published in 1897, occupies a uniquely interesting place in the long history of Henry James's literary career. It was the first substantial piece of fiction that he wrote after the collapse of his ambitions to find fame and fortune as a playwright, and the first to be written in what has come to be known as his 'later' manner. These two facts are connected.

In 1890 James was commissioned to adapt his early novel *The American* (1877) for the stage. It had a qualified success, and the experience encouraged him to try writing original plays. His career as a novelist was in the doldrums. The reception of his last two major works, *The Princess Casamassima* (1886) and *The Tragic Muse* (1890), had been disappointing, both critically and commercially. He was worried and piqued by the small financial reward he derived from his books. He saw in the theatre the chance to make a lot of money in a short space of time, enough to ensure 'real freedom for one's general artistic life'.[1] He accordingly wrote three comedies in the next few years, none of which managed to find a producer. All his hopes now hung upon the success of *Guy Domville*, a costume drama set in eighteenth-century England about a young Catholic gentleman who is torn between his vocation to become a priest and a felt obligation, on the sudden death of his elder brother, to marry and ensure the continuation of the family. A popular actor-manager, George Alexander, accepted the play for production at the St James's theatre in London early in 1895.

The story of the first night of *Guy Domville*, superbly narrated by Leon Edel in his *Life of Henry James*,[2] is itself as full of suspense, pathos, comedy and irony as any novel. Among the newspaper critics present, at that time unknown to each other and to James, were three men shortly destined to become the most celebrated writers of the age – George Bernard Shaw, Arnold Bennett and H. G. Wells. They appreciated James's intelligent dialogue, as did most of the stalls, well packed with James's friends and admirers of his fiction. The gallery, however, was impatient with the play's clumsy stagecraft and began to barrack the production in its later stages. James himself, unable to bear the strain of sitting through the performance, had spent the evening watching Oscar Wilde's highly successful *An Ideal Husband*. With the applause for this play still ringing in his ears, James walked the short distance to the St James's theatre, arriving in the wings just as Alexander was taking his bow. The actor-manager, either foolishly or mischievously, led James onto the stage, where this most sensitive and dignified of writers was roundly booed by the gallery.

Guy Domville was a flop and had to be hurriedly replaced (ironically enough by Wilde's *The Importance of Being Earnest*), but it was the personal humiliation of the first night that determined James to abandon his theatrical ambitions. It was one of the darkest episodes of his literary life. Yet he was able to turn this apparent failure to positive account. He returned to writing fiction with a confirmed sense that this was his true *métier*, but he began to develop a new kind of narrative method that owed much to his experiments with drama – first in short novels such as *The Spoils of Poynton* and *What Maisie Knew* (1897), and eventually in the three great masterpieces of his mature years, *The Wings of the Dove* (1902), *The Ambassadors* (1903) and *The Golden Bowl* (1904).

On superficial inspection the later novels of Henry James seem anything but theatrical. They are much concerned with consciousness, with representing mental acts of perception, speculation and inference; and usually the story is conveyed to us through the consciousness of a single character whose understanding of the actions and motives of the others is necessarily limited and often unreliable. These are effects that are very difficult to achieve in the theatre, except by the comparatively clumsy conventions of the soliloquy and the aside.

What Henry James's later work owes to drama is essentially structural, what he himself referred to as 'the scenic method'. The story is unfolded in a series of scenes or dramatic encounters between the main characters, in which the issues of the plot are discussed or alluded to in dialogue. The import of what is said is often obscure or problematical, and the effort of interpreting it is depicted in the consciousness of the central or focalizing character, rendered in prose of great complexity and delicacy of nuance. Many of these scenes give the illusion of 'real time', like scenes in a naturalistic play. Examples in *The Spoils of Poynton* would be Fleda's meeting with Owen at Ricks in Chapter VIII, and her subsequent discussions with Mrs Gereth in Chapters X and XI. There is another kind of scene in which there is more physical movement through space and a more overt condensation of real time, in which speech is more often reported than quoted. Examples would be the opening chapter at Waterbath, and Owen's meeting with and escorting of Fleda in London in Chapter VI. Both kinds of scene may be linked by passages of introspection by the focalizing character (the whole of Chapter IX is an example) or narrative passages that summarize the actions – or inaction – of the principal characters between their important confrontations (for example Chapter V).

This method constitutes a considerable modification of the form of the classic nineteenth-century novel on which James's earlier fiction was modelled. Instead of an even balance between 'telling' and 'showing', between expansive authorial description and commentary on the one hand, and the dramatic interaction of characters on the other, the balance has shifted radically in favour of 'showing'. The authorial voice rarely intrudes, and when it does its comments are ambiguous. Instead of being given a detailed visual description of the physical setting of the action and appearance of the characters, we get only the *impressions* of the focalizing character. (Fleda's enraptured introduction to Poynton at the beginning of Chapter III is a good example – there is not a single reference to a specific object.) One consequence of this narrative method is that the interpretative effort required of the reader becomes equivalent to that required of the central character. To James it represented an enormous gain in intensity and economy of effect, very different from the 'loose baggy monsters' of classic nineteenth-century fiction, from Balzac to George Eliot; and it was a gain he attributed to his experience of writing plays. 'When I ask myself what there may have been to show for my long tribulation, my wasted years and patiences and pangs, of theatrical experiment,' James wrote in his notebook at the time of writing *The Spoils of Poynton*, 'the answer comes up as just possibly *this*: what I have gathered from it will perhaps have been exactly some such mastery of fundamental statement – of the art and secret of it, of expression, of the sacred mystery of structure.'[3]

Another distinction of *The Spoils of Poynton* is that James left a more detailed account of its genesis and composition in his notebooks than of any other of his novels. This, as I shall suggest later, is a double-edged tool for interpreting the story, but, supplemented by the Preface James wrote for the New York Edition of 1908, the notebook entries afford an unequalled insight into the laboratory of the writer's mind. (They are included as an appendix to this edition.)

The original 'germ' of the story came to James, as so often, in the form of an anecdote related at a dinner party, in 1893. It concerned a legal dispute between a Scottish widow and her son about the possession of the family house, which was full of 'valuable things' collected by the former. According to James's informant, the mother was prepared to deny her son's legitimacy to win her case, a melodramatic twist which James characteristically eschewed, along with other particulars, in his own working out of the situation. ('Clumsy Life at her stupid work,' as he disdainfully observes in the Preface.)

The potential story James saw in the anecdote was about the effect of aesthetic taste on personal relationships, arising from the injury to the mother's pride and possessiveness at being forced to relinquish the house she has made into a thing of beauty to a son who is not only indifferent to her connoisseurship, but who chooses an equally Philistine wife, instead of the discriminating protégée the mother had intended for him. According to the Preface, James at first thought of the contents of the house themselves, the 'things', as being the centre of the story, but quickly realized that this would not do. The things were in themselves inarticulate, and to render them with the lavish descriptive detail of a Balzac would take up far too much space for what he then conceived of as a short story, and (more significantly) would work against the interests of 'the muse of dialogue'. Hence the 'growth and predominance of Fleda Vetch' as 'a centre' for the tale, a process which we can trace through its various stages in the notebook entries from May 1895 when, a few months after the débâcle of *Guy Domville*, he commenced work on the story.

From the beginning James saw the mainspring of the narrative as the mother's removal of the 'things' from the house. Originally this was to have happened after the son's marriage, and Fleda was to have assisted in their restoration out of wholly altruistic motives. When the plot was revised so that Mrs Gereth made a pre-emptive strike, removing the things *before* the marriage, the question of their restoration became entangled with the question of Fleda's personal destiny, especially when James, rather to his own surprise, made Owen fall in love with her while engaged to Mona Brigstock. For Fleda the dispute between mother and son becomes morally complex because she stands to gain or lose by what she does or does not do in relation to it. The overarching narrative question of the text becomes, not what will happen to the things, but will Fleda come to possess them, along with her Prince Charming? For, like many other great English novels, from *Pamela* to *Mansfield Park* and *Jane Eyre*, *The Spoils of Poynton* is a variation on the Cinderella myth, albeit an ironic one. The crucial interpretative question is: at whom, or at what, is the irony directed?

Most of the critics who have commented on *The Spoils of Poynton* fall into two groups. Either they take Fleda to be the heroine of the story in the traditional sense – heroic in her readiness to sacrifice her own happiness rather than compromise her principles, sensitive and perceptive in her dealings with the other characters, to whom she is morally superior; or they have taken her to be neurotic and self-deceiving, pathologically fearful of sex, and contributing more harm than balm to the domestic row between the Gereths. According to the editors of the Notebooks, F. O. Matthiessen and Kenneth B. Murdock, Fleda is 'one of James's most extreme embodiments of imagination, taste and renouncing sensibility'.[4] Wayne Booth says she comes 'close to representing the author's ideal of taste, judgement and moral sense'.[5] Philip L. Greene asserts: 'James produces in Fleda Vetch a reliable reflector of his values. She is the renouncing sensibility who is capable of love.'[6] According to Nina Baym, on the other hand, Fleda is 'a stumbling bungler'.[7] According to William Bysshe Stein, 'She sacrifices her love for moral mummery' and 'her hypocritical respectability converts social behaviour into a game that is a comic perversion of life.'[8] John Lucas claims that 'Fleda invents most of her experience and in particular she invents Owen's love for her'.[9] This is only a sample of the contradictory opinions to be found in the criticism of *The Spoils of Poynton* (which has followed a very similar course to that of *The Turn of the Screw*, for similar reasons).

Both schools of thought can muster plausible arguments for their respective readings of the tale, and the impossibility of choosing between them has led some critics to conclude that here is something deeply unsatisfactory about the work. 'If there is a line in good literature between complexity and self-contradiction,' says A. W. Bellringer, 'the possibility is that James's treatment of his material has overstepped that line,' and he cites the similar opinions of F. R. Leavis and Ivor Winters.[10] A number of recent critics, however, without discussing *The Spoils of Poynton* in detail, have in various ways suggested that James's later fiction constantly aspired to the condition of ambiguity – that the impossibility of arriving at a single, simple version of the 'truth' about any human action or experience is, in the broadest sense, what that fiction is about.[11] I shall argue that this is the appropriate perspective in which to read *The Spoils of Poynton*. What Fleda says to Mrs Gereth – 'You simplify far too much . . . The tangle of life is much more intricate than you've ever, I think, felt it to be' (p. 186) – could be turned against many critics of the novel. It is, however, instructive to consider the arguments that have divided them.

What one might call the pro-Fleda party relies heavily on James's own remarks in the Preface and Notebooks. (The controversy is therefore a classic instance of a general theoretical question about the bearing of authorial intention on interpretation.[12]) It seems clear that James intended his readers to admire and identify with Fleda. 'Fleda becomes rather fine, DOES something, distinguishes herself (to the reader),' he writes in the notebook (p. 223). In the Preface, justifying his choice of Fleda as the story's centre of consciousness, he describes her as a 'free spirit' surrounded by 'fools' (p. 31).

The anti-Fleda party are likely to be anti-intentionalists, arguing that whatever James thought he was going to write beforehand, or thought he had written afterwards (many years afterwards in the case of the Preface), is irrelevant to the interpretation of what he did write. In the Notebook scenario for instance, Fleda was to have demonstrated her heroism by sending Owen away from

Ricks with a firm recommendation that he should marry Mona immediately. She makes no such declaration in the text. Indeed, the Fleda of the text is generally notable for what she does not do, rather than for what she does. (Matthiessen and Murdock note how many positive actions in the scenario were finally treated negatively.[13]) Fleda vacillates, hesitates, and delays rather than acts. Chapter IV concludes:

She dodged and dreamed and fabled and trifled away the time. Instead of inventing a remedy or a compromise, instead of preparing a plan by which a scandal might be averted, she gave herself, in her sacred solitude, up to a mere fairy-tale, up to the very taste of the beautiful peace she would have scattered on the air if only something might have been that could never have been. [p. 62]

This is less damaging to Fleda if we read it as rendering a self-accusation rather than as an authorial judgement, but it does seem to hold her partly responsible for the family 'war' that follows.

As to the Preface, James's tributes to Fleda are in fact always equivocal, giving with one hand and taking away with the other. 'Fleda almost demoniacally both sees and feels, while the others but feel without seeing' (p. 31). This assertion of Fleda's superior sensibility is qualified by an adverb that suggests all the hysteria and capacity for mischief unsympathetic readers have attributed to her. Such readers are however unable, or unwilling, to entertain both terms of the paradox; and in seeking to establish that Fleda is a deeply flawed character whose exposure is the whole point of the novel they usually overstate the case and make assumptions and inferences quite unwarranted by the text.

Central to this reading is the claim that Fleda is neurotic about sex, though the precise diagnosis of her condition varies. Either she wants Owen as a husband only as a means of bettering herself, or she desires him sexually but is guilty about her desire and represses it, or she doesn't really want a heterosexual relationship but a lesbian or mother-daughter one with Mrs Gereth. There is some evidence for all of these interpretations (and some counter-evidence, as we shall see). In the first chapter Fleda is shown as rather priggishly disapproving of Owen's 'romping' with Mona, and Mona's physical charms and putative 'permissions' figure prominently in Fleda's thoughts. She herself allows Owen only one embrace, and is most characteristically seen as running away from him or shutting doors in his face whenever he shows signs of becoming amorous. She is however constantly kissing or being kissed by Mrs Gereth.

Because of its subjective method of representing experience, the later fiction of Henry James lends itself to psychoanalytical interpretation. Whether Owen's umbrella and the Maltese cross are phallic symbols; whether, as Arnold Edelstein has ingeniously argued,[14] Fleda is arrested at the anal stage of personal development, seeking a mother-substitute in Mrs Gereth, but forfeiting her regard because she 'holds on' (to her modesty) when Mrs Gereth urges her to 'let herself go', and lets go of Owen when Mrs Gereth wishes her to hold on – these are interpretations which it is impossible absolutely to prove or falsify, and their persuasiveness will depend ultimately on the credence the reader gives to the Freudian discourse itself. But there are limits to interpretative licence. When William Bysshe Stein,[15] for instance, bids us note Fleda's 'insidious conversion of [Owen's] quick speech into an erotic association' in her reflection that 'It was usually as desperate as a "rush" at some violent game', we must protest that there is nothing erotic about a game like football or rugby which is obviously being alluded to here, one of a string of sporting motifs associated with Owen.

Fleda is certainly sexually inexperienced, and this contributes to the difficulties in which she finds herself. She lacks confidence in her physical attractiveness, and is disturbed by Mrs Gereth's hints that she should use it to captivate Owen. Her one embrace with Owen is, however, passionate, and rendered with an orgasmic lyricism rare in James's writing (p. 161). Defending herself later against Mrs Gereth's accusation that she has lost Owen by her scruples and her reserve, she says: 'I don't know what girls may do; but if he doesn't know that there isn't an inch of me that isn't his – !' (p. 181). The conjunction of Fleda's confession of sexual inexperience with the assertion of her passion is significant. James was intensely and sympathetically interested in the plight of the genteel young woman or adolescent girl in late-Victorian society who, brought up largely in ignorance of the sexual life, has to make her way in a knowing and corrupt adult world. He returned to this theme again and again – sometimes combined with the 'international theme', as in *Daisy Miller* and *The Portrait of a Lady*, sometimes more directly as in *What Maisie Knew* and *The Awkward Age* – often increasing the vulnerability of the heroine by making her motherless, like Fleda Vetch. Critics who regard Fleda as neurotic are apt to be judging her in the light of modern sexual mores.

Her defenders often cite the speech just quoted as evidence that, within the limits of her experience, she is capable of genuine passion. But when we look at those words in context we find that their import, typically, is qualified by a suggestion of calculation on Fleda's part:

'I don't know what girls may do; but if he doesn't know that there isn't an inch of me that isn't his – !' Fleda sighed as if she couldn't express it; she piled it up, as she would have said; holding Mrs Gereth with dilated eyes she seemed to sound her for the effect of these professions.

There is a small but significant deviation in the narrative discourse, here, from Fleda's 'point of view', which frames the story after the first chapter. We glimpse Fleda momentarily from some impersonal vantage-point, with her dilated eyes anxiously calculating whether Mrs Gereth is convinced. She is not. Fleda feels 'more and more in her companion's attitude a quality that treated her speech as a desperate rigmarole and even perhaps a piece of cold immodesty' (p. 181). There is a poignant irony in that final phrase, since Mrs Gereth has frequently appeared in relation to Fleda as a kind of bawd or female pander. Fleda's aposiopesis (i.e. a sentence left incomplete for rhetorical effect) echoes another in Mrs Gereth's speech a few pages before:

'When once I get you [and Owen] abroad together – !' Mrs Gereth checked herself as if from excess of meaning; what might happen when she should get them abroad together was to be gathered only from the way she slowly rubbed her hands. [p. 173]

The 'sounding' of other people's unspoken thoughts by observation of their body language, facial expressions, or oblique hints and allusions in speech, is a characteristic activity of Fleda Vetch, as of most Jamesian protagonists. It is how she first becomes aware that Owen is attracted to her – in Chapter VI when, on meeting her in Oxford Street, he insists on escorting her on her shopping expedition and back across the Park to Kensington.

He wanted to stay with her – he wanted not to leave her: he had dropped into complete silence, but that was what his silence said. [p. 76]

Is it? At this point the reader has no way of knowing. It could be wishful thinking, since we already know that Fleda has indulged in a fantasy of winning Owen's love. The same question is raised, even more acutely, in Chapter VIII when, towards the end of Owen's interview with Fleda at Ricks, he shuts the door which she has opened to let him out of the drawing room.

He had done this before she could stop him, and he stood there with his hand on the knob and smiled at her strangely. Clearer than he could have spoken it was the sense of those seconds of silence.

'When I got into this I didn't know you, and now that I know you how can I tell you the difference? And *she's* so different, so ugly and vulgar, in the light of this squabble. No, like *you* I've never known one. It's another thing, it's a new thing altogether. Listen to me a little: can't something be done?' [p. 99]

It is easy to assume that because they appear in quotation marks these words are actually spoken by Owen. Even as careful a reader as Bernard Richards seems to make this mistake, describing the italicized '*she*' as:

a typical Jamesian device: the unspecified pronoun. It is quite probable that Owen is referring to his mother, but readers who want a romance between Owen and Fleda will assume that he has Mona in mind.[16]

In fact these words are Fleda's verbalization of what she thinks, or would like to think, Owen's silence means, and it is the truth of her interpretation, not the reference of the pronoun, that is doubtful (Fleda is obviously interested in how Owen compares herself to Mona). That Owen himself has not spoken is confirmed as the passage continues:

It was what had been in the air in those moments at Kensington, and it only wanted words to be a committed act. The more reason, to the girl's excited mind, why it shouldn't have words . . . [p. 99]

Critics who would have us believe that Owen's attraction to Fleda is a complete fabrication of her 'excited mind' have, however, some difficulty in explaining away his declaration and proposal of marriage in Chapter XVI. According to Robert C.

McLean, Owen is deceiving Fleda in order to get the spoils back.[17] This theory requires us to believe that, had Fleda accepted his suit, Owen, with the collusion of the Brigstocks, would have broken off his engagement to Mona, and engaged himself to Fleda, for just so long as it took his mother to return the spoils to Poynton, and then reversed the process, with all the scandal and dishonour to himself that would entail. This seems improbable, to say the least, and inconsistent with McLean's own judgement that Owen is 'the most humane figure in the book'.[18]

But if Owen's declaration of love for Fleda is not a callous trick, why does he marry Mona after all? Fleda suggests that he recognized where his duty lay, but her words sound more like a self-justification: 'That he has done it, that he couldn't *not* do it, shows how right I was' (p. 196). Mrs Gereth has a coarser explanation: taking advantage of Fleda's foolish scruples, Mona compromised Owen into marrying her by seducing him (p. 197). This theory is somewhat undermined, however, when her confident assertion that Owen 'hates' Mona for this ploy and will not cohabit with her, is falsified, as she herself later admits (pp. 206–7).

Owen's motivation remains an enigma till the end, but the most likely explanation is that he is a weak and, in personal relations, cowardly man. Mrs Gereth calls him 'disgustingly weak' (p. 186) and Fleda accepts the verdict, adding only that 'it's because he's weak that he needs me' (p. 186). This has been Fleda's attitude to Owen from her very first encounter with him, when he strikes her as being 'absolutely beautiful and delightfully dense . . . She herself was prepared, if she should ever marry, to contribute all the cleverness, and she liked to figure it out that her husband would be a force grateful for direction' (p. 40). Such, apparently, has also been the nature of the marriage between Mrs Gereth and her late husband (see p. 186), and such, we may guess, will be the marriage of Mona and Owen. One of the many ironies of *The Spoils of Poynton* is the spectacle of three, in their different ways, strong-willed women fighting for the allegiance of a decidedly weak man.

The mystery of Owen's motivation is sealed by the wonderfully ambiguous conclusion to his letter asking Fleda to choose some treasure from Poynton as a gift: 'You won't refuse if you'll simply think a little what it must be that makes me ask' (p. 209). It is an epitome of the whole book, and Fleda enacts in relation to it our own experience of reading the book:

Fleda read that last sentence over more times even than the rest: she was baffled – she couldn't think at all of what in particular made him ask. This was indeed because it might be one of so many things.

Reviewing the critical discussion of *The Spoils of Poynton* reveals the difficulties and dangers of reading this text with the aim of wresting from it a single answer to the questions it raises. It is possible to make a plausible case for almost any answer by selective quotation, but as soon as we return to the text itself we find that nearly every speech or action is capable of a double interpretation, and that every hint is balanced by a counter-suggestion. At the heart of the story is the ambiguity of Fleda's character and conduct. Does it arise from authentic conflict or neurotic contradiction? Is her anxiety to protect her 'secret' (i.e., that she loves Owen) reasonable and honourable (given that he is engaged to another woman) or obsessive and perverse (given that she has reason to think he loves her and is disillusioned in the other woman)? Is her refusal to take any of the several opportunities she has to attach Owen to herself and detach him from Mona indicative of high moral principle and selflessness, or of moral egotism and sexual neurosis? Is her sudden change of mind in Chapter XVIII, when she declares herself ready to 'go to the Registry Office' and takes steps to recall Owen, an example of moral pragmatism, responding to Mrs Gereth's changed status as the 'victim' of the situation,[19] or is it typical of her confused and illogical mind that she acts when it is too late to have any effect? To read the text carefully is to be swayed back and forth between these alternatives, without ever finding a conclusive answer.

Some deep imaginative fascination with symmetrically opposed ideas has left its mark on every level of the text. Rhetorical figures of parallelism and antithesis abound, for example:

If he didn't dislike Mona what was the matter with him? And if he did, Fleda asked, what was the matter with her own silly self? [p. 105]

If her friend should really keep the spoils she would never return to her.

If that friend should on the other hand part with them what on earth would there be to return to? [p. 132]

'Where is . . . your freedom? . . . If it's real there's plenty of time, and if it isn't there's more than enough.' [p. 162]

'If he's at Waterbath he doesn't care for you. If he cares for you he's not at Waterbath.' [p. 186]

This last is a good example of the figure of chiasmus (repetition of words or phrases in reverse order) which Ralf Norrman has plausibly argued is the key to James's imagination.[20] The plot of *The Spoils of Poynton* exhibits the same pattern in the movement of the spoils themselves: present at Poynton – absent from Poynton – present at Ricks: absent from Ricks – present at Poynton – absent from Poynton. This brings us to the ending of the story, which is as ambiguous as everything else about it.

Fleda eagerly accepts Owen's offer of a souvenir from Poynton:

The passion for which what had happened had made no difference, the passion that had taken this into account before as well as after, found here an issue that there was nothing whatever to choke. [p. 209]

The passage is typically complex and allusive, but evidently means that Fleda, who still loves Owen, in spite of his marriage, a contingency she had always taken into account, sees no reason why she should not find some relief or satisfaction of her feelings by accepting a precious gift from Poynton. When she goes to the house, in a state of high excitement, to make her choice (she inclines to the Maltese cross), she finds that Poynton and all its contents have been destroyed by fire, a disaster that is attributed by the station-master partly to the carelessness of the servants left in charge by the absent Owen and Mona.

Mixed with the horror, with the kindness of the station-master, with the smell of cinders and the riot of sound was the raw bitterness of a hope that she might never again in life have to give up so much at such short notice. [p. 213]

This conclusion can be and has been interpreted in a number of different ways: as vindicating Mrs Gereth by showing that Owen and Mona are unworthy custodians of Poynton; as implying that

Fleda is responsible for the disaster because she could have been mistress of Poynton; as punishing Fleda for her pride and folly by denying her the much-desired present; as vindicating Fleda's refusal to compromise her moral principles for the sake of worldly goods; as impressing Fleda with a final, painful awareness of the meaning of renunciation; as a judgement on all the chief characters for their egotistical obsession with the 'things'.

It is important to realize that the latter are not major works of art, but what are usually called 'antiques'. Discussing the original germ of the story in the Preface, James observes:

One thing was 'in it' . . . on the first blush . . . the sharp light it might project on that most modern of our current passions, the fierce appetite for the upholsterer's and joiner's and brazier's work, the chairs and tables, the cabinets and presses, the material odds and ends, of the more labouring ages. [p. 26]

Although this theme was overlaid, in the development of the story, by a concern with character, it never disappeared entirely, and the terms in which James describes it here are extremely interesting. His use of the epithet 'labouring' suggests a quasi-Marxist explanation of the modern cult of antiques, while his references to 'passion' and 'fierce appetite' hint at a Freudian diagnosis.

The cult probably had its origin in the aesthetic nostalgia of the Romantic Revival. Later in the nineteenth century, the Pre-Raphaelite Movement, art historians like Ruskin, aesthetes like Pater and Wilde, and the Arts and Crafts Movement led by William Morris, all contributed to a growing enthusiasm among people with claims to good taste for domestic artefacts of pre-industrial design or manufacture. By the time James was writing *The Spoils of Poynton*, as Bernard Richards observes,[21] magazines were springing up to cater for the new passion for collecting (*The Studio* in 1893, *The Connoisseur* in 1901, for instance).

The overt justification for collecting antiques is that the artefacts of the past are aesthetically superior to those of the present. But James's description of the past as 'the more labouring ages' implies another explanation: the value of the antique is a function of the difference between pre- and post-industrial methods of production. As industrial techniques of mass-production made domestic furnishings and ornaments cheaply and plentifully available, the upper-classes could only demonstrate their superior status in this sphere in one of two ways – either by conspicuous consumption of the products of the new technology, or by collecting the artefacts of pre-industrial times and, preferably, foreign countries. Waterbath epitomizes the first way, and Poynton the second. That the former is the object of irony in *The Spoils of Poynton* hardly needs to be stated: some of its funniest pages concern the vulgarity of Waterbath and its inhabitants. But it is a vulgarity perceived by Mrs Gereth and Fleda Vetch, and if we identify too uncritically with their attitude we miss the more subtle irony directed at Poynton and the cult of its 'things'.

The cult of antiques might be described as a special case of what Marxist theory calls 'commodity fetishism' and 'reification'. Commodity fetishism is the tendency of commodities to conceal the social nature of their production behind their exchange value, and reification (literally, 'making into a thing') is the false consciousness that allows this to happen by treating economic laws and institutions as if they are absolute and unchangeable.[22] By surrounding themselves with commodities produced in the pre-industrial past, that have acquired the status of art, the Mrs Gereths of this world can suppress the knowledge that they inhabit a capitalist society based on the exploitation of labour; and their obsessive collecting is a kind of inverted reification, treating 'things' as absolute and irreplaceable.

'Fetishism' also has a meaning in Freudian discourse which seems relevant, namely, the displacement of erotic desire on to some non-sexual part of the human body (for example, the foot) or inanimate object (for example, clothing). *The Spoils of Poynton* is a story of erotic desire displaced on to 'things'. All the energy of Mrs Gereth's marriage went into collecting 'things'. Mona is ineligible as a mate for Owen, in his mother's view, because she does not appreciate the 'things', yet she covets them enough to make their possession a condition of her marriage. Fleda is made available to Owen as an alternative partner only by virtue of sharing Mrs Gereth's taste, and reflects that, if she had been in a position to actually marry Owen, 'she might, should she have wished to keep her secret, have found it possible to pass off the motive of her conduct as a mere passion for his property' (p. 58). 'Passion' is a floating signifier in *The Spoils of Poynton*, attaching itself now to sexuality, now to decor, and trailing with it connotations of religious ecstasy and suffering. As noted above, Fleda's 'passion' seeks its final outlet in the acquisition of one of the 'things' at Poynton, and if we see the Maltese cross as symbolically phallic rather than sacrificial, we may accuse Fleda of sexual fetishism too.

The word 'fetish' literally denotes an object invested with magic or supernatural properties in primitive religion, and when we say colloquially that somebody 'makes a fetish' of something, we mean they attribute an exaggerated or irrational importance to it. The religious imagery associated with the beauty of Poynton is characteristically ambiguous in import, but there are frequent suggestions that Mrs Gereth's obsession has warped her human nature. Fleda, for instance, early on recognizes

the poor lady's strange, almost maniacal disposition to thrust in everywhere the question of 'things,' to read all behaviour in the light of some fancied relation to them. 'Things' were of course the sum of the world; only, for Mrs. Gereth, the sum of the world was rare French furniture and oriental china. [p. 49]

It is a measure of Fleda's moral superiority that she can take no pleasure in the things when they are illicitly removed to Ricks: 'there was a wrong about them all that turned them to ugliness' (p. 85). They become 'a torment of taste' (p. 86).

James originally thought of calling his tale 'The House Beautiful', the Paterian title of a lecture Oscar Wilde was trailing around the country in 1893.[23] When it was serialized in the *Atlantic Monthly* he called it *The Old Things*, and finally settled on *The Spoils of Poynton* for the first book publication. The shift from a metonymic to a metaphoric title suggests a wish to moralize the theme. The 'things' are 'spoils' in a multiple sense: they are booty brought back by Mrs Gereth from her Continental travels, they are the cause of a war between the principal characters to possess them (imagery of battle is persistent) and they are finally 'spoiled' by the fire.

This conclusion to the tale must carry some implication of *vanitas vanitatum*. 'Vanity of vanities, all is vanity. What profit hath a man of all his labours which he taketh under the sun?' asks the preacher in *Ecclesiastes*. Mrs Gereth, whose marriage had seemed to her 'a long sunny harvest of taste and curiosity' (p. 41), comes to acknowledge the force of this question. In that remarkable scene in

Chapter XVIII, when she faces the prospect of losing the 'war', she reproaches herself for having adopted Fleda as her protégée in these terms: 'It was your clever sympathy that did it – your beautiful feeling for those accursed vanities' (p. 185). To Fleda, Mrs Gereth in final defeat seems to 'represent the final vanity of everything' (p. 196). Yet Fleda herself, a page or two earlier, consoles herself, in the ominous silence and absence of Owen, by imagining the restoration of the spoils to Poynton in rapturous religious language:

It was really her obliterated passion that had revived, and with it an immense assent to Mrs Gereth's early judgment of her. She equally, she felt, was of the religion, and like any other of the passionately pious she could worship now even in the desert. Yes, it was all for *her*, far round as she had gone she had been strong enough: her love had gathered them in. . . . They were nobody's at all – too proud, unlike base animals and humans, to be reducible to anything so narrow. It was Poynton that was theirs; they had simply recovered their own. The joy of that for them was the source of the strange peace that had descended like a charm. [p. 194]

It is difficult to decide whether this flight of fancy is sublime or ridiculous – and whether its reversal in the last chapter is a spectacle of tragic suffering or poetic justice.

In the first edition of *The Spoils of Poynton* James frequently describes his characters as 'hesitating'. The text itself is continually hesitating between alternative meanings, and the attentive reader perforce must do the same. In the New York edition of 1908, S. P. Rosenbaum has noted, James substituted several variations for the verb 'hesitated': *gasped, wondered, debated, dropped, faltered, cast about, hung fire, hung back, took it so, rather floundered, thought again, waited for thought, had a pause, failed of presence of mind for a moment*, and *seemed for an instant to have to walk round it*. These verbs also apply well enough to the experience of reading *The Spoils of Poynton*.

NOTES

[Place of publication is London unless otherwise indicated.]
1. Leon Edel, *The Life of Henry James* (Harmondsworth, 1977), Vol 2, p. 15.
2. Ibid., pp. 137–52.
3. *The Notebooks of Henry James*, ed. F. O. Matthiessen and Kenneth B. Murdock (New York, 1961), p. 208.

4. Ibid., p. 138.

5. Wayne Booth, *The Rhetoric of Fiction* (1961), p. 159.

6. Philip L. Greene, 'Point of view in *The Spoils of Poynton*', *Nineteenth-Century Fiction*, 21 (1967), p. 368.

7. Nina Baym, 'Fleda Vetch and the plot of *The Spoils of Poynton*', *PMLA*, 84 (1969), p. 106.

8. William Bysshe Stein, 'The method at the heart of madness: *The Spoils of Poynton*', *Modern Fiction Studies*, 14 (1968), pp. 198 and 202.

9. John Lucas, '*The Spoils of Poynton*: James's intended uninvolvement', *Essays in Criticism*, 16 (1966), p. 482. (A reply to the article by Bellringer cited in the next note.)

10. A. W. Bellringer, '*The Spoils of Poynton*: James's unintended involvement', *Essays in Criticism*, 16 (1966), p. 185.

11. Tzvetan Todorov, 'The Secret of Narrative', in *The Poetics of Prose* (Oxford, 1971), pp. 143–78; Ralf Norrman, *Techniques of Ambiguity in the Fiction of Henry James* (Abo, Finland, 1977) and *The Insecure World of Henry James's Fiction* (1982); Shlomith Rimmon, *The Concept of Ambiguity: the Case of Henry James* (1977); Christine Brooke-Rose, *A Rhetoric of The Unreal* (Chaps. 6–8) (Cambridge, 1981).

12. See 'The intentional fallacy', in *The Verbal Icon* by W. K. Wimsatt and Monroe C. Beardsley (Lexington, Ky., 1954).

13. Matthiessen and Murdock, *op. cit.*, p. 251.

14. Arnold Edelstein, 'The tangle of life: levels of meaning in *The Spoils of Poynton*', *Hartford Studies in Literature*, 2 (1970), pp. 133–50.

15. Stein, *op. cit.*, p. 193.

16. *The Spoils of Poynton*, ed. Bernard Richards (1982), p. 189.

17. Robert C. McLean, 'The subjective adventure of Fleda Vetch', in *Henry James: Modern Judgements*, ed. Tony Tanner (1968), pp. 204–21.

18. Ibid., p. 220.

19. The suggestion of C. B. Cox (*The Free Spirit* (1963), pp. 52–3) who cites Henry James's endorsement of the pragmatic philosophy of his brother William.

20. Norrman, *The Insecure World of Henry James's Fiction* (1982).

21. Richards, *op. cit.*, p.185.

22. See the relevant articles in *A Dictionary of Political Thought* by Roger Scruton (1982).

23. In the Postscript to his book *Appreciations* (1889), Walter Pater referred to 'that *House Beautiful* which the creative minds of all generations – the artists and those who have treated life in the spirit of art – are always building together, for the refreshment of the human spirit . . .'. I am indebted to Ian Small for this information.

A NOTE ON THE TEXT

The Spoils of Poynton was first published, in serial form, in the
Atlantic Monthly, from April to October 1896, under the title
The Old Things. It was first published in book form, entitled
The Spoils of Poynton, in February 1897, by Heinemann in
England and by Houghton, Mifflin in America. The text of
the serial version was extensively revised by James for book
publication, and there are slight variations between the English
and American first editions. James revised the text once more,
in 1908, for the 'New York' edition of his collected works,
published by Scribner's in America and by Macmillan in
England. For this volume, which included the stories *A London
Life* and *The Chaperon*, James wrote a Preface.

The evolution of the text of *The Spoils of Poynton* has been
carefully studied by S. P. Rosenbaum ('*The Spoils of Poynton*:
revisions and editions', *Studies in Bibliography*, 19 (1966), pp.
161–74), who calculates that 'nearly 3,400 changes are to be
found between the four texts', 1,500 of which were made for
the New York edition. Many of these are trivial and none of
them substantially affects the development of the narrative or
helps to resolve its ambiguities. Most are matters of emphasis
and nuance. In preparing the text for the New York edition,
for instance, James took the opportunity to add some additional
war imagery, and to change the word 'things' to 'spoils' in three
places. As indicated at the end of the Introduction, he also
indulged a taste for elegant variation which is a general characteristic of his later style. Some readers find the later style irritatingly
mannered, and regret James's revisions of his early work for
the New York edition. *The Spoils of Poynton*, however, inaugur-
ates the later period, and there is no discontinuity of style
between the 1897 and 1908 versions. Rosenbaum concludes that
there is 'no good bibliographical reason' for ignoring James's
final revisions. The text of this Penguin edition accordingly

follows the text of the New York edition with two exceptions: a garbled sentence in Chapter VII has been emended by reference to the 1897 version (see note 3 to p. 80); and on page 61, line 24, the 1897 reading, 'It was the furniture she wouldn't give up', has been preferred to the New York edition's 'It was the furniture he wouldn't give up'.

THE SPOILS OF POYNTON

PREFACE

IT was years ago, I remember, one Christmas Eve when I was dining with friends: a lady beside me made in the course of talk one of those allusions that I have always found myself recognising on the spot as 'germs.' The germ, wherever gathered, has ever been for me the germ of a 'story,' and most of the stories straining to shape under my hand have sprung from a single small seed, a seed as minute and wind-blown as that casual hint for *The Spoils of Poynton* dropped unwitting by my neighbour, a mere floating particle in the stream of talk. What above all comes back to me with this reminiscence is the sense of the inveterate minuteness, on such happy occasions, of the precious particle – reduced, that is, to its mere fruitful essence. Such is the interesting truth about the stray suggestion, the wandering word, the vague echo, at touch of which the novelist's imagination winces as at the prick of some sharp point:[1] its virtue is all in its needle-like quality, the power to penetrate as finely as possible. This fineness it is that communicates the virus[2] of suggestion, anything more than the minimum of which spoils the operation. If one is given a hint at all designedly one is sure to be given too much; one's subject is in the merest grain, the speck of truth, of beauty, of reality, scarce visible to the common eye – since, I firmly hold, a good eye for a subject is anything but usual. Strange and attaching, certainly, the consistency with which the first thing to be done for the communicated and seized idea is to reduce almost to nought the form, the air as of a mere disjoined and lacerated lump of life, in which we may have happened to meet it. Life being all inclusion and confusion, and art being all discrimination and selection, the latter, in search of the hard latent *value* with which alone it is concerned, sniffs round the mass as instinctively and unerringly as a dog suspicious of some buried bone. The difference here, however, is that, while the dog desires his bone but to destroy it, the artist finds in *his* tiny nugget, washed free of awkward accretions and hammered into a sacred hardness, the very stuff for a clear affirmation, the happiest chance for the indestructible. It at the same time amuses him again and again to note how, beyond the first step of the actual case, the case that constitutes for him his germ, his vital particle, his grain of gold, life persistently blunders and deviates, loses herself in the sand. The reason is of course that life has no direct sense whatever for the subject and is capable, luckily for us, of nothing but splendid waste. Hence the opportunity for the sublime economy of art, which rescues, which saves and hoards and 'banks,' investing and reinvesting these fruits of toil in wondrous useful 'works' and thus making up for us, desperate spendthrifts that we all naturally are, the most princely of incomes. It is the subtle secrets of that system, however, that are meanwhile the charming study, with an endless attraction, above all, in the question – endlessly baffling indeed – of the method at the heart of the madness; the madness, I mean, of a zeal, among the reflective sort, so disinterested. If life, presenting us the germ, and left merely to herself in such a business, gives the case away, almost always, before we can stop her, what are the signs for our guidance, what the primary laws for a saving selection, how do we know when and where to intervene, where do we place the beginnings of the wrong or the right deviation? Such would be the elements of an inquiry upon which, I hasten to say, it is quite forbidden me here to embark: I but glance at them in evidence of the rich pasture that at every turn surrounds the ruminant critic. The answer may be after all that mysteries here elude us, that general considerations fail or mislead, and that even the fondest of artists need ask no wider range than the logic of the particular case. The particular case, or in other words his relation to a given subject, once the relation is established, forms in itself a little world of exercise and agitation. Let him hold himself perhaps supremely fortunate if he can meet half the questions with which that air alone may swarm.

So it was, at any rate, that when my amiable friend, on the Christmas Eve, before the table that glowed safe and fair through the brown London night, spoke of such an odd matter as that a good lady in the north, always well looked on, was at daggers drawn with her only son, ever hitherto exemplary, over the ownership of the valuable furniture of a fine old house just accruing to the young man by his father's death, I instantly became aware with my 'sense for the subject,' of the prick of inoculation; the *whole* of the virus, as I have called it, being infused by that single touch. There had been but ten words, yet I had recognised in them, as in a flash, all the possibilities of the little drama of my *Spoils*, which glimmered then and there into life; so that when in the next breath I began to hear of action taken, on the beautiful ground, by our engaged adversaries, tipped each, from that instant, with the light of the highest distinction, I saw clumsy Life again at her stupid work. For the action taken, and on which my friend, as I knew she would, had already begun all complacently and benightedly further to report, I had absolutely, and could have, no scrap of use; one had been so perfectly qualified to say in advance, 'It's the perfect little workable thing, but she'll strangle it in the cradle, even while she pretends, all so cheeringly, to rock it; wherefore I'll stay her hand while yet there's time.' I didn't, of course, stay her hand – there never *is* in such cases 'time'; and I had once more the full demonstration of the fatal futility of Fact. The turn taken by the excellent situation – excellent, for development, if arrested in the right place, that is in the germ – had the full measure of the classic ineptitude; to which with the full measure of the artistic irony one could once more, and for the thousandth time, but take off one's hat. It was not, however, that this in the least mattered, once the seed had been transplanted to richer soil; and I dwell on that almost inveterate redundancy of the wrong, as opposed to the ideal right, in any free flowering of the actual, by reason only of its approach to calculable regularity.

If there was nothing regular meanwhile, nothing more so than the habit of vigilance, in my quickly feeling where interest would really lie, so I could none the less acknowledge afresh that these small private cheers of recognition made the spirit easy and the temper bland for the confused whole. I 'took' in fine, on the spot, to the rich bare little fact of the two related figures, embroiled perhaps all so sordidly; and for reasons of which I could most probably have given at the moment no decent account. Had I been asked why they were, in that stark nudity, to say nothing of that ugliness of attitude, 'interesting,' I fear I could have said nothing more to the point, even to my own questioning spirit, than 'Well, you'll see!' By which of course I should have meant 'Well, *I* shall see' – confident meanwhile (as against the appearance or the imputation of poor taste) that interest would spring as soon as one should begin really to see *anything*. That points, I think, to a large part of the very source of interest for the artist: it resides in the strong consciousness of his seeing all for himself. He has to borrow his motive, which is certainly half the battle; and this motive is his ground, his site, and his foundation. But after that he only lends and gives, only builds and piles high, lays together the blocks quarried in the deeps of his imagination and on his personal premises. He thus remains all the while in intimate commerce with his motive, and can say to himself – what really more than anything else inflames and sustains him – that he alone has the *secret* of the particular case, he alone can measure the truth of the direction to be taken by his developed data. There can be for him, evidently, only one logic for these things; there can be for him only one truth and one direction – the quarter in which his subject most completely expresses itself. The careful ascertainment of how it shall do so, and the art of guiding it with consequent authority – since this sense of 'authority' is for the master-builder the treasure of treasures, or at least the joy of joys – renews in the modern alchemist something like the old dream of the secret of life.

Extravagant as the mere statement sounds, one seemed accordingly to handle the secret of life in drawing the positive right truth out of the so easy muddle of wrong truths in which the interesting possibilities of that 'row,' so to call it, between mother and son over their household gods might have been stifled. I find it odd to consider, as I thus revert, that I could have had none but the most general warrant for 'seeing anything in it,' as the phrase would have been; that I couldn't in the least, on the spot, as I have already hinted, have justified my faith. One thing was 'in it,' in the sordid situation, on the first blush, and one thing only – though this, in its limited way, no doubt, a curious enough value: the sharp light it might project on that most modern of our current passions, the fierce appetite for the upholsterer's and joiner's and brazier's work, the chairs and tables, the cabinets and presses, the material odds and ends, of the more labouring ages. A lively mark of our manners indeed the diffusion of this curiosity and this avidity, and full of suggestion, clearly, as to their possible influence on other passions and other relations. On the face of it the 'things' them-selves would form the very centre of such a crisis; these grouped objects, all conscious of their eminence and their price, would enjoy, in any picture of a conflict, the heroic importance. They would have to be presented, they would have to be painted – arduous and desperate thought; something would have to be done for them not too ignobly unlike the great array in which Balzac,[3] say, would have marshalled them: *that* amount of workable inter-est at least would evidently be 'in it.'

It would be wrapped in the silver tissue of some such conviction, at any rate, that I must have laid away my prime impression for a rest not disturbed till long afterwards, till the year 1896, I make out, when there arose a question of my contributing three 'short stories' to *The Atlantic Monthly*; or supplying rather perhaps a third to complete a trio two members of which had appeared.[4] The echo of the situation mentioned to me at our Christmas Eve dinner awoke again, I recall, at that touch – I recall, no doubt, with true humility, in view of my renewed mismeasurement of my charge. Painfully associated for me had *The Spoils of Poynton* remained, until recent re-perusal, with the awkward consequence of that fond error. The subject had emerged from cool reclusion all suf-fused with a flush of meaning; thanks to which irresistible air, as I could but plead in the event, I found myself – as against a mere commercial austerity – beguiled and led on. The thing had 'come,' the flower of conception had bloomed – all in the happy dusk of indifference and neglect; yet, strongly and frankly as it might now appeal, my idea wouldn't surely overstrain a *natural* brevity. A story that couldn't possibly be long would have inevitably to be 'short,' and out of the depths of that delusion it accordingly began to struggle. To my own view, after the 'first number,' this compo-sition (which in the magazine bore another title) conformed but to its nature, which was not to transcend a modest amplitude; but, dispatched in instalments, it felt itself eyed, from month to month, I seem to remember, with an editorial ruefulness excellently well founded – from the moment such differences of sense could exist, that is, as to the short and the long. The sole impression it made, I woefully gathered, was that of length, and it has till lately, as I say, been present to me but as the poor little 'long' thing.

It began to appear in April 1896, and, as is apt blessedly to occur for me throughout this process of revision, the old, the shrunken concomitants muster again as I turn the pages. They lurk between the lines; these serve for them as the barred seraglio-windows behind which, to the outsider in the glare of the Eastern street, forms indistinguishable seem to move and peer; 'association' in fine bears upon them with its infinite magic. Peering through the lattice from without inward I recapture a cottage on a cliff-side, to which, at the earliest approach of the summer-time, redoubtable in London through the luxuriance of still other than 'natural' forces, I had betaken myself to finish a book in quiet and to begin another in fear. The cottage was, in its kind, perfection; mainly by reason of a small paved terrace which, curving forward from the cliff-edge like the prow of a ship, overhung a view as level, as purple, as full of rich change, as the expanse of the sea. The horizon was in fact a band of sea; a small red-roofed town, of great antiquity, perched on its sea-rock, clustered within the picture off to the right; while above one's head rustled a dense summer shade, that of a trained and arching ash, rising from the middle of the terrace, brushing the parapet with a heavy fringe and covering the place like a vast umbrella. Beneath this umbrella and really under exquisite protection *The Spoils of Poynton* managed more or less symmetrically to grow.

I recall that I was committed to begin, the day I finished it, short of dire penalties, *The Other House*, with which work, however, of whatever high profit the considerations springing from it might be too, we have nothing to do here – and to the felt jealousy of which, as that of a grudging neighbour, I allude only for sweet recovery of the fact, mainly interesting to myself I admit, that the rhythm of the earlier book shows no flurry of hand. I 'liked' it – the earlier book: I venture now, after years, to welcome the sense of that amenity as well; so immensely refreshing is it to be moved, in any case, toward these retrospective simplicities. Painters and writers, I gather, are, when easily accessible to such appeals, frequently questioned as to those of their productions they may most have delighted in; but the profession of delight has always struck me as the last to consort, for the artist, with any candid account of his troubled effort – ever the sum, for the most part, of so many lapses and compromises, simplifications and surrenders. Which is the work in which he hasn't surrendered, under dire difficulty, the best thing he meant to have kept? In which indeed, before the dreadful *done*, doesn't he ask himself what has become of the thing all for the sweet sake of which it was to proceed to that extremity? Preference and complacency, on these terms, riot in general as they best may; not disputing, however, a grain of which weighty truth, I still make out, between my reconsidered lines, as it were, that I must – my opera-box of a terrace and my great green umbrella indeed aiding – have assisted at the growth and predominance of Fleda Vetch.

For something like Fleda Vetch had surely been latent in one's first apprehension of the theme; it wanted, for treatment, a centre, and, the most obvious centre being 'barred,' this image, while I still wondered, had, with all the assurance in the world, sprung up in its place. The real centre, as I say, the citadel of the interest, with the fight waged round it, would have been the felt beauty and value of the prize of battle,[5] the Things, always the splendid Things, placed in the middle light, figured and constituted, with each identity made vivid, each character discriminated, and their common consciousness of their great dramatic part established. The rendered tribute of these honours, however, no vigilant editor, as I have intimated, could be conceived as allowing room for; since, by so much as the general glittering presence should spread, by so much as it should suggest the gleam of brazen idols[6] and precious metals and inserted gems in the tempered light of some arching place of worship, by just so much would the muse of 'dialogue,'[7] most usurping influence of all the romancingly invoked, be routed without ceremony, to lay her grievance at the feet of her gods. The spoils of Poynton were not directly articulate, and though they might have, and constantly did have, wondrous things to say, their message fostered about them a certain hush of cheaper sound – as a consequence of which, in fine, they would have been costly to keep up. In this manner Fleda Vetch, maintainable at less expense – though even she, I make out, less expert in spreading chatter thin than the readers of romance mainly like their heroines to-day – marked her place in my foreground at one ingratiating stroke. She planted herself centrally, and the stroke, as I call it, the demonstration after which she couldn't be gainsaid, was the simple act of letting it be seen she had character.

For somehow – that was the way interest broke out, once the

germ had been transferred to the sunny south window-sill of one's fonder attention – character, the question of what my agitated friends should individually, and all intimately and at the core, show themselves, would unmistakably be the key to my modest drama, and would indeed alone make a drama of any sort possible. Yes, it is a story of cabinets and chairs and tables; they formed the bone of contention, but what would merely 'become' of them, magnificently passive, seemed to represent a comparatively vulgar issue. The passions, the faculties, the forces their beauty would, like that of antique Helen of Troy,[8] set in motion, was what, as a painter, one had really wanted of them, was the power in them that one had from the first appreciated. Emphatically, by that truth, there would have to be moral developments – dreadful as such a prospect might loom for a poor interpreter committed to brevity. A character is interesting as it comes out, and by the process and duration of that emergence; just as a procession is effective by the way it unrolls, turning to a mere mob if all of it passes at once. My little procession, I foresaw then from an early stage, would refuse to pass at once; though I could keep it more or less down, of course, by reducing it to three or four persons. Practically, in *The Spoils*, the reduction is to four, though indeed – and I clung to that as to my plea for simplicity – the main agents, with the others all dependent, are Mrs. Gereth and Fleda. Fleda's ingratiating stroke, for importance, on the threshold, had been that she would understand; and positively, from that moment, the progress and march of my tale became and remained that of her understanding.

Absolutely, with this, I committed myself to making the affirmation and the penetration of it my action and my 'story'; once more, too, with the re-entertained perception that a subject so lighted, a subject residing in somebody's excited and concentrated feeling about something – both the something and the somebody being of course as important as possible – has more beauty to give out than under any other style of pressure. One is confronted obviously thus with the question of the importances; with that in particular, no doubt, of the weight of intelligent consciousness, consciousness of the whole, or of something ominously like it, that one may decently permit a represented figure to appear to throw. Some plea for this cause, that of the intelligence of the moved mannikin, I have already had occasion to make, and can scarce hope too often to evade it. This intelligence, an honourable amount of it, on the part of the person to whom one most invites attention, has but to play with sufficient freedom and ease, or call it with the right grace, to guarantee us that quantum of the impression of beauty which is the most fixed of the possible advantages of our producible effect. It may fail, as a positive presence, on other sides and in other connexions; but more or less of the treasure is stored safe from the moment such a quality of inward life is distilled, or in other words from the moment so fine an interpretation and criticism as that of Fleda Vetch's – to cite the present case – is applied without waste to the surrounding tangle.[9]

It is easy to object of course 'Why the deuce then Fleda Vetch, why a mere little flurried bundle of petticoats, why not Hamlet or Milton's Satan at once, if you're going in for a superior display of "mind"?' To which I fear I can only reply that in pedestrian prose, and in the 'short story,' one is, for the best reasons, no less on one's guard than on the stretch; and also that I have ever recognised, even in the midst of the curiosity that such displays may quicken, the rule of an exquisite economy. The thing is to lodge somewhere at the heart of one's complexity an irrepressible *appreciation*, but where a light lamp will carry all the flame I incline to look askance at a heavy. From beginning to end, in *The Spoils of Poynton*, appreciation, even to that of the very whole, lives in Fleda; which is precisely why, as a consequence rather grandly imposed, every one else shows for comparatively stupid; the tangle, the drama, the tragedy and comedy of those who appreciate consisting so much of their relation with those who don't. From the presented reflexion of this truth my story draws, I think, a certain assured appearance of roundness and felicity. The 'things' are radiant, shedding afar, with a merciless monotony, all their light, exerting their ravage without remorse; and Fleda almost demoniacally both sees and feels, while the others but feel without seeing. Thus we get perhaps a vivid enough little example, in the concrete, of the general truth, for the spectator of life, that the fixed constituents of almost any reproducible action are the fools who minister, at a particular crisis, to the intensity of the free spirit engaged with them. The fools are interesting by contrast, by the salience they acquire, and by a hundred other of their advantages;

and the free spirit, always much tormented, and by no means always triumphant, is heroic, ironic, pathetic or whatever, and, as exemplifed in the record of Fleda Vetch, for instance, 'successful,' only through having remained free.

I recognise that the novelist with a weakness for that ground of appeal is foredoomed to a well-nigh extravagant insistence on the free spirit, seeing the possibility of one in every bush; I may perhaps speak of it as noteworthy that this very volume happens to exhibit in two other cases my disposition to let the interest stand or fall by the tried spontaneity and vivacity of the freedom. It is in fact for that respectable reason that I enclose *A London Life* and *The Chaperon* between these covers; my purpose having been here to class my reprintable productions as far as possible according to their kinds. The two tales I have just named are of the same 'kind' as *The Spoils*, to the extent of their each dealing with a human predicament in the light, for the charm of the thing, of the amount of 'appreciation' to be plausibly imputed to the subject of it. They are each – and truly there are more of such to come – 'stories about women,' very young women, who, affected with a certain high lucidity, thereby become characters; in consequence of which their doings, their sufferings or whatever, take on, I assume, an importance. Laura Wing, in *A London Life*, has, like Fleda Vetch, acuteness and intensity, reflexion and passion, has above all a contributive and participant view of her situation; just as Rose Tramore, in *The Chaperon*, rejoices, almost to insolence, very much in the same cluster of attributes and advantages. They are thus of a family – which shall have also for us, we seem forewarned, more members, and of each sex.

As to our young woman of *The Spoils*, meanwhile, I briefly come back to my claim for a certain definiteness of beauty in the special effect wrought by her aid. My problem had decently to be met – that of establishing for the other persons the vividness of their appearance of comparative stupidity, that of exposing them to the full thick wash of the penumbra[10] surrounding the central light, and yet keeping their motions, within it, distinct, coherent and 'amusing.' But these are exactly of course the most 'amusing' things to do; nothing, for example, being of a higher reward artistically than the shade of success aimed at in such a figure as Mrs. Gereth. A character she too, absolutely, yet the very reverse of a free spirit. I have found myself so pleased with Mrs. Gereth, I confess, on resuming acquaintance with her, that, complete and all in equilibrium as she seems to me to stand and move there, I shrink from breathing upon her any breath of qualification; without which, however, I fail of my point that, thanks to the 'value' represented by Fleda, and to the position to which the elder woman is confined by that irradiation, the latter is at the best a 'false' character, floundering as she does in the dusk of disproportionate passion. She is a *figure*, oh definitely – which is a very different matter; for you may be a figure with all the blinding, with all the hampering passion in life, and may have the grand air in what shall yet prove to the finer view (which Fleda again, *e.g.*, could at any time strike off) but a perfect rage of awkwardness. Mrs. Gereth was, obviously, with her pride and her pluck, of an admirable fine paste;[11] but she was not intelligent, was only clever, and therefore would have been no use to us at all as centre of our subject – compared with Fleda, who was only intelligent, not distinctively able. The little drama confirms at all events excellently, I think, the contention of the old wisdom that the question of the personal will has more than all else to say to the verisimilitude of these exhibitions. The will that rides the crisis quite most triumphantly is that of the awful Mona Brigstock, who is *all* will, without the smallest leak of force into taste or tenderness or vision, into any sense of shades or relations or proportions. She loses no minute in that perception of incongruities in which half Fleda's passion is wasted and misled, and into which Mrs. Gereth, to her practical loss, that is by the fatal grace of a sense of comedy, occasionally and disinterestedly strays. Every one, every thing, in the story is accordingly sterile *but* the so thriftily constructed Mona, able at any moment to bear the whole of her dead weight at once on any given inch of a resisting surface. Fleda, obliged to neglect inches, sees and feels but in acres and expanses and blue perspectives; Mrs. Gereth too, in comparison, while her imagination broods, drops half the stitches of the web she seeks to weave.[12]

I

MRS. GERETH had said she would go with the rest to church, but suddenly it seemed to her she shouldn't be able to wait even till church-time for relief: breakfast was at Waterbath a punctual meal and she had still nearly an hour on her hands. Knowing the church to be near she prepared in her room for the little rural walk, and on her way down again, passing through corridors and observing imbecilities of decoration, the esthetic misery of the big commodious house, she felt a return of the tide of last night's irritation, a renewal of everything she could secretly suffer from ugliness and stupidity. Why did she consent to such contacts? why did she so rashly expose herself? She had had, heaven knew, her reasons, but the whole experience was to be sharper than she had feared. To get away from it and out into the air, into the presence of sky and trees, flowers and birds, was a necessity of every nerve. The flowers at Waterbath would probably go wrong in colour and the nightingales sing out of tune; but she remembered to have heard the place described as possessing those advantages that are usually spoken of as natural. There were advantages enough it clearly didn't possess. It was hard for her to believe a woman could look presentable who had been kept awake for hours by the wall-paper in her room; yet none the less, as she rustled in her fresh widow's weeds across the hall, she was sustained by the consciousness, which always added to the unction of her social Sundays, that she was, as usual, the only person in the house incapable of wearing in her preparation the horrible stamp of the same exceptional smartness that would be conspicuous in a grocer's wife. She would rather have perished than have looked *endimanchée*.[1]

She was fortunately not challenged, the hall being empty of the other women, who were engaged precisely in arraying themselves to that dire end. Once in the grounds she recognised that, with a site, a view, that struck the note, set an example to all inmates, Waterbath ought to have been charming. How she herself, with such elements to handle, would have taken the fine hint of nature! Suddenly, at the turn of a walk, she came on a member of the party, a young lady seated on a bench in deep and lonely meditation. She had observed the girl at dinner and afterwards: she was always looking at girls with reference, apprehensive or speculative, to her son. Deep in her heart was a conviction that Owen would, in spite of all her spells², marry at last a frump; and this from no evidence she could have represented as adequate, but simply from her deep uneasiness, her belief that such a special sensibility as her own could have been inflicted on a woman only as a source of anguish. It would be her fate, her discipline, her cross, to have a frump brought hideously home to her. This girl, one of the two Vetches³, had no beauty, but Mrs. Gereth, scanning the dulness for a sign of life, had been straightway able to classify such a figure as for the moment the least of her afflictions. Fleda Vetch was dressed with an idea, though perhaps not with much else; and that made a bond when there was none other, especially as in this case the idea was real, not imitation. Mrs. Gereth had long ago generalised the truth that the temperament of the frump may easily consort with a certain casual prettiness. There were five girls in the party, and the prettiness of this one, slim, pale, and black-haired, was less likely than that of the others ever to occasion an exchange of platitudes. The two less developed Brigstocks, daughters of the house, were in particular tiresomely 'lovely.' A second glance, a sharp one, at the young lady before her conveyed to Mrs. Gereth the soothing assurance that she also was guiltless of looking hot and fine. They had had no talk as yet, but here was a note that would effectually introduce them if the girl should show herself in the least conscious of their community. She got up from her seat with a smile that but partly dissipated the prostration Mrs. Gereth had recognised in her attitude. The elder woman drew her down again, and for a minute, as they sat together, their eyes met and sent out mutual soundings. 'Are you safe? Can I utter it?' each of them said to the other, quickly recognising, almost proclaiming, their common need to escape. The tremendous fancy, as it came to be called, that Mrs. Gereth was destined to take to Fleda Vetch virtually began with this discovery that the poor child had been moved to flight even more promptly than herself. That the poor child no less quickly perceived how far

36

she could now go was proved by the immense friendliness with which she instantly broke out: 'Isn't it too dreadful?'

'Horrible – horrible!' cried Mrs. Gereth with a laugh; 'and it's really a comfort to be able to say it.' She had an idea, for it was her ambition, that she successfully made a secret of that awkward oddity her proneness to be rendered unhappy by the presence of the dreadful. Her passion for the exquisite was the cause of this, but it was a passion she considered she never advertised nor gloried in, contenting herself with letting it regulate her steps and show quietly in her life, remembering at all times that there are few things more soundless than a deep devotion. She was therefore struck with the acuteness of the little girl who had already put a finger on her hidden spring. What was dreadful now, what was horrible, was the intimate ugliness of Waterbath, and it was of that phenomenon these ladies talked while they sat in the shade and drew refreshment from the great tranquil sky, whence no cheap blue plates depended. It was an ugliness fundamental and systematic, the result of the abnormal nature of the Brigstocks, from whose composition the principle of taste had been extravagantly omitted. In the arrangement of their home some other principle, remarkably active, but uncanny and obscure, had operated instead, with consequences depressing to behold, consequences that took the form of a universal futility. The house was bad in all conscience, but it might have passed if they had only let it alone. This saving mercy was beyond them; they had smothered it with trumpery ornament and scrapbook art, with strange excrescences and bunchy draperies, with gimcracks that might have been keepsakes for maid-servants and nondescript conveniences that might have been prizes for the blind. They had gone wildly astray over carpets and curtains; they had an infallible instinct for gross deviation and were so cruelly doom-ridden that it rendered them almost tragic. Their drawing-room, Mrs. Gereth lowered her voice to mention, caused her face to burn, and each of the new friends confided to the other that in her own apartment she had given way to tears. There was in the elder lady's a set of comic water-colours, a family joke by a family genius, and in the younger's a souvenir from some centennial or other Exhibition, that they shudderingly alluded to. The house was perversely full of souvenirs of places even more ugly than itself and of things it would have been a pious duty to forget. The worst horror was the acres of varnish, something advertised and smelly, with which everything was smeared: it was Fleda Vetch's conviction that the application of it, by their own hands and hilariously shoving each other, was the amusement of the Brigstocks on rainy days.

When, as criticism deepened, Fleda dropped the suggestion that some people would perhaps see something in Mona, Mrs. Gereth caught her up with a groan of protest, a smothered familiar cry of 'Oh my dear!' Mona was the eldest of the three, the one Mrs. Gereth most suspected. She confided to her young friend how it was her suspicion that had brought her to Waterbath; and this was going very far, for on the spot, as a refuge, a remedy, she had clutched at the idea that something might be done with the girl before her. It was her fancied exposure at any rate that had sharpened the shock, made her ask herself with a terrible chill if fate could really be plotting to saddle her with a daughter-in-law brought up in such a place. She had seen Mona in her appropriate setting and had seen Owen, handsome and heavy, dangle beside her; but the effect of these first hours had happily not been to darken the prospect. It was clearer to her that she could never accept Mona, but it was after all by no means certain Owen would ask her to. He had sat by somebody else at dinner and afterwards had talked to Mrs. Firmin, who was as dreadful as all the rest, but redeemingly married. His heaviness, which in her need of expansion she freely named, had two aspects: one of them his monstrous lack of taste, the other his exaggerated prudence. If it should come to a question of carrying Mona with a high hand there would be no need to worry, for that was rarely his mode of proceeding.

Invited by her companion, who had asked if it weren't wonderful, Mrs. Gereth had begun to say a word about Poynton; but she heard a sound of voices that made her stop short. The next moment she rose to her feet, and Fleda could then see her alarm to be by no means quenched. Behind the place where they had been sitting the ground dropped with some steepness, forming a long grassy bank up which Owen Gereth and Mona Brigstock, dressed for church but making a familiar joke of it, were in the act of scrambling and helping each other. When they had reached the even ground Fleda was able to read the meaning of the exclamation in which Mrs. Gereth had expressed her reserves on the subject of Miss Brigstock's personality. Miss Brigstock had been laughing and even romping, but the circumstance hadn't contributed the ghost of an expression to her countenance. Tall, straight and fair, long-limbed and strangely festooned, she stood there without a look in her eye or any perceptible intention of any sort in any other feature. She belonged to the type in which speech is an unaided emission of sound, in which the secret of being is impenetrably and incorruptibly kept. Her expression would probably have been beautiful if she had had one, but whatever she communicated she communicated, in a manner best known to herself, without signs. This was not the case with Owen Gereth, who had plenty of them, and all very simple and immediate. Robust and artless, eminently natural yet perfectly correct, he looked pointlessly active and pleasantly dull. Like his mother and like Fleda Vetch, but not for the same reason, this young pair had come out to take a turn before church.

The meeting of the two couples was sensibly awkward, and Fleda, who had perceptions, and these now more and more roused, took the measure of the shock inflicted on Mrs. Gereth. There had been intimacy – oh yes, intimacy as well as puerility – in the horse-play of which they had just had a glimpse. The party began to stroll together to the house, and Fleda had again a sense of Mrs. Gereth's quick management in the way the lovers, or whatever they were, found themselves separated. She strolled behind with Mona, the mother possessing herself of her son, her exchange of remarks with whom, however, remained, as they went, vividly inaudible. That member of the party in whose intenser consciousness we shall most profitably seek a reflexion of the little drama with which we are concerned drew a yet livelier impression of Mrs. Gereth's intervention from the fact that ten minutes later, on the way to church, still another pairing had been effected. Owen walked with Fleda, and it was an amusement to the girl to feel sure this was by his mother's direction. Fleda had other amusements as well: such as noting that Mrs. Gereth was now with Mona Brigstock; such as observing that she was all affability to that young woman; such as reflecting that, masterful and clever, with a great bright spirit, she was one of those who impose, who interfuse themselves; such as feeling finally that

Owen Gereth was absolutely beautiful and delightfully dense. This young person had even from herself wonderful secrets of delicacy and pride; but she came as near distinctness as in the consideration of such matters she had ever come at all in now embracing the idea that it was of a pleasant effect and rather remarkable to be stupid without offence – of a pleasanter effect and more remarkable indeed than to be clever and horrid. Owen Gereth at any rate, with his inches, his features and his lapses, was neither of these latter things. She herself was prepared, if she should ever marry, to contribute all the cleverness, and she liked to figure it out that her husband would be a force grateful for direction. She was in her small way a spirit of the same family as Mrs. Gereth. On that flushed and huddled Sunday a great matter occurred; her little life became aware of a singular quickening. Her meagre past fell away from her like a garment of the wrong fashion, and as she came up to town on the Monday what she stared at from the train in the suburban fields was a future full of the things she particularly loved.

II

THESE were neither more nor less than the things with which she had had time to learn from Mrs. Gereth that Poynton overflowed. Poynton, in the south of England, was this lady's established, or rather her disestablished, home: it had recently passed into the possession of her son. The father of the boy, an only child, had died two years before, and in London, with his mother, Owen was occupying for May and June a house good-naturedly lent them by Colonel Gereth, their uncle and brother-in-law. His mother had laid her hand so engagingly on Fleda Vetch that in a very few days the girl knew it was possible they should suffer together in Cadogan Place[1] almost as much as they had suffered together at Waterbath. The kind soldier's house was also an ordeal, but the two women, for the ensuing month, had at least the relief of their confessions. The great drawback of Mrs. Gereth's situation was that, thanks to the rare perfection of Poynton, she was condemned to wince wherever she turned. She had lived for a quarter of a century in such warm closeness with the beautiful that, as she frankly admitted, life had become for her a true fool's paradise. She couldn't leave her own house without peril of exposure. She didn't say it in so many words, but Fleda could see she held nothing in England really comparable to Poynton. There were places much grander and richer, but no such complete work of art, nothing that would appeal so to those really informed. In putting such elements into her hand destiny had given her an inestimable chance; she knew how rarely well things had gone with her and that she had enjoyed an extraordinary fortune.

There had been in the first place the exquisite old house itself, early Jacobean,[2] supreme in every part; a provocation, an inspiration, the matchless canvas for a picture. Then there had been her husband's sympathy and generosity, his knowledge and love, their perfect accord and beautiful life together, twenty-six years of planning and seeking, a long, sunny harvest of taste and curiosity.

Lastly, she never denied, there had been her personal gift, the genius, the passion, the patience of the collector – a patience, an almost infernal cunning, that had enabled her to do it all with a limited command of money. There wouldn't have been money enough for any fumbler, she said with pride, but there had been money enough for her. They had saved on lots of things in life, and there were lots of things they hadn't had at all, but they had had in every corner of Europe their swing among the demons of Jews.[2] It was fascinating to poor Fleda, who hadn't a penny in the world nor anything nice at home, and whose only treasure was her subtle mind, to hear this genuine English lady, fresh and fair, young in the fifties, admit with gaiety and conviction that she was herself the craftiest stalker who had ever tracked big game. Fleda, with her mother dead, hadn't so much even as a home, and her nearest chance of one was that there was some appearance her sister would become engaged to a curate whose eldest brother was supposed to have property and would perhaps allow him something. Her father paid some of her bills but didn't like her to live with him; and she had lately, in Paris, with several hundred other young women, spent a year at a studio, arming herself for the battle of life by a course with an impressionist painter.[4] She was determined to work, but her impressions, or somebody's else, were as yet her only material. Mrs. Gereth had told her she liked her because she had an extraordinary *flair*; but under the circumstances a *flair* was a questionable boon: in the dry spaces in which she had mainly moved she could have borne a chronic catarrh. She was now much summoned to Cadogan Place and before the month elapsed was kept to stay, to pay a visit of which the end, it was agreed, should have nothing to do with the beginning. She had a sense partly exultant and partly alarmed of having quickly become necessary to her imperious friend, who indeed gave a reason quite sufficient for it in telling her there was nobody else who understood. From Mrs. Gereth there was in these days an immense deal to understand, though it might freely be summed up in the circumstance that she was wretched. Fleda was thus assured she couldn't completely know why till she should have seen the things at Poynton. She could perfectly grasp this connexion, which was exactly one of the matters that, in their inner mystery, were a blank to everybody else.

The girl had a promise that the wonderful house should be shown her early in July, when Mrs. Gereth would return to it as to her home; but even before this initiation she put her finger on the spot that in the poor lady's troubled soul ached hardest. This was the misery haunting her, the dread of the inevitable surrender. What Fleda had to sit up to was the confirmed appearance that Owen Gereth would marry Mona Brigstock, marry her in his mother's teeth, and that such an act would have incalculable bearings. They were present to Mrs. Gereth, her companion could see, with a vividness that at moments almost ceased to be that of sanity. She would have to give up Poynton, and give it up to a product of Waterbath – that was the wrong that rankled, the humiliation at which one would be able adequately to shudder only when one should know the place. She did know Waterbath and despised it – she had that qualification for sympathy. Her sympathy was intelligent, for she read deep into the matter: she stared, aghast, as it came home to her for the first time, at the cruel English custom of the expropriation of the lonely mother. Mr. Gereth had apparently been a very amiable man, but Mr. Gereth had left things in a way that made the girl marvel. The house and its contents had been treated as a single splendid object; everything was to go straight to his son, his widow being assured but a maintenance and a cottage in another county. No account whatever had been taken of her relation to her treasures, of the passion with which she had waited for them, worked for them, picked them over, made them worthy of each other and the house, watched them, loved them, lived with them. He appeared to have assumed she would settle questions with her son and that he could depend on Owen's affection and Owen's fairness. And in truth, as poor Mrs. Gereth inquired, how could he possibly have had a prevision – he who turned his eyes instinctively from everything repulsive – of anything so abnormal either as a Waterbath Brigstock or as a Brigstock Waterbath? He had been in ugly houses enough, but had escaped that particular nightmare. Nothing so perverse could have been expected to happen as that the heir to the loveliest thing in England should be inspired to hand it over to a girl so exceptionally tainted. Mrs. Gereth spoke of poor Mona's taint as if to mention it were almost a violation of decency, and a person who had listened without enlightenment would have wondered of what fault the girl had been or had indeed not been guilty. But Owen had from a boy never cared, never taken the least pride or pleasure in his home.

'Well then if he doesn't care – !' Fleda exclaimed with some impetuosity; stopping short, however, before she completed her sentence.

Mrs. Gereth looked at her rather hard. 'If he doesn't care?'

Fleda cast about; she had not quite had a definite idea. 'Well – he'll give them up.'

'Give what up?'

'Why, those beautiful things.'

'Give them up to whom?' Mrs. Gereth more boldly stared.

'To you of course – to enjoy, to keep for yourself.'

'And leave his house as bare as your hand? There's nothing in it that isn't precious.'

Fleda considered; her friend had taken her up with a smothered ferocity by which she was slightly disconcerted. 'I don't mean, naturally, that he should surrender everything; but he might let you pick out the things to which you're most attached.'

'I think he would if he were free,' said Mrs. Gereth.

'And do you mean, as it is, that she'll prevent him?' Mona Brigstock, between these ladies, was now nothing but 'she.'

'By every means in her power.'

'But surely not because she understands and appreciates them?'

'No,' Mrs. Gereth replied, 'but because they belong to the house and the house belongs to Owen. If I should wish to take anything she would simply say, with that motionless mask, "It goes with the house." And day after day, in the face of every argument, of every consideration of generosity, she would repeat, without winking, in that voice like the squeeze of a doll's stomach, "It goes with the house – it goes with the house." In that attitude they'll shut themselves up.'

Fleda was struck, was even a little startled by the way Mrs. Gereth had turned this over – had faced, if indeed only to recognise its futility, the notion of a battle with her only son. These words led her to take a sounding she had not thought it discreet to take before: she brought out the idea of the possibility, after all, of her friend's continuing to live at Poynton. Would they really wish to proceed to extremities? Was no good-humoured graceful compro-

44

mise to be imagined or brought about? Couldn't the same roof cover them? Was it so very inconceivable that a married son should for the rest of her days share with so charming a mother the home she had devoted more than a score of years to making beautiful for him? Mrs. Gereth hailed this question with a wan compassionate smile: she replied that a common household was in such a case just so inconceivable that Fleda had only to glance over the fair face of the English land to see how few people had ever conceived it. It was always thought a wonder, a 'mistake,' a piece of overstrained sentiment; and she confessed she was as little capable of a flight of that sort as Owen himself. Even if they both had been capable they would still have Mona's hatred to reckon with. Fleda's breath was sometimes taken away by the great fierce bounds and elisions which, on Mrs. Gereth's lips, the course of discussion could take.

This was the first she had heard of Mona's hatred, though she certainly had not needed Mrs. Gereth to tell her that in close quarters that young lady would prove secretly mulish. Later Fleda perceived indeed that perhaps almost any girl would hate a person who should be so markedly averse to having anything to do with her. Before this, however, in conversation with her young friend, Mrs. Gereth furnished a more vivid motive for her despair by asking how she could possibly be expected to sit there with the new proprietors and accept – or call it, for a day, endure – the horrors they would perpetrate in the house. Fleda argued that they wouldn't after all smash things nor burn them up; and Mrs. Gereth admitted when pushed that she didn't quite suppose they would. What she meant was that they would neglect them, ignore them, leave them to clumsy servants[5] – there wasn't an object of them all but should be handled with perfect love – and in many cases probably wish to replace them by pieces answerable to some vulgar modern notion of the 'handy.' Above all she saw in advance with dilated eyes the abominations they would inevitably mix up with them – the maddening relics of Waterbath, the little brackets and pink vases, the sweepings of bazaars, the family photographs and illuminated texts, the 'household art' and household piety of Mona's hideous home. Wasn't it enough simply to contend that Mona would approach Poynton in the spirit of a Brigstock and that in the spirit of a Brigstock she would deal with her acquisition? Did Fleda really see *her*, Mrs. Gereth demanded, spending the remainder of her days with such a creature's elbow half-way down her throat?

Fleda had to declare that she certainly didn't and that Waterbath had been a warning it would be frivolous to overlook. At the same time she privately reflected that they were taking a great deal for granted and that, inasmuch as to her knowledge Owen Gereth had positively denied his betrothal, the ground of their speculations was by no means firm. It struck our young lady that in a difficult position Owen conducted himself with some natural art; treating this domesticated confidant of his mother's wrongs with a simple civility that almost troubled her conscience, so deeply she felt she might have had for him the air of siding with that lady against him. She wondered if he would ever know how little really she did this and that she was there, since Mrs. Gereth had insisted, not to betray but essentially to plead and protect. The fact that his mother disliked Mona Brigstock might have made him dislike the object of her preference, and it was detestable to Fleda to remember that she might have appeared to him to offer herself as an exemplary contrast. It was clear enough, however, that the happy youth had no more sense for a motive than a deaf man for a tune; a limitation by which, after all, she could gain as well as lose. He came and went very freely on the business with which London abundantly furnished him, but he found time more than once to say to her 'It's awfully nice of you to look after poor Mummy.' As well as his quick speech, which shyness made obscure – it was usually as desperate as a 'rush' at some violent game – his child's eyes in his man's face put it to her that, you know, this really meant a good deal for him and that he hoped she would stay on. With a person in the house who, like herself, was clever, poor Mummy was conveniently occupied. Fleda found a beauty in the candour and even in the modesty which apparently kept him from suspecting that two such wiseheads could possibly be occupied with Owen Gereth.

THEY went at last, the wiseheads, down to Poynton, where the palpitating girl had the full revelation. '*Now* do you know how I feel?' Mrs. Gereth asked when in the wondrous hall, three minutes after their arrival, her pretty associate dropped on a seat with a soft gasp and a roll of dilated eyes. The answer came clearly enough, and in the rapture of that first walk through the house Fleda took a prodigious span. She perfectly understood how Mrs. Gereth felt – she had understood but meagrely before; and the two women embraced with tears over the tightening of their bond – tears which on the younger one's part were the natural and usual sign of her submission to perfect beauty. It was not the first time she had cried for the joy of admiration, but it was the first time the mistress of Poynton, often as she had shown her house, had been present at such an exhibition. She exulted in it; it quickened her own tears; she assured her companion that such an occasion made the poor old place fresh to her again and more precious than ever. Yes, nobody had ever, that way, *cared*, ever felt what she had achieved: people were so grossly ignorant, and everybody, even the knowing ones as they thought themselves, more or less dense. What Mrs. Gereth had achieved was indeed a supreme result; and in such an art of the treasure-hunter, in selection and comparison refined to that point, there was an element of creation, of personality. She had commended Fleda's *flair*, and Fleda now gave herself up to satiety. Preoccupations and scruples fell away from her; she had never known a greater happiness than the week passed in this initiation.

Wandering through clear chambers where the general effect made preferences almost as impossible as if they had been shocks, pausing at open doors where vistas were long and bland, she would, even hadn't she already known, have discovered for herself that Poynton was the record of a life. It was written in great syllables of colour and form, the tongues of other countries and the hands of rare artists. It was all France and Italy with their ages composed to rest. For England you looked out of old windows – it was England that was the wide embrace. While outside, on the low terraces, she contradicted gardeners and refined on nature, Mrs. Gereth left her guest to finger fondly the brasses that Louis Quinze[1] might have thumbed, to sit with Venetian velvets just held in a loving palm, to hang over cases of enamels and pass and repass before cabinets. There were not many pictures – the panels and the stuffs were themselves the picture; and in all the great wainscoted house there was not an inch of pasted paper. What struck Fleda most in it was the high pride of her friend's taste, a fine arrogance, a sense of style which, however amused and amusing, never compromised nor stooped. She felt indeed, as this lady had promised her she should, both a respect and a compassion she had not known before; thus the vision of the coming surrender could but fill her with an equal pain. To give it all up, to die to it – that thought ached in her breast. She herself could imagine clinging there with a clutch indifferent to dignity. To have created such a place was to have had dignity enough; when there was a question of defending it the fiercest attitude was the right one. After so intense a taking of possession she too was to give it up; for she reflected that if Mrs. Gereth's remaining would have offered her an apology for a future – stretching away in safe years on the other side of a gulf – the advent of the others could only be, by the same law, a great vague menace, the ruffling of a still water. Such were the emotions of a hungry girl whose sensibility was almost as great as her opportunities for comparison had been small. The museums had done something for her, but nature had done more.

If Owen had not come down with them nor joined them later it was because he still found London jolly;[2] yet the question remained of whether the jollity of London were not merely the only name his small vocabulary yielded for the jollity of Mona Brigstock. There was indeed in his conduct another ambiguity – something that required explaining so long as his motive didn't come to the surface. If he was in love what was the matter? And what was the matter still more if he wasn't? The mystery was at last cleared up: this Fleda gathered from the tone in which, one morning at breakfast, a letter just opened made Mrs. Gereth cry out. Her dismay was almost a shriek: 'Why he's bringing her down

– he wants her to see the house!' They flew, the two women, into each other's arms and, with their heads together, soon made out the reason, the baffling reason why nothing had yet happened, to be that Mona didn't know, or Owen didn't, whether Poynton would really please her. She was coming down to judge; and could anything in the world be more like poor Owen than the ponderous probity that had kept him from pressing her for a reply till she should have learned if she approved what he had to offer her? That was a scruple it had naturally been impossible to impute. If only they might fondly hope, Mrs. Gereth wailed, that the girl's expectations would be dashed! There was a fine consistency, a sincerity quite affecting, in her arguing that the better the place should happen to look, the better it should express the conceptions to which it owed its origin, the less it would speak to an intelligence so primitive. How could a Brigstock possibly understand what it was all about? How, really, could a Brigstock logically do anything but hate it? Mrs. Gereth, even as she whisked away linen shrouds,[3] persuaded herself of the likelihood on Mona's part of some bewildered blankness, some collapse of admiration that would prove disconcerting to her swain – a hope of which Fleda at least could see the absurdity and which gave the measure of the poor lady's strange, almost maniacal disposition to thrust in everywhere the question of 'things,' to read all behaviour in the light of some fancied relation to them. 'Things' were of course the sum of the world;[4] only, for Mrs. Gereth, the sum of the world was rare French furniture and oriental china. She could at a stretch imagine people's not 'having,' but she couldn't imagine their not wanting and not missing.

The young people were to be accompanied by Mrs. Brigstock, and with a prevision of how fiercely they would be watched Fleda became conscious, before the party arrived, of an amused diplomatic pity for them. Almost as much as Mrs. Gereth's her taste was her life, though her life was somehow the larger for it. Besides, she had another care now: there was some one she wouldn't have liked to see humiliated even in the person of a young lady formed to foster his never suspecting so much delicacy. When this young lady appeared Fleda tried, so far as the wish to efface herself allowed, to be mainly the person to take her about, show her the house and cover up her ignorance. Owen's

49

announcement had been that, as trains made it convenient, they would present themselves for luncheon and depart before dinner; but Mrs. Gereth, true to her system of glaring civility, proposed and obtained an extension, a dining and a spending of the night. She made her young friend wonder against what rebellion of fact she was sacrificing in advance so profusely to appearance. Fleda was appalled after the first hour by the rash innocence with which Mona had accepted the responsibility of observation, and indeed by the large levity with which, sitting there like a bored tourist in fine scenery, she exercised it. She felt in her nerves the effect of such a manner on her companion's, and it was this that made her want to entice the girl away, give her some merciful warning or some jocular cue. Mona met intense looks, however, with eyes that might have been blue beads, the only ones she had – eyes into which Fleda thought it strange Owen Gereth should have to plunge for his fate and his mother for a confession of whether Poynton were a success. She made no remark that helped to supply this light; her impression at any rate had nothing in common with the feeling that, as the beauty of the place throbbed out like music, had caused Fleda Vetch to burst into tears. She was as content to say nothing as if, their hostess afterwards exclaimed, she had been keeping her mouth shut in a railway tunnel.[5] Mrs. Gereth contrived at the end of an hour to convey to Fleda that it was plain she was brutally ignorant; but Fleda more finely discovered that her ignorance was obscurely active.

Mona was not so stupid as not to see that something, though she scarcely knew what, was expected of her that she couldn't give; and the only mode her intelligence suggested of meeting the expectation was to plant her big feet and pull another way. Mrs. Gereth wanted her to rise, somehow or somewhere, and was prepared to hate her if she didn't: very well, she couldn't, wouldn't rise; she had already moved at the altitude that suited her and was able to see that since she was exposed to the hatred she might at least enjoy the calm. The smallest trouble, for a girl with no nonsense about her, was to earn what she incurred; so that, a dim instinct teaching her she would earn it best by no fond overflow, and combining with the conviction that she now definitely held Owen, and therefore the place, she had the pleasure of her honesty as well as of her security. Didn't her very honesty lead her to be belligerently blank about Poynton, inasmuch as it was just Poynton that was forced upon her as a subject for effusiveness? Such subjects, to Miss Brigstock, had an air almost of indecency; so that the house became uncanny to her by the very appeal in its name – an appeal that somewhere in the twilight of her being, as Fleda was sure, Mona thanked heaven she *was* the girl stiffly to draw back from. She was a person whom pressure at a given point infallibly caused to expand in the wrong place instead of, as it is usually administered in the hope of doing, the right one. Her mother, to make up for this, broke out universally, pronounced everything 'most striking,' and was visibly happy that Owen's captor should be so far on the way to strike: but she jarred upon Mrs. Gereth by her formula of admiration, which was that anything she looked at was 'in the style' of something else. This was to show how much she had seen, but it only showed she had seen nothing; everything at Poynton was in the style of Poynton, and poor Mrs. Brigstock, who at least was determined to rise and had brought with her a trophy of her journey, a 'lady's magazine'[6] purchased at the station, a horrible thing with patterns of antimacassars,[7] which, as it was quite new, the first number, and seemed so clever, she kindly offered to leave for the house, was in the style of a vulgar old woman who wore silver jewelry and tried to pass off a gross avidity as a sense of the beautiful.

By the day's end it was clear to Fleda Vetch that, however Mona judged, the day had been determinant. Whether or no she felt the charm she felt the challenge: at an early moment Owen Gereth would be able to tell his mother the worst. Nevertheless when the elder lady, at bedtime, coming in a dressing-gown and a high fever to the younger one's room, cried out 'She hates it: but what will she do?' Fleda pretended vagueness, played at obscurity and assented disingenuously to the proposition that they at least had a respite. The future was dark to her, but there was a silken thread[8] she could clutch in the gloom – she would never give Owen away. He might give himself – he even certainly would; but that was his own affair, and his blunders, his innocence, only added to the appeal he made to her. She would cover him, she would protect him, and beyond thinking her a cheerful inmate he would never guess her intention, any more than, beyond thinking her clever enough for anything, his astute mother would discover it. From this hour, with Mrs. Gereth, there was a flaw in her frankness. Her admirable friend continued to know everything she did: what was to remain unknown was her general motive.

From the window of her room, the next morning before breakfast, the girl saw Owen in the garden with Mona, who strolled beside him under a listening parasol but without a visible look for the great florid picture hung there from so far back by Mrs. Gereth's hand. Mona kept dropping her eyes, as she walked, to catch the sheen of her patent-leather shoes, which resembled a man's and which she kicked forward a little – it gave her an odd movement – to help her see what she thought of them. When Fleda came down Mrs. Gereth was in the breakfast-room; and at that moment Owen, through a long window, passed in alone from the terrace and very endearingly kissed his mother. It immediately struck their guest that she was in their way, for hadn't he been borne on a wave of joy exactly to announce, before the Brigstocks departed, that Mona had at last faltered out the sweet word he had been waiting for? He shook hands with his friendly violence, but Fleda contrived not to look into his face: what she liked most to see in it was not the reflexion of Mona's big boot-toes. She could bear well enough that young lady herself, but she couldn't bear Owen's opinion of her. She was on the point of slipping into the garden when the movement was checked by Mrs. Gereth's suddenly drawing her close, as if for the morning embrace, and then, while she kept her there with the bravery of the night's repose, breaking out: 'Well, my dear boy, what *does* your young friend there make of our odds and ends?'

'Oh she thinks they're all right!'

Fleda immediately guessed from his tone that he had not come in to say what she supposed: there was even something in it to confirm Mrs. Gereth's belief that their danger had dropped. She was sure, moreover, that his tribute to Mona's taste was a repetition of the eloquent words in which the girl had herself recorded it; she could indeed hear with all vividness the probable pretty passage between the pair. 'Don't you think it's rather jolly, the old shop?' 'Oh it's all right!' Mona had graciously remarked; and then they had probably, with a slap on a back, run another race up or down a green bank. Fleda knew Mrs. Gereth hadn't yet uttered a word to her son that would have shown him how much she feared; but it was impossible to feel her friend's arm round her and not become aware that this friend was now throbbing with a strange intention. Owen's reply had scarcely been of a nature to usher in a discussion of Mona's sensibilities, but Mrs. Gereth went on in a moment with an innocence of which Fleda could measure the cold hypocrisy. 'Has she any sort of feeling for nice old things?' The question was as fresh as the morning light.

'Oh of course she likes everything that's nice.' And Owen, who constitutionally shirked questions – an answer was almost as hateful to him as a 'trick' to a big dog – smiled kindly at Fleda and conveyed that she'd understand what he meant even if his mother didn't. Fleda, however, mainly understood that Mrs. Gereth, with an odd wild laugh, held her so hard as to hurt her.

'I could give up everything without a pang, I think, to a person I could trust, I could respect.' The girl heard her voice tremble under the effort to show nothing but what she wanted to show, and felt the sincerity of her implication that the piety most real to her was to be on one's knees before one's high standard. 'The best things here, as you know, are the things your father and I collected, things all that we worked for and waited for and suffered for. Yes,' cried Mrs. Gereth with a fine freedom of fancy, 'there are things in the house that we almost starved for! They were our religion, they were our life, they were *us*! And now they're only *me* – except that they're also *you*, thank God, a little, you dear!' she continued, suddenly inflicting on Fleda a kiss intended by every sign to knock her into position. 'There isn't one of them I don't know and love – yes, as one remembers and cherishes the happiest moments of one's life. Blindfold, in the dark, with the brush of a finger, I could tell one from another. They're living things to me; they know me, they return the touch of my hand. But I could let them all go, since I have to so strangely, to another affection, another conscience. There's a care they want, there's a sympathy that draws out their beauty. Rather than make them over to a woman ignorant and vulgar I think I'd deface them with my own hands. Can't you see me, Fleda, and wouldn't you do it yourself?' – she appealed to her companion with glittering eyes. 'I couldn't bear the thought of such a woman here – I *could*n't. I don't know what she'd do: she'd be sure to invent some deviltry, if it should be only to bring in her own little belongings and horrors! The world is full of cheap gimcracks in this awful age, and they're thrust in at one at every turn. They'd be thrust in here on top of my treasures, my own. Who'd save *them* for me – I ask you who *would*?' and she turned again to Fleda with a dry strained smile. Her handsome high-nosed excited face might have been that of Don Quixote[10] tilting at a windmill. Drawn into the eddy of this outpouring the girl, scared and embarrassed, laughed off her exposure; but only to feel herself more passionately caught up and, as it seemed to her, thrust down the fine open mouth (it showed such perfect teeth) with which poor Owen's slow cerebration gaped. '*You* would, of course – only you, in all the world, because you know, you feel as I do myself, what's good and true and pure.' No severity of the moral law could have taken a higher tone in this implication of the young lady who lacked the only virtue Mrs. Gereth actively esteemed. '*You* would replace me, *you* would watch over them, *you* would keep the place right,' she austerely pursued, 'and with you here – yes, with you, I believe I might rest at last in my grave!' She threw herself on Fleda's neck, and before that witness, horribly shamed, could shake her off, had burst into tears which couldn't have been explained but which might perhaps have been understood.

IV

A WEEK later Owen came down to inform his mother he had settled with Mona Brigstock; but it was not at all a joy to Fleda, aware of how much to himself it would be a surprise, that he should find her still in the house. That dreadful scene before breakfast had made her position false and odious; it had been followed, after they were left alone, by a scene of her own making with her extravagant friend. She notified Mrs. Gereth of her instant departure: she couldn't possibly remain after being offered to Owen so distinctly, before her very face, as his mother's candidate for the honour of his hand. That was all he could have seen in such an outbreak and in the indecency of her standing there to enjoy it. Fleda had on the prior occasion dashed out of the room by the shortest course and, while still upset, had fallen on Mona in the garden. She had taken an aimless turn with her and they had had some talk, rendered at first difficult, thoroughly thankless, by Mona's apparent suspicion that she had been sent out to spy, as Mrs. Gereth had tried to spy, into her opinions. Fleda was wise enough to treat these opinions as a mystery almost awful; which had an effect so much more than reassuring that at the end of five minutes the young lady from Waterbath suddenly and perversely said: 'Why has she never had a winter garden thrown out? If ever I have a place of my own I mean to have one.' Fleda, dismayed, could see the thing – something glazed and piped, on iron pillars, with untidy plants and cane sofas; a shiny excrescence on the noble face of Poynton. She remembered at Waterbath a conservatory where she had caught a bad cold in the company of a stuffed cockatoo fastened to a tropical bough and a waterless fountain composed of shells stuck into some hardened paste. She asked Mona if her idea would be to make something like this conservatory; to which Mona replied: 'Oh no, much finer; we haven't got a winter garden at Waterbath.' Fleda wondered if she meant to convey that it was the only grandeur they lacked, and in a moment she went on: 'But we *have* got a billiard-room – that I *will* say for us!' There was no billiard-room at Poynton, but there would evidently be one, and it would have, hung on its walls, framed at the 'Stores,'[1] caricature-portraits of celebrities taken from a 'society paper.'

When the two girls had gone in to breakfast it was for Fleda to see at a glance that there had been a further passage, of some high colour, between Owen and his mother; and she had turned pale in guessing to what extremity, at her expense, Mrs. Gereth had found occasion to proceed. Hadn't she after her clumsy flight been pressed upon Owen in still clearer terms? Mrs. Gereth would practically have said to him: 'If you'll take *her* I'll move away without a sound. But if you take any one else, any one I'm not sure of as I am of her – heaven help me, I'll fight to the death!' Breakfast this morning at Poynton had been a meal singularly silent, in spite of the vague little cries with which Mrs. Brigstock turned up the underside of plates[2] and the knowing but alarming raps administered by her big knuckles to porcelain cups. Some one had to respond to her, and the duty assigned itself to Fleda, who, while pretending to meet her on the ground of explanation, wondered what Owen thought of a girl still indelicately anxious, after she had been grossly hurled at him, to prove by exhibitions of her fine taste that she was really what his mother pretended. This time at any rate their fate was sealed: Owen, as soon as he should get out of the house, would describe to Mona the extraordinary display made to him, and if anything more had been wanted to 'fetch' her,[3] as he would call it, the deficiency was now made up. Mrs. Gereth in fact took care of that – took care of it by the way, at the last, on the threshold, she said to the younger of her departing guests, with an irony of which the sting was wholly in the sense, not at all in the sound: 'We haven't had the talk we might have had, have we? You'll feel I've neglected you and you'll treasure it up against me. *Don't*, because really, you know, it has been quite an accident, and I've all sorts of information at your disposal. If you should come down again (only you won't, ever – I feel that!) I should give you plenty of time to worry it out of me. Indeed there are some things I should quite insist on your learning; not permit you at all, in any settled way, *not* to learn. Yes indeed, you'd put me through, and I should put you, my dear! We should have each other to reckon with and you'd see me as I really am. I'm not a bit the vague mooning easy creature I daresay you think. However, if you won't come you won't; *n'en parlons plus.*[4] It *is* stupid here after what you're accustomed to. We can only, all round, do *what* we can, eh? For heaven's sake don't let your mother forget her precious publication, the female magazine with the what-do-you-call-'em? – the greasecatchers. There!'

Mrs. Gereth, delivering herself from the doorstep, had tossed the periodical[5] higher in air than was absolutely needful – tossed it toward the carriage the retreating party was about to enter. Mona, from the force of habit, the reflex action of the custom of sport, had popped out, with a little spring, a long arm and intercepted the missile as easily as she would have caused a tennis-ball to rebound from a racket. 'Good catch!' Owen had cried, so genuinely pleased that practically no notice was taken of his mother's impressive remarks. It was to the accompaniment of romping laughter, as Mrs. Gereth afterwards said, that the carriage had rolled away; but it was while that laughter was still in the air that Fleda Vetch, white and terrible, had turned on her hostess with her scorching 'How *could* you? Great God, how *could* you?' This lady's perfect blankness was from the first a sign of her smooth conscience; and the fact that till indoctrinated she didn't even know what Fleda meant by resenting her late offence to every susceptibility gave our young woman a sore scared perception that her own value in the house was the mere value, as one might say, of a good agent. Mrs. Gereth was generously sorry, but was still more surprised – surprised at Fleda's not having liked to be shown off to Owen as the right sort of wife for him. Why not, in the name of wonder, if she absolutely *was* the right sort? She had admitted on explanation that she could see what her young friend meant by having been laid, as Fleda called it, at his feet; but it struck the girl that the admission was only made to please her and that Mrs. Gereth was secretly surprised at her not being as happy to be sacrificed to the supremacy of a high standard as she was happy to sacrifice her. She had taken a tremendous fancy to her, but that was on account of the fancy – to Poynton of course – taken by Fleda herself. Wasn't this latter fancy then so great after all? Fleda felt she could pronounce it great indeed when really forgiving for the sake of it what she had suffered and, after re-

57

proaches and tears, asseverations and kisses, after practical proof that she was cared for only as a priestess of the altar and a view of her bruised dignity which left no alternative to flight, accepting the shame with the balm, consenting not to depart, taking refuge in the thin comfort of the truth at least brought home to her. The truth was simply that all Mrs. Gereth's scruples were on one side and that her ruling passion had in a manner despoiled her of her humanity. On the second day, when the tide of emotion had somewhat ebbed, she said soothingly to her companion: 'But you *would*, after all, marry him, you know, darling, wouldn't you, if that girl were not there? I mean of course if he were to ask you,' Mrs. Gereth had thoughtfully added. Yet she made the strangest free reach over all such preliminaries.

'Marry him if he were to ask me? Most distinctly not!'

The question had not come up with this definiteness before, and Mrs. Gereth was clearly more surprised than ever. She marvelled a moment. 'Not even to have Poynton?'

'Not even to have Poynton.'

'But why on earth?' Mrs. Gereth's sad eyes were fixed on her.

Fleda coloured; she hung fire. 'Because he's too stupid!' Save on one other occasion at which we shall in time arrive she never came nearer to betraying to Mrs. Gereth that she was in love with Owen. She found a vain charm in reflecting that if Mona had not been there and he had not been too stupid and he verily had asked her, she might, should she have wished to keep her secret, have found it possible to pass off the motive of her conduct as a mere passion for his property.

Mrs. Gereth evidently thought in these days of little but things hymeneal; for she broke out with sudden rapture in the middle of the week: 'I know what they'll do: they *will* marry, but they'll go and live at Waterbath!' There was positive joy in that form of the idea, which she embroidered and developed: it seemed so much the safest thing that could happen. 'Yes, I'll have you, but I won't go *there*!' Mona would have said with a vicious nod at the southern horizon: 'we'll leave your horrid mother alone there for life.' It would be an ideal solution, this ingress the lively pair, with their spiritual need of a warmer medium, would playfully punch in the ribs of her ancestral home; for it would not only prevent recurring panic at Poynton – it would offer them, as in one of their gimcrack baskets or other vessels of ugliness, a diurnal round of felicity that Poynton could never give. Owen might manage his estate just as he managed it now, and Mrs. Gereth would manage everything else. When in the hall, on the unforgettable day of his return, she had heard his voice ring out like a call to a terrier she had still, as Fleda afterwards learned, clutched frantically at the conceit that he had come, at the worst, to announce some compromise; to tell her she would have to put up with the girl yes, but that some way would be arrived at of leaving her in personal possession. Fleda Vetch, whom from the earliest hour no illusion had brushed with its wing, now held her breath, went on tiptoe, wandered in out-lying parts of the house and through delicate muffled rooms while the mother and son faced each other below. From time to time she stopped to listen; but all was so quiet she was almost fright-ened: she had vaguely expected a sound of contention. It lasted longer than she would have supposed, whatever it was they were doing; and when finally, from a window, she saw Owen stroll out of the house, stop and light a cigarette and then pensively lose himself in the plantations, she found other matter for trepidation in the fact that Mrs. Gereth didn't immediately come rushing up into her arms. She wondered if she oughtn't to go down to her, and measured the gravity of what had occurred by the circum-stance, which she presently ascertained, that the poor lady had retired to her room and wished not to be disturbed. This admon-ition had been for her maid, with whom Fleda conferred as at the door of a death-chamber; but the girl, without either fatuity or resentment, judged that, since it could render Mrs. Gereth indif-ferent even to the ministrations of disinterested attachment, the scene had been tremendous.

She was absent from luncheon, where indeed Fleda had enough to do to look Owen in the face: there would be so much to make that hateful in their common memory of the passage in which his last visit had terminated. This had been her apprehension at least; but as soon as he stood there she was constrained to surprise at the practical simplicity of the ordeal – a simplicity that was altogether his own simplicity, the particular thing that, for Fleda Vetch, some other things of course aiding, made almost any direct relation with him pleasant. He had neither wit nor tact nor inspiration: all she could say was that in his presence, uncontrolled as it might be, the alienation these charms were usually depended on to allay didn't occur. On this occasion for instance he did so much better than 'carry off' an awkward remembrance: he simply didn't have it. He had clean forgotten she was the girl his mother would have fobbed off on him; he was conscious only of her being there as for decent service – conscious of the dumb instinct that from the first had made him regard her not as complicating his intercourse with that personage, but as simplifying it. Fleda found it beautiful that this theory should have survived the incident of the other day; found it exquisite that whereas she was aware, through faint reverberations, that for her kind little circle at large, who didn't now at all matter, her tendency had begun to define itself as parasitical, this strong young man, who had a right to judge and even a reason to loathe her, didn't judge and didn't loathe, let her down gently, treated her as if she pleased him – in fact evidently liked her to be just where she was. She asked herself what he did when Mona denounced her, and the only answer to the question was that perhaps Mona didn't denounce her. If Mona was inarticulate he wasn't such a fool then to marry her. That he was glad Fleda was there was at any rate sufficiently shown by the domestic familiarity with which he said to her: 'I must tell you I've been having an awful row with my mother. I'm engaged to be married to Miss Brigstock.'

'Ah really?' cried Fleda, achieving a radiance of which she was secretly proud. 'How very exciting!'

'Too exciting for poor Mummy. She won't hear of it. She has been slating her fearfully. She says she's a regular barbarian.⁶'

'Why she's lovely!' Fleda exclaimed.

'Oh she's all right. Mother must come round.'

'Only give her time,' said Fleda. She had advanced to the threshold of the door thus thrown open to her and, without exactly crossing it, she threw in an appreciative glance. She asked Owen when his marriage would take place, and in the light of his reply read that Mrs. Gereth's wretched attitude would have no influence at all on the event, absolutely fixed when he had come down and distant by only three months. He liked Fleda's seeming to be on his side, though that was a secondary matter; for what actually most concerned him was the line his mother took about Poynton, her declared unwillingness to give it up.

'Naturally I want my own house, you know,' he said, 'and my father made every arrangement for me to have it. But she may make it devilish awkward. What in the world's a fellow to do?' This it was that Owen wanted to know, and there could be no better proof of his friendliness than his air of depending so utterly on Fleda Vetch to tell him. She questioned him, they spent an hour together, and, as he spoke of the force of the concussion from which he had rebounded she found herself scared and depressed by the material he seemed to offer her to deal with. It *was* devilish awkward, and it was so in part because Owen had no imagination. It had lodged itself in that empty chamber that his mother hated the surrender because she hated Mona. He didn't of course understand why she hated Mona, but this belonged to an order of mysteries that never troubled him: there were lots of things, especially in people's minds, that a fellow didn't understand. Poor Owen went through life with a frank dread of people's minds: there were explanations he would have been almost as shy of receiving as of giving. There was therefore nothing that accounted for anything, though on its own free lines it was vivid enough, his picture to Fleda of his mother's all but express refusal to move. That was what it came to; for didn't she refuse to move when she as good as declared that she would move only with the furniture? It was the furniture she wouldn't give up; and what was the good of Poynton pray without the furniture? Besides, the furniture happened to be his, just as everything else happened to be. The furniture—the word, on his lips, had somehow to Fleda the sound of washing-stands and copious bedding, and she could well imagine the note it might have struck for Mrs. Gereth. The girl herself, in this interview with him, spoke of the contents of the house only as 'the works of art.' It didn't, however, in the least matter to Owen what they were called; what did matter, she easily guessed, was that it had been laid upon him by Mona, been made in effect a condition of her consent, that he should hold his mother to the strictest accountability for them. Mona had already entered upon the enjoyment of her rights. She had made him feel that Mrs. Gereth had been liberally provided for, and had asked him strikingly enough what room there would be at Ricks for the innumerable treasures of the big house. Ricks, the sweet little place offered to the mistress of Poynton as the refuge of her declining years, had been left to the late Mr. Gereth a considerable time before his death by an old maternal aunt, a good lady who had spent most of her life there. The house had in recent times been let, but it was amply furnished, it contained all the defunct aunt's possessions. Owen had lately inspected it, and he communicated to Fleda that he had quietly taken Mona to see it. It wasn't a place like Poynton – what dower-house ever was? – but it was an awfully jolly little place, and Mona had taken a tremendous fancy to it. If there were a few things at Poynton that were Mrs. Gereth's peculiar property she must of course take them away with her; but one of the matters that became clear to Fleda was that this transfer would be now wholly subject to Miss Brigstock's approval. The special business she herself thus became aware of being charged with was that of seeing Mrs. Gereth safely and singly off the premises.

Her heart failed her, after Owen had returned to London, with the ugliness of this duty – with the ugliness indeed of the whole close contest. She saw nothing of Mrs. Gereth that day; she spent it in roaming with sick sighs, in feeling, as she passed from room to room, that what was expected of her companion was really dreadful. It would have been better never to have had such a place than to have had it and lose it. It was odious to *her* to have to look for solutions: what a strange relation between mother and son when there was no fundamental tenderness out of which a solution would irrepressibly spring! Was it Owen who was mainly responsible for that poverty? Fleda couldn't think so when she remembered that, so far as he was concerned, Mrs. Gereth would still have been welcome to keep her seat by the Poynton fire. The fact that from the moment one accepted his marrying one saw no very different course for him to take – this fact made her all the rest of that aching day find her best relief in the mercy of not having yet to face her hostess. She dodged and dreamed and fabled and trifled away the time. Instead of inventing a remedy or a compromise, instead of preparing a plan by which a scandal might be averted, she gave herself, in her sacred solitude, up to a mere fairy-tale, up to the very taste of the beautiful peace she would have scattered on the air if only something might have been that could never have been.

V

'I'LL give up the house if they'll let me take what I require!' – that, on the morrow, was what Mrs. Gereth's stifled night had qualified her to say with a tragic face at breakfast. Fleda reflected that what she 'required' was simply every object that surrounded them. The poor woman would have admitted this truth and accepted the conclusion to be drawn from it, the reduction to the absurd of her attitude, the exaltation of her claim. The girl's dread of a scandal, of spectators and critics, grew less the more she saw how little vulgar avidity had to do with this rigour. It was not the crude love of possession; it was the need to be faithful to a trust and loyal to an idea. The idea was surely noble; it was that of the beauty Mrs. Gereth had so patiently and consummately wrought. Pale but radiant, her back to the wall, she planted herself there as a heroine guarding a treasure. To give up the ship was to flinch from her duty; there was something in her eyes that declared she would die at her post. If their difference should become public the shame would be all for the others. If Waterbath thought it could afford to expose itself, then Waterbath was welcome to the folly. Her fanaticism gave her a new distinction, and Fleda remarked almost with awe that she had never carried herself so well. She trod the place like a reigning queen or a proud usurper; full as it was of splendid pieces it could show in these days no ornament so effective as its menaced mistress.

Our young lady's spirit was strangely divided; she had a tenderness for Owen which she deeply concealed, yet it left her occasion to marvel at the way a man was made who could care in any relation for a creature like Mona Brigstock when he had known in any relation a creature like Adela Gereth. With such a mother to give him the pitch how could he take it so low? She wondered she didn't despise him for this, but there was something that kept her from it. If there had been nothing else it would have sufficed

63

that she really found herself from this moment, between the pair, the sole messenger and mediator.

'He'll come back to assert himself,' Mrs. Gereth had said; and the following week Owen in fact reappeared. He might merely have written, Fleda could see, but he had come in person because it was at once 'nicer' for his mother and stronger for his cause. He didn't like such a row, though Mona probably did; if he hadn't a sense of beauty he had after all a sense of justice; but it was inevitable he should clearly announce at Poynton the date at which he must look to find the house vacant. 'You don't think I'm rough or hard, do you?' he asked of Fleda, his impatience shining in his idle eyes as the dining-hour shines in club-windows. 'The place at Ricks stands there with open arms. And then I give her lots of time. Tell her she can remove everything that belongs to her.' Fleda recognised the elements of the sort of case the newspapers called a deadlock in the circumstance that nothing at Poynton belonged to Mrs. Gereth either more or less than anything else. She must either take everything or nothing, and the girl's suggestion was that it might perhaps be an inspiration to do the latter and begin again on a clean page. What, however, was the poor woman in that event to begin with? What was she to do at all on her meagre income but make the best of the *objets d'art* of Ricks, the treasures collected by Mr. Gereth's maiden-aunt? She had never been near the place: for long years it had been let to strangers, and after this the foreboding that it would be her doom had kept her from positively courting abasement. She had felt she should see it soon enough, but Fleda (who was careful not to betray to her that Mona had seen it and had been gratified) knew her reasons for believing that the maiden-aunt's principles had had much in common with the principles of Waterbath. In short the only thing she would ever have to do with the *objets d'art* of Ricks would be to turn them out into the road. What belonged to her at Poynton, as Owen said, would conveniently mitigate the void resulting from that demonstration.

The exchange of observations between the friends had grown very direct by the time Fleda asked Mrs. Gereth if she literally meant to shut herself up and stand a siege, or if it might be her idea to expose herself, more informally, to be dragged out of the house by constables. 'Oh I prefer the constables and the dragging!'

the heroine of Poynton had readily answered. 'I want to make Owen and Mona do everything that will be most publicly odious.' She gave it out as her one thought now to force them to a line that would dishonour them and dishonour the tradition they embodied, though Fleda was privately sure she had visions of an alternative policy. The strange thing was that, proud and fastidious all her life, she now showed so little distaste for the world's hearing of the broil. What had taken place in her above all was that a long resentment had ripened. She hated the effacement to which English usage reduced the widowed mother; she had discoursed of it passionately to Fleda; contrasted it with the beautiful homage paid by other countries to women in that position, women no better than herself, whom she had seen acclaimed and enthroned, whom she had known and envied; made in short as little as possible a secret of the injury, the bitterness she found in it. The great wrong Owen had done her was not his 'taking up' with Mona – that was disgusting, but it was a detail, an accidental form; it was his failure from the first to understand what it was to have a mother at all, to appreciate the beauty and sanctity of the character. She was just his mother as his nose was just his nose, and he had never had the least imagination or tenderness or gallantry about her. One's mother, gracious goodness, if one were the kind of fine young man one ought to be, the only kind Mrs. Gereth cared for, was a subject for poetry, for idolatry. Hadn't she often told Fleda of her friend Madame de Jaume, the wittiest of women, but a small black crooked person, each of whose three boys, when absent, wrote to her every day of their lives? She had the house in Paris, she had the house in Poitou, she had more than in the lifetime of her husband – to whom, in spite of her appearance, she had afforded repeated cause for jealousy – because she was to have till the end of her days the supreme word about everything. It was easy to see how Mrs. Gereth would have given again and again her complexion, her figure, and even perhaps the spotless virtue she had still more successfully retained, to have been the consecrated Madame de Jaume. She wasn't, alas, and this was what she had at present a splendid occasion to protest against. She was of course fully aware of Owen's concession, his willingness to let her take away with her the few things she liked best; but as yet she only declared that to meet him on this ground would be to give him a triumph, to put him impossibly in the right. 'Liked best?' There wasn't a thing in the house she didn't like best, and what she liked better still was to be left where she was. How could Owen use such an expression without being conscious of his hypocrisy? Mrs. Gereth, whose criticism was often gay, dilated with sardonic humour on the happy look a dozen objects from Poynton would wear, and the charming effect they would conduce to, when interspersed with the peculiar features of Ricks. What had her whole life been but an effort toward completeness and perfection? Better Waterbath at once, in its cynical sameness, than the ignominy of such a mixture!

All this was of no great help to Fleda, in so far as Fleda tried to rise to her mission of finding a way out. When at the end of a fortnight Owen came down once more it was ostensibly to tackle a tenant on the property¹ whose course with them had not been straight; the girl was sure, however, that he had really come, on the instance of Mona, to see what his mother was up to. He wanted to convince himself that she was preparing her departure, and he desired to perform a duty, distinct but not less imperative, in regard to the question of the perquisites with which she would retreat. The tension between them was now such that he had thus to reconnoitre without meeting the enemy. Mrs. Gereth was as willing as himself that he should address to Fleda Vetch whatever cruel remarks he might have to make; she only pitied her poor young friend for repeated encounters with a person as to whom she perfectly understood the girl's repulsion. Fleda found it of a fine dim inspiration on Owen's part not to have expected her to write to him: he wouldn't have wished any more than herself that she should have the air of spying on his mother in his interest. What made it of good effect to deal with him in this more familiar way was the sense that she understood so perfectly how poor Mrs. Gereth suffered and that she measured so adequately the sacrifice the other side did take rather monstrously for granted. She understood equally how Owen himself suffered, now that Mona had already begun to make him do things he didn't like. Vividly Fleda apprehended how *she* would have first made him like anything she would have made him do; anything even as disagreeable as this appearing there to state, virtually on Mona's behalf, that of course there must be a definite limit to the number of articles appropriated. She took a longish stroll with him in order to talk the matter over; to say if she didn't think a dozen pieces, chosen absolutely at will, would be a handsome allowance; and above all to consider the very delicate question of whether the advantage enjoyed by Mrs. Gereth mightn't be left – well, to her honour. To leave it so was what Owen wished; but there was plainly a young lady at Waterbath to whom, on his side, he already had to render an account. He was as touching in his off-hand annoyance as his mother was tragic in her intensity; for if he couldn't help having a sense of propriety about the whole matter he could as little help hating it. It was for his hating it, Fleda reasoned, that she liked him so, and her insistence to his mother on the hatred perilously resembled on one or two occasions a revelation of the liking. There were moments when, in conscience, that revelation pressed her inasmuch as it was just on the ground of her not liking him that Mrs. Gereth trusted her so much. Mrs. Gereth herself didn't in these days like him at all, and she was of course always on Mrs. Gereth's side. He ended really, while the preparations for his marriage went on, by quite a little custom of coming and going; but at no one of these junctures would his mother receive him. He talked only with Fleda and strolled with Fleda; and when he asked her, in regard to the great matter, if Mrs. Gereth were really doing nothing, the girl usually replied: 'She pretends not to be, if I may say so; but I think she's really thinking over what she'll take.' When her friend at the great house asked her in turn what 'those monsters' were doing she could have but one answer. 'They're waiting, dear lady, to see what *you* do!'

Mrs. Gereth, a month after she had received her great shock, did something abrupt and extraordinary: she caught up her companion and went over to have a look at Ricks. They had come to London first and taken a train from Liverpool Street,[2] and the least of the sufferings they were armed against was that of passing the night. Fleda's admirable dressing-bag had been given her by her high benefactress. 'Why it's charming!' she exclaimed a few hours later, turning back again into the small prim parlour from a friendly advance to the single plate[3] of the window. Mrs. Gereth hated such windows, the one flat glass sliding up and down, especially when they enjoyed a view of four iron pots on pedestals, painted white and containing ugly geraniums, ranged on the edge of a gravel path and doing their best to give it the air of a terrace. Fleda had instantly averted her eyes from these ornaments, but Mrs. Gereth grimly gazed, wondering of course how a place in the deepest depths of Essex and three miles from a small station could contrive to look so suburban. The room was practically a shallow box, with the junction of the walls and ceiling guiltless of curve or cornice and marked merely by the little band of crimson paper glued round the top of the other paper, a turbid grey sprigged with silver flowers. This decoration was rather new and quite fresh; and there was in the centre of the ceiling a big square beam papered over in white,[4] as to which Fleda hesitated about throwing out that it was rather picturesque. She recognised in time that this venture would be weak and that she should, all through, be able to say nothing either for the mantelpieces or for the doors, of which she saw her companion become sensible with a soundless moan. On the subject of doors especially Mrs. Gereth had the finest views: the thing in the world she most despised was the meanness of the undivided opening. From end to end of Poynton there swung high double leaves. At Ricks the entrances to the rooms were like the holes of rabbit-hutches.

It was all, none the less, not so bad as Fleda had feared; it was faded and melancholy, whereas there had been a danger it would be contradictious and positive, cheerful and loud. The place was crowded with objects of which the aggregation somehow made a thinness and the futility a grace; things that told her they had been gathered as slowly and as lovingly as the golden flowers of the other house. She too, for a home, could have lived with them: they made her fond of the old maiden-aunt; they made her even wonder if it didn't work more for happiness not to have tasted, as she herself had done, of knowledge. Without resources, without a stick, as she said, of her own, Fleda was moved, after all, to some secret surprise at the pretensions of a shipwrecked woman who could hold such an asylum cheap. The more she looked about the surer she felt of the character of the maiden-aunt, the sense of whose dim presence urged her to pacification: the maiden-aunt had been a dear; she should have adored the maiden-aunt. The poor lady had passed shyly, yet with some bruises, through life; had been sensitive and ignorant and exquisite: that too was a sort of origin, a sort of atmosphere for relics and rarities, though different from the sorts most prized at Poynton. Mrs. Gereth had of course more than once said that one of the deepest mysteries of life was the way that – given certain natures – hideous objects could be loved. But it wasn't a question of love at present for these; it was only a question of some practical patience. Perhaps a thought of that kind had stolen over her when, at the end of a brooding hour, she exclaimed, taking in the house with a strenuous sigh: 'Well, something can be done with it!' Fleda had repeated to her more than once the indulgent fancy about the maiden-aunt – she was so sure she had deeply suffered. 'I'm sure I thoroughly hope she did!' was, however, all the more austere of the pilgrims to Ricks had replied.

VI

IT was a great relief to the girl at last to feel sure that the dreadful move would really be made. What might happen if it shouldn't had been from the first indefinite. It was absurd to pretend that any violence was probable – a tussle, dishevelment, pushes, scratches, shrieks; yet Fleda had an imagination of drama, of a 'great scene,' a thing, somehow, of indignity and misery, of wounds inflicted and received, in which indeed, though Mrs. Gereth's presence, with movements and sounds, loomed large to her, Owen remained indistinct and on the whole unaggressive. He wouldn't be there with a cigarette in his teeth, very handsome and insolently quiet: that was only the way he would be in a novel, across whose interesting page some such figure, as she half-closed her eyes, seemed to her to walk. Fleda harboured rather, and indeed with shame, the confused, pitying vision of Mrs. Gereth with her great scene left in a manner on her hands, Mrs. Gereth missing her effect and having to appear merely hot and injured and in the wrong. The symptoms that she would be spared even that spectacle resided not so much, through the chambers of Poynton, in an air of concentration as in the hum of uneasy alternatives. There was no common preparation, but one day, at the turn of a corridor, she found her hostess standing very still, with the hanging hands of despair and yet with the active eyes of adventure. These eyes appeared to Fleda to meet her own with a strange dim bravado, and there was a silence almost awkward before either of the friends spoke. The girl afterwards thought of the moment as one in which her hostess mutely accused her of an accusation, meeting it at the same time, however, by a kind of defiant acceptance. Yet it was with mere melancholy candour that Mrs. Gereth at last sighingly exclaimed: 'I'm thinking over what I had better take!' Fleda could have embraced her for this virtual promise of a concession, the announcement that she had finally accepted the problem of knocking together a shelter with the small salvage of the wreck.

It was true that when after their return from Ricks they tried to lighten the ship the great embarrassment was still immutably there, the odiousness of sacrificing the exquisite things one wouldn't take to the exquisite things one would. This immediately made the things one wouldn't the very things one ought to, and, as Mrs. Gereth said, condemned one, in the whole business, to an eternal vicious circle. In such a circle, for days, she had been tormentedly moving, prowling up and down, comparing incomparables. It was for that one had to cling to them – for their faces of supplication. Fleda herself could judge of these faces, so conscious of their race and their danger, and she had little enough to say when her companion asked her if the place, all perversely fair on October afternoons, looked like a place to give up. It looked, to begin with, through some effect of season and light, larger than ever, immense, and it brimmed over as with the hush of sorrow, which was in turn all charged with memories. Everything was in the air – each history of each find, each circumstance of each capture. Mrs. Gereth had drawn back every curtain and removed every cover; she prolonged the vistas, opened wide the whole house, gave it an appearance of awaiting a royal visit. The shimmer of wrought substances spent itself in the brightness; the old golds and brasses, old ivories and bronzes, the fresh old tapestries and deep old damasks threw out a radiance in which the poor woman saw in solution all her old loves and patiences, all her old tricks and triumphs.

Fleda had a depressed sense of not, after all, helping her much: this was relieved indeed by the fact that Mrs. Gereth, letting her off easily, didn't now seem to expect it. Her sympathy, her interest, her feeling for everything for which her hostess felt, were a force that really worked to prolong the deadlock. 'I only wish I bored you and my possessions bored you,' that lady declared with some humour; 'then you'd make short work with me, bundle me off, tell me just to pile certain things into a cart and have done.' Fleda's sharpest difficulty was in having to act up to the character of thinking Owen a brute, or in having at least to carry off the inconsistency of seeing him when he came down. By good fortune it was her indicated duty, her prescribed function, as well as a due protection to Mrs. Gereth. She thought of him perpetually and her eyes had come to rejoice in his manly magnificence more even than they rejoiced in the royal cabinets of the red saloon. She wondered, very faintly at first, why he came so often: but of course she knew nothing of the business he had in hand, over which, with men red-faced and leather-legged,[1] he was sometimes closeted for an hour in a room of his own that was the one monstrosity of Poynton: all tobacco-pots and bootjacks, his mother had said – such an array of arms of aggression and castigation that he himself had confessed to eighteen rifles and forty whips. He was arranging for settlements on his wife, he was doing things that would meet the views of the Brigstocks. Considering the house was his own Fleda thought it nice of him to keep himself in the background while his mother remained; making his visits, at some cost of ingenuity about trains from town, only between meals, taking pains to let it press lightly on her that he was there. This was rather a check to her meeting Mrs. Gereth on the ground of his being a brute; the most possible really at last was not to contradict her when she repeated that he was posted – just insultingly posted to watch. He *was* watching, no doubt; but he watched somehow with his head turned away. He knew Fleda to know at present what he wanted of her, so that it would be gross of him to say it over and over. It existed as a confidence between them and made him sometimes, with his wandering stare, meet her eyes as if a silence so pleasant could only unite them the more. He had no great flow of speech, certainly, and at first the girl took it for granted that this only exhausted any conceivable statement of the matter. Yet little by little she speculated as to whether, with a person who, like herself, could after all put him at some domestic ease, it was not supposable he would have more conversation if he were not keeping some of it back for Mona.

From the moment she suspected he might be thinking how Mona would judge his chattering so to an underhand 'companion,' an inmate all but paid in shillings, this young lady's repressed emotion began to require still more repression. She grew impatient of her posture at Poynton, privately pronouncing it false and horrid. She said to herself that she had let Owen know of her having, to the best of her power, directed his mother in the general sense he desired; that he quite understood this and that he also understood how unworthy it was of either of them to stand over the good lady with a note-book and a lash. Wasn't this practical unanimity just practical success? Fleda became aware of a sudden desire, as well as of pressing reasons, for the cessation of her long stay. She had not, on the one hand, like a minion of the law, undertaken to see Mrs. Gereth down to the train and locked, in sign of her abdication, into a compartment; neither had she on the other committed herself to hold Owen indefinitely in dalliance while his mother gained time or worked with the spade at a counter-mine. Besides, people *were* saying that she fastened like a leech on other people – people who had houses where something was to be picked up: this disclosure was frankly made her by her sister, now distinctly doomed to the curate and in view of whose nuptials she had almost finished, as a present, a wonderful piece of embroidery suggested, and precisely at Poynton, by an old Spanish altar-cloth. She would have to exert herself still further for the intended recipient of this offering, turn her out for the altar and subsequent straits with more than that drapery. She would go up to town, in short, to dress Maggie; and their father, in lodgings at West Kensington,[2] would stretch a point and take them in. He, to do him justice, never reproached her with profitable devotions;[3] so far as they existed he rather studied to glean from the same supposed harvest. Mrs. Gereth gave her up as heroically as if she had been a great bargain, and Fleda knew she shouldn't herself miss any imminent visit of the young man's, since the young man was shooting at Waterbath. Owen shooting was Owen lost, and there was scant sport at Poynton.

The first news she had from Mrs. Gereth was news of that lady's having accomplished, in form at least, her dread migration. The letter was dated from Ricks, to which place she had been transported by an impulse apparently as sudden as the inspiration she had obeyed before. 'Yes, I've literally come,' she wrote, 'with a band-box and a kitchen-maid; I've crossed the Rubicon,[4] I've taken possession. It has been like plumping into cold water. I saw the only thing was to do it, not to stand shivering. I shall have warmed the place a little by simply being here for a week; when I come back the ice will have been broken. I didn't write to you to meet me on my way through town, because I know how busy you are and because, besides, I'm too savage and odious to be fit company even for you. You'd say I really go too far, and there's no doubt whatever I do. I'm here, at any rate, just to look round

73

once more, to see certain things done before I enter in force. I shall probably be at Poynton all next week. There's more room than I quite measured the other day, and a rather good set of old Worcester. But what are space and time, what's even old Worcester,[5] to your wretched and affectionate A. G.?'

The day after Fleda received this letter she had occasion to enter a big shop in Oxford Street – a journey she achieved circuitously, first on foot and then by the aid of two omnibuses. The second of these vehicles put her down on the side of the street opposite her shop, and while, on the curbstone, she humbly waited, with a parcel, an umbrella and a tucked-up frock,[6] to cross in security, she became aware that, close beside her, a hansom[7] had pulled up short and in obedience to the brandished stick of a demonstrative occupant. This occupant was exactly Owen Gereth, who had caught sight of her as he rattled along and who, with an exhibition of white teeth that, from under the hood of the cab, had almost flashed through the fog, now alighted to ask her if he couldn't give her a lift. On learning her destination to be just over the way he dismissed his vehicle and joined her, not only piloting her to the shop but taking her in: with the assurance that his errands didn't matter and that it amused him to be concerned with hers. She told him she had come to buy a trimming for her sister's frock, and he expressed a joyous interest in the purchase. His joy, always hilarious, was apt to be out of proportion to the case, but it struck her at present as higher-pitched than ever; especially when she had suggested he might find it a good time to buy a garnishment of some sort for Mona. After wondering an instant whether he read the full satiric meaning, such as it was, into this remark, Fleda dismissed the possibility as inconceivable. He stammered out that it was for *her* he should like to buy something, something 'ripping,' and that she must give him the pleasure of telling him what would best please her. He couldn't have a better opportunity for making her a present – the tribute of recognition of all she had done for Mummy that he had had in his head for weeks.

Fleda had more than one small errand in the big bazaar, and he went up and down with her, pointedly patient, pretending to be interested in questions of tape and of change. She had now not the least hesitation in wondering what Mona would think of such proceedings. But they were not her doing – they were Owen's;

and Owen, inconsequent and even extravagant, was unlike anything she had ever seen him before. He broke off, he came back, he repeated questions without heeding answers, he made vague and abrupt remarks about the resemblances of shop-girls and the uses of chiffon. He unduly prolonged their business together, giving Fleda a sense of his putting off something particular that he had to face. If she had ever dreamed of Owen Gereth as finely fluttered she would have seen him with some such manner as this. But why should he be finely fluttered? Even at the height of the crisis his mother hadn't made him flagrantly nervous, and at present he was satisfied about his mother. The one idea he stuck to was that Fleda should mention something she would let him give her: there was everything in the world in the wonderful place, and he made her incongruous offers – a travelling-rug, a massive clock, a table for breakfast in bed, and above all, in a resplendent binding, a set of somebody's 'works.' His notion was a testimonial, something of the sort usually done by subscription – and in this case indeed perhaps the Brigstocks would contribute; so that the 'works' in especial would be a graceful intimation that it was her cleverness he wished above all to commemorate. He was immensely in earnest, but the articles he pressed upon her betrayed a delicacy that went to her heart: what he would really have liked, as he saw them tumbled about, was one of the splendid stuffs for a gown – a choice proscribed by his fear of seeming to patronise her, to refer to her small means and her deficiencies. Fleda found it easy to chaff him about his exaggeration of her deserts; she gave the just measure of them in consenting to accept a small pincushion, costing sixpence, in which the letter F was marked out with pins. A sense of loyalty to Mona was not needed to enforce this discretion, and she was careful not to renew her reference to their beautiful friend. She noticed on this occasion more things in Owen Gereth than she had ever noticed before, but what she noticed most was that he said no word of his intended. She asked herself what he had done, in so long a parenthesis, with his loyalty or at least with his 'form'; and then reflected that even had he done something very good the situation in which such a question could come up was already a little strange. Of course he wasn't thinking of anything so vulgar as to make love to her; but there was a kind of punctilio for a man known to be engaged.

That punctilio didn't prevent Owen's remaining with her after they had left the shop, nor his hoping she had a lot more to do, nor yet his pressing her to look with him, for a possible glimpse of something she might really let him give her, into the windows of other establishments. There was a moment when, under this pressure, she made up her mind that his tribute would be, if analysed, a tribute to her insignificance. But all the same he wanted her to come somewhere and have luncheon with him: what was that a tribute to? She must have counted very little if she didn't count too much for a romp in a restaurant. She had to get home with her trimming, and the most she was amenable to in his company was a retracing of her steps to the Marble Arch[8] and then, after a discussion when they had reached it, a walk with him across the Park.[9] She knew Mona would have considered she ought now to take the 'penny bus' again; but she had by this time to think for Owen as well as for herself – she couldn't think for Mona. Even in the Park the autumn air was thick, and as they moved westward over the grass, which was what Owen preferred, the cool greyness made their words soft, made them at last rare and everything else dim. He wanted to stay with her – he wanted not to leave her: he had dropped into complete silence, but that was what his silence said. What was it he had postponed? What was it he wanted still to postpone? She grew a little scared while they strolled together and while she thought. The indication, all indirect, was too vague to be flagrant, but it was as if somehow he were feeling differently. Fleda Vetch didn't suspect him at first of feeling differently to *her*, but only of feeling differently to Mona; yet she was not unconscious that this latter difference would have had something to do with his being on the grass there beside her. She had read in novels about gentlemen who on the eve of marriage, winding up the past, had surrendered themselves for the occasion to the influence of a former tie; and there was something in Owen's behaviour now, something in his very face, that suggested a resemblance to one of those gentlemen. But whom and what, in that case, would Fleda herself resemble? She wasn't a former tie, she wasn't any tie at all; she was only a deep little person for whom happiness was a kind of pearl-diving plunge.[10] Happiness was down at the very bottom of all that had lately occurred; for all that had lately occurred was that Owen Gereth had come and gone at Poynton. That was the small sum of her experience, and what it had made for her was her own affair, quite consistent with her not having dreamed it had made a relation – at least what *she* called one – for Owen. The old relation, at any rate, was with Mona – Mona whom he had known so very much longer.

They walked far, to the south-west corner of the great Gardens,[11] where, by the old round pond and the old red palace,[12] when she had put out her hand to him in farewell, declaring that from the gate she must positively take a conveyance, it seemed suddenly to rise between them that this was a real separation. She was on his mother's side, she belonged to his mother's life, and his mother, in the future, would never, never come to Poynton. After what had passed she wouldn't even be at his wedding, and it was not possible now that Mr. Gereth should mention that ceremony to the girl, much less express a wish that the girl should be present at it. Mona, from decorum and with reference less to the bridegroom than to the bridegroom's mother, would of course not invite any such creature as Miss Vetch. Everything therefore was ended; they would go their different ways; it was the last time they should stand face to face. They looked at each other with the fuller sense of it and, on Owen's part, with an expression of dumb trouble, the intensification of his frequent appeal to any interlocutor to add the right thing to what he said. It struck Fleda at this moment that the right thing might easily be the wrong. At any rate he only said: 'I want you to understand, you know – I want you to understand.'

What did he want her to understand? He seemed unable to bring it out, and this understanding was moreover exactly what she wished not to arrive at. Bewildered as she was she had already taken in as much as she should know what to do with; the blood also was rushing into her face. He liked her – it was stupefying – more than he really ought: that was what was the matter with him and what he desired her to swallow; so that she was suddenly as frightened as some thoughtless girl who finds herself the object of an overture from a married man.

'Good-bye, Mr. Gereth – I *must* get on!' she declared with a cheerfulness that she felt to be an unnatural grimace. She broke away from him sharply, smiling, backing across the grass and then turning altogether and moving as fast as she could. 'Good-bye, good-bye!' she threw off again as she went, wondering if he would overtake her before she reached the gate; conscious with a red disgust that her movement was almost a run; conscious too of the very confused handsome face with which he would look after her. She felt as if she had answered a kindness with a great flouncing snub, but in any case she had got away – though the distance to the gate, her ugly gallop down the Broad Walk, every graceless jerk of which hurt her, seemed endless. She signed from afar to a cab on the stand in the Kensington Road[13] and scrambled into it, glad of the encompassment of the four-wheeler[14] that had officiously obeyed her summons and that, at the end of twenty yards, when she had violently pulled up a glass, permitted her to feel herself all wretchedly ready to burst into tears.

VII

AS soon as her sister had been married she went down to Mrs.
Gereth at Ricks – a promise to this effect having been promptly
exacted and given; and her inner vision was much more fixed
on the alterations there, complete now as she understood, than
on the success of her plotting and pinching for Maggie's happiness. Her imagination, in the interval, had indeed had plenty
to do and numerous scenes to visit; for when on the summons
just mentioned it had taken a flight from West Kensington to
Ricks, it had hung but an hour over the terrace of painted pots
and then yielded to a current of the upper air that swept it
straight off to Poynton and to Waterbath. Not a sound had
reached her of any supreme clash, and Mrs. Gereth had communicated next to nothing; giving out that, as was easily conceivable, she was too busy, too bitter and too tired for vain
civilities. All she had written was that she had got the new place
well in hand and that Fleda would be surprised at the way
it was turning out. Everything was even yet upside down;
nevertheless, in the sense of having passed the threshold of
Poynton for the last time, the amputation, as she called it, had
been performed. Her leg had come off – she had now begun to
stump along with the lovely wooden substitute; she would
stump for life, and what her young friend was to come and
admire was the beauty of her movement and the noise she made
about the house. The reserve of Poynton, as well as that of
Waterbath, had been matched by the austerity of Fleda's own
secret, under the discipline of which she had repeated to herself
a hundred times a day that she rejoiced in cares so heavy as to
exclude all thought of it. She had lavished herself, in act, on
Maggie and the curate, and had opposed to her father's selfish-
ness a heavenly patience. The young couple wondered why they
had waited so long, since everything seemed after all so easy.
She had thought of everything, even to how the 'quietness' of

the wedding should be relieved by champagne and her father – very firmly – kept brilliant on a single bottle. Fleda knew, in short, and liked the knowledge, that for several weeks she had appeared exemplary in every relation of life.

She had been perfectly prepared to be surprised at Ricks, for Mrs. Gereth was a wonder-working wizard, with a command, when all was said, of good material; but the impression in wait for her on the threshold made her catch her breath and falter. Dusk had fallen when she arrived, and in the plain square hall, one of the few good features, the glow of a Venetian lamp just showed on either wall, in perfect proportion, a small but splendid tapestry. This instant perception that the place had been dressed at the expense of Poynton was a shock: it was as if she had abruptly seen herself in the light of an accomplice. The next moment, folded in Mrs. Gereth's arms, her eyes were diverted; but she had already had, in a flash, the vision of great gaps in the other house. The two tapestries, not the biggest pieces but those most splendidly toned by time, had been on the whole its most uplifted pride. When she could really see again she was on a sofa in the drawing-room, staring with intensity at an object soon distinct as the great Italian cabinet that had been in the red saloon.[1] All without looking she was sure the room was occupied by just such other objects, stuffed with as many as it could hold of the trophies of her friend's struggle. By this time the very fingers of her glove, resting on the seat of the sofa, had thrilled at the touch of an old velvet brocade, a wondrous texture she could recognise, would have recognised among a thousand, without dropping her eyes on it. They stuck to the cabinet with dissimulated dread while she painfully asked herself if she should notice it, notice everything, or just pretend not to be affected. How could she pretend not to be affected with the very pendants of the lustres tinkling at her and with Mrs. Gereth, beside her, staring at her even as she herself stared at the cabinet, hunching up a back like Atlas[2] under his globe?[3] She was appalled at this image of what Mrs. Gereth had on her shoulders. That lady was waiting and watching her, bracing herself and preparing the same face of confession and defiance she had shown at Poynton the day she had been surprised in the corridor. It was farcical not to speak; and yet to exclaim, to participate, would give one a bad sense of being mixed up with a theft. This ugly word sounded, for herself, in Fleda's silence, and the very violence of it jarred her into a scared glance, as of a creature detected, to right and left. But what again the full picture most showed her was the far-away empty sockets, a scandal of nakedness between high bleak walls. She at last uttered something formal and incoherent – she didn't know what: it had no relation to either house. Then she felt all her friend's weight, as it were, once more on her arm. 'I've arranged a charming room for you – it's really lovely. You'll be very happy there.' This was spoken with extraordinary sweetness and with a smile that meant: 'Oh I know what you're thinking; but what does it matter when you're so loyally on my side?' It had come indeed to a question of 'sides,' Fleda thought, for the whole place was in battle array. In the soft lamplight, with one fine feature after another looming up into sombre richness, it defied her not to pronounce it a triumph of taste. Her passion for beauty leaped back into life; and was not what now most appealed to it a certain gorgeous audacity? Mrs. Gereth's high hand was, as mere great effect, the climax of the impression.

'It's too wonderful what you've done with the house!' – the visitor met her friend's eyes. They lighted up with joy, that friend herself was so pleased with what she had done. This was not at all, in its accidental air of enthusiasm, what Fleda wanted to have said: it offered her as stupidly announcing from the first minute on whose side she was. Such was clearly the way Mrs. Gereth took it; she threw herself upon the delightful girl and tenderly embraced her again; so that Fleda soon went on with a studied difference and a cooler inspection. 'Why you brought away absolutely everything!'

'Oh no, not everything. I saw how little I could get into this scrap of a house. I only brought away what I required.'

Fleda had got up; she took a turn round the room. 'You "required" the very best pieces – the *morceaux de musée*,[4] the individual gems!'

'I certainly didn't want the rubbish, if that's what you mean.' Mrs. Gereth, on the sofa, followed the direction of her companion's eyes; with the light of her satisfaction still in her face she slowly rubbed her large handsome hands. Wherever she was she was herself the great piece in the gallery. It was the first Fleda had heard of there being 'rubbish' at Poynton, but she didn't for the

81

moment take up this false plea; she only, from where she stood in the room, called out, one after the other, as if she had had a list before her, the items that in the great house had been scattered and that now, if they had a fault, were too much like a minuet danced on a hearth-rug. She knew them each by every inch of their surface and every charm of their character – knew them by the personal name their distinctive sign or story had given them; and a second time she felt how, against her intention, this uttered knowledge struck her hostess as so much free approval. Mrs. Gereth was never indifferent to approval, and there was nothing she could so love you for as for doing justice to her deep morality. There was a particular gleam in her eyes when Fleda exclaimed at last, dazzled by the display, 'And even the Maltese cross!'[5] That description, though technically incorrect, had always been applied at Poynton to a small but marvellous crucifix of ivory, a masterpiece of delicacy, of expression and of the great Spanish period,[6] the existence and precarious accessibility of which she had heard of at Malta, years before, by an odd and romantic chance – a clue followed through mazes of secrecy till the treasure was at last unearthed.

' "Even" the Maltese cross?' Mrs. Gereth rose as she sharply echoed the words. 'My dear child, you don't suppose I'd have sacrificed *that*! For what in the world would you have taken me?'

'A *bibelot* the more or less,' Fleda said, 'could have made little difference in this grand general view of you. I take you simply for the greatest of all conjurors. You've operated with a quickness – and with a quietness!' Her voice just trembled as she spoke, for the plain meaning of her words was that what her friend had achieved belonged to the class of operations essentially involving the protection of darkness. Fleda felt she really could say nothing at all if she couldn't say she took in the risks heroically run, all the danger surmounted. She completed her thought by a resolute and perfectly candid question. 'How in the world did you get off with them?'

Mrs. Gereth confessed to the fact of great evasions with a cynicism that surprised her. 'By calculating, by choosing my time. I *was* quiet and I *was* quick. I manoeuvred, prepared my ground; then at the last I rushed!' Fleda drew a long breath: she saw in the poor woman something much better than sophistical ease, a crude elation that was a comparatively simple state to deal with. Her elation, it was true, was not so much from what she had done as from the way she had done it – by as brilliant a stroke as any commemorated in the annals of punished crime. 'I succeeded because I had thought it all out and left nothing to chance. The whole business was organised in advance, so that the mere carrying it into effect took but a few hours. It was largely a matter of money: oh I was horribly extravagant – I had to turn on so many people. But they were all to be had – a little army of workers, the packers, the porters, the helpers of every sort, the men with the mighty vans. It was a question of arranging in Tottenham Court Road[7] and of paying the price. I haven't paid it yet; there'll be a horrid bill; but at least the thing's done! Expedition pure and simple was the essence of the bargain. "I can give you two days," I said; "I can't give you another second." They undertook the job, and the two days saw them through. The people came down on a Tuesday morning; they were off on the Thursday. I admit that some of them worked all Wednesday night. I had thought it all out; I stood over them; I showed them how. Yes, I coaxed them, I made love to them. Oh I was inspired – they found me wonderful. I neither ate nor slept, but I was as calm as I am now. I didn't know what was in me: it was worth finding out. I'm very remarkable, my dear: I lifted tons with my own arms. I'm tired, very, very tired; but there's neither a scratch nor a nick, there isn't a teacup missing.' Magnificent both in her exhaustion and in her triumph she sank on the sofa again, the sweep of her eyes a rich synthesis and the restless friction of her hands a clear betrayal. 'Upon my word,' she laughed, 'they really look better here!'

Fleda had listened in awe. 'And no one at Poynton said anything? There was no alarm?'

'What alarm should there have been? Owen left me almost defiantly alone. I had taken a special time I had reason to believe safe from a descent.' Fleda had another wonder, which she hesitated to express: it would scarcely do to ask if such a heroine hadn't stood in fear of her servants. She knew moreover some of the secrets of the heroine's humorous household rule, all made up of shocks to shyness and provocations to curiosity – a diplomacy so artful that several of the maids quite yearned to accompany her to Ricks. Mrs. Gereth, reading sharply the whole of her visitor's thought, caught it up with fine frankness. 'You mean that I was watched – that he had his myrmidons,[8] pledged to wire him if they should see what I was "up to"? Precisely. I know the three persons you have in mind: I had them in mind myself. Well, I took a line with them – I settled them.'

Fleda had had no one in particular in mind and had never believed in the myrmidons; but the tone in which Mrs. Gereth spoke added to her suspense. 'What did you do to them?'

'I took hold of them hard – I put them in the forefront. I made them work.'

'To move the furniture?'

'To help, and to help so as to please me. That was the way to take them: it was what they had least expected. I marched up to them and looked each straight in the eye, giving him the chance to choose if he'd gratify me or gratify my son. He gratified *me*. They were too stupid!'

She massed herself more and more as an immoral woman, but Fleda had to recognise that another person too would have been stupid and another person too would have gratified her. 'And when did all this take place?'

'Only last week; it seems a hundred years. We've worked here as fast as we worked there, but I'm not settled yet: you'll see in the rest of the house. However, the worst's over.'

'Do you really think so?' Fleda presently inquired. 'I mean does he after the fact, as it were, accept it?'

'Owen – what I've done? I haven't the least idea,' said Mrs. Gereth.

'Does Mona?'

'You mean that she'll be the soul of the row?'

'I hardly see Mona as the "soul" of anything,' the girl replied. 'But have they made no sound? Have you heard nothing at all?'

'Not a whisper, not a step, in all the eight days. Perhaps they don't know. Perhaps they're crouching for a leap.'

'But wouldn't they have gone down as soon as you left?'

'They may not have known of my leaving.' Fleda wondered afresh; it struck her as scarcely supposable that some sign shouldn't have flashed from Poynton to London. If the storm was taking this term of silence to gather, even in Mona's breast, it would probably discharge itself in some thunderburst. The great hush of every one concerned was strange; but when she pressed Mrs. Gereth for the sense of it that lady only replied with her brave irony: 'Oh I took their breath away!' She had no illusions, however; she was still prepared to fight. What indeed was her spoliation of Poynton but the first engagement of a campaign?

All this was exciting, but Fleda's spirit dropped, at bedtime, in the quarter embellished for her particular pleasure, where she found several of the objects that in her earlier room she had most admired. These had been re-enforced by other pieces from other rooms, so that the quiet air of it was a harmony without a break, the finished picture of a maiden's bower. It was the sweetest Louis Seize,⁹ all assorted and combined – old, chastened, figured, faded France. Fleda was impressed anew with her friend's genius for composition. She could say to herself that no girl in England, that night, went to rest with so picked a guard; but there was no joy for her in her privilege, no sleep even for the tired hours that made the place, in the embers of the fire and the winter dawn, look grey, somehow, and loveless. She couldn't care for such things when they came to her in such ways; there was a wrong about them all that turned them to ugliness. In the watches of the night she saw Poynton dishonoured; she had cherished it as a happy whole, she reasoned, and the parts of it now around her seemed to suffer like chopped limbs. To lie there in the stillness was partly to listen for some soft low plaint from them. Before going to bed she had walked about with Mrs. Gereth and seen at whose expense the whole house had been furnished. At poor Owen's from top to bottom – there wasn't a chair he hadn't sat upon. The maiden-aunt had been exterminated – no trace of her to tell her tale. Fleda tried to think of some of the things at Poynton still unappropriated, but her memory was a blank about them, and in the effort to focus the old combinations she saw again nothing but gaps and scars, a vacancy that gathered at moments into something worse. This concrete image was her greatest trouble, for it was Owen Gereth's face, his sad, strange eyes, fixed upon her now as they had never been. They stared at her out of the darkness and their expression was more than she could bear: it seemed to say that he was in pain and that it was somehow her fault. He had looked to her to help him, yet this was what her help had been. He had done her the honour to ask her to exert herself in his interest, confiding to her a task of difficulty but of the highest delicacy. Hadn't that been exactly the sort of service she longed to render him? Well, her way of rendering it had been simply to betray him and hand him over to his enemy. Shame, pity, resentment oppressed her in turn; in the last of these feelings the others were soon submerged. Mrs. Gereth had imprisoned her in that torment of taste, but it was clear to her for an hour at least that she might hate Mrs. Gereth.

Something else, however, when morning came, was even more intensely definite: the most odious thing in the world for her would be ever again to meet Owen. She took on the spot a resolve to neglect no precaution that could lead to her going through life without that calamity. After this, while she dressed, she took still another. Her position had become in a few hours intolerably false; in as few more hours as possible she would therefore put an end to it. The way to put an end would be to let her friend know that, to her great regret, she couldn't be with her now, couldn't cleave to her to the point that everything about them so plainly urged. She dressed with a sort of violence, a symbol of the manner in which this purpose had been precipitated. The more they parted company the less likely she was to come across Owen; for Owen would be drawn closer to his mother now by the very necessity of bringing her down. Fleda, in the inconsequence of distress, wished to have nothing to do with her fall; she had had too much to do with everything. She was well aware of the importance, before breakfast and in view of any light they might shed on the question of motive, of not suffering her invidious expression of a difference to be accompanied by the traces of tears; but it none the less came to pass, downstairs, that after she had subtly put her back to the window to make a mystery of the state of her eyes she stupidly let a rich sob escape her before she could properly meet the consequences of being asked if she wasn't delighted with her room. This accident struck her on the spot as so grave that she felt the only refuge to be instant hypocrisy, some graceful impulse that would charge her emotion to the quickened sense of her friend's generosity – a demonstration entailing a flutter round the table and a renewed embrace, yet not so successfully improvised but that Fleda fancied Mrs. Gereth to have been only half-reassured. She had been startled at any rate and might remain suspicious: this reflexion interposed by the time, after breakfast, our young woman had recovered sufficiently to say what was in her heart. She accordingly didn't say it that morning at all. She had absurdly veered about; she had encountered the shock of the fear that Mrs. Gereth, with sharpened eyes, might wonder why the deuce (she often wondered in that phrase) she had grown so warm about Owen's rights. She would doubtless at a pinch be able to defend them on abstract grounds, but that would involve a discussion, and the idea of a discussion made her nervous for her secret. Until in some way Poynton should return the blow and give her a cue she must keep nervousness down; and she called herself a fool for having forgotten, however briefly, that her one safety was in silence.

Directly after luncheon her friend took her into the garden for a glimpse of the revolution[10] – or at least, said the mistress of Ricks, of the great row – that had been decreed there; but the ladies had scarcely placed themselves for this view before the younger one found herself embracing a prospect that opened in quite another quarter. Her attention was called to it, oddly, by the streamers of the parlour-maid's cap, which, flying straight behind the neat young woman who unexpectedly burst from the house and showed a long red face as she ambled over the grass, seemed to articulate in their flutter the name that Fleda lived at present only to catch. 'Poynton – Poynton!' said the morsels of muslin; so that the parlour-maid became on the instant an actress in the drama, and Fleda, assuming pusillanimously that she herself was only a spectator, looked across the footlights at the exponent of the principal part. The manner in which this artist returned the look showed her as equally preoccupied. Both were haunted alike by possibilities, but the apprehension of neither, before the announcement was made, had taken the form of the arrival at Ricks, in the flesh, of Mrs. Gereth's victim. When the messenger informed them that Mr. Gereth was in the drawing-room the blank 'Oh!' emitted by Fleda was quite as precipitate as the sound on her hostess's lips, besides being, as she felt, much less pertinent. 'I thought it would be somebody,' that lady afterwards said; 'but I expected on the whole a solicitor's clerk.' Fleda didn't mention that she herself had expected on the whole a brace of constables. She wondered at Mrs. Gereth's question to the parlour-maid.

'For whom did he ask?'

'Why for *you* of course, dearest friend!' Fleda interjected, falling instinctively into the address that embodied the intensest pressure. She wanted to put Mrs. Gereth between her and her danger.

'He asked for Miss Vetch, mum,' the girl replied with a face that brought startlingly to Fleda's ear the muffled chorus of the kitchen.''

'Quite proper,' said Mrs. Gereth austerely. Then to Fleda: 'Please go to him.'

'But what to do?'

'What you always do – see what he wants.' Mrs. Gereth dismissed the maid. 'Tell him Miss Vetch will come.' Fleda saw that nothing was in the mother's imagination at this moment but the desire not to meet her son. She had completely broken with him and there was little in what had just happened to repair the rupture. It would now take more to do so than his presenting himself uninvited at her door. 'He's right in asking for you – he's aware that you're still our communicator; nothing has occurred to alter that. To what he wishes to transmit through you I'm ready, as I've been ready before, to listen. As far as *I'm* concerned, if I couldn't meet him a month ago how am I to meet him to-day? If he has come to say "My dear mother, you're here, in the hovel into which I've flung you, with consolations that give me pleasure," I'll listen to him; but on no other footing. That's what you're to ascertain, please. You'll oblige me as you've obliged me before. There!' Mrs. Gereth turned her back and with a fine imitation of superiority began to redress the miseries immediately before her. Fleda meanwhile hesitated, lingered for some minutes where she had been left, feeling secretly that her fate still had her in hand. It had put her face to face with Owen Gereth and evidently meant to keep her so. She was reminded afresh of two things: one of which was that, though she judged her friend's rigour, she had never really had the story of the scene enacted in the great awe-stricken house between the intimate adversaries weeks before – the day the elder took to her bed in her overthrow. The other was that at Ricks as at Poynton it was before all things her own place to accept thankfully a usefulness not, she must remember, universally acknowledged. What determined her at the last, while Mrs. Gereth disappeared in the shrubbery, was that, though at a distance from the house and with the drawing-room turned the other way, she could absolutely see the young man alone there with the sources of his pain. She saw his simple stare at his tapestries, heard his heavy tread on his carpets and the hard breath of his sense of unfairness. At this she went to him fast.

VIII

❊

'I ASKED for you,' he said when she stood there, 'because I heard from the flyman[1] who drove me from the station to the inn that he had brought you here yesterday. We had some talk – he mentioned it.'

'You didn't know I was here?'

'No. I knew only you had had in London all you told me that day to do; and it was Mona's idea that after your sister's marriage you were staying on with your father. So I thought you were with him still.'

'I am,' Fleda replied, idealising a little the fact. 'I'm here only for a moment. But do you mean,' she went on, 'that if you had known I was with your mother you wouldn't have come down?'

The way Owen hung fire at this question made it sound more playful than she had intended. She had in fact no consciousness of any intention but to confine herself rigidly to her function. She could already see that in whatever he had now braced himself for she was an element he had not reckoned with. His preparation had been of a different sort – the sort congruous with his having been careful to go first and lunch solidly at the inn. He had not been forced to ask for her, but she became aware in his presence of a particular desire to make him feel that no harm could really come to him. She might upset him, as people called it, but she should take no advantage of having done so. She had never seen a person with whom she wished more to be light and easy, to be exceptionally human. The account he presently gave of the matter was that he indeed wouldn't have come if he had known she was on the spot; because then, didn't she see? he could have written to her. He would have had her there to let fly at his mother.

'That would have saved me – well, it would have saved me a lot. Of course I'd rather see you than her,' he somewhat awkwardly added. 'When the fellow spoke of you I assure you I quite jumped at you. In fact I've no real desire to see Mummy at all. If

90

she thinks I *like* it – !' He sighed disgustedly. 'I only came because it seemed better than any other way. I didn't want her to be able to say I hadn't been all right. I daresay you know she has taken everything; or if not quite everything at least a lot more than one ever dreamed. You can see for yourself – she has got half the place down. She has got them crammed – you can see for yourself!' He had his old trick of artless repetition, his helpless iteration of the obvious; but he was sensibly different for Fleda, if only by the difference of his clear face mottled over and almost disfigured by little points of pain. He might have been a fine young man with a bad toothache, with the first even of his life. What ailed him above all, she felt, was that trouble was new to him. He had never known a difficulty; he had taken all his fences, his world wholly the world of the personally possible, rounded indeed by a grey suburb into which he had never had occasion to stray. In this vulgar and ill-lighted region he had evidently now lost himself. 'We left it quite to her honour, you know,' he said ruefully.

'Perhaps you've a right to say you left it a little to mine.' Mixed up with the spoils there, rising before him as if she were in a manner their keeper, she felt she must absolutely dissociate herself. Mrs. Gereth had made it impossible to do anything but give her away. 'I can only tell you that on my side I left it to her. I never dreamed either that she would pick out so many things.'

'And you don't really think it's fair, do you? You *don't*!' He spoke very quickly; he really seemed to plead.

Fleda just faltered. 'I think she has gone too far.' Then she added: 'I shall immediately tell her I've said that to you.'

He appeared puzzled by this statement, but he presently rejoined: 'You haven't then said to her what you think?'

'Not yet; remember that I got here only last night.' She struck herself as ignobly weak. 'I had had no idea what she was doing. I was taken completely by surprise. She managed it wonderfully.'

'It's the sharpest thing I ever saw in *my* life!' They looked at each other with intelligence, in appreciation of the sharpness, and Owen quickly broke into a loud laugh. The laugh was in itself natural, but the occasion of it strange; and stranger still to Fleda, so that she too almost laughed, the inconsequent charity with which he added: 'Poor dear old Mummy! That's one of the reasons I asked for you,' he went on – 'to see if you'd back her up.'

Whatever he said or did she somehow liked him the better for it. 'How can I back her up, Mr. Gereth, when I think, as I tell you, that she has made a great mistake?'

'A great mistake! That's all right.' He spoke – it wasn't clear to her why – as if this attestation had been a great point gained.

'Of course there are many things she hasn't taken,' Fleda continued.

'Oh yes, a lot of things. But you wouldn't know the place, all the same.' He looked about the room with his discoloured, swindled face, which deepened Fleda's compassion for him, conjuring away any smile at so candid an image of the dupe. 'You'd know this one soon enough, wouldn't you? These are just the things she ought to have left. Is the whole house full of them?'

'The whole house,' said Fleda uncompromisingly. She thought of her lovely room.

'I never knew how much I cared for them. They're awfully valuable, aren't they?' Owen's manner mystified her; she was conscious of a return of the agitation he had produced in her on that last bewildering day, and she reminded herself that, now she was warned, it would be inexcusable of her to allow him to justify the fear that had dropped on her. 'Mother thinks I never took any notice, but I assure you I was awfully proud of everything. Upon my honour I *was* proud, Miss Vetch.'

There was an oddity in his helplessness; he appeared to wish to persuade her and to satisfy himself that she sincerely felt how worthy he really was to treat what had happened as an injury. She could only exclaim almost as helplessly as himself: 'Of course you did justice! It's all most painful. I shall instantly let your mother know,' she again declared, 'the way I've spoken of her to you.' She clung to that idea as to the sign of her straightness.

'You'll tell her what you think she ought to do?' he asked with some eagerness.

'What she ought to do?'

'*Don't* you think it – I mean that she ought to give them up?'

'To give them up?' Fleda cast about her again.

'To send them back – to keep it quiet.' The girl had not felt the impulse to ask him to sit down among the monuments of his wrong, so that, nervously, awkwardly, he fidgeted over the room with his hands in his pockets and an effect of returning a little into possession through the formulation of his view. 'To have them packed and despatched again, since she knows so well how. She does it beautifully' – he looked close at two or three precious pieces. 'What's sauce for the goose is sauce for the gander!'

He had laughed at his way of putting it, but Fleda remained grave. 'Is that what you came to say to her?'

'Not exactly those words. But I did come to say' – he stammered, then brought it out – 'I did come to say we must have them right back.'

'And did you think your mother would see you?'

'I wasn't sure, but I thought it right to try – to put it to her kindly, don't you see? If she won't see me then she has herself to thank. The only other way would have been to set the lawyers at her.'

'I'm glad you didn't do that.'

'I'm dashed if I want to!' Owen honestly responded. 'But what's a fellow to do if she won't meet a fellow?'

'What do you call meeting a fellow?' Fleda asked with a smile.

'Why letting *me* tell her a dozen things she can have.'

This was a transaction that Fleda had after a moment to give up trying to represent to herself. 'If she won't do that – ?' she went on.

'I'll leave it all to my solicitor. *He* won't let her off, by Jove. I know the fellow!'

'That's horrible!' said Fleda, looking at him in woe.

'It's utterly beastly.'

His want of logic as well as his vehemence startled her; and with her eyes still on his she considered before asking him the question these things suggested. At the last she asked it. 'Is Mona very angry?'

'Oh dear yes!' said Owen.

She had noted that he wouldn't speak of Mona without her beginning. After waiting fruitlessly now for him to say more she continued: 'She has been there again? She has seen the state of the house?'

'Oh dear yes!' he repeated.

Fleda disliked to appear not to take account of his brevity, but it was just because she was struck by it that she felt the pressure of the desire to know more. What it suggested was simply what

her intelligence supplied, for he was incapable of any art of insinu-
ation. Wasn't it at all events the rule of communication with him
for her to say on his behalf what he couldn't say? This truth was
present to the girl as she inquired if Mona greatly resented what
Mrs. Gereth had done. He satisfied her promptly; he was standing
before the fire, his back to it, his long legs apart, his hands, behind
him, rather violently jiggling his gloves. 'She hates it awfully. In
fact she refuses to put up with it at all. Don't you see? – she saw
the place with all the things.'

'So that of course she misses them.'

'Misses them – rather! She was awfully sweet on them.' Fleda
remembered how sweet Mona had been, and reflected that if that
was the sort of plea he had prepared it was indeed as well he
shouldn't see his mother. This was not all she wanted to know,
but it came over her that it was all she needed. 'You see it puts me
in the position of not carrying out what I promised,' Owen said.
'As she says herself' – he hung fire an instant – 'it's just as if I had
obtained her under false pretences.' Just before, when he spoke
with more drollery than he knew, it had left Fleda serious; but
now his own clear gravity had the effect of exciting her mirth. She
laughed out, and he looked surprised, but went on: 'She regards
it as a regular sell.'

Fleda was silent; yet finally, as he added nothing, she exclaimed:
'Of course it makes a great difference!' She knew all she needed,
but none the less she risked after another pause an interrogative
remark. 'I forgot when it is your marriage takes place?'

He came away from the fire and, apparently at a loss where to
turn, ended by directing himself to one of the windows. 'It's a
little uncertain. The date isn't quite fixed.'

'Oh I thought I remembered that at Poynton you had told me
a day and that it was near at hand.'

'I daresay I did; it was for the nineteenth. But we've altered that
– she wants to shift it.' He looked out of the window; then he said:
'In fact it won't come off till Mummy has come round.'

'Come round?'

'Put the place as it was.' In his off-hand way he added: 'You
know what I mean!'

He spoke not impatiently, but with a kind of intimate familiarity, the mildness of which made her feel a pang for having forced

him to tell her what was embarrassing to him, what was even humiliating. Yes indeed, she knew all she needed: all she needed was that Mona had proved apt at putting down that wonderful patent-leather foot. Her type was misleading only to the superficial, and no one in the world was less superficial than Fleda. She had guessed the truth at Waterbath and had suffered from it at Poynton; at Ricks the only thing she could do was to accept it with the dumb exaltation that she felt rising. Mona had been prompt with her exercise of the member in question, for it might be called prompt to do that sort of thing before marriage. That she had indeed been premature who might say save those who should have read the matter in the full light of results? Neither at Waterbath nor at Poynton had even Fleda's thoroughness discovered all there was – or rather all there wasn't – in Owen Gereth. 'Of course it makes all the difference!' she said in answer to his last words. She pursued the next moment: 'What you wish me to say from you then to your mother is that you demand immediate and practically complete restitution?'

'Yes, please. It's tremendously good of you.'

'Very well then. Will you wait?'

'For Mummy's answer?' Owen stared and looked perplexed; he was more and more fevered with so much vivid expression of his case. 'Don't you think that if I'm here she may hate it worse – suppose I may want to make her reply bang off?'

Fleda weighed it. 'You don't then?'

'I want to take her in the right way, don't you know? – treat her as if I gave her more than just an hour or two.'

'I see,' said Fleda. 'Then if you don't wait – good-bye.'

This again seemed not what he wanted. 'Must *you* do it bang off?'

'I'm only thinking she'll be impatient – I mean, you know, to learn what will have passed between us.'

'I see,' said Owen, looking at his gloves. 'I can give her a day or two, you know. Of course I didn't come down to sleep,' he went on. 'The inn seems a beastly hole. I know all about the trains – having no idea you were here.' Almost as soon as his entertainer he was struck with the absence of the visible, in this, as between effect and cause. 'I mean because in that case I should have felt I could stop over. I should have felt I could talk with you a blessed sight longer than with Mummy.'

'We've already talked a long time,' smiled Fleda.

'Awfully, haven't we?' He spoke with the stupidity she didn't object to. Inarticulate as he was he had more to say; he lingered perhaps because vaguely aware of the want of sincerity in her encouragement to him to go. 'There's one thing, please,' he mentioned, as if there might be a great many others too. 'Please don't say anything about Mona.'

She didn't understand. 'About Mona?'

'About it being *her* that thinks she has gone too far.' This was still slightly obscure, but now Fleda understood. 'It mustn't seem to come from *her* at all, don't you know? That would only make Mummy worse.'

Fleda knew exactly how much worse, but felt a delicacy about explicitly assenting: she was already immersed moreover in the deep consideration of what might make 'Mummy' better. She couldn't see as yet at all, could only clutch at the hope of some inspiration after he should go. Oh there was a remedy, to be sure, but it was out of the question; in spite of which, in the strong light of Owen's troubled presence, of his anxious face and restless step, it hung there before her for some minutes. She guessed that, remarkably, beneath the decent rigour of his errand, the poor young man, for reasons, for weariness, for disgust, would have been ready not to insist. His fitness to fight his mother had left him – he wasn't in fighting trim. He had no natural avidity and even no special wrath; he had none that had not been taught him, and it was his doing his best to learn the lesson that had made him so sick. He had his delicacies, but he hid them away like presents before Christmas. He was hollow, perfunctory, pathetic; he had been girded by another hand. That hand had naturally been Mona's, and it was heavy even now on his strong, broad back. Why then had he originally rejoiced so in its touch? Fleda dashed aside this question, for it had nothing to do with her problem. Her problem was to help him to live as a gentleman and carry through what he had undertaken; her problem was to reinstate him in his rights. It was quite irrelevant that Mona had no intelligence of what she had lost – quite irrelevant that she was moved not by the privation but by the insult. She had every reason to be moved, though she was so much more movable, in the vindictive way at any rate, than one might have supposed – assuredly more than Owen himself had imagined.

'Certainly I shall not mention Mona,' Fleda said, 'and there won't be the slightest necessity for it. The wrong's quite sufficiently yours, and the demand you make perfectly justified by it.'

'I can't tell you what it is to me to feel you on my side!' Owen exclaimed.

'Up to this time,' said Fleda after a pause, 'your mother has had no doubt of my being on hers.'

'Then of course she won't like your changing.'

'I daresay she won't like it at all.'

'Do you mean to say you'll have a regular kick-up with her?'

'I don't exactly know what you mean by a regular kick-up. We shall naturally have a great deal of discussion – if she consents to discuss at all. That's why you must decidedly give her two or three days.'

'I see you think she *may* refuse to discuss at all,' said Owen.

'I'm only trying to be prepared for the worst. You must remember that to have to withdraw from the ground she has taken, to make a public surrender of what she had publicly appropriated, will go uncommonly hard with her pride.'

Owen considered; his face seemed to broaden, but not into a smile. 'I suppose she's tremendously proud, isn't she?' This might have been the first time it had occurred to him.

'You know better than I,' said Fleda, speaking with high extravagance.

'I don't know anything in the world half so well as you. If I were as clever as you I might hope to get round her.' Owen waited for more thought; then he went on: 'In fact I don't quite see what even you can say or do that will really fetch her.'

'Neither do I, as yet. I must think – I must pray!' the girl pursued, smiling. 'I can only say to you that I'll try. I *want* to try, you know – I want to help you.' He stood looking at her so long on this that she added with much distinctness: 'So you must leave me, please, quite alone with her. You must go straight back '

'Back to the inn?'

'Oh no, back to town. I'll write to you to-morrow.'

He turned about vaguely for his hat. 'There's the chance of course that she may be afraid.'

'Afraid you mean of the legal steps you may take?'

'I've got a perfect case – I could have her up. The Brigstocks say it's simply stealing.'

'I can easily fancy what the Brigstocks say!' Fleda permitted herself to remark without solemnity.

'It's none of their business, is it?' was Owen's unexpected rejoinder. Fleda had already noted that no one so slow could ever have had such quick transitions.

She showed her amusement. 'They've a much better right to say it's none of mine.'

'Well, at any rate, you don't call her names.'

Fleda wondered if Mona did; and this made it all the finer of her to exclaim in a moment: 'You don't know what I shall call her if she holds out!'

Owen gave her a gloomy glance; then he blew a speck off the crown of his hat. 'But if you do have a set-to with her?'

He paused so long for a reply that Fleda said: 'I don't think I know what you mean by a set-to.'

'Well, if she calls *you* names.'

'I don't think she'll do that.'

'What I mean to say is if she's angry at your backing me up – what will you do then? She can't possibly like it, you know.'

'She may very well not like it; but everything depends. I must see what I shall do. You mustn't worry about me.'

She spoke with decision, but Owen seemed still unsatisfied. 'You won't go away, I hope?'

'Go away?'

'If she does take it ill of you.'

Fleda moved to the door and opened it. 'I'm not prepared to say. You must have patience and see.'

'Of course I must,' said Owen – 'of course, of course.' But he took no more advantage of the open door than to say: 'You want me to be off, and I'm off in a minute. Only before I go please answer me a question. If you *should* leave my mother where would you go?'

She blinked a little at the immensity of it. 'I haven't the least idea.'

'I suppose you'd go back to London.'

'I haven't the least idea,' Fleda repeated.

'You don't – a – live anywhere in particular, do you?' the young man went on. He looked conscious as soon as he had spoken; she could see that he felt himself to have alluded more grossly than he meant to the circumstance of her having, if one were plain about it, no home of her own. He had meant it as an allusion of a highly considerate sort to all she would sacrifice in the case of a quarrel with his mother; but there was indeed no graceful way of touching on that. One just couldn't be plain about it.

Fleda, wound up as she was, shrank from any treatment at all of the matter; she simply neglected his question. 'I *won't* leave your mother,' she said instead. 'I'll produce an effect on her. I'll convince her absolutely.'

'I believe you will if you look at her like that!'

She was wound up to such a height that there might well be a light in her pale, fine little face – a light that, while for all return at first she simply shone back at him, was intensely reflected in his own. 'I'll make her see it, I'll make her see it!' – she rang out like a silver bell. She had at that moment a perfect faith she should succeed; but it passed into something else when, the next instant, she became aware that Owen, quickly getting between her and the door she had opened, was sharply closing it, as might be said, in her face. He had done this before she could stop him, and he stood there with his hand on the knob and smiled at her strangely. Clearer than he could have spoken it was the sense of those seconds of silence.

'When I got into this I didn't know you, and now that I know you how can I tell you the difference? And *she's* so different, so ugly and vulgar, in the light of this squabble. No, like *you* I've never known one. It's another thing, it's a new thing altogether. Listen to me a little: can't something be done?' It was what had been in the air in those moments at Kensington, and it only wanted words to be a committed act. The more reason, to the girl's excited mind, why it shouldn't have words; her one thought was not to hear, to keep the act uncommitted. She would do this if she had to be horrid.

'Please let me out, Mr. Gereth,' she said; on which he opened the door with a debate so very brief that in thinking of these things afterwards – for she was to think of them for ever – she wondered in what tone she must have spoken. They went into the hall, where she came upon the parlour-maid, of whom she asked if Mrs. Gereth had come in.

'No, miss; and I think she has left the garden. She has gone up the back road.' In other words they had the whole place to themselves. It would have been a pleasure, in a different mood, to converse with that parlour-maid.

'Please open the house-door,' said Fleda.

Owen, as if in quest of his umbrella, looked vaguely about the hall – looked even wistfully up the staircase – while the neat young woman complied with Fleda's request. Owen's eyes then wandered out of the framed aperture. 'I think it's awfully nice here,' he struck off. 'I assure you I could do with it myself.'

'I should think you might, with half your things here! It's Poynton itself – almost. Good-bye, Mr. Gereth,' Fleda added. Her intention had naturally been that the neat young woman, releasing the guest, should remain to close the door on his departure. That functionary, however, had acutely vanished behind a swinging screen of green baize[2] garnished with brass nails, a horror Mrs. Gereth had not yet had time to abolish. Fleda put out her hand, but Owen turned away – he couldn't find his umbrella. She passed into the open air – she was determined to get him out; and in a moment he joined her in the little plastered portico which had small resemblance to any feature of Poynton. It was, as Mrs. Gereth had said, the portico of a house in Brompton[3].

'Oh I don't mean with all the things here,' he explained in regard to the opinion he had just expressed. 'I mean I could put up with it just as it was; it had a lot of good things, don't you think? I mean if everything was back at Poynton, if everything was all right.' But the high flight of this idea showed somehow the broken wing. Fleda didn't understand his explanation unless it had reference to another and more wonderful exchange – the restoration to the great house not only of its tables and chairs but of its alienated mistress. This would imply the installation of his own life at Ricks, and obviously that of another person. Such another person could scarcely be Mona Brigstock. He put out his hand now; and once more she heard his unsounded words. 'With everything patched up at the other place I could live here with *you*. Don't you see what I mean?'

She saw perfectly and, with a face in which she yet flattered herself that nothing of her vision appeared, simply gave him her hand. 'Good-bye, good-bye.'

He held her very firmly, keeping her even after the effort she made for release – an effort not repeated, as she felt it best not to show she was flurried. That solution – of her living with him at Ricks – disposed of him beautifully and disposed not less so of herself; it disposed admirably too of Mrs Gereth. Fleda could only vainly wonder how it provided for poor Mona. While he looked at her, grasping her still, she felt that now indeed she was paying for his mother's extravagance at Poynton – the vividness of that lady's public plea that little Fleda Vetch was the person to ensure the general peace. It was to this vividness poor Owen had come back, and if Mrs. Gereth had had more discretion little Fleda Vetch wouldn't have been in a predicament. She saw that Owen had now his sharpest necessity of speech, and so long as he didn't let go her hand she could only submit to him. Her defence would be perhaps to look blank and hard; so she looked as blank and as hard as she could, with the reward of an immediate sense that this was not a bit what he wanted. It even made him flounder as for sudden compunction, some recall to duty and to honour. Yet he none the less brought out: 'There's one thing I daresay I ought to tell you, if you're going so kindly to act for me; though of course you'll see for yourself it's a thing it won't do to tell *her*.' What was it? He made her wait again, and while she waited, under firm coercion, she had the extraordinary impression that his simplicity was in eclipse. His natural honesty was like the scent of a flower, and she felt at this moment as if her nose had been brushed by the bloom without the odour. The allusion was undoubtedly to his mother; and was not what he meant about the matter in question the opposite of what he said – that it just *would* do to tell her? It would have been the first time he had intended the opposite of what he said, and there was certainly an interest in the example as well as a challenge to suspense in the ambiguity. 'It's just that I understand from Mona, you know,' he stammered; 'it's just that she has made no bones about bringing home to me – !' He tried to laugh and in the effort faltered again.

'About bringing home to you?' – Fleda encouraged him.

He was sensible of it, he surmounted his difficulty. 'Why, that if I don't get the things back – every blessed one of them except a few *she*'ll pick out – she won't have anything more to say to me.'

Fleda after an instant encouraged him again. 'To say to you?'

'Why she simply won't have me, don't you see?'

Owen's legs, not to mention his voice, had wavered while he spoke, and she felt his possession of her hand loosen so that she was free again. Her stare of perception broke into a lively laugh. 'Oh you're all right, for you *will* get them. You will; you're quite safe; don't worry!' She fell back into the house with her hand on the door. 'Good-bye, good-bye.' She repeated it several times, laughing bravely, quite waving him away and, as he didn't move and save that he was on the other side of it, closing the door in his face quite as he had closed that of the drawing-room in hers. Never had a face, never at least had such a handsome one, been presented so straight to that offence. She even held the door a minute lest he should try to come in again. At last as she heard nothing she made a dash for the stairs and ran up.

IX

❈

IN knowing a while before all she needed she had been far from knowing as much as that; so that once above, where, in her room, with her sense of danger and trouble, the age of Louis Seize suddenly struck her as wanting in taste and point, she felt she now for the first time knew her temptation. Owen had put it before her with an art beyond his own dream. Mona would cast him off if he didn't proceed to extremities – if his negotiation with his mother should fail he would be completely free. That negotiation depended on a young lady to whom he had pressingly suggested the condition of his freedom; and as if to aggravate the young lady's predicament designing fate had sent Mrs. Gereth, as the parlour-maid said, 'up the back road.' This would give the young lady the more time to make up her mind that nothing should come of the negotiation. There would be different ways of putting the question to Mrs. Gereth, and Fleda might profitably devote the moments before her return to a selection of the way that would most surely be tantamount to failure. This selection indeed required no great adroitness; it was so conspicuous that failure would be the reward of an effective introduction of Mona. If that abhorred name should be properly invoked Mrs. Gereth would resist to the death, and before envenomed resistance Owen would certainly retire. His retirement would be into single life, and Fleda reflected that he had now gone away conscious of having practically told her so. She could only say as she waited for the back road to disgorge that she hoped it was a consciousness he enjoyed. There was something *she* enjoyed, but that was a very different matter. To know she had become to him an object of desire gave her wings that she felt herself flutter in the air: it was like the rush of a flood into her own accumulations. These stored depths had been fathomless and still, but now, for half an hour, in the empty house, they spread till they overflowed. He seemed to have made it right for her to confess to herself her secret. Strange then there

103

should be for him in return nothing that such a confession could make right! How could it make right his giving up Mona for another woman? His position was a sorry appeal to Fleda to legitimate that. But he didn't believe it himself, he had none of the courage of his perversity. She could easily see how wrong everything must be when a man so made to be manly was wanting in courage. She had upset him, yes, and he had spoken out from the force of the jar of finding her there. He had upset her too, goodness knew, but she was one of those who could pick themselves up. She had the real advantage, she considered, of having kept him from seeing she had been overthrown.

She had moreover at present completely recovered her feet, though there was in the intensity of the effort required for this a vibration that throbbed away into an immense allowance for the young man. How could she after all know what, in the disturbance wrought by his mother, Mona's relations with him might have become? If he had been able to keep his wits, such as they were, more about him he would probably have felt – as sharply as she felt on his behalf – that so long as those relations were not ended he had no right to say even the little he had said. He had no right to appear to wish to draw in another girl to help him to run away. If he was in a plight he must get out of the plight himself, he must get out of it first, and anything he should have to say to any one else must be deferred and detached. She herself at any rate – it was her own case that emerged – couldn't dream of assisting him save in the sense of their common honour. She could never be the girl to be drawn in; she could never lift her finger against Mona. There was something in her that would make it a shame to her for ever to have owed her happiness to an interference. It would seem intolerably vulgar to her to have 'ousted' the daughter of the Brigstocks; and merely to have abstained even wouldn't sufficiently assure her she had been straight. Nothing was really straight but to justify her little pensioned[1] presence by her use; and now, won over as she was to heroism, she could see her use only as some high and delicate deed. She couldn't in short do anything at all unless she could do it with a degree of pride, and there would be nothing to be proud of in having arranged for poor Owen to get off easily. Nobody had a right to get off easily from pledges so deep and sacred. How could Fleda doubt they had been tremendous when she knew so well what any pledge of her own would be? If Mona was so formed that she could hold such vows light this was Mona's particular affair. To have loved Owen apparently, and yet to have loved him only so much, only to the extent of a few tables and chairs, was not a thing she could so much as try to grasp. Of a different manner of loving she was herself ready to give an instance, an instance of which the beauty indeed would not be generally known. It would not perhaps if revealed be generally understood, inasmuch as the effect of the special pressure she proposed to exercise would be, should success attend it, to keep him tied to an affection that had died a sudden and violent death. Even in the ardour of her meditation Fleda remained in sight of the truth that it would be an odd result of her magnanimity to prevent her friend's shaking off a woman he disliked. If he didn't dislike Mona what was the matter with him? And if he did, Fleda asked, what was the matter with her own silly self?

Our young lady met this branch of the temptation it pleased her frankly to recognise by declaring that to encourage any such cruelty would be tortuous and base. She had nothing to do with his dislikes; she had only to do with his good nature and his good name. She had joy of him just as he was, but it was of these things she had the greatest. The worst aversion and the liveliest reaction wouldn't alter the fact – since one was facing facts – that but the other day his strong arms must have clasped a remarkably handsome girl as close as she had permitted. Fleda's emotion at this time was a wondrous mixture, in which Mona's permissions and Mona's beauty figured powerfully as aids to reflexion. She herself had no beauty, and *her* permissions were the stony stares she had just practised in the drawing-room – a consciousness of a kind appreciably to add to the strange sense of triumph that made her generous. We may not perhaps too much diminish the merit of that generosity if we mention that it could take the flight we are considering just because really, with the telescope of her long thought, Fleda saw what might bring her out of the wood. Mona herself would bring her out; at the least Mona possibly might. Deep down plunged the idea that even should she achieve what she had promised Owen there was still the contingency of Mona's independent action. She might by that time, under stress of temper or of whatever it was that was now moving her, have said or done the things there is no patching up. If the rupture should come from Waterbath they might all be happy yet. This was a calculation that Fleda wouldn't have committed to paper, but it affected the total of her sentiments. She was meanwhile so remarkably constituted that while she refused to profit by Owen's mistake, even while she judged it and hastened to cover it up, she could drink a sweetness from it that consorted little with her wishing it mightn't have been made. There was no harm done, because he had instinctively known, poor dear, with whom to make it, and it was a compensation for seeing him worried that he hadn't made it with some horrid mean girl who would immediately have dished him by making a still bigger one. Their protected error (for she indulged a fancy that it was hers too) was like some dangerous, lovely, living thing that she had caught and could keep – keep vivid and helpless in the cage of her own passion and look at and talk to all day long. She had got it well locked up there by the time that from an upper window she saw Mrs. Gereth again in the garden. At this she went down to meet her.

X

※

FLEDA'S line had been taken, her word was quite ready: on the terrace of the painted pots she broke out before her benefactress could put a question. 'His errand was perfectly simple: he came to demand that you shall pack everything straight up again and send it back as fast as the railway will carry it.'

The back road had apparently been fatiguing to Mrs. Gereth; she rose there rather white and wan with her walk. A certain sharp thinness was in her ejaculation of 'Oh!' – after which she glanced about her for a place to sit down. The movement was a criticism of the order of events that offered such a piece of news to a lady coming in tired; but Fleda could see that in turning over the possibilities this particular peril was the one that during the last hour her friend had turned up oftenest. At the end of the short grey day, which had been moist and mild, the sun was out; the terrace looked to the south, and a bench, formed as to legs and arms of iron representing knotted boughs, stood against the warmest wall of the house. The mistress of Ricks sank upon it and presented to her companion the handsome face she had composed to hear everything. Strangely enough it was just this fine vessel of her attention that made the girl most nervous about what she must drop in. 'Quite a "demand," dear, is it?' asked Mrs. Gereth, drawing in her cloak.

'Oh that's what I should call it!' – Fleda laughed to her own surprise.

'I mean with the threat of enforcement and that sort of thing.'

'Distinctly with the threat of enforcement – of what would be called, I suppose, coercion.'

'What sort of coercion?' said Mrs. Gereth.

'Why legal, don't you know? – what he calls setting the lawyers at you.'

'Is that what he calls it?' She seemed to speak with disinterested curiosity.

'That's what he calls it,' said Fleda.

Mrs. Gereth considered an instant. 'Oh the lawyers!' she exclaimed lightly. Seated there almost cosily in the reddening winter sunset, only with her shoulders raised a little and her mantle tightened as if from a slight chill, she had never yet looked to Fleda so much in possession nor so far from meeting unsuspectedness halfway. 'Is he going to send them down here?'

'I daresay he thinks it may come to that.'

'The lawyers can scarcely do the packing,' Mrs. Gereth playfully remarked.

'I suppose he means them – in the first place at least – to try to talk you over.'

'In the first place, eh? And what does he mean in the second?'

Fleda debated; she hadn't foreseen that so simple an inquiry could disconcert her. 'I'm afraid I don't know.'

'Didn't you ask?' Mrs. Gereth spoke as if she might have said, 'What then were you doing all the while?'

'I didn't ask very much,' said her companion. 'He has been gone some time. The great thing seemed to be to understand clearly that he wouldn't be content with anything less than what he mentioned.'

'My just giving everything back?'

'Your just giving everything back.'

'Well, darling, what did you tell him?' Mrs. Gereth blandly proceeded.

Fleda faltered again, wincing at the term of endearment, at what the words took for granted, charged with the confidence she had now committed herself to betray. 'I told him I'd tell you!' She smiled, but felt her smile too poor a thing and even that Mrs. Gereth had begun to look at her with some fixedness.

'Did he seem very angry?'

'He seemed very sad. He takes it very hard,' Fleda added.

'And how does *she* take it?'

'Ah that – that I felt a delicacy about asking.'

'So you didn't get it out of him?' The words had the note of surprise.

Fleda was embarrassed; she had not made up her mind definitely to lie. 'I didn't think you'd care.' That small untruth she would risk.

'Well – I don't!' Mrs. Gereth declared; and Fleda felt less guilty to hear her, for the words were as far from the purpose as her own. 'Didn't you say anything in return?' the elder woman continued.

'Do you mean in the way of justifying you?'

'I didn't mean to trouble you to do that. My justification,' said Mrs. Gereth, sitting there warmly and, in the lucidity of her thought, which nevertheless hung back a little, dropping her eyes on the gravel – 'my justification was all the past. My justification was the cruelty –' But at this, with a short sharp gesture, she checked herself. 'It's too good of me to talk – now.' She produced these sentences with a cold patience, as if addressing Fleda in the girl's virtual and actual character of Owen's representative. Our young lady crept to and fro before the bench, combating the sense that it was occupied by a judge, looking at her boot-toes, reminding herself in doing so of Mona, and lightly crunching the pebbles as she walked. She moved about because she was afraid, putting off from moment to moment the exercise of the courage she had been sure she possessed. That courage would all come to her if she could only be equally sure that what she should be called upon to do for Owen would be to suffer. She had wondered, while Mrs. Gereth spoke, how that lady would describe her justification. She had described it as if to be irreproachably fair, give her adversary the benefit of every doubt and then dismiss the question for ever. 'Of course,' Mrs. Gereth went on, 'if we didn't succeed in showing him at Poynton the ground we took it's simply that he shuts his eyes. What I supposed was that you would have given him your opinion that if I was the woman so signally to assert myself I'm also the woman to rest on it unshakably enough.'

Fleda stopped in front of her hostess. 'I gave him my opinion that you're very logical, very obstinate and very proud.'

'Quite right, my dear: I'm a rank bigot – about that sort of thing!' Mrs. Gereth jerked her head at the contents of the house. 'I've never denied it. I'd kidnap – to save them, to convert them – the children of heretics. When I know I'm right I go to the stake. Oh he may burn me alive!' she cried with a happy face. 'Did he abuse me?' she then demanded.

Fleda had remained there, gathering in her purpose. 'How little you know him!'

Mrs. Gereth stared, then broke into a laugh that her companion had not expected. 'Ah my dear, certainly not so well as you!' The girl, at this, turned away again – she felt she looked too conscious; and she was aware that during a pause Mrs. Gereth's eyes watched her as she went. She faced about afresh to meet them, but what she met was a question that re-enforced them. 'Why had you a "delicacy" as to speaking of Mona?'

She stopped again before the bench, and an inspiration came to her. 'I should think *you* would know,' she said with proper dignity.

Blankness was for a moment on Mrs. Gereth's brow; then light broke – she visibly remembered the scene in the breakfast-room after Mona's night at Poynton. 'Because I contrasted you – told him *you* were the one?' Her eyes looked deep. 'You were – you are still!'

Fleda gave a bold dramatic laugh. 'Thank you, my love – with all the best things at Ricks!'

Mrs. Gereth considered, trying to penetrate, as it seemed; but at last she brought out roundly: 'For you, you know, I'd send them back!'

The girl's heart gave a tremendous bound; the right way dawned upon her in a flash. Obscurity indeed the next moment engulfed this course, but for a few thrilled seconds she had understood. To send the things back 'for her' meant of course to send them back if there was even a dim chance that she might become mistress of them. Fleda's palpitation was not allayed as she asked herself what portent Mrs. Gereth had suddenly descried of such a chance: the light could be there but by a sudden suspicion of her secret. This suspicion in turn was a tolerably straight consequence of that implied view of the propriety of surrender from which she was well aware she could say nothing to dissociate herself. What she first felt was that if she wished to rescue the spoils she wished also to rescue her secret. So she looked as innocent as she could and said as quickly as she might: 'For me? Why in the world for me?'

'Because you're so awfully keen.'

'Am I? Do I strike you so? You know I hate him,' Fleda went on.

She had the sense for a while of Mrs. Gereth's regarding her with the detachment of some stern clever stranger. 'Then what's the matter with you? Why do you want me to give in?'

Fleda hesitated; she felt herself reddening. 'I've only said your son wants it. I haven't said *I* do.'

'Then say it and have done with it!'

This was more peremptory than any word her friend, though often speaking in her presence with much point, had ever yet deliberately addressed her. It affected her like the crack of a whip, but she confined herself with an effort to taking it as a reminder that she must keep her head. 'I know he has his engagement to carry out.'

'His engagement to marry? Why, it's just that engagement we loathe?'

'Why should *I* loathe it?' Fleda asked with a strained smile. Then before Mrs. Gereth could reply she pursued: 'I'm thinking of his general undertaking – to give her the house as she originally saw it.'

'To give her the house!' – Mrs. Gereth brought up the words from the depth of the unspeakable. The effect was like the moan of an autumn wind, and she turned as pale as if she had heard of the landing, there on her coast, of a foreign army.

'I'm thinking,' Fleda continued, 'of the simple question of his keeping faith on an important clause of his contract: it doesn't matter whether with a stupid person or with a monster of cleverness. I'm thinking of his honour and his good name.'

'The honour and good name of a man you hate?'

'Certainly,' the girl resolutely answered. 'I don't see why you should talk as if one had a petty mind. You don't think so. It's not on that assumption you've ever dealt with me. I can do your son justice – as he put his case to me.'

'Ah then he did put his case to you!' Mrs. Gereth cried with an accent of triumph. 'You seemed to speak just now as if really nothing of any consequence had passed between you.'

'Something always passes when one has a little imagination,' our young lady declared.

'I take it you don't mean that Owen has any!' Mrs. Gereth answered with her large laugh.

Fleda had a pause. 'No, I don't mean that Owen has any,' she returned at last.

'Why is it you hate him so?' her hostess abruptly put to her.

'Should I love him for all he has made you suffer?'

Mrs. Gereth slowly rose at this and, coming over the walk, took her young friend to her breast and kissed her. She then passed into one of Fleda's an arm perversely and imperiously sociable. 'Let us move a little,' she said, holding her close and giving a slight shiver. They strolled along the terrace and she brought out another question. 'He *was* eloquent then, poor dear – he poured forth the story of his wrongs?'

Fleda smiled down at her companion, who, cloaked and perceptibly bowed, leaned on her heavily and gave her an odd unwonted sense of age and cunning. She took refuge in an evasion. 'He couldn't tell me anything I didn't know pretty well already.'

'It's very true you know everything. No, dear, you haven't a petty mind; you've a lovely imagination and you're the nicest creature in the world. If you were inane, like most girls – like every one in fact – I'd have insulted you, I'd have outraged you, and then you'd have fled from me in terror. No, now that I think of it,' Mrs. Gereth went on, 'you wouldn't have fled from me: nothing, on the contrary, would have made you budge. You'd have cuddled into your warm corner, but you'd have been wounded and weeping and martyrised, and have taken every opportunity to tell people I'm a brute – as indeed I should have been!' They went to and fro, and she wouldn't allow Fleda, who laughed and protested, to attenuate with any light civility this spirited picture. She praised her cleverness and her patience; then she said it was getting cold and dark and they must go in to tea. She delayed quitting the place, however, and reverted instead to Owen's ultimatum, about which she asked another question or two; in particular whether it had struck Fleda that he really believed she'd give way.

'I think he really believes that if I try hard enough I can make you.' After uttering which words our young woman stopped short and emulated the embrace she had received a few moments before.

'And you've promised to try: I see. You didn't tell me that either,' Mrs. Gereth added as they moved. 'But you're rascal enough for anything!' While Fleda was occupied in thinking in what terms she could explain why she had indeed been rascal enough for the reticence thus denounced, her companion broke out with a question somewhat irrelevant and even in form somewhat profane. 'Why the devil, at any rate, doesn't it come off?'

Fleda hesitated. 'You mean their marriage?'

'Of course I mean their marriage!'

She thought again. 'I haven't the least idea.'

'You didn't ask him?'

'Oh how in the world can you fancy?' She spoke in a shocked tone.

'Fancy your putting a question so indelicate? *I* should have put it – I mean in your place; but I'm quite coarse, thank God!' Fleda felt privately that she herself was coarse, or at any rate would presently have to be; and Mrs. Gereth, with a purpose that struck her as increasing, continued: 'What then *was* the day to be? Wasn't it just one of these?'

'I'm sure I don't remember.'

It was part of the great rupture and an effect of Mrs. Gereth's character that up to this moment she had been completely and haughtily indifferent to that detail. Now, however, she had a visible reason for being sure. She bethought herself and she broke out: 'Isn't the day past?' Then stopping short she added: 'Upon my word they must have put it off!' As Fleda made no answer to this she became insistent. '*Have* they put it off?'

'I haven't the least idea,' said the girl.

Her hostess was again looking at her hard. 'Didn't he tell you – didn't he say anything about it?'

Fleda meanwhile had had time to make her reflexions, which were moreover the continued throb of those that had occupied the interval between Owen's departure and his mother's return. If she should now repeat his words this wouldn't at all play the game of her definite vow; it would only play the game of her little gagged and blinded desire. She could calculate well enough the result of telling Mrs. Gereth, how she had had it from Owen's troubled lips that Mona was only waiting for the restitution and would do nothing without it. The thing was to obtain the restitution without imparting that knowledge. The only way also not to impart it was not to tell any truth at all about it; and the only way to meet this last condition was to reply to her companion as she presently did. 'He told me nothing whatever. He didn't touch on the subject.'

'Not in any way?'

'Not in any way.'

Mrs. Gereth watched her and considered. 'You haven't the notion they're waiting for the things?'

'How should I have? I'm not in their counsels.'

'I dare say they are – or that Mona is.' Mrs. Gereth weighed it again; she had a bright idea. 'If I don't give in I'll be hanged if she'll not break off.'

'She'll never, never break off,' said Fleda.

'Are you sure?'

'I can't be sure, but it's my belief.'

'Derived from *him*?'

The girl hung fire a few seconds. 'Derived from him.'

Mrs. Gereth gave her a long last look, then turned abruptly away. 'It's an awful bore you didn't really get it out of him! Well, come to tea,' she added rather dryly, passing straight into the house.

XI

✳

THE sense of her dryness, which was ominous of a complication, made Fleda, before complying, linger a little on the terrace: she felt the need moreover of taking breath after such a flight into the cold air of denial. When at last she rejoined Mrs. Gereth she found her erect before the drawing-room fire. Their tea had been set out in the same quarter, and the mistress of the house, for whom the preparation of it was generally a high and undelegated function, preserved a posture to which the hissing urn made no appeal. This omission was such a further sign of something to come that to disguise her apprehension Fleda straightway and without apology took the duty in hand; only however to be promptly reminded that she was performing it confusedly and not counting the journeys of the little silver shovel she emptied into the pot. 'Not *five*, my dear – the usual three,' said her hostess with the same irony; watching her then in silence while she clumsily corrected her mistake. The tea took some minutes to draw, and Mrs. Gereth availed herself of them suddenly to exclaim: 'You haven't yet told me, you know, how it is you propose to "make" me!'

'Give everything back?' Fleda looked into the pot again and uttered her question with a briskness that she felt to be a trifle overdone. 'Why, by putting the question well before you; by being so eloquent that I shall persuade you, shall act on you; by making you sorry for having gone so far,' she said boldly. 'By simply and earnestly asking it of you, in short; and by reminding you at the same time that it's the first thing I ever have so asked. Oh you've done things for me – endless and beautiful things,' she exclaimed; 'but you've done them all from your own generous impulse – I've never so much as hinted to you to lend me a postage-stamp.'

'Give me a cup of tea,' said Mrs. Gereth. A moment later, taking the cup, she replied: 'No, you've never asked me for a postage-stamp.'

'That gives me a pull!' Fleda returned with briskness.

'Puts you in the situation of expecting I shall do this thing just simply to oblige you?'

Well, the girl took it so. 'You said a while ago that for me you *would* do it.'

'For you, but not for your eloquence. Do you understand what I mean by the difference?' Mrs. Gereth asked as she stood stirring her tea.

Fleda, to postpone answering, looked round, while she drank it, at the beautiful room. 'I don't in the least like, you know, your having brought away so much. It was a great shock to me, on my arrival here, to find how you had plunged.'

'Give me some more tea,' said Mrs. Gereth; and there was a moment's silence as Fleda poured out another cup. 'If you were shocked, my dear, I'm bound to say you concealed your shock.'

'I know I did. I was afraid to show it.'

Mrs. Gereth drank off her second cup. 'And you're·not afraid now?'

'No, I'm not afraid now.'

'What has made the difference?'

'I've pulled myself together.' Fleda paused; then she added: 'And I've seen Mr. Owen.'

'You've seen Mr. Owen' – Mrs. Gereth concurred. She put down her cup and sank into a chair in which she leaned back, resting her head and gazing at her young friend. 'Yes, I did tell you a while ago that for you I'd do it. But you haven't told me yet what you'll do in return.'

Fleda cast about. 'Anything in the wide world you may require.'

'Oh, "anything" is nothing at all! That's too easily said.' Mrs. Gereth, reclining more completely, closed her eyes with an air of disgust, an air indeed of yielding to drowsiness.

Fleda looked at her quiet face, which the appearance of oblivious sleep always made particularly handsome: she noted how much the ordeal of the last few weeks had added to its indications of age. 'Well then, try me with something. What is it you demand?'

At this, opening her eyes, Mrs. Gereth sprang straight up. 'Get him away from her!'

Fleda marvelled: her companion had in an instant become young again. 'Away from Mona? How in the world – ?'

'By not looking like a fool!' cried Mrs. Gereth very sharply. She kissed her, however, on the spot, to make up for this roughness, and with an officious hand took off the hat which, on coming into the house, our young lady had not removed. She applied a friendly touch to the girl's hair and gave a business-like pull to her jacket. 'I say don't look like an idiot, because you happen not to be one – not the least bit. I'm idiotic; I've been so, I've just discovered, ever since our first days together. I've been a precious donkey. But that's another affair.'

Fleda, as if she humbly assented, went through no form of controverting this; she simply stood passive to her friend's sudden invocation of her personal charms. 'How can I get him away from her?' she presently demanded.

'By letting yourself go.'

'By letting myself go?' She spoke mechanically, still more like an idiot, and felt as if her face flamed out the insincerity of her question. It was vividly back again, the vision of the real way to act on Mrs. Gereth. This lady's movements were now rapid; she turned off from her as quickly as she had seized her, and Fleda sat down to steady herself for full responsibility.

Her hostess, without taking up her appeal, gave a violent poke at the fire and again dealt with her. 'You've done two things then to-day – haven't you? – that you've never done before. One has been asking me the service or favour or concession – whatever you call it – that you just mentioned; the other has been telling me (certainly too for the first time!) an immense little fib.'

'An immense little fib?' Fleda felt weak; she was glad of the support of her seat.

'An immense big one then!' Mrs. Gereth said sharply. 'You don't in the least "hate" Owen, my darling. You care for him very much. In fact, my own, you're in love with him – there! Don't tell me any more lies!' she cried with a voice and a face under which Fleda recognised that there was nothing but to hold one's self and bear up. When once the truth was out it was out, and she could see more and more every instant that it offered the only way. She accepted therefore what had to come; she leaned back her head and closed her eyes as her companion had done just before. She would have covered her face with her hands but for the still greater shame. 'Oh you're a wonder, a wonder,' said Mrs.

Gereth; 'you're magnificent, and I was right, as soon as I saw you, to pick you out and trust you!' Fleda closed her eyes tighter at this last word, but her friend kept it up. 'I never dreamed of it till a while ago – when, after he had come and gone, we were face to face. Then something stuck out of you; it strongly impressed me, and I didn't know at first quite what to make of it. It was that you had just been with him and that you were not natural. Not natural to *me*,' she added with a smile. 'I sat forward, I promise you, and all that this might mean was to dawn upon me when you said you had asked nothing about Mona. It put me on the scent, but I didn't show you, did I? I felt it was *in* you, deep down, and that I must draw it out. Well, I *have* drawn it, and it's a blessing. Yesterday, when you shed tears at breakfast, I was awfully puzzled. What has been the matter with you all the while? Why Fleda, it isn't a crime, don't you know that?' cried the delighted amazing woman. 'When I was a girl I was always in love, and not always with such nice people as Owen. I didn't behave so well as you; compared with you I think I must have been odious. But if you're proud and reserved it's your own affair; I'm proud too, though I'm not reserved – that's what spoils it. I'm stupid above all – that's what I am; so dense I really blush for it. However, no one but you could have deceived me. If I trusted you moreover it was exactly to be cleverer than myself. You must be so now more than ever!' Suddenly Fleda felt her hands grasped: Mrs. Gereth had plumped down at her feet and was leaning on her knees. 'Save him – save him: you *can*!' she passionately pleaded. 'How could you not like him when he's such a dear? He *is* a dear, darling; there's no harm in my own boy! You can do what you will with him – you know you can! What else does he give us all this time for? Get him away from her: it's as if he entreated you, poor wretch! Don't abandon him to such a fate, and I'll never abandon *you*. Think of him with that creature, that family, that future! If you'll take him I'll give up everything. There, it's a solemn promise, the most sacred of my life. Get the better of her and he shall have every stick I grabbed. Give me your word and I'll accept it. I'll write for the packers to-night!'

Fleda, before this, had fallen forward on her companion's neck, and the two women, clinging together, had got up while the younger wailed on the other's bosom. 'You smooth it down because you see more in it than there can ever be; but after my hideous double game how will you be able to believe in me again?'

'I see in it simply what *must* be, if you've a single spark of pity. Where on earth was the double game when you've behaved like such a saint? You've been beautiful, you've been exquisite, and all our trouble's over.'

Fleda, drying her eyes, shook her head ever so sadly. 'No, Mrs. Gereth, it isn't over. I can't do what you ask – I can't meet your condition.'

Mrs. Gereth stared; the cloud again darkened her face. 'Why, in the name of goodness, when you adore him? I know what you see in him,' she declared in another tone. 'You're quite right!'

Fleda gave a faint stubborn smile. 'He cares for her too much.'

'Then why doesn't he marry her? He's giving you an extraordinary chance.'

'He doesn't dream I've ever thought of him,' said Fleda. 'Why should he if you didn't?'

'It wasn't with me you were in love, my duck.' Then Mrs. Gereth added: 'I'll go and tell him.'

'If you do any such thing you shall never see me again – absolutely, literally never!'

Mrs. Gereth looked hard at her young friend, betraying how she saw she must believe her. 'Then you're perverse, you're wicked. Will you swear he doesn't know?'

'Of course he doesn't know!' cried Fleda indignantly.

Her benefactress was silent a little. 'And that he has no feeling on *his* side?'

'For me?' Fleda stared. 'Before he has even married her?'

Mrs. Gereth gave a sharp laugh at this. 'He ought at least to appreciate your wit. Oh my dear, you *are* a treasure! Doesn't he appreciate anything? Has he given you absolutely no symptom – not looked a look, not breathed a sigh?'

'The case,' said Fleda coldly, 'is as I've had the honour to state it.'

'Then he's as big a donkey as his mother! But you know you've got to account for their delay,' Mrs. Gereth remarked.

'Why have I got to?' Fleda asked after a moment.

'Because you were closeted with him here so long. You can't pretend at present, you know, not to have any art.'

The girl debated; she was conscious that she must choose between two risks. She had had a secret and the secret was spoiled. Owen had one, ripe but from yesterday, still unbruised, and the greater risk now was that his mother should lay her formidable hand upon it. All Fleda's tenderness for him moved her to protect it; so she faced the smaller peril. 'Their delay,' she brought herself to reply, 'may perhaps be Mona's doing. I mean because he has lost her the things.'

Mrs. Gereth jumped at this. 'So that she'll break altogether if I keep them?'

Fleda winced. 'I've told you what I believe about that. She'll make scenes and conditions; she'll worry him. But she'll hold him fast; she'll never let him go.'

Mrs. Gereth turned it over. 'Well, I'll keep them to try her,' she finally pronounced; at which Fleda felt quite sick, as for having given everything and got nothing.

XII

✖

'I MUST in common decency let him know I've talked of the matter with you,' she said to her hostess that evening. 'What answer do you wish me to write him?'

'Write him that you must see him again,' said Mrs. Gereth.

Fleda looked very blank. 'What on earth am I to see him for?'

'For anything you like!'

The girl would have been struck with the levity of this had she not already, in an hour, felt the extent of the change suddenly wrought in her commerce with her friend – wrought above all, to that friend's view, in her relation to the great issue. The effect of all that had followed Owen's visit was to make this relation the very key of the crisis. Pressed upon her, goodness knew, the crisis had been, but it now put forth big encircling arms – arms that squeezed till they hurt and she must cry out. It was as if everything at Ricks had been poured into a common receptacle, a public ferment of emotion and zeal, out of which it was ladled up, with a splash, to be tasted and talked about; everything at least but the one little treasure of knowledge that she kept back. She ought to have liked this, she reflected, because it meant sympathy, meant a closer union with the source of so much in her life that had been beautiful and renovating; but there were fine instincts in her that stood off. She had had – and it was not merely at this time – to recognise that there were things for which Mrs. Gereth's famous *flair* was not so happy as for bargains and 'marks.'¹ It wouldn't be happy now as to the best action on the knowledge she had just gained; yet as from this moment they were still more intimately together, so a person deeply in her debt would simply have to stand and meet what was to come. There were ways in which she could sharply incommode such a person, and not only with the best conscience in the world but with a high brutality of good intentions. One of the straightest of these strokes, Fleda saw, would be the dance of delight over the mystery she, terrible woman, had profaned; the loud lawful tactless joy of the explorer leaping upon the strand.[2] Like any other lucky discoverer she would take possession of the fortunate island. She was nothing if not practical: almost the only thing she took account of in her young friend's soft secret was the excellent use she could make of it – a use so much to her taste that she refused to feel a hindrance in the quality of the material. Fleda put into Mrs. Gereth's answer to her question a good deal more meaning than it would have occurred to her a few hours before that she was prepared to put, but she had on the spot a foreboding that even so broad a hint would live to be bettered.

'Do you suggest I shall propose to him to come down here again?' she soon proceeded.

'Dear no. Say you'll go up to town and meet him.' It *was* bettered, the broad hint; and Fleda felt this to be still more the case when, returning to the subject before they went to bed, her companion said: 'I make him over to you wholly, you know – to do what you like with. Deal with him in your own clever way – I ask no questions. All I ask is that you put it through.'

'That's charming,' Fleda replied, 'but it doesn't tell me a bit, you'll be so good as to consider, in what terms to write to him. It's not an answer from you to the message I was to give you.'

'The answer to his message is perfectly distinct. He shall have everything in the place the minute he'll say he'll marry you.'

'You really pretend,' Fleda asked, 'to think me capable of transmitting him that news?'

'What else can I really pretend – when you threaten so to cast me off if I speak the word myself?'

'Oh if *you* speak the word – !' the girl murmured very gravely; yet happy at least to know that in this direction Mrs. Gereth confessed herself warned and helpless. Then she added: 'How can I go on living with you on a footing of which I so deeply disapprove? Thinking as I do that you've despoiled him far more than is just or merciful – for if I expected you to take something I didn't in the least expect you to take everything – how can I stay here without a sense that I'm backing you up in your cruelty and participating in your ill-gotten gains?' Fleda was determined that if she had the chill of her exposed and investigated state she should also have the convenience of it, and that if Mrs. Gereth popped in and out of the chamber of her soul she would at least return the freedom. 'I shall quite hate, you know, in a day or two, every object that surrounds you – become blind to all the beauty and rarity that I formerly delighted in. Don't think me harsh; there's no use in my not being frank now. If I leave you everything's at an end.'

Mrs. Gereth, however, was imperturbable: Fleda had to recognise that her advantage had become too real. 'It's too beautiful, the way you care for him; it's music in my ears. Nothing else but such a passion could make you say such things; that's the way I should have been too, my dear. Why didn't you tell me sooner? I'd have gone right in for you; I never would have moved a candlestick. Don't stay with me if it torments you: don't, if it costs you so much, be where you see all the plunder. Go up to town – go back for a little to your father's. It need be only for a little; two or three weeks will make us all right. Your father will take you and be glad, if you'll only make him understand what it's a question of – of your getting yourself off his hands for ever. *I'll* make him understand, you know, if you feel shy. I'd take you up myself, I'd go with you to spare your being bored: we'd put up at an hotel and we might amuse ourselves a bit. We haven't had much innocent pleasure since we met, have we? But of course that wouldn't suit our book. I should be a bugaboo to Owen – I should be fatally in the way. Your chance is there – your chance is to be alone. For God's sake use it to the right end. If you're in want of money I've a little I can give you. But I ask no questions – not a question as small as your shoe!'

She asked no questions, but she took the most extraordinary things for granted: Fleda felt this still more at the end of a couple of days. On the second of these our young lady wrote to Owen: her emotion had to a certain degree cleared itself – there was something she could briefly say. If she had given everything to Mrs. Gereth and as yet got nothing, so she had on the other hand quickly reacted – it took but a night – against the discouragement of her first check. Her desire to serve him was too passionate, the sense that he counted upon her too sweet: these things caught her up again and gave her a new patience and a new subtlety. It shouldn't really be for nothing she had given so much; deep within her burned again the resolve to get something back. So what she wrote to Owen was simply that she had had a great scene with his mother, but that he must be patient and give her time. It was difficult, as they both had expected, but she was working her hardest for him. She had made an impression – she would do everything to follow it up. Meanwhile he must keep intensely quiet and take no other steps; he must only trust her and pray for her and believe in her perfect loyalty. She made no allusion whatever to Mona's attitude, nor to his not being, as regarded that young lady, master of the situation; but she said in a postscript, referring to his mother, 'Of course she wonders a good deal why your marriage doesn't take place.' After the letter had gone she regretted having used the word 'loyalty'; there were two or three vaguer terms she might as well have employed. The answer she immediately received from Owen was a little note the deficiencies of which she met by describing it to herself as pathetically simple, but which, to prove that Mrs. Gereth might ask as many questions as she liked, she at once made his mother read. He had no art with his pen, he had not even a good hand, and his letter, a short profession of friendly confidence, was couched but in a few familiar and colourless words of acknowledgment and assent. The gist of it was that he would certainly, since Miss Vetch recommended it, not hurry mamma too much. He wouldn't for the present cause her to be approached by any one else, but would nevertheless continue to hope she'd see she must really come round. 'Of course, you know,' he added, 'she can't keep me waiting indefinitely. Please give her my love and tell her that. If it can be done peaceably I know you're just the one to do it.'

Fleda had awaited his rejoinder in deep suspense; such was her imagination of the possibility of his having, as she tacitly phrased it, let himself go on paper that when it arrived she was at first almost afraid to open it. There was indeed a distinct danger, for if he should take it into his head to write her love-letters the whole chance of aiding him would drop: she should have to return them, she should have to decline all further communication with him; it would be the end alike of dreams and of realities. This imagination of Fleda's was a faculty that easily embraced all the heights and depths and extremities of things; that made a single mouthful in particular of any tragic or desperate necessity. She was perhaps at first just a trifle disappointed not to find in the risky note some syllable that strayed from the text; but the next moment she had risen to a point of view from which it presented itself as a production almost inspired in its simplicity. It was simple even for Owen, and she wondered what had given him the cue to be more so than usual. Then she admirably saw how natures that are right just do the things that are right. He wasn't clever – his manner of writing showed it; but the cleverest man in England couldn't have had more the instinct that in the conditions was the supremely happy one, the instinct of giving her something that would do beautifully to be shown to Mrs. Gereth. This was deep divination, for naturally he couldn't know the line Mrs. Gereth was taking. It was furthermore explained – and that was the most touching part of all – by his wish that she herself should notice how awfully well he was behaving. His very bareness called her attention to his virtue, and these were the exact fruits of her beautiful and terrible admonition. He was cleaving to Mona; he was doing his duty; he was making tremendously sure he should be without reproach.

If Fleda handed her friend the letter as a triumphant gage of the innocence of the young man's heart her elation lived but a moment after Mrs. Gereth had pounced on the tell-tale spot in it. 'Why in the world then does he still not breathe a breath about the day, the *day*, the DAY?' She repeated the word with a crescendo of superior acuteness; she proclaimed that nothing could be more marked than its absence – an absence that simply spoke volumes. What did it prove in fine but that she was producing the effect she had toiled for – that she had settled or was rapidly settling Mona?

Such a challenge Fleda was obliged in some manner to take up. 'You may be settling Mona,' she returned with a smile, 'but I can hardly regard it as sufficient evidence that you're settling Mona's lover.'

'Why not, with such a studied omission on his part to gloss over in any manner the painful tension existing between them – the painful tension that, under Providence, I've been the means of bringing about? He gives you by his silence clear notice that his marriage is practically off.'

'He speaks to me of the only thing that concerns me. He gives me clear notice that he abates not one jot of his demand.'

'Well then let him take the only way to get it satisfied!'

Fleda had no need to ask again what such a way might be, nor was the ground supplied her cut away by the almost irritating confidence with which Mrs. Gereth could make her own arguments wait on her own wishes. These days, which dragged their length into a strange uncomfortable fortnight, had already borne more testimony to that element than all the other time the conspirators had lived through. Our young woman had been at first far from measuring the extent of an element that Owen himself would probably have described as her companion's 'cheek.' She lived now in a kind of bath of boldness, felt as if a fierce light poured in upon her from windows opened wide; and the singular part of the ordeal was that she couldn't protest against it fully without incurring even to her own mind some reproach of ingratitude, some charge of smallness. If Mrs. Gereth's apparent determination to hustle her into Owen's arms was accompanied with an air of holding her dignity rather cheap, this was after all only as a consequence of her being held in respect to some other attributes rather dear. It was a new version of the old story of being kicked upstairs. The wonderful woman was the same woman who, in the summer, at Poynton, had been so puzzled to conceive why a good-natured girl shouldn't have contributed more to the personal rout of the Brigstocks – shouldn't have been grateful even for the handsome published puff of Fleda Vetch. Only her passion was keener now and her scruple more absent; the prolonged contest made a demand on her, and her pugnacity had become one with her constant habit of using such weapons as she could pick up. She had no imagination about anybody's life save on the side she bumped against. Fleda was quite aware that she would have otherwise been a rare creature, but a rare creature was originally just what she had struck her as being. Mrs. Gereth had really no perception of anybody's nature – had only one question about persons: were they clever or stupid? To be clever meant to know the 'marks.' Fleda knew them by direct inspiration, and a warm recognition of this had been her friend's tribute to her character. The girl now had hours of sombre hope she might never see anything 'good' again: that kind of experience was clearly so broken a reed, so fallible a source of peace. One would be more at peace in some vulgar little place that should owe its *cachet* to a Universal

Provider.³ There were nice strong simplifying horrors in West Kensington; it was as if they beckoned her and wooed her back to them. She had a relaxed recollection of Waterbath; and of her reasons for staying on at Ricks the force was rapidly ebbing. One of these was her pledge to Owen – her vow to press his mother close; the other was the fact that of the two discomforts, that of being prodded by Mrs. Gereth and that of appearing to run after somebody else, the former remained for a while the more endurable.

As the days passed, however, it became plainer that her only chance of success would be in lending herself to this low appearance. Then moreover, at last, her nerves settling the question, the choice was simply imposed by the violence done her taste – done whatever was left of that high principle, at least, after the free and reckless satisfaction, for months, of great drafts and appeals. It was all very well to try to evade discussion: Owen Gereth was looking to her for a struggle, and it wasn't a bit of a struggle to be disgusted and dumb. She was on too strange a footing – that of having presented an ultimatum and having had it torn up in her face. In such a case as that the envoy always departed; he never sat gaping and dawdling before the city. Mrs. Gereth every morning looked publicly into *The Morning Post*,⁴ the only newspaper she received; and every morning she treated the blankness of that journal as fresh evidence that everything was 'off.' What did the *Post* exist for but to tell you your children were wretchedly married? – so that if such a fount of misery was dry what could you do but infer that for once you had miraculously escaped? She almost taunted Fleda with supineness in not getting something out of somebody – in the same breath indeed in which she drenched her with a kind of appreciation more onerous to the girl than blame. Mrs. Gereth herself had of course washed her hands of the matter; but Fleda knew people who knew Mona and would be sure to be in her confidence – inconceivable people who admired her and had the 'entrée' of Waterbath. What was the use therefore of being the most natural and the easiest of letter-writers, if no sort of side-light – in some pretext for correspondence – was, by a brilliant creature, to be got out of such barbarians? Fleda was not only a brilliant creature, but she heard herself commended in these days for attractions new and strange: she figured suddenly in the queer conversations of Ricks as a distinguished, almost as a dangerous, beauty. That retouching of her hair and dress in which her friend had impulsively indulged on a first glimpse of her secret was by implication very frequently repeated. She had the impression not only of being advertised and offered, but of being counselled, enlightened, initiated in ways she scarcely understood – arts obscure even to a poor girl who had had, in good society and motherless poverty, to look straight at realities and fill out blanks.

These arts, when Mrs. Gereth's spirits were high, were handled with a brave and cynical humour with which Fleda's fancy could keep no step: they left our young lady wondering what on earth her companion wanted her to do. 'I want you to cut in!' – that was Mrs. Gereth's familiar and comprehensive phrase for the course she prescribed. She challenged again and again Fleda's picture, as she called it (though the sketch was too slight to deserve the name), of the indifference to which a prior attachment had committed the proprietor of Poynton. 'Do you mean to say that, Mona or no Mona, he could see you that way, day after day, and not have the ordinary feelings of a man? Don't you know a little more, you absurd affected thing, what men *are*, the brutes?' This was the sort of interrogation to which Fleda was fitfully and irrelevantly treated. She had grown almost used to the refrain. 'Do you mean to say that when, the other day, one had quite made you over to him, the great gawk, and he was, on this very spot, utterly alone with you – ?' The poor girl at this point never left any doubt of what she meant to say; but Mrs. Gereth could be trusted to break out in another place and at another time. At last Fleda wrote to her father that he must take her in a little, take her in while she looked about; and when, to her companion's delight, she returned to London that lady went with her to the station and wafted her on her way. *The Morning Post* had been delivered as they left the house, and Mrs. Gereth had brought it with her for the traveller, who never spent a penny on a newspaper. On the platform, however, when this young person was ticketed, labelled and seated, she opened it at the window of the carriage, exclaiming as usual, after looking into it a moment, 'Nothing, nothing, nothing: don't tell *me*!' Every day that there was nothing was a nail in the coffin of the marriage. An instant later the train was off, but, moving quickly beside it, while Fleda leaned inscrutably forth, Mrs. Gereth grasped her friend's hand and looked up with wonderful eyes. 'Only let yourself go, darling – only let yourself go!'

XIII

✳

THAT she desired to ask no prudish questions Mrs. Gereth conscientiously proved by closing her lips tight after Fleda had gone to London. No letter from Ricks arrived at West Kensington, and Fleda, with nothing to communicate that could be to the taste of either party, forbore to open a correspondence. If her heart had been less heavy she might have been amused to feel how much free rope this reticence of Ricks seemed to signify to her she could take. She had at all events no good news for her friend save in the sense that her silence was not bad news. She was not yet in a position to write that she had 'cut in'; but neither, on the other hand, had she gathered material for announcing that Mona was undisseverable from her prey. She had made no use of the pen so glorified by Mrs. Gereth to wake up the echoes of Waterbath; she had sedulously abstained from inquiring what in any quarter, far or near, was said or suggested or supposed. She only spent a matutinal penny on *The Morning Post*; she only saw on each occasion that that inspired sheet had as little to say about the imminence as about the collapse of certain nuptials. It was at the same time obvious that Mrs. Gereth triumphed on these occasions much more than she trembled, and that with a few such triumphs repeated she should cease to tremble at all. What came out most, however, was that she had had a rare preconception of the circumstances that would have ministered, had Fleda been disposed, to the girl's cutting in. It was brought home to Fleda that these circumstances would have particularly favoured intervention; she was promptly forced to do them a secret justice. One of the effects of her intimacy with Mrs. Gereth was that she had quite lost all sense of intimacy with any one else. The lady of Ricks had made a desert round her, possessing and absorbing her so utterly that other partakers had fallen away. Hadn't she been admonished, months before, that people considered they had lost her and were reconciled on the whole to the privation? Her present position in the great unconscious town showed distinctly for obscure: she regarded it at any rate with eyes suspicious of that lesson. She neither wrote notes nor received them; she indulged in no reminders nor knocked at any doors; she wandered vaguely in the western wilderness or cultivated shy forms of that 'household art' for which she had had a respect before tasting the bitter tree of knowledge.[1] Her only plan was to be as quiet as a mouse, and when she failed in the attempt to lose herself in the flat suburb she resembled – or thought she did – a lonely fly crawling over a dusty chart.

How had Mrs. Gereth known in advance that if she had chosen to be 'vile' (that was what Fleda called it) everything would happen to help her? – especially the way her poor father doddered after breakfast off to his club, giving the impression of seventy when he was really fifty-seven and leaving her richly alone for the day. He came back about midnight, looking at her very hard and not risking long words – only making her feel by inimitable touches that the presence of his family compelled him to alter all his hours. She had in their common sitting-room the company of the objects he was fond of saying he had collected – objects, shabby and battered, of a sort that appealed little to his daughter: old brandy-flasks and match-boxes, old calendars and hand-books, intermixed with an assortment of penwipers and ash-trays, a harvest gathered in from penny bazaars.[2] He was blandly unconscious of that side of Fleda's nature which had endeared her to Mrs. Gereth, and she had often heard him wish to goodness there was something intelligible she cared for. Why didn't she try collecting something? – it didn't matter what. She would find it gave an interest to life – there was no end to the little curiosities one could easily pick up. He was conscious of having a taste for fine things which his children had unfortunately not inherited. This indicated the limits of their acquaintance with him – limits which, as Fleda was now sharply aware, could only leave him to wonder what the mischief she was there for. As she herself echoed this question to the letter she was not in a position to clear up the mystery. She couldn't have given a name to her business nor have explained it save by saying that she had had to get away from Ricks. It was intensely provisional, but what was to come next? Nothing could come next but a deeper anxiety. She had neither a home nor an outlook

– nothing in all the wide world but a feeling of suspense. It was, morally speaking, like figuring in society with a wardrobe of one garment.

Of course she had her duty – her duty to Owen – a definite undertaking, re-affirmed, after his visit to Ricks, under her hand and seal; but no sense of possession was attached to that, only a horrible sense of privation. She had quite moved from under Mrs. Gereth's wide wing; and now that she was really among the pen-wipers and ash-trays she was swept, at the thought of all the beauty she had forsworn, by short wild gusts of despair. If her friend should really keep the spoils[3] she would never return to her. If that friend should on the other hand part with them what on earth would there be to return to? The chill struck deep as Fleda thought of the mistress of Ricks also reduced, in vulgar parlance, to what she had on her back: there was nothing to which she could compare such an image but her idea of Marie Antoinette in the Concier-gerie,[4] or perhaps the vision of some tropical bird, the creature of hot, dense forests, dropped on a frozen moor to pick up a living. The mind's eye could indeed see Mrs. Gereth only in her thick, coloured air; it took all the light of her treasures to make her concrete and distinct. She loomed for a moment, in any mere house of compartments and angles, gaunt and unnatural; then she vanished as if she had suddenly sunk into a quicksand. Fleda lost herself in the rich fancy of how, if *she* were mistress of Poynton, a whole province, as an abode, should be assigned there to the great queen-mother. She would have returned from her campaign with her baggage-train and her loot, and the palace would unbar its shutters and the morning flash back from its halls. In the event of a surrender the poor woman would never again be able to begin to collect: she was now too old and too moneyless, and times were altered and good things impossibly dear.[5] A surrender, further-more, to any daughter-in-law save an oddity like Mona needn't at all be an abdication in fact; any other fairly nice girl whom Owen should have taken it into his head to marry would have been positively glad to have, for the museum, a custodian equal to a walking catalogue, a custodian versed beyond any one any-where in the mysteries of ministration to rare pieces. A fairly nice girl would somehow be away a good deal and would at such times count it a blessing to feel Mrs. Gereth at her post.

Fleda had from the first days fully recognised that, quite apart from any question of letting Owen know where she was, it would be a charity to give him some sign: it would be weak, it would be ugly to be diverted from this kindness by the fact that Mrs. Gereth had attached a tinkling bell to it. A frank relation with him was only superficially discredited: she ought for his own sake to send him a word of cheer. So she repeatedly reasoned, but as repeatedly delaying performance: if her general plan had been to be as still as a mouse an interview like the interview at Ricks would be an odd contribution to that ideal. Therefore with a confused preference of practice to theory she let the days go by; she judged nothing so imperative as the gain of precious time. She shouldn't be able to stay with her father for ever, but she might now reap the benefit of having married her sister – Maggie's union had been built up round a small spare room. Concealed in this retreat she might try to paint again, and abetted by the grateful Maggie – for Maggie at least was grateful – she might try to dispose of her work. She had not indeed struggled with a brush since her visit to Waterbath, where the sight of the family splotches had put her immensely on her guard. Poynton, moreover, had been an impossible place for producing; no art more active than a Buddhistic contemplation[6] could lift its head there. It had stripped its mistress clean of all feeble accomplishments[7]; she sometimes unrolled, her needles and silks, her gold and silver folded in it, a big, brave, flowery square of ancient unfinished 'work';[8] but her hand had sooner been imbrued with blood than with ink or with water-colour. Close to Fleda's present abode was the little shop of a man who mounted and framed pictures and desolately dealt in artists' materials. She sometimes paused before it to look at a couple of shy experiments for which its dull window constituted publicity; small studies placed there on sale and full of warning to a young lady without fortune and without talent. Some such young lady had brought them forth in sorrow; some such young lady, to see if they had been snapped up, had passed and re-passed as helplessly as she herself was doing. They never had been, they never would be snapped up; yet they were quite above the actual attainment of some other young ladies. It was a matter of discipline with Fleda to take an occasional lesson from them; besides which when she now quitted the house she had to look for reasons after she was out. The only place to find them was in the shop-windows. They likened her to a servant-girl taking her 'afternoon,'[9] but that didn't signify: perhaps some day she would resemble such a person still more closely. This continued a fortnight, at the end of which the feeling was suddenly dissipated. She had stopped as usual in the presence of the little pictures and then, as she turned away, had found herself face to face with Owen Gereth.

At the sight of him two fresh waves passed quickly across her heart, one at the heels of the other. The first was an instant perception that their meeting was not an accident; the second a consciousness as prompt that the best place for it was the street. She knew before he told her that he had been to see her, and the next thing she knew was that he had had information from his mother. Her mind grasped these things while he said with a smile: 'I saw only your back, but I knew like a shot. I was over the way. I've been at your house.'

'How came you to know my house?' Fleda asked.

'I like that!' he laughed. 'How came you not to let me know you were there?'

Fleda, at this, thought it best also to laugh. 'Since I didn't let you know why did you come?'

'Oh I say!' cried Owen. 'Don't add insult to injury. Why in the world didn't you let me know? I came because I want awfully to see you.' He rather floundered, then added: 'I got the tip from mother. She has written to me – fancy!'

They still stood where they had met. Fleda's instinct was to keep him there; the more that she could already see him take for granted they would immediately proceed together to her door. He rose before her with a different air: he looked less ruffled and bruised than he had done at Ricks; he showed a recovered freshness. Perhaps, however, this was only because she had scarcely seen him at all till now in London form, as he would have called it – 'turned out' as he was turned out in town. In the country, heated with the chase and splashed with the mire, he had always much reminded her of a picturesque peasant in national costume. This costume, as Owen wore it, varied from day to day; it was as copious as the wardrobe of an actor; but it never failed of suggestions of the earth and the weather, the hedges and ditches, the beasts and birds. There had been days when he struck her as all potent nature in one pair of boots. It didn't make him now another person that he was delicately dressed, shining and splendid, that he had a higher hat and light gloves with black seams and an umbrella as fine as a lance; but it made him, she soon decided, really handsomer, and this in turn gave him – for she never could think of him, or indeed of some other things, without the aid of his vocabulary – a tremendous pull. Yes, that was for the moment, as he looked at her, the great fact of their situation – his pull was tremendous. She tried to keep the acknowledgment of it from trembling in her voice as she said to him with more surprise than she really felt: 'You've then reopened relations with her?'

'It's she who has reopened them with me. I got her letter this morning. She told me you were here and that she wished me to know it. She didn't say much; she just gave me your address. I wrote her back, you know, "Thanks no end. Shall go to-day." So we *are* in correspondence again, aren't we? She means of course that you've something to tell me from her, hey? But if you have why haven't you let a fellow know?' He waited for no answer to this, he had so much to say. 'At your house, just now, they told me how long you've been here. Haven't you known all the while that I'm counting the hours? I left a word for you – that I would be back at six; but I'm awfully glad to have caught you so much sooner. You don't mean to say you're not going home!' he exclaimed in dismay. 'The young woman there told me you went out early.'

'I've been out a very short time,' said Fleda, who had hung back with the general purpose of making things difficult for him. The street would make them difficult; she could trust the street. She reflected in time, however, that to betray she was afraid to admit him would give him more a feeling of facility than of anything else. She moved on with him after a moment, letting him direct their course to her door, which was only round a corner; she considered as they went that it mightn't prove such a stroke to have been in London so long and yet not have called him. She desired he should feel she was perfectly simple with him, and there was no simplicity in that. None the less, on the steps of the house, though she had a key, she rang the bell; and while they waited together and she averted her face she looked straight into the depths of what Mrs. Gereth had meant by giving him the 'tip.' This had been perfidious, had been monstrous of Mrs. Gereth, and Fleda wondered if her letter had contained only what Owen repeated.

XIV

WHEN they had passed together into her father's little place and, among the brandy-flasks and pen-wipers, still more disconcerted and divided, the girl – to do something, though it would make him stay – had ordered tea, he put the letter before her quite as if he had guessed her thought. 'She's still a bit nasty – fancy!' He handed her the scrap of a note he had pulled out of his pocket and from its envelope. 'Fleda Vetch,' it ran, 'is at West Kensington – 10 Raphael Road.[1] Go to see her and try, for God's sake, to cultivate a glimmer of intelligence.' When, handing it back to him, she took in his face she saw how his heightened colour was the effect of watching her read such an allusion to his want of wit. Fleda knew what it was an allusion to, and his pathetic air of having received this buffet, tall and fine and kind as he stood there, made her conscious of not quite concealing her knowledge. For a minute she was kept mute by an angered sense of the trick thus played her. It was a trick because she considered there had been a covenant; and the trick consisted of Mrs. Gereth's having broken the spirit of their agreement while conforming in a fashion to the letter. Under the girl's menace of a complete rupture she had been afraid to make of her secret the use she itched to make; but in the course of these days of separation she had gathered pluck to hazard an indirect betrayal. Fleda measured her hesitations and the impulse she had finally obeyed, which the continued procrastination of Waterbath had encouraged, had at last made irresistible. If in her high-handed manner of playing their game she had not named the thing hidden she had named the hiding-place. It was over the sense of this wrong that Fleda's lips closed tight: she was afraid of aggravating her case by some sound that would quicken her visitor's attention. A strong effort, however, helped her to avoid the danger; with her constant idea of keeping cool and repressing a visible flutter she found herself able to choose her words. Meanwhile he had exclaimed with his uncomfortable laugh: 'That's a good one for me, Miss Vetch, isn't it?'

'Of course you know by this time that your mother's very direct,' said Fleda.

'I think I can understand well enough when I know what's to be understood,' the young man returned. 'But I hope you won't mind my saying that you've kept me pretty well in the dark about that. I've been waiting, waiting, waiting – so much has depended on your news. If you've been working for me I'm afraid it has been a thankless job. Can't she say what she'll do, one way or the other? I can't tell in the least where I am, you know. I haven't really learnt from you, since I saw you there, where *she* is. You wrote me to be patient, and I should like to know what else I've been. But I'm afraid you don't quite realise what I'm to be patient *with*. At Waterbath, don't you know? I've simply to account and answer, piece by piece, for my damned property. Mona glowers at me and waits, and I, hang it, I glower at *you* and do the same.' Fleda had gathered fuller confidence as he continued; so plain was it that she had succeeded in not dropping into his mind the spark that might produce the glimmer his mother had tried to rub up. But even her small safety gave a start when after an appealing pause he went on: 'I hope, you know, that all this time you're not keeping anything back from me.'

In the full face of what she was keeping back such a hope could only make her wince; but she was prompt with her explanations in proportion as she felt they failed to meet him. The smutty maid came in with tea-things, and Fleda, moving several objects, eagerly accepted the diversion of arranging a place for them on one of the tables. 'I've been trying to break your mother down because it has seemed there may be some chance of it. That's why I've let you go on expecting it. She's too proud to veer round all at once, but I think I speak correctly in saying I've made an impression.'

In spite of ordering tea she had not invited him to sit down; she herself made a point of standing. He hovered by the window that looked into Raphael Road; she kept at the other side of the room; the stunted slavey,[2] gazing wide-eyed at the beautiful gentleman and either stupidly or cunningly bringing but one thing at a time, came and went between the tea-tray and the open door.

'You pegged at her so hard?' Owen asked.

'I explained to her fully your position and put before her much more strongly than she liked what seemed to me her absolute duty.'

He waited a little. 'And having done that you came away?'

She felt the full need of giving a reason for her movement, but at first only said with cheerful frankness: 'I came away.'

Her companion again seemed to search her. 'I thought you had gone to her for several months.'

'Well,' Fleda replied, 'I couldn't stay. I didn't like it. I didn't like it at all – I couldn't bear it,' she went on. 'In the midst of those trophies of Poynton, living with them, touching them, using them, I felt as if backing her up. As I wasn't a bit of an accomplice, as I hate what she has done, I didn't want to be, even to the extent of the mere look of it – what is it you call such people? – an accessory after the fact.' There was something she kept back so rigidly that the joy of uttering the rest was double. She yielded to the sharp need of giving him all the other truth. There was a matter as to which she had deceived him, and there was a matter as to which she had deceived Mrs. Gereth, but her lack of pleasure in deception as such came home to her now. She busied herself with the tea and, to extend the occupation, cleared the table still more, spreading out the coarse cups and saucers and the vulgar little plates. She was aware she produced more confusion than symmetry, but she was also aware she was violently nervous. Owen tried to help her with something: this made indeed for disorder. 'My reason for not writing to you,' she pursued, 'was simply that I was hoping to hear more from Ricks. I've waited from day to day for that.'

'But you've heard nothing?'

'Not a word.'

'Then what I understand,' said Owen, 'is that practically you and Mummy have quarrelled. And you've done it – I mean you personally – for *me*.'

'Oh no, we haven't quarrelled a bit!' Then with a smile: 'We've only diverged.'

'You've diverged uncommonly far!' – Owen laughed pleasantly back. Fleda, with her hideous crockery and her father's collections, could conceive that these objects, to her visitor's perception even more strongly than to her own, measured the length of the swing from Poynton and Ricks; she couldn't forget either that her high standards must figure vividly enough even to Owen's simplicity to make him reflect that West Kensington was a tremendous fall. If she had fallen it was because she had acted for him. She was all the more content he should thus see she *had* acted, as the cost of it, in his eyes, was none of her own showing. 'What seems to have happened,' he said, 'is that you've had a row with her and yet not moved her!'

She felt her way; she was full of the impression that, notwithstanding her scant help, he saw his course clearer than he had seen it at Ricks. He might mean many things, and what if the many should mean in their turn only one? 'The difficulty is, you understand, that she doesn't really see into your situation.' She had a pause. 'She doesn't make out why your marriage hasn't yet taken place.'

Owen stared. 'Why, for the reason I told you: that Mona won't take another step till mother has given full satisfaction. Everything must be there, every blessed "stolen" thing. You see everything *was* there the day of that fatal visit.'

'Yes, that's what I understood from you at Ricks,' said Fleda; 'but I haven't repeated it to your mother.' She had hated at Ricks to talk with him about Mona, but now that scruple was swept away. If he could speak of Mona's visit as fatal she need at least not pretend not to notice it. It made all the difference that she had tried to assist him and had failed: to give him any faith in her service she must give him all her reasons but one. She must give him, in other words, with a corresponding omission, all Mrs. Gereth's. 'You can easily see that, as she dislikes your marriage, anything that may seem to make it less certain works in her favour. Without my telling her, she has suspicions and views that are simply suggested by your delay. Therefore it didn't seem to me right to make them worse. By holding off long enough she thinks she may put an end to your engagement. If Mona's waiting she believes she may at last tire Mona out.' This, in all conscience, Fleda felt to be lucid enough.

So the young man, following her attentively, appeared equally to feel. 'So far as that goes,' he promptly declared, 'she *has* at last tired Mona out.' He uttered the words with a strange approach to hilarity.

Fleda's surprise at this aberration left her a moment looking at him. 'Do you mean your marriage is off?'

He answered with the oddest gay pessimism. 'God knows, Miss Vetch, where or when or what my marriage is! If it isn't "off" it certainly, at the point things have reached, isn't *on*. I haven't seen Mona for ten days, and for a week I haven't heard from her. She used to write to me every week, don't you know? She won't budge from Waterbath and I haven't budged from town.' Then he put it plain. 'If she does break will mother come round?'

Fleda, at this, felt her heroism meet its real test – felt that in telling him the truth she should effectively raise a hand to push his impediment out of the way. Was the knowledge that such a motion would probably dispose for ever of Mona capable of yielding to the conception of still giving her every chance she was entitled to? That conception was heroic, but at the same moment it reminded our young woman of the place it had held in her plan she was also reminded of the not less urgent claim of the truth. Ah the truth – there was a limit to the impunity with which one could juggle with that value, which in itself never shifted. Wasn't what she had most to remember the fact that Owen had a right to his property, and that he had also her vow to stand by him in the recovery of it? How did she stand by him if she hid from him the only process of recovery of which she was quite sure? For an instant that seemed to her the fullest of her life she debated. 'Yes,' she said at last, 'if your marriage really drops she'll give up everything she has taken.'

'That's just what makes Mona hesitate!' Owen honestly stated. 'I mean the idea that I shall get back the things only if she gives me up.'

Fleda thought an instant. 'You mean makes her hesitate to keep you – not hesitate to renounce you?'

He looked a trifle befogged. 'She doesn't see the use of hanging on, as I haven't even yet put the matter into legal hands. She's awfully keen about that, and awfully disgusted that I don't. She says it's the only real way and she thinks I'm afraid to take it. She has given me time and then has given me again more. She says I give Mummy too much. She says I'm a muff to go pottering on. That's why she's drawing off so hard, don't you see?'

'I don't see very clearly. Of course you must give her what you offered her; of course you must keep your word. There must be no mistake about *that!*' the girl declared.

His bewilderment visibly increased. 'You think then, as she does, that I *must* send down the police?'

The mixture of reluctance and dependence in this made her feel how much she was failing him: she had the sense of 'breaking' too. 'No, no, not yet!' she said, though she had really no other and no better course to prescribe. 'Doesn't it occur to you,' she asked in a moment, 'that if Mona is, as you say, drawing away, she may have in doing so a very high motive? She knows the immense value of all the objects detained by your mother, and to restore the spoils of Poynton she's ready – is that it? – to make a sacrifice. The sacrifice is that of an engagement she had entered upon with joy.'

He had been blank a moment before, but he followed this argument with success – a success so immediate that it enabled him to produce with decision: 'Ah she's not that sort! She wants them herself,' he added; 'she wants to feel they're hers; she doesn't care whether I have them or not. And if she can't get them she doesn't want *me*. If she can't get them she doesn't want anything at all.'

This was categoric: Fleda drank it in. 'She takes such an interest in them?'

'So it appears.'

'So much that they're *all*, in the whole business, and that she can let everything else absolutely depend upon them?'

Owen weighed it as if he felt the responsibility of his answer; but that answer nevertheless came, and, as Fleda could see, out of a wealth of memory. 'She never wanted them particularly till they seemed to be in danger. Now she has an idea about them, and when she gets hold of an idea – oh dear me!' He broke off, pausing and looking away as with a sense of the futility of expression: it was the first time she had heard him explain a matter so pointedly or embark at all on a generalisation. It was striking, it was touching to her, as he faltered, that he appeared but half capable of floating his generalisation to the end. The girl, however, was so far competent to fill up his blank as that she had divined on the occasion of Mona's visit to Poynton what would happen in case of the accident at which he glanced. She had there with her own eyes seen Owen's betrothed get hold of an idea. 'I say, you know, *do* give me some tea!' he went on irrelevantly and familiarly.

Her profuse preparations had all this time had no sequel, and with a laugh that she felt to be awkward she hastily prepared his draught. 'It's sure to be horrid,' she said; 'we don't have at all good things.' She offered him also bread and butter, of which he partook, holding his cup and saucer in his other hand and moving slowly about the room. She poured herself a cup, but not to take it; after which, without wanting it, she began to eat a small stale biscuit. She was struck with the extinction of the unwillingness she had felt at Ricks to contribute to the bandying between them of poor Mona's name; and under this influence she presently resumed: 'Am I to understand that she engaged herself to marry you without caring for you?'

He looked into Raphael Road. 'She *did* care for me awfully. But she can't stand the strain.'

'The strain of what?'

'Why of the whole wretched thing.'

'The whole thing has indeed been wretched, and I can easily conceive its effect on her,' Fleda sagaciously said.

Her visitor turned sharp round. 'You *can*?' There was a light in his strong stare. 'You can understand its spoiling her temper and making her come down on *me*? She behaves as if I were of no use to her at all!'

Fleda wondered even to extravagance. 'She's rankling under the sense of her wrong.'

'Well, was it I, pray, who perpetrated the wrong? Ain't³ I doing what I can to get the thing arranged?'

The ring of his question made his anger at Mona almost resemble for a minute an anger at Fleda; and this resemblance in turn caused our young lady to observe how it became him to speak, as he did for the first time in her hearing, with that degree of heat, and to use, for the first time too, such a term as 'perpetrated.'⁴ In addition his challenge rendered still more vivid to her the mere flimsiness of her own aid. 'Yes, you've been perfect,' she said. 'You've had a most difficult part. You've had to show tact and patience as well as firmness with your mother, and you've

143

strikingly shown them. It's I who, quite unintentionally, have deceived you. I haven't helped you at all to your remedy.'

'Well, you wouldn't at all events have ceased to like me, would you?' Owen demanded. It evidently mattered to him to know if she really justified Mona. 'I mean of course if you *had* liked me – liked me as *she* liked me,' he explained.

Fleda looked this appeal in the face only long enough to recognise that in her embarrassment she must take instant refuge in a higher one. 'I can answer that better if I know how kind to her you've been. *Have* you been kind to her?' she asked as simply as she could.

'Why rather, Miss Vetch! I've done every blessed thing she has ever wished,' he protested. 'I rushed down to Ricks, as you saw, with fire and sword, and the day after that I went to see her at Waterbath.' At this point he checked himself, though it was just the point at which her interest deepened. A different look had come into his face as he put down his empty teacup. 'But why should I tell you such things for any good it does me? I gather you've no suggestion to make me now except that I shall request my solicitor to act. *Shall* I request him to act?'

Fleda scarce caught his words: something new had suddenly come into her mind. 'When you went to Waterbath after seeing me,' she asked, 'did you tell her all about that?'

Owen looked conscious. 'All about it?'

'That you had had a long talk with me without seeing your mother at all?'

'Oh yes, I told her exactly, and that you had been most awfully kind and that I had placed the whole thing in your hands.'

Fleda gazed as at the scene he reported. 'Perhaps that displeased her,' she at last suggested.

'It displeased her fearfully.' He brought it out with a rush.

'Fearfully?' broke from the girl. Somehow, at the word, she was startled.

'She wanted to know what right you had to meddle. She said you weren't honest.'

'Oh!' Fleda cried with a long wail. Then she controlled herself. 'I see.'

'She abused you and I defended you. She denounced you –

She checked him with a gesture. 'Don't tell me what she did!'

She had coloured up to her eyes, where, as with the effect of a blow in the face, she quickly felt the tears gathering. It was a sudden drop in her great flight, a shock to her attempt to watch over Mona's interests. While she had been straining her very soul in this attempt the subject of her magnanimity had been practically pronouncing her vile. She took it all in, however, and after an instant was able to speak with a smile. She wouldn't have been surprised to learn indeed that her smile was queer. 'You spoke a while ago of your mother's and my quarrelling about you. It's much more true that you and Mona have quarrelled about *me*.'

The proposition was fairly simple, but he seemed for an instant to have to walk round it. 'What I mean to say is, don't you know, that Mona, if you don't mind my saying so, has taken into her head to be jealous.'

'I see,' said Fleda. 'Well, I daresay our conferences have looked very odd.'

'They've looked very beautiful and they've *been* very beautiful. Oh I've told her the sort you are!' the young man pursued.

'That of course hasn't made her love me better.'

'No, nor love me,' – he jumped at it now. 'Of course, you know, she *says* – so far as that goes – that she loves me.'

'And do you say you love her?'

'I say nothing else – I say it all the while. I said it the other day about ninety times.' Fleda made no immediate rejoinder to this, and before she could choose one he repeated his question of a moment before. '*Am* I to tell my solicitor to act?'

She had at that moment turned away from this solution, precisely because she saw in it the great chance for herself. If she should determine him to adopt it she might put out her hand and take him. It would shut in Mrs. Gereth's face the open door of surrender: she would flare up and fight, flying the flag of a passionate, an heroic defence. The case would obviously go against her, but the proceedings would last longer than Mona's patience or Owen's propriety. With a formal rupture he would be at large; and she had only to tighten her fingers round the string that would raise the curtain on that scene. 'You tell me you "say" you love her, but is there nothing more in it than your saying so? You wouldn't say so, would you, if it's not true? What in the world has become in so short a time of the affection that led to your engagement?'

'The deuce knows what has become of it, Miss Vetch!' Owen cried. 'It seemed all to go to pot as this horrid struggle came on.' He was close to her now and, with his face lighted again by the relief of it, he looked all his helpless history into her eyes. 'As I saw you and noticed you more, as I knew you better and better, I felt less and less – I couldn't help it – about anything or any one else. I wished I had known you sooner – I knew I should have liked you better than any one in the world. But it wasn't you who made the difference,' he eagerly continued, 'and I was awfully determined to stick to Mona to the death. It was she herself who made it, upon my soul, by the state she got into, the way she sulked, the way she took things and the way she let me have it! She destroyed our prospects and our happiness – upon my honour she destroyed them. She made just the same smash of them as if she had kicked over that tea-table. She wanted to know all the while what was passing between us, between you and me; and she wouldn't take my solemn assurance that nothing was passing but what might have directly passed between me and old Mummy. She said a pretty girl like you was a nice old Mummy for me, and, if you'll believe it, she never called you anything else but that. I'll be hanged if I haven't been good, haven't I? I haven't breathed a breath of any sort to you, have I? You'd have been down on me hard if I had, wouldn't you? You're down on me pretty hard as it is, I think, aren't you? But I don't care what you say now, or what Mona says either, or a single rap what any one says: she has given me at last by her confounded behaviour a right to speak out, to utter the way I feel about it. The way I feel about it, don't you know? is that it had all better come to an end. You ask me if I don't love her, and I suppose it's natural enough you should. But you ask it at the very moment I'm half-mad to say to you that there's only one person on the whole earth I *really* love, and that that person – ' Here he pulled up short, and Fleda wondered if it were from the effect of his perceiving, through the closed door, the sound of steps and voices on the landing of the stairs. She had caught this sound herself with surprise and a vague uneasiness: it was not an hour at which her father ever came in, and there was no present reason why she should have a visitor. She had a fear which after a few seconds deepened: a visitor was at hand; the visitor would be simply Mrs. Gereth. That lady wished for a near view of the consequence of her note to Owen. Fleda straightened herself with the instant thought that if this was what Mrs. Gereth desired Mrs. Gereth should have it in a form not to be mistaken. Owen's pause was the matter of a moment, but during that moment our young couple stood with their eyes holding each other's eyes and their ears catching the suggestion, still through the door, of a murmured conference in the hall. Fleda had begun to move to cut it short when Owen stopped her with a grasp of her arm. 'You're surely able to guess,' he said with his voice down and her arm pressed as she had never known such a tone or such a pressure – 'you're surely able to guess the one person on earth I love?'

The handle of the door turned and she had only time to jerk at him: 'Your mother!'

But as the door opened the smutty maid, edging in, announced 'Mrs. Brigstock!'

XV

MRS. BRIGSTOCK, in the doorway, stood looking from one of the occupants of the room to the other; then they saw her eyes attach themselves to a small object that had lain hitherto unnoticed on the carpet. This was the biscuit of which, on giving Owen his tea, Fleda had taken a perfunctory nibble: she had immediately laid it on the table, and that subsequently, in some precipitate movement, she should have brushed it off was doubtless a sign of the agitation that possessed her. For Mrs. Brigstock there was apparently more in it than met the eye. Owen at any rate picked it up, and Fleda felt as if he were removing the traces of some scene that the newspapers would have characterised as lively. Mrs. Brigstock clearly took in also the sprawling tea-things and the marks as of a high tide in the full faces of her young friends. These elements made the little place a vivid picture of intimacy. A minute was filled by Fleda's relief at finding her visitor not to be Mrs. Gereth, and a longer space by the later sense of what was really more compromising in the case presented. It dimly occurred to her that the lady of Ricks had also written to Waterbath. Not only had Mrs. Brigstock never paid her a call, but Fleda would have been unable to figure her so employed. A year before[1] the girl had spent a day under her roof, but never feeling that Mrs. Brigstock regarded this as constituting a bond. She had never stayed in any house but Poynton in which the imagination of a bond, on one side or the other, prevailed. After the first astonishment she dashed gaily at her guest, emphasising her welcome and wondering how her whereabouts had become known at Waterbath. Hadn't Mrs. Brigstock quitted that residence for the very purpose of laying her hand on the associate of Mrs. Gereth's misconduct? The spirit in which this hand was to be laid our young woman was yet to ascertain; but she was a person who could think ten thoughts at once – a circumstance which, even putting her present plight at its worst, gave her a great advantage over a person who required easy conditions for dealing even with one. The very vibration of the air, however, told her that whatever Mrs. Brigstock's sense might originally have been it was now sharply affected by the sight of Owen. He was essentially a surprise: she had reckoned with everything that concerned him but his personal presence. With that, in awkward silence, she had begun to deal, as Fleda could see, while she effected with friendly aid an embarrassed transit to the sofa. Owen would be useless, would be deplorable: this aspect of the case Fleda had taken in as well. Another aspect was that he would admire her, adore her, exactly in proportion as she herself should rise gracefully superior. Fleda felt for the first time free to let herself 'go,' as Mrs. Gereth had said, and she was full of the sense that to 'go' meant now to aim straight at the effect of moving Owen to rapture at her simplicity and tact. It was her impression that he had no positive dislike of Mona's mother; but she couldn't entertain that notion without a glimpse of the implication that he had a positive dislike of Mrs. Brigstock's daughter. Mona's mother declined tea, declined a better seat, declined a cushion, declined to remove her boa:[2] Fleda guessed that she had not come on purpose to be dry, but that the voice of the invaded room had itself given her the hint.

'I just came on the mere chance,' she said. 'Mona found yesterday somewhere the card of invitation to your sister's marriage that you sent us, or your father sent us, some time ago. We couldn't be present – it was impossible; but as it had this address on it I said to myself that I might find you here.'

'I'm very glad to be at home,' Fleda responded.

'Yes, that doesn't happen very often, does it?' Mrs. Brigstock looked round afresh at Fleda's home.

'Oh I came back a while ago from Ricks. I shall be here now till I don't know when.'

'We thought it very likely you'd have come back. We knew of course of your having been at Ricks. If I didn't find you I thought I might perhaps find Mr. Vetch,' Mrs. Brigstock went on.

'I'm sorry he's out. He's always out – all day long.'

Mrs. Brigstock's round eyes grew rounder. 'All day long?'

'All day long,' Fleda smiled.

'Leaving you quite to yourself?'

'A good deal to myself, but a little, to-day, as you see, to Mr.

Gereth' – and the girl looked at Owen to draw him into their sociability. For Mrs. Brigstock he had immediately sat down; but the movement had not corrected the sombre stiffness possessing him at sight of her. Before he found a response to the appeal addressed to him Fleda turned again to her other visitor. 'Is there any purpose for which you would like my father to call on you?'

Mrs. Brigstock received this question as if it were not to be unguardedly answered; upon which Owen intervened with pale irrelevance. 'I wrote to Mona this morning of Miss Vetch's being in town; but of course the letter hadn't arrived when you left home.'

'No, it hadn't arrived. I came up for the night – I've several matters to attend to.' Then looking with an intention of fixedness from one of her companions to the other, 'I'm afraid I've interrupted your conversation,' Mrs. Brigstock said. She spoke without effectual point, had the air of merely announcing the fact. Fleda had not yet been confronted with the question of the sort of person Mrs. Brigstock was; she had only been confronted with the question of the sort of person Mrs. Gereth scorned her for being. She was really somehow no sort of person at all, and it came home to Fleda that if Mrs. Gereth could see her at this moment she would scorn her more than ever. She had a face of which it was impossible to say anything but that it was pink, and a mind it would be possible to describe only had one been able to mark it in a similar fashion. As nature had made this organ neither green nor blue nor yellow there was nothing to know it by: it strayed and bleated like an unbranded sheep. Fleda felt for it at this moment much of the kindness of compassion, since Mrs. Brigstock had brought it with her to do something for her that she regarded as delicate. Fleda was quite prepared to assist its use might she only divine what it wanted to do. What she divined however, more and more, was that it wanted to do something different from what it had wanted to do in leaving Waterbath. There was still nothing to enlighten her more specifically in the way her visitor continued: 'You must be very much taken up. I believe you quite espouse his dreadful quarrel.'

Fleda gained time by a vague echo. 'His dreadful quarrel?'

'About the contents of the house. Aren't you looking after them for him?'

'She knows how awfully kind you've been to me,' Owen explained to their young friend. He showed such discomfiture that he really gave away their situation; and Fleda found herself divided between the hope that he would take leave and the wish that he should see the whole of what the occasion might enable her to bring to pass for him.

She addressed herself to Mrs. Brigstock. 'Mrs. Gereth, at Ricks the other day, asked me particularly to see him for her.'

'And did she ask you also particularly to see him here in town?' Mrs. Brigstock's hideous bonnet seemed to argue for the unsophisticated truth; and it was on Fleda's lips to reply that such had indeed been Mrs. Gereth's request. But she checked herself, and before she could say anything else Owen had taken up the question.

'I made a point of letting Mona know that I should be here, don't you see? That's exactly what I wrote her this morning.'

'She would have had little doubt you'd be here if you had a chance,' Mrs. Brigstock returned. 'If your letter had arrived it might have prepared me for finding you here at tea. In that case I certainly wouldn't have come.'

'I'm glad then it didn't arrive. Shouldn't you like him to leave us?' Fleda asked.

Mrs. Brigstock looked at Owen and considered: nothing showed in her face but that it turned a deeper pink. 'I should like him to come with *me*.' There was no menace in her tone, but she evidently knew what she wanted. As Owen made no response to this Fleda glanced at him to invite him to assent; then for fear he wouldn't, and thus would make his case worse, she took upon herself to express for him all such readiness. She had no sooner spoken than she felt in the words a bad effect of intimacy: she had answered for him as if she had been his wife. Mrs. Brigstock continued to regard him without passion and spoke only to Fleda. 'I've not seen him for a long time – I've particular things to say to him.'

'So have I things to say to you, Mrs. Brigstock,' Owen interjected. With this he took up his hat as for prompt departure.

The other visitor meanwhile kept at their hostess. 'What's Mrs. Gereth going to do?'

'Is that what you came to ask me?' Fleda demanded.

'That and several other things.'

'Then you had much better let Mr. Gereth go, and stay by yourself and make me a pleasant visit. You can talk with him when you like, but it's the first time you've been to see me.'

This appeal had evidently a certain effect; Mrs. Brigstock visibly wavered. 'I can't talk with him whenever I like,' she returned; 'he hasn't been near us since I don't know when. But there are things that have brought me here.'

'They can't be things of any importance,' Owen, to Fleda's surprise, suddenly asserted. He had not at first taken up Mrs. Brigstock's expression of a wish to carry him off: Fleda could see the instinct at the bottom of this to be that of standing by her, of seeming not to abandon her. But abruptly, all his soreness working within him, it had struck him he should abandon her still more if he should leave her to be dealt with by the messenger from Waterbath. 'You must allow me to say, you know, Mrs. Brigstock, that I don't think you should come down on Miss Vetch about anything. It's very good of her to take the smallest interest in us and our horrid vulgar little squabble. If you want to talk about it talk about it with *me*.' He was flushed with the idea of protecting Fleda, of exhibiting his consideration for her. 'I don't like you cross-questioning her, don't you see? She's as straight as a die: *I'll* tell you all about her!' he declared with a reckless laugh. 'Please come off with me and let her alone.'

Mrs. Brigstock, at this, became vivid at once; Fleda thought her look extraordinary. She stood straight up – a queer distinction in her whole person and in everything of her face but her mouth, which she gathered into a small, tight orifice. The girl was painfully divided; her joy was deep within, but it was more relevant to the situation that she shouldn't appear to associate herself with the tone of familiarity in which Owen addressed a lady who had been, and was perhaps still, about to become his mother-in-law. She laid on Mrs. Brigstock's arm a repressive, persuasive hand. Mrs. Brigstock, however, had already exclaimed on her having so wonderful a defender. 'He speaks, upon my word, as if I had come here to be rude to you!'

At this, grasping her hard, Fleda laughed; then she achieved the exploit of delicately kissing her. 'I'm not in the least afraid to be alone with you or of your tearing me to pieces. I'll answer any question that you can possibly dream of putting to me.'

'I'm the proper person to answer Mrs. Brigstock's questions,' Owen broke in again, 'and I'm not a bit less ready to meet them than you are.' He was firmer than she had ever seen him; it was as if she hadn't dreamed he could be so firm.

'But she'll only have been here a few minutes. What sort of a visit is that?' Fleda cried.

'It has lasted long enough for my purpose,' Mrs. Brigstock judiciously declared. 'There was something I wanted to know, but I think I know it now.'

'Anything you don't know I daresay I can tell you!' Owen observed as he impatiently smoothed his hat with the cuff of his coat.

Fleda by this time desired immensely to keep his companion, but she saw she could do so only at the cost of provoking on his part a further exhibition of the sheltering attitude which he exaggerated precisely because it was the first thing, since he had begun to 'like' her, that he had been able frankly to do for her. It was not to her advantage that Mrs. Brigstock should be more struck than she already was with that benevolence. 'There may be things you know that I don't,' she presently said to her all reasonably and brightly. 'But I've a sort of sense that you're labouring under some great mistake.'

Mrs. Brigstock, at this, looked into her eyes more deeply and yearningly than she had supposed Mrs. Brigstock could look: it was the flicker of a mild, muddled willingness to give her a chance. Owen, however, quickly spoiled everything. 'Nothing's more probable than that Mrs. Brigstock is doing what you say; but there's no one in the world to whom you owe an explanation. I may owe somebody one – I daresay I do. But not you – no!'

'But what if there's one that it's no difficulty at all for me to give?' Fleda sweetly argued. 'I'm sure that's the only one Mrs. Brigstock came to ask, if she came to ask any at all.'

Again the good lady looked hard at her young friend. 'I came, I believe, Fleda, just – you know – to plead with you.'

Fleda, with her lighted face, hesitated a moment. 'As if I were one of those bad women in a play?'[3]

The remark was disastrous: Mrs. Brigstock, on whom the grace of it was lost, evidently thought it singularly free. She turned away as from a presence that had really defined itself as objectionable, and the girl had a vain sense that her good humour, in which there was an idea, was taken for impertinence, or at least for levity. Her allusion was improper even if she herself wasn't. Mrs. Brigstock's emotion simplified: it came to the same thing. 'I'm quite ready,' that lady said to Owen rather grandly and woundedly. 'I do want to speak to you very much.'

'I'm completely at your service.' Owen held out his hand to Fleda. 'Good-bye, Miss Vetch. I hope to see you again to-morrow.' He opened the door for Mrs. Brigstock, who passed before Miss Vetch with an oblique, averted salutation. Owen and Fleda, while he stood at the door, then faced each other darkly and without speaking. Their eyes met once more for a long moment, and she was conscious there was something in hers that the darkness didn't quench, that he had never seen before and that he was perhaps never to see again. He stayed long enough to take it – to take it with a sombre stare that just showed the dawn of wonder; then he followed Mrs. Brigstock out of the house.

HE had uttered the hope that he should see her the next day, but Fleda could easily reflect that he wouldn't see her if she were not there to be seen. If there was a thing in the world she desired at that moment it was that the next day should have no point of resemblance with the day that had just elapsed. She accordingly rose to the conception of an absence: she would go immediately down to Maggie. She ran out that evening and telegraphed to her sister, and in the morning she quitted London by an early train. She required for this step no reason but the sense of necessity. It was a strong personal need; she wished to interpose something, and there was nothing she could interpose but distance, but time. If Mrs. Brigstock had to deal with Owen she would allow Mrs. Brigstock the chance. To be there, to be in the midst of it, was the reverse of what she craved; she had already been more in the midst of it than had ever entered into her plan. At any rate she had renounced her plan; she had no plan now but the plan of separation. This was to abandon Owen, to give up the fine office of helping him back to his own; but when she had undertaken that office she had not foreseen that Mrs. Gereth would defeat it by a manoeuvre so remarkably simple. The scene at her father's rooms had extinguished all offices, and the scene at her father's rooms was of Mrs. Gereth's producing. Owen must at all events now act for himself: he had obligations to meet, he had satisfactions to give, and Fleda fairly ached with the wish he might be equal to them. She never knew the extent of her tenderness for him till she became conscious of the present force of her desire that he should be superior, be perhaps even sublime. She obscurely made out that superiority, that sublimity mightn't after all be fatal. She closed her eyes and lived for a day or two in the mere beauty of confidence. It was with her on the short journey; it was with her at Maggie's; it glorified the mean little house in the stupid little town. Owen had grown larger to her: he would do, like a man, whatever he should have to do. He wouldn't be weak – not as she was: she herself was weak exceedingly.

Arranging her few possessions in Maggie's fewer receptacles she caught a glimpse of the bright side of the fact that her old things were not such a problem as Mrs. Gereth's. Picking her way with Maggie through the local puddles, diving with her into smelly cottages[1] and supporting her, at smellier shops, in firmness over the weight of joints and the taste of cheese, it was still her own secret that was universally interwoven. In the puddles, the cottages, the shops she was comfortably alone with it; that comfort prevailed even while, at the evening meal, her brother-in-law invited her attention to a diagram, drawn with a fork on too soiled a tablecloth, of the scandalous drains[2] of the Convalescent Home. To be alone with it she had come away from Ricks, and now she knew that to be alone with it she had come away from London. This advantage was of course menaced, though not immediately destroyed, by the arrival on the second day of the note she had been sure she should receive from Owen. He had gone to West Kensington and found her flown, but he had got her address from the little maid and then hurried to a club and written to her. 'Why have you left me just when I want you most?' he demanded. The next words, it was true, were more reassuring on the question of his steadiness. 'I don't know what your reason may be,' they went on, 'nor why you've not left a line for me; but I don't think you can feel that I did anything yesterday that it wasn't right for me to do. As regards Mrs. Brigstock certainly I just felt what was right and I did it. She had no business whatever to attack you that way, and I should have been ashamed if I had left her there to worry you. I won't have you worried by any one. No one shall be disagreeable to you but me. I didn't mean to be so yesterday, and I don't to-day; but I'm perfectly free now to want you, and I want you much more than you've allowed me to explain. You'll see how right I am if you'll let me come to you. Don't be afraid – I'll not hurt you nor trouble you. I give you my honour I'll not hurt any one. Only I *must* see you about what I had to say to Mrs. B. She was nastier than I thought she could be, but I'm behaving like an angel. I assure you I'm all right – that's exactly what I want you to see. You owe me something, you know, for what you said you would do and haven't done; what your departure without a word gives me to understand – doesn't it? – that you definitely can't do. Don't simply forsake me. See me if you only see me once. I shan't wait for any leave, I shall come down to-morrow. I've been looking into trains and find there's something that will bring me just after lunch and something very good for getting me back. I won't stop long. For God's sake be there.'

This communication arrived in the morning, but Fleda would still have time to wire a protest. She debated on that alternative; then she read the note over and found in one phrase an exact statement of her duty. Owen's simplicity had so expressed it that her subtlety had nothing to answer. She owed him something for her obvious failure – what she owed him was to receive him. If indeed she had known he would make this attempt she might have been held to have gained nothing by flight. Well, she had gained what she had gained – she had gained the interval. She had no compunction for the greater trouble she should give the young man; it was now doubtless right he should have as much trouble as possible. Maggie, who thought she was in her confidence, yet was immensely not, had reproached her for having quitted Mrs. Gereth, and Maggie was just in this proportion gratified to hear of the visitor with whom, early in the afternoon, Fleda would have to ask to be left alone. Maggie liked to see far, and now she could sit upstairs and rake the whole future. She had known that, as she familiarly said, there was something the matter with Fleda, and the value of that knowledge was augmented by the fact that there was apparently also something the matter with Mr. Gereth.

Fleda, downstairs, learned soon enough what this was. It was simply that, as he insisted afresh the moment he stood before her, he was now all right. When she asked him what he meant by that term he replied that he meant he could practically regard himself henceforth as a free man: he had had at West Kensington, as soon as they got into the street, such a beastly horrid scene with Mrs. Brigstock.

'I knew what she wanted to say to me: that's why I was determined to get her off. I knew I shouldn't like it, but I was perfectly prepared,' said Owen. 'She brought it out as soon as we got round the corner. She asked me point-blank if I was in love with you.'

'And what did you say to that?'

'That it was none of her business.'

'Ah,' said Fleda, 'I'm not so sure!'

'Well *I* am, and I'm the person most concerned. Of course I didn't use just those words: I was perfectly civil, quite as civil as she. But I told her I didn't consider she had a right to put me any such question. I said I wasn't sure that even Mona had, with the extraordinary line, you know – I mean that *she* knew – Mona had taken. At any rate the whole thing, the way *I* put it, was between Mona and me; and between Mona and me, if she didn't mind, it would just have to remain.'

Fleda waited for more. 'All that didn't answer her question.'

'Then you think I ought to have told her?'

Again our young lady reflected. 'I think I'm rather glad you didn't.'

'I knew what I was about,' said Owen. 'It didn't strike me she had the least right to come down on us that way and try to overhaul us.'

Fleda looked very grave, weighing the whole matter. 'I daresay that when she started, when she arrived, she didn't mean to "come down."'

'What then did she mean to do?'

'What she said to me just before she went: she meant to plead with me.'

'Oh, I heard her – rather!' said Owen. 'But plead with you for what?'

'For you, of course – to entreat me to give you up. She thinks me awfully designing – that I've taken some sort of possession of you.'

Owen stared. 'You haven't lifted a finger! It's I who have taken possession.'

'Very true, you've done it all yourself.' Fleda spoke gravely and gently, without a breath of coquetry. 'But those are shades between which she's probably not obliged to distinguish. It's enough for her that we're repulsively intimate.'

'I am, but you're not!' Owen exclaimed.

Fleda gave a dim smile. 'You make me at least feel that I'm learning to know you very well when I hear you say such a thing as that. Mrs. Brigstock came to get round me, to supplicate me,' she went on; 'but to find you there looking so much at home, paying me a friendly call and shoving the tea-things about – that was too much for her patience. She doesn't know, you see, that I'm after all a decent girl. She simply made up her mind on the spot that I'm a very bad case.'

'I couldn't stand the way she treated you, and that was what I had to say to her,' Owen returned.

'She's simple and slow, but she's not a fool: I think she treated me on the whole very well.' Fleda remembered how Mrs. Gereth had treated Mona when the Brigstocks came down to Poynton.

Owen evidently thought her painfully perverse. 'It was you who carried it off; you behaved like a brick. And so did I, I consider. If you only knew the difficulty I had! I told her you were the noblest and straightest of women.'

'That can hardly have removed her impression that there are things I put you up to.'

'It didn't,' Owen replied with candour. 'She said our relation, yours and mine, isn't innocent.'

'What did she mean by that?'

'As you may suppose, I put it to her straight. Do you know what she had the cheek to tell me?' Owen asked. 'She didn't better it much. She said she meant that it's jolly unnatural.'

Fleda considered afresh. 'Well, it is!' she brought out at last.

'Then, upon my honour, it's only you who make it so!' Her perversity was distinctly too much for him. 'I mean you make it so by the way you keep me off.'

'Have I kept you off to-day?' Fleda sadly shook her head, raising her arms a little and dropping them.

Her gesture of resignation gave him a pretext for catching at her hand, but before he could take it she had put it behind her. They had been seated together on Maggie's single sofa, and her movement brought her to her feet while Owen, looking at her reproachfully, leaned back in discouragement. 'What good does it do me to be here when I find you only a stone?'

She met his eyes with all the tenderness she had not yet uttered, and she had not known till this moment how great was the accumulation. 'Perhaps, after all,' she risked, 'there may be even in a stone still some little help for you.'

He sat there a minute staring at her. 'Ah you're beautiful, more beautiful than any one,' he broke out, 'but I'll be hanged if I can ever understand you! On Tuesday, at your father's, you were beautiful – as beautiful, just before I left, as you are at this instant. But the next day, when I went back, I found it had apparently meant nothing; and now again that you let me come here and you shine at me like an angel, it doesn't bring you an inch nearer to saying what I want you to say.' He remained a moment longer in the same position, then jerked himself up. 'What I want you to say is that you like me – what I want you to say is that you pity me.' He sprang up and came to her. 'What I want you to say is that you'll *save* me!'

Fleda cast about. 'Why do you need saving when you announced to me just now that you're a free man?'

He too hesitated, but he was not checked. 'It's just for the reason that I'm free. Don't you know what I mean, Miss Vetch? I want you to marry me.'

Miss Vetch, at this, put out her hand in charity; she held his own, which quickly grasped it a moment, and if he had described her as shining at him it may be assumed that she shone all the more in her deep still smile. 'Let me know what you mean by your "freedom" first,' she said. 'I gather that Mrs. Brigstock was not wholly satisfied with the way you disposed of her question.'

'I daresay she wasn't. But the less she's satisfied the more I'm free.'

'What bearing have *her* feelings, pray?' Fleda asked.

'Why, Mona's much worse than her mother, you know. She wants much more to give me up.'

'Then why doesn't she do it?'

'She will, as soon as her mother gets home and tells her.'

'Tells her what?' Fleda went on.

'Why, that I'm in love with *you*!'

Fleda debated. 'Are you so very sure she will?'

'Certainly I'm sure, with all the evidence I already have. That will finish her!' Owen declared.

This made his companion thoughtful again. 'Can you take such pleasure in her being "finished" – a poor girl you've once loved?'

He waited long enough to take in the question; then with a serenity startling even to her knowledge of his nature, 'I don't think I can have *really* loved her, you know,' he pronounced.

She broke into a laugh that gave him a surprise as visible as the emotion it represented. 'Then how am I to know you "really" love – anybody else?'

'Oh I'll show you that!' said Owen.

'I must take it on trust,' the girl pursued. 'And what if Mona doesn't give you up?' she added.

He was baffled but a few seconds; he had thought of everything. 'Why, that's just where you come in.'

'To save you? I see. You mean I must get rid of her for you.' His blankness showed for a little that he felt the chill of her cold logic, but as she waited for his rejoinder she knew to which of them it cost most. He gasped a minute, and that gave her time to say: 'You see, Mr. Owen, how impossible it is to talk of such things yet!'

Like lightning he had grasped her arm. 'You mean you *will* talk of them?' Then as he began to take the flood of assent from her eyes: 'You *will* listen to me? Oh you dear, you dear – when, when?'

'Ah when it isn't mere misery!' The words had broken from her in a sudden loud cry, and what next happened was that the very sound of her pain upset her. She heard her own true note; she turned short away from him; in a moment she had burst into sobs; in another his arms were round her; the next she had let herself go so far that even Mrs. Gereth might have seen it. He clasped her, and she gave herself – she poured out her tears on his breast. Something prisoned and pent throbbed and gushed; something deep and sweet surged up – something that came from far within and far off, that had begun with the sight of him in his indifference and had never had rest since then. The surrender was short, but the relief was long: she felt his warm lips on her face and his arms tighten with his full divination. What she did, what she *had* done, she scarcely knew: she only was aware, as she broke from him again, of what had taken place on his own amazed part. What had taken place was that, with the click of a spring, he saw. He had cleared the high wall at a bound; they were together without a veil. She had not a shred of a secret left; it was as if a whirlwind had come and gone, laying low the great false front she had built up stone by stone. The strangest thing of all was the momentary sense of desolation.

'Ah all the while you *cared*?' Owen read the truth with a wonder so great that it was visibly almost a sadness, a terror caused by his sudden perception of where the impossibility was not. That treacherously placed it perhaps elsewhere.

'I cared, I cared, I cared!' – she wailed it as to confess a misdeed. 'How couldn't I care? But you mustn't, you must never, never ask! It isn't for us to talk about,' she protested. 'Don't speak of it, don't speak!'

It was easy indeed not to speak when the difficulty was to find words. He clasped his hands before her as he might have clasped them at an altar; his pressed palms shook together while he held his breath and while she stilled herself in the effort to come round again to the real and the thinkable. He assisted this effort, soothing her into a seat with a touch as anxious as if she had been truly something sacred. She sank into a chair and he dropped before her on his knees; she fell back with closed eyes and he buried his face in her lap. There was no way to thank her but this act of prostration, which lasted, in silence, till she laid consenting hands on him, touched his head and stroked it, let her close possession of it teach him his long blindness. He made the whole fall, as she yet felt it, seem only his – made her, when she rose again, raise him at last, softly, as if from the abasement of it. If in each other's eyes now, however, they saw the truth, this truth, to Fleda, looked harder even than before – all the harder that when, at the very moment she recognised it, he murmured to her ecstatically, in fresh possession of her hands, which he drew up to his breast, holding them tight there with both his own: 'I'm saved, I'm saved – I *am*! I'm ready for anything. I have your word. Come!' he cried, as if from the sight of a response slower than he needed and in the tone he so often had of a great boy at a great game.

She had once more disengaged herself with the private vow that he shouldn't yet touch her again. It was all too horribly soon – her sense of this had come straight back. 'We mustn't talk, we mustn't talk; we must wait!' – she had to make that clear. 'I don't know what you mean by your freedom; I don't see it, I don't feel it. Where is it yet, where, your freedom? If it's real there's plenty of time, and if it isn't there's more than enough. I hate myself,' she insisted, 'for having anything to say about her: it's like waiting for dead men's shoes! What business is it of mine what she does? She has her own trouble and her own plan. It's too hideous to watch her so and count on her!'

Owen's face, at this, showed a reviving dread, the fear of some darksome process of her mind. 'If you speak for yourself I can understand. But why is it hideous for me?'

'Oh I mean for myself!' Fleda quickly cried.

'*I* watch her, *I* count on her: how can I do anything else? If I count on her to let me definitely know how we stand I do nothing in life but what she herself has led straight up to. I never thought of asking you to "get rid of her" for me, and I never would have spoken to you if I hadn't held that I *am* rid of her, that she has backed out of the whole thing. Didn't she do so from the moment she began to put it off? I had already applied for the licence; the very invitations were half-addressed. Who but she, all of a sudden, required an unnatural wait? It was none of *my* doing: I had never dreamed of anything but coming up to the scratch.' Owen grew more and more lucid and more confident of the effect of his lucidity. 'She called it "taking a stand" – taking it to see what mother would do. I told her mother would do what I'd make her do; and to that she replied that she'd like to see me make her first. I said I'd arrange that everything should be all right, and she said she really preferred to arrange it herself. It was a flat refusal to trust me in the smallest degree. Why then had she pretended so tremendously to care for me? And of course at present,' said Owen, 'she trusts me, if possible, still less.'

Fleda paid this statement the homage of a minute's muteness. 'As to that, naturally, she has reason.'

'Why on earth has she reason?' Then as his companion, moving away, simply threw up her hands, 'I never looked at you – not to call looking – till she had regularly driven me to it,' he went on. 'I know what I'm about. I do assure you I'm all right!'

'You're not all right – you're all wrong!' Fleda cried in sudden despair. 'You mustn't stay here, you mustn't!' she repeated in still greater anxiety. 'You make me say dreadful things, and I feel as if I made *you* say them.' But before he could reply she took it up in another tone. 'Why in the world, if everything had changed, didn't you break off?'

'I – ?' The words moved him to visible stupefaction. 'Can you ask me that when I only wanted to please you? Didn't you seem to show me, in your wonderful way, that that was exactly how? If I didn't break off it was just on purpose to leave it to

Mona. If I didn't break off it was just so that there shouldn't be a thing to be said against me.'

The instant after her challenge she had faced him again in self-reproof. 'There *isn't* a thing to be said against you, and I don't know what folly you make me talk! You *have* pleased me, and you've been right and good, and it's the only comfort, and you must go. Everything must come from Mona, and if it doesn't come we've said entirely too much. You must leave me alone – for ever.'

'For ever?' Owen gasped.

'I mean unless everything's different.'

'Everything *is* different when I know you!'

Fleda winced at his knowledge; she made a wild gesture which seemed to whirl it out of the room. The mere allusion was like another attack from him. 'You don't know me – you don't – and you must go and wait! You mustn't break down at this point.'

He looked about him and took up his hat: it was as if in spite of frustration he had got the essence of what he wanted and could afford to agree with her to the extent of keeping up the forms. He covered her with his fine simple smile, but made no other approach. 'Oh I'm so awfully happy!' he cried.

She hung back now; she would only be impeccable even though she should have to be sententious. 'You'll be happy if you're per-fect!' she risked.

He laughed out at this, and she wondered if, with a new-born acuteness, he saw the absurdity of her speech and that no one was happy just because no one could be what she so easily prescribed. 'I don't pretend to be perfect, but I shall find a letter to-night!'

'So much the better, if it's the kind of one you desire.' That was the most she could say, and having made it sound as dry as possible she lapsed into a silence so pointed as to deprive him of all pretext for not leaving her. Still, nevertheless, he stood there, playing with his hat and filling the long pause with a strained and unsatis-fied smile. He wished to obey her thoroughly, to appear not to presume on any advantage he had won from her; but there was clearly something he longed for besides. While he showed this by hanging on she thought of two other things. One of these was that the look of him after all failed to bear out his description of his bliss. As for the other, it had no sooner come into her head than she found it seated, in spite of her resolution, on her lips. It took the form of an inconsequent question. 'When did you say Mrs. Brigstock was to have gone back?'

Owen stared. 'To Waterbath? She was to have spent the night in town, don't you know? But when she left me after our talk I said to myself that she'd take an evening train. I know I made her want to get home.'

'Where did you separate?' Fleda asked.

'At the West Kensington Station – she was going to Victoria. I had walked with her there, and our talk was all on the way.'

Fleda turned it over. 'If she did go back that night you'd have heard from Waterbath by this time.'

'I don't know,' said Owen. 'I thought I might hear this morning.'

'She can't have gone back,' Fleda declared. 'Mona would have written on the spot.'

'Oh yes, she *will* have written bang off!' he cheerfully conceded.

She thought again. 'So that even in the event of her mother's not having got home till the morning you'd have had your letter at the latest to-day. You see she has had plenty of time.'

Owen took it in; then 'Oh she's all right!' he laughed. 'I go by Mrs. Brigstock's certain effect on her – the effect of the temper the old lady showed when we parted. Do you know what she asked me?' he sociably continued. 'She asked me in a kind of nasty manner if I supposed you "really" cared anything about me. Of course I told her I supposed you didn't – not a solitary rap. How could I ever suppose you did – with your extraordinary ways? It doesn't matter. I could see she thought I lied.'

'You should have told her, you know, that I had seen you in town only that one time,' Fleda said.

'By Jove, I did – for *you*! It was only for you.'

Something in this touched the girl so that for a moment she couldn't trust herself to speak. 'You're an honest man,' she said at last. She had gone to the door and opened it. 'Good-bye.'

Even yet, however, he hung back. 'But say there's no letter – ' he anxiously began. He began, but there he left it.

'You mean even if she doesn't let you off? Ah you ask me too much!' Fleda spoke from the tiny hall, where she had taken refuge between the old barometer and the old mackintosh. 'There are things too utterly for yourselves alone. How can I tell? What do I know? Good-bye, good-bye! If she doesn't let you off it will be because she *is* attached to you.'

'She's not, she's not: there's nothing in it! Doesn't a fellow know? – except with *you*!' Owen ruefully added. With this he came out of the room, lowering his voice to secret-supplication, pleading with her really to meet him on the ground of the negation of Mona. It was this betrayal of his need of support and sanction that made her retreat, harden herself in the effort to save what might remain of all she had given, given probably for nothing. The very vision of him as he thus morally clung to her was the vision of a weakness somewhere at the core of his bloom, a blessed manly weakness which, had she only the valid right, it would be all easy and sweet to take care of. She faintly sickened, however, with the sense that there was as yet no valid right poor Owen could give. 'You can take it from my honour, you know,' he painfully brought out, 'that she quite loathes me.'

Fleda had stood clutching the knob of Maggie's little painted stair-rail; she took, on the stairs, a step backward. 'Why then doesn't she prove it in the only clear way?'

'She *has* proved it. Will you believe it if you see the letter?'

'I don't want to see any letter,' said Fleda. 'You'll miss your train.'

Facing him, waving him away, she had taken another upward step; but he sprang to the side of the stairs, and brought his hand, above the banister, down hard on her wrist. 'Do you mean to tell me that I must marry a woman I hate?'

From her step she looked down into his raised face. 'Ah you see it's not true that you're free!' She seemed almost to exult. 'It's not true, it's not true!'

He only, at this, like a buffeting swimmer, gave a shake of his head and repeated his question: 'Do you mean to tell me I must marry such a woman?'

Fleda gasped too; he held her fast. 'No. Anything's better than that.'

'Then in God's name what must I do?'

'You must settle that with Mona. You mustn't break faith. Anything's better than that. You must at any rate be utterly sure. She must love you – how can she help it? *I* wouldn't give you up!'

said Fleda. She spoke in broken bits, panting out her words. 'The great thing is to keep faith. Where's a man if he doesn't? If he doesn't he may be so cruel. So cruel, so cruel, so cruel!' Fleda repeated. 'I couldn't have a hand in that, you know: that's my position – that's mine. You offered her marriage. It's a tremendous thing for her.' Then looking at him another moment, '*I* wouldn't give you up!' she said again. He still had hold of her arm; she took in his blank dread. With a quick dip of her face she reached his hand with her lips, pressing them to the back of it with a force that doubled the force of her words. 'Never, never, never!' she cried; and before he could succeed in seizing her she had turned and, flashing up the stairs, got away from him even faster than she had got away at Ricks.

XVII

※

TEN days after his visit she received a communication from Mrs. Gereth – a telegram of eight words, exclusive of signature and date. 'Come up immediately and stay with me here' – it was characteristically sharp, as Maggie said; but, as Maggie added, it was also characteristically kind. 'Here' was an hotel in London, and Maggie had embraced a condition of life which already began to produce in her some yearning for hotels in London. She would have responded on the spot and was surprised that her sister seemed to wait. Fleda's demur, which lasted but an hour, was expressed in that young lady's own mind by the reflexion that in obeying her friend's call she shouldn't know what she should be 'in for.' Her friend's call, however, was but another name for her friend's need, and Mrs. Gereth's bounty had laid her under obligations more marked than any hindrance. In the event – that is at the end of her hour – she testified to her gratitude by taking the train and to her mistrust by leaving her luggage. She went as if going up for the day. In the train, however, she had another thoughtful hour, during which it was her mistrust that mainly deepened. She felt as if for ten days she had sat in darkness and looked to the east for a dawn that had not glimmered. Her mind had lately been less occupied with Mrs. Gereth; it had been so exceptionally occupied with Mona. If the sequel was to justify Owen's prevision of Mrs. Brigstock's action on her daughter this action was at the end of a week still thoroughly obscure. The stillness all round had been exactly what Fleda desired, but it gave her for a time a deep sense of failure, the sense of a sudden drop from a height at which she had had all things beneath her. She had nothing beneath her now; she herself was at the bottom of the heap. No sign had reached her from Owen – poor Owen who had clearly no news to give about his precious letter from Waterbath. If Mrs. Brigstock had hurried back to obtain that this letter should be written Mrs. Brigstock might then have spared herself so great an inconvenience. Owen had been silent for the best of all reasons – the reason that he had had nothing in life to say. If the letter had not been written he would simply have had to introduce some large qualification into his account of his freedom. He had left his young friend under her refusal to listen to him till he should be able, on the contrary, to extend that picture; and his present submission was all in keeping with the rigid honesty that his young friend had prescribed.

It was this that formed the element through which Mona loomed large; Fleda had enough imagination, a fine enough feeling for life, to be impressed with such an image of successful immobility. The massive maiden at Waterbath *was* successful from the moment she could entertain her resentments as if they had been poor relations who needn't put her to expense. She was a magnificent dead weight; there was something positive and portentous in her quietude. 'What game are they all playing?' poor Fleda could only ask; for she had an intimate conviction that Owen was now under the roof of his betrothed. That was stupefying if he really hated his betrothed; and if he didn't really hate her what had brought him to Raphael Road and to Maggie's? Fleda had no real light, but she felt that to account for the absence of any sequel to their last meeting would take a supposition of the full sacrifice to charity that she had held up before him. If he had gone to Waterbath it had been simply because he had had to go. She had as good as told him he would have to go; that this was an inevitable incident of his keeping perfect faith – faith so literal that the smallest subterfuge would always be a reproach to him. When she tried to remember that it was for herself he was taking his risk she felt how weak a way that was of expressing Mona's supremacy. There would be no need of keeping him up if there was nothing to keep him up to. Her eyes grew wan as she discerned in the impenetrable air that Mona's thick outline never wavered an inch. She wondered fitfully what Mrs. Gereth had by this time made of it, and reflected with a strange elation that the sand on which the mistress of Ricks had built a momentary triumph was quaking beneath the surface. As *The Morning Post* still held its peace she would be of course more confident; but the hour was at hand at which Owen would have absolutely to do either one thing or the other. To keep perfect faith was to inform against his mother, and to hear the police at her door would be Mrs. Gereth's awakening. How much she was beguiled Fleda could see from her having been for a whole month quite as deep and dark as Mona. She had left her young friend alone because of the certitude, cultivated at Ricks, that Owen had done the opposite. He had done the opposite indeed, but much good had that brought forth! To have sent for her now, Fleda felt, was from this point of view wholly natural: she had sent for her to show at last how largely she had scored. If, however, Owen was really at Waterbath the refutation of that boast would be easy even to a primitive critic.

Fleda found Mrs. Gereth in modest apartments and with an air of fatigue in her distinguished face, a sign, as she privately remarked, of the strain of that effort to be discreet of which she herself had been having the benefit. It was a constant feature of their relation that this lady could made Fleda blench a little, and that the effect proceeded from the intense pressure of her confidence. If the confidence had been heavy even when the girl, in the early flush of devotion, had been able to feel herself yield most, it drew her heart into her mouth now that she had reserves and conditions, now that she couldn't simplify with the same bold hand as her protectress. In the very brightening of the tired look and at the moment of their embrace Fleda felt on her shoulders the return of the load; whereupon her spirit quailed as she asked herself what she had brought up from her trusted seclusion to support it. Mrs. Gereth's free manner always made a joke of weakness, and there was in such a welcome a richness, a kind of familiar nobleness, that suggested shame to a harried conscience. Something had happened, she could see, and she could also see, in the bravery that seemed to announce it had changed everything, a formidable assumption that what had happened was what a healthy young woman must like. The absence of luggage had made this young woman feel meagre even before her companion, taking in the bareness at a second glance, exclaimed upon it and roundly rebuked her. Of course she had expected her to stay.

Fleda thought best to show bravery too and to show it from the first. 'What you expected, dear Mrs. Gereth, is exactly what I came up to ascertain. It struck me as right to do that first. Right, I mean, to ascertain without making preparations.'

'Then you'll be so good as to make them on the spot!' Mrs. Gereth was most emphatic. 'You're going abroad with me.'

Fleda wondered, but she also smiled. 'To-night – to-morrow?'

'In as few days as possible. That's all that's left for me now.' Fleda's heart, at this, gave a bound; she wondered to what particular difference in Mrs. Gereth's situation as last known to her it referred. 'I've made my plan,' her friend continued: 'I go at least for a year. We shall go straight to Florence; we can manage there. I of course don't look to you, however,' she added, 'to stay with me all that time. That will require to be settled. Owen will have to join us as soon as possible; he may not be quite ready to get off with us. But I'm convinced it's quite the right thing to go. It will make a good change. It will put in a decent interval.'

Fleda listened; she was deeply mystified. 'How kind you are to me!' she presently said. The picture suggested so many questions that she scarce knew which to ask first. She took one at a venture. 'You really have it from Mr. Gereth that he'll give us his company?'

If Mr. Gereth's mother smiled in response to this Fleda knew that her smile was a tacit criticism of such a mode of dealing with her son. Fleda habitually spoke of him as Mr. Owen, and it was a part of her present system to appear to have relinquished that right. Mrs. Gereth's manner confirmed a certain betrayal of her pretending to more than she felt; her very first words had conveyed it, and it reminded Fleda of the conscious courage with which, weeks before, the lady had met her visitor's first startled stare at the clustered spoils of Poynton. It was her practice to take immensely for granted whatever she wished. 'Oh if you'll answer for him it will do quite as well!' With this answer she put her hands on the girl's shoulders and held them at arm's length, as to shake them a little, while in the depths of her shining eyes Fleda saw something obscure and unquiet. 'You bad false thing, why didn't you tell me?' Her tone softened her harshness, and her visitor had never had such a sense of her indulgence. Mrs. Gereth could show patience; it was a part of the general bribe, but it was also like the presentation of a heavy bill before which Fleda could only fumble in a penniless pocket. 'You must perfectly have known at Ricks, and yet you practically denied it. That's why I call you bad and false!' It was apparently also why she again almost roughly kissed her.

'I think that before I satisfy you I had better know what you're talking about,' Fleda said.

Mrs. Gereth looked at her with a slight increase of hardness. 'You've done everything you need for modesty, my dear! If he's sick with love of you, you haven't had to wait for me to inform you.'

Fleda knew herself turn pale. 'Has he informed *you*, dear Mrs. Gereth?'

Dear Mrs. Gereth smiled sweetly. 'How could he when our situation is such that he communicates with me only through you and that you're so tortuous you conceal everything?'

'Didn't he answer the note in which you let him know I was in town?' Fleda asked.

'He answered it sufficiently by rushing off on the spot to see you.'

Mrs. Gereth met this allusion with a prompt firmness that made almost insolently light of any ground of complaint, and Fleda's own sense of responsibility was now so vivid that all resentments comparatively shrank. She had no heart to produce a grievance; she could only, left as she was with the little mystery on her hands, produce after a moment a question. 'How then do you come to know that your son has ever thought – ?'

'That he would give his ears to get you?' Mrs. Gereth broke in. 'I had a visit from Mrs. Brigstock.'

Fleda opened her eyes. 'She went down to Ricks?'

'The day after she had found Owen at your feet. She knows everything.'

Fleda shook her head sadly: she was more startled than she cared to show. This odd journey of Mrs. Brigstock's, which, with a simplicity equal for once to Owen's, she had not divined, now struck her as at bottom of the hush of the last ten days. 'There are things she doesn't know!' she presently returned.

'She knows he'd do anything to marry you.'

'He hasn't told her so,' Fleda said.

'No, but he has told *you*. That's better still!' laughed Mrs. Gereth. 'My dear child,' she went on with an air that affected the girl as a blind profanity, 'don't try to make yourself out better than you are. *I* know what you are – I haven't lived with you so much for nothing. You're not quite a saint in heaven yet. Lord, what a creature you'd have thought me in my good time! But you do like it fortunately, you idiot. You're pale with your passion, you sweet thing. That's exactly what I wanted to see. I can't for the life of me think where the shame comes in.' Then with a finer significance, a look that seemed to Fleda strange, she added: 'It's all right.'

'I've seen him but twice,' said Fleda.

'But twice?' Mrs. Gereth still smiled.

'On the occasion, at papa's, that Mrs. Brigstock told you of, and one day, since then, down at Maggie's.'

'Well, those things are between yourselves, and you seem to me both poor creatures at best.' She spoke with a rich humour which made her attitude indeed a complacency. 'I don't know what you've got in your veins. You absurdly exaggerate the difficulties. But enough's as good as a feast, and when once I get you abroad together – !' Mrs. Gereth checked herself as from excess of meaning; what might happen when she should get them abroad together was to be gathered only from the way she slowly rubbed her hands.

The gesture, however, made the promise so definite that for a moment her companion was almost beguiled. Yet there was still nothing to account for the wealth of her certitude: the visit of the lady of Waterbath appeared but half to explain it. 'Is it permitted to be surprised,' Fleda deferentially asked, 'at Mrs. Brigstock's thinking it would help her to see you?'

'It's never permitted to be surprised at the aberrations of born fools,' said Mrs. Gereth. 'If a cow should try to calculate, that's the kind of happy thought she'd have. Mrs. Brigstock came down to plead with me.'

Fleda mused a moment. 'That's what she came to do with *me*,' she then honestly returned. 'But what did she expect to get of you – with your opposition so marked from the first?'

'She didn't know I want *you*, my dear. It's a wonder, with all my violence – the gross publicity I've given my desires. But she's as stupid as an owl – she doesn't feel your charm.'

Fleda felt herself flush slightly, and her amusement at this was ineffective. 'Did you tell her all about my charm? Did you make her understand you want me?'

'For what do you take me? I wasn't such a booby.'

'So as not to aggravate Mona?' Fleda suggested.

'So as not to aggravate Mona, naturally. We've had a narrow course to steer, but thank God we're at last in the open!'

'What do you call the open, Mrs. Gereth?' Fleda demanded. Then as that lady faltered: 'Do you know where Mr. Owen is to-day?'

His mother stared. 'Do you mean he's at Waterbath? Well, that's your own affair. I can bear it if *you* can.'

'Wherever he is I can bear it,' Fleda said. 'But I haven't the least idea where he is.'

'Then you ought to be ashamed of yourself!' her friend broke out with a change of note that showed how deep a passion underlay everything she had said. The poor woman, catching her hand, however, the next moment, as if to retract something of this harshness, spoke more patiently. 'Don't you understand, Fleda, how immensely, how devotedly I've trusted you!' Her tone was indeed a supplication.

Fleda was infinitely shaken; she couldn't immediately speak. 'Yes, I understand. Did she go to you to complain of me?'

'She came to see what she could do. She had been tremendously upset the day before by what had taken place at your father's, and she had posted down to Ricks on the inspiration of the moment. She hadn't meant it on leaving home; it was the sight of you closeted there with Owen that had suddenly determined her. The whole story, she said, was written in your two faces: she spoke as if she had never seen such an exhibition. Owen was on the brink, but there might still be time to save him, and it was with this idea she had bearded me in my den. 'What won't a mother do, you know!' – that was one of the things she said. What wouldn't a mother do indeed? I thought I had sufficiently shown her what! She tried to break me down by an appeal to my good nature, as she called it, and from the moment she opened on *you*, from the moment she denounced Owen's falsity, I was as good-natured as she could wish. I understood it as a plea for mere mercy – because you and he between you were killing her child. Of course I was delighted that Mona should be killed, but I was studiously kind to Mrs. Brigstock. At the same time I was honest, I didn't pretend to anything I couldn't feel. I asked her why the marriage hadn't taken place months ago, when Owen was perfectly ready; and I showed her how completely that fatuous mistake on Mona's part cleared his responsibility. It was she who had killed *him* – it was she who had destroyed his affection, his illusions. Did she want him now when he was estranged, when he was disgusted, when he had a sore grievance? She reminded me that Mona had a sore grievance too, but admitted she hadn't come to me to speak of that. What she had come for was not to get the old things back, but simply to get Owen. What she wanted was that I would, in simple pity, see fair play. Owen had been awfully bedevilled – she didn't call it that, she called it "misled"; but it was simply you who had bedevilled him. He would be all right still if I would only see you well out of the way. She asked me point-blank if it was possible I could want him to marry you.'

Fleda had listened in unbearable pain and growing terror, as if her companion, stone by stone, were piling some fatal mass upon her breast. She had the sense of being buried alive, smothered in the mere expansion of another will; and now there was but one gap left to the air. A single word, she felt, might close it, and with the question that came to her lips as Mrs. Gereth paused she seemed to herself to ask, in cold dread, for her doom. 'What did you say to that?' she gasped.

'I was embarrassed, for I saw my danger – the danger of her going home and saying to Mona that I was backing you up. It had been a bliss to learn that Owen had really turned to you, but my joy didn't put me off my guard. I reflected intensely a few seconds; then I saw my issue.'

'Your issue?' Fleda echoed.

'I remembered how you had tied my hands about saying a word to Owen.'

Fleda wondered. 'And did you remember the little letter that, with your hands tied, you still succeeded in writing him?'

'Perfectly; my little letter was a model of reticence. What I remembered was all that in those few words I forbade myself to say. I had been an angel of delicacy – I had effaced myself like a saint. It wasn't for me to have done all that and then figure to such a woman as having done the opposite. Besides, it was none of her business.'

'Is that what you said to her?' the girl asked.

'I said to her that her question revealed a total misconception of the nature of my present relations with my son. I said to her that I had no relations with him at all and that nothing had passed between us for months. I said to her that my hands were spotlessly clean of any attempt to make up to you. I said to her that I had taken from Poynton what I had a right to take, but had done nothing else in the world. I was determined that since I had bitten my tongue off to oblige you I would at least have the righteousness that my sacrifice gave me.'

'And was Mrs. Brigstock satisfied with your answer?'

'She was visibly relieved.'

'It was fortunate for you,' said Fleda, 'that she's apparently not aware of the manner in which, almost under her nose, you advertised me to him at Poynton.'

Mrs. Gereth appeared to recall that scene; she smiled with a serenity remarkably effective as showing how cheerfully used she had grown to invidious allusions to it. 'How should she be aware of it?'

'She would if Owen had described your outbreak to Mona.'

'Yes, but he didn't describe it. All his instinct was to conceal it from Mona. He wasn't conscious, but he was already in love with you!' Mrs. Gereth declared.

Fleda shook her head wearily. 'No – I was only in love with *him*!'

Here was a faint illumination with which Mrs. Gereth instantly mingled her fire. 'You dear old wretch!' she exclaimed; and she again, with ferocity, embraced her young friend.

Fleda submitted like a sick animal: she would submit to everything now. 'Then what further passed?'

'Only that she left me thinking she had got something.'

'And what had she got?'

'Nothing but her luncheon. But *I* got everything!'

'Everything?' Fleda quavered.

Mrs. Gereth, struck apparently by something in her tone, looked at her from a tremendous height. 'Don't fail me now!'

It sounded so like a menace that, with a full divination at last, the poor girl fell weakly into a chair. 'What on earth have you done?'

Mrs. Gereth stood there in all the glory of a great stroke. 'I've settled you.' She filled the room, to Fleda's scared vision, with the glare of her magnificence. 'I've sent everything back.'

'Everything?' Fleda wailed.

'To the smallest snuff-box. The last load went yesterday. The same people did it. Poor little Ricks is empty.' Then as if, for a crowning splendour, to check all deprecation, 'They're yours, you goose!' the wonderful woman concluded, holding up her handsome head and rubbing her white hands. But there were tears none, the less in her deep eyes.

XVIII

FLEDA was slow to take in the announcement, but when she had done so she felt it to be more than her cup of bitterness would hold. Her bitterness was her anxiety, the taste of which suddenly sickened her. What had she on the spot become but a dire traitress to her friend? The treachery increased with the view of the friend's motive, a motive splendid as a tribute to her value. Mrs. Gereth had wished to make sure of her and had reasoned that there would be no such way as by a large appeal to her honour. If it be true, as men have declared, that the sense of honour is weak in women, some of the bearings of this stroke might have thrown a light on the question. What was now at all events put before Fleda was that she had been made sure of, since the greatness of the surrender imposed an obligation as great. There was an expression she had heard used by young men with whom she danced: the only word to fit Mrs. Gereth's intention was that Mrs. Gereth had designed to 'fetch' her. It was a calculated, it was a crushing bribe; it looked her in the eyes and said awfully: 'That's what I do for you!' What Fleda was to do in return required no pointing out. The sense at present of how little she had done it made her almost cry out with pain; but her first endeavour in face of the fact was to keep such a cry from reaching her companion. How little she had done it Mrs. Gereth didn't yet know, and possibly there would be still some way of turning round before the discovery. On her own side too Fleda had almost made one: she had known she was wanted, but she had not after all conceived how magnificently much. She had been treated by her friend's act as a conscious prize, but her value consisted all in the power the act itself imputed to her. As high bold diplomacy it dazzled and carried her off her feet. She admired the noble risk of it, a risk Mrs. Gereth had faced for the utterly poor creature the girl now felt herself. The change it instantly wrought in her was moreover extraordinary: it transformed at a touch her feeling on the subject of concessions. A few weeks earlier

she had jumped at the duty of pleading for them, practically quarrelling with the lady of Ricks for her refusal to restore what she
had taken. She had been sore with the wrong to Owen, she had
bled with the wounds of Poynton; now, however, as she heard of
the replenishment of the void that had so haunted her she came as
near sounding an alarm as if from the deck of a ship she had seen
a person she loved jump into the sea. Mrs. Gereth had become in
a flash the victim; poor little Ricks had yielded up its treasure in a
night. If Fleda's present view of the 'spoils' had taken precipitate
form the form would have been a frantic command. It was indeed
for mere want of breath she didn't shout 'Oh stop them – it's no
use; bring them back – it's too late!' And what most kept her
breathless was her companion's very grandeur. Fleda distinguished as never before the purity of the passion concerned; it
made Mrs. Gereth august and almost sublime. It was absolutely
unselfish – she cared nothing for mere possession. She thought
solely and incorruptibly of what was best for the objects themselves; she had surrendered them to the presumptive care of the
one person of her acquaintance who felt about them as she felt
herself and whose long lease of the future would be the nearest
approach that could be compassed to committing them to a
museum. Now it was indeed that Fleda knew what rested on her;
now it was also that she measured as for the first time her friend's
notion of the natural influence of a grand 'haul.' Mrs. Gereth had
risen to the idea of blowing away the last doubt of what her young
charge would gain, of making good still more than she was obliged
to make it the promise of weeks before. It was one thing for the
girl to have learnt that in a certain event restitution would be made;
it was another for her to see the condition, with a noble trust,
treated in advance as performed, and to know she should have
only to open a door to find very old piece in every old corner.
To have played such a card would be thus, for so grand a gambler,
practically to have won the game. Fleda had certainly to recognise
that, so far as the theory of the matter went, the game had been
won. Oh she had been made sure of!

She couldn't, however, succeed for so very many minutes in
putting off her exposure. 'Why didn't you wait, dearest? Ah why
didn't you wait?' – if that inconsequent appeal kept rising to her
lips to be cut short before it was spoken, this was only because at

first the humility of gratitude helped her to gain time, enabled her to present herself very honestly as too overcome to be clear. She kissed her companion's hands, she did homage at her feet, she murmured soft snatches of praise, and yet in the midst of it all was conscious that what she really showed most was the dark despair at her heart. She saw the poor woman's glimpse of this strange reserve suddenly widen, heard the quick chill of her voice pierce through the false courage of endearments. 'Do you mean to tell me at such an hour as this that you've really lost him?'

The tone of the question made the idea a possibility for which Fleda had nothing from this moment but terror. 'I don't know, Mrs. Gereth; how can I say?' she asked. 'I've not seen him for so long; as I told you just now, I don't even know where he is. That's by no fault of his,' she hurried on: 'he would have been with me every day if I had consented. But I made him understand, the last time, that I'll receive him again only when he's able to show me his release as quite signed and sealed. Oh he can't yet, don't you see? – and that's why he hasn't been back. It's far better than his coming only that we should both be miserable. When he does come he'll be in a better position. He'll be tremendously moved by the wonderful thing you've done. I know you wish me to feel you've done it as much for me as for Owen, but your having done it for me is just what will delight him most! When he hears of it,' said Fleda in panting optimism, 'when he hears of it – !' There indeed, regretting her advance and failing of every confidence, she quite broke down. She was wholly powerless to say what Owen would do when he heard of it. 'I don't know what he won't make of you and how he won't hug you!' she had to content herself with meanly declaring. She had drawn her terrible dupe and judge to a sofa with a vague instinct of pacifying her and still, after all, gaining time; but it was a position in which that extraordinary character, portentously patient again during this demonstration, looked far from inviting a 'hug.' Fleda found herself tricking out the situation with artificial flowers, trying to talk even herself into the fancy that Owen, whose name she now made simple and sweet,[1] might come in upon them at any moment. She felt an immense need to be understood and justified; she abjectly averted her face from all she might have to be forgiven. She pressed on her hostess's arm as if to keep her quiet till she should really know, and then, after a minute, she poured out the clear essence of what in happier days had been her 'secret.' 'You mustn't think I don't adore him when I've told him so to his face. I love him so that I'd die for him – I love him so that it's horrible. Don't look at me therefore as if I hadn't been kind, as if I hadn't been as tender as if he were dying and my tenderness were what would save him. Look at me as if you believe me, as if you feel what I've been through. Darling Mrs. Gereth, I could kiss the ground he walks on. I haven't a rag of pride; I used to have, but it's gone. I used to have a secret, but every one knows it now, and any one who looks at me can say, I think, what's the matter with me. It's not so very fine, my secret, and the less one really says about it the better; but I want you to have it from me because I was stiff before. I want you to see for yourself that I've been brought as low as a girl can very well be. It serves me right,' Fleda laughed, 'if I was ever proud and horrid to you! I don't know what you wanted me, in those days at Ricks, to do, but I don't think you can have wanted much more than what I've done. The other day at Maggie's I did things that made me afterwards think of you! I don't know what girls may do; but if he doesn't know that there isn't an inch of me that isn't his – !' Fleda sighed as if she couldn't express it; she piled it up, as she would have said; holding Mrs. Gereth with dilated eyes she seemed to sound her for the effect of these professions. 'It's idiotic,' she wearily smiled; 'it's so strange that I'm almost angry for it, and the strangest part of all is that it isn't even happiness. It's anguish – it was from the first; from the first there was a bitterness and a dread.[2] But I owe you every word of the truth. You don't do him justice either; he's a dear, I assure you he's a dear: I'd trust him to the last breath. I don't think you really know him. He's ever so much cleverer than he makes any show of; he's remarkable in his own shy way. You told me at Ricks that you wanted me to let myself go, and I've "gone" quite far enough to discover as much as that, as well as all sorts of other delightful things about him. You'll tell me I make myself out worse than I am,' said the girl, feeling more and more in her companion's attitude a quality that treated her speech as a desperate rigmarole and even perhaps as a piece of cold immodesty. She wanted to make herself out 'bad' – it was a part of her justification; but it suddenly occurred to her that such a picture of her extravagance imputed a want of gallantry

181

to the young man. 'I don't care for anything you think,' she declared, 'because Owen, don't you know? sees me as I am. He's so kind that it makes up for everything!'

This attempt at gaiety was futile; the silence with which for a minute her great swindled benefactress greeted her troubled plea brought home to her afresh that she was on the bare defensive. 'Is it a part of his kindness never to come near you?' Mrs. Gereth inquired at last. 'Is it a part of his kindness to leave you without an inkling of where he is?' She rose again from where Fleda had kept her down; she seemed to tower there in the majesty of her gathered wrong. 'Is it a part of his kindness that after I've toiled as I've done for six days, and with my own weak hands, which I haven't spared, to denude myself, in your interest, to that point that I've nothing left, as I may say, but what I have on my back – is it a part of his kindness that you're not even able to produce him for me?'

There was a high contempt in this which was for Owen quite as much, and in the light of which Fleda felt that her effort at plausibility had been mere grovelling. She rose from the sofa with an humiliated sense of rising from ineffectual knees. That discomfort, however, lived but an instant: it was swept away in a rush of loyalty to the absent. She herself could bear his mother's scorn, but to avert it from all *his* decency she broke out with a quickness that was like the raising of an arm. 'Don't blame him – don't blame him: he'd do anything on earth for me! It was I,' said Fleda eagerly, 'who sent him back to her. I made him go, I pushed him out of the house. I declined to have anything to say to him except on another footing.'

Mrs. Gereth stared as at some gross material ravage. 'Another footing? What other footing?'

'The one I've already made so clear to you: my having it from her in black and white, as you may say, that she freely gives him up.'

'Then you think he lies when he tells you he has recovered his liberty?'

Fleda failed of presence of mind a moment; after which she exclaimed with a certain hard pride: 'He's enough in love with me for anything!'

'For anything apparently save to act like a man and impose his

182

reason and his will on your incredible folly. For anything save to put an end, as any man worthy of the name would have put it, to your systematic, to your idiotic perversity. What are you, after all, my dear, I should like to know, that a gentleman who offers you what Owen offers should have to meet such wonderful exactions, to take such extraordinary precautions about your sweet little scruples?' Her resentment rose to a high insolence which Fleda took full in the face and which, for the moment at least, had the horrible force to present to her vengefully a showy side of the truth. It gave her a blinding glimpse of lost alternatives. 'I don't know what to think of him,' Mrs. Gereth went on; 'I don't know what to call him: I'm so ashamed of him that I can scarcely speak of him even to *you*. But indeed I'm so ashamed of you both together that I scarcely know in common decency where to look.' She paused to give Fleda the full benefit of this harsh statement; then she exclaimed with the very best of her coarseness: 'Any one but a jackass would have tucked you under his arm and marched you off to the Registrar[3]!'

Fleda wondered; with her free imagination she could wonder even while her cheek stung from a slap. 'To the Registrar?'

'That would have been the sane sound immediate course to adopt. With a grain of gumption you'd both instantly have felt it. *I* should have found a way to take you, you know, if I had been what Owen's supposed to be. *I* should have got the business over first – then the rest could come when you liked! Good God, girl, your place was to stand before me as a woman honestly married. One doesn't know what one has hold of in touching you, and you must excuse my saying that you're literally unpleasant to me to meet as you are. Then at least we could have talked, and Owen, if he had the ghost of a sense of humour, could have snapped his fingers at your refinements.'

This stirring speech affected our young lady as if it had been the shake of a tambourine borne toward her from a gipsy dance: her head seemed to go round and she felt a sudden passion in her feet. The thrill, however, was but meagrely expressed in the flatness with which she heard herself presently say: 'I'll go to the Registrar now.'

'Now?' Magnificent was the sound Mrs. Gereth threw into this monosyllable. 'And pray who's to take you?' Fleda gave a colourless smile, and her companion continued: 'Do you literally mean that you can't put your hand upon him?' Fleda's sick grimace appeared to irritate her; she made a short imperious gesture. 'Find him for me, you fool – *find* him for me!'

'What do you want of him,' Fleda dismally asked – 'feeling as you do to both of us?'

'Never mind how I feel, and never mind what I say when I'm furious!' Mrs. Gereth still more incisively added. 'Of course I cling to you, you wretches, or I shouldn't suffer as I do. What I want of him is to see that he takes you; what I want of him is to go with you myself to the place.' She looked round the room as if, in feverish haste, for a mantle to catch up; she bustled to the window as if to spy out a cab: she would allow half an hour for the job. Already in her bonnet, she had snatched from the sofa a garment for the street: she jerked it on as she came back. 'Find him, find him,' she repeated; 'come straight out with me to try at least and get *at* him!'

'How can I get *at* him? He'll come when he's ready,' our young woman quavered.

Mrs. Gereth turned on her sharply. 'Ready for what? Ready to see me ruined without a reason or a reward?'

Fleda could at first say nothing; the worst of it all was the something still unspoken between them. Neither of them dared utter it, but the influence of it was in the girl's tone when she returned at last with great gentleness: 'Don't be cruel to me – I'm very unhappy.' The words produced a visible impression on Mrs. Gereth, who held her face averted and sent off through the window a gaze that kept pace with the long caravan of her treasures. Fleda knew she was watching it wind up the avenue of Poynton – Fleda participated indeed fully in the vision; so that after a little the most consoling thing seemed to her to add: 'I don't see why in the world you take so for granted that he's, as you say, "lost." '

Mrs. Gereth continued to stare out of the window, and her stillness denoted some success in controlling herself. 'If he's not lost why are you unhappy?'

'I'm unhappy because I torment you and you don't understand me.'

'No, Fleda, I don't understand you,' said Mrs. Gereth, finally facing her again. 'I don't understand you at all, and it's as if you and Owen were of quite another race and another flesh. You make me feel very old-fashioned and simple and bad. But you must take me as I am, since you take so much else *with* me!' She spoke now with the drop of her resentment, with a dry and weary calm. 'It would have been better for me if I had never known you,' she pursued, 'and certainly better if I hadn't taken such an extraordinary fancy to you. But that too was inevitable: everything, I suppose, is inevitable. It was all my own doing – you didn't run after me: I pounced on you and caught you up. You're a stiff little beggar, in spite of your pretty manners: yes, you're hideously misleading. I hope you feel how handsome it is of me to recognise the independence of your character. It was your clever sympathy that did it – your beautiful feeling for those accursed vanities. You were sharper about them than any one I had ever known, and that was a thing I simply couldn't resist. Well,' the poor lady concluded after a pause, 'you see where it has landed us!'

'If you'll go for him yourself I'll wait here,' said Fleda.

Mrs. Gereth, holding her mantle together, appeared for a while to consider. 'To his club, do you mean?'

'Isn't it there, when he's in town, that he has a room? He has at present no other London address,' Fleda said. 'It's there one writes to him.

'How do *I* know, with my wretched relations with him?' Mrs. Gereth cried.

'Mine have not been quite so bad as that,' Fleda desperately smiled. Then she added: 'His silence, *her* silence, our hearing nothing at all – what are these but the very things on which, at Poynton and at Ricks, you rested your assurance that everything is at an end between them?'

Mrs. Gereth looked dark and void. 'Yes, but I hadn't heard from you then that you could invent nothing better than, as you call it, to send him back to her.'

'Ah but on the other hand' – the girl sprung to this – 'you've learned from them what you didn't know, you've learned by Mrs. Brigstock's visit that he cares for me.' She found herself in the position of availing herself of optimistic arguments that she formerly had repudiated; her refutation of her companion had completely changed its ground. A fever of ingenuity had started to burn in her, though she was painfully conscious, on behalf of

185

her success, that it was visible as fever. She could herself see the reflexion of it gleam in her critic's sombre eyes.

'You plunge me in stupefaction,' that personage answered, 'and at the same time you terrify me. Your account of Owen's inconceivable, and yet I don't know what to hold on by. He cares for you, it does appear, and yet in the same breath you tell me that nothing is more possible than that he's spending these days at Waterbath. Pardon me if I'm so dull as not to see my way in such darkness. If he's at Waterbath he doesn't care for you. If he cares for you he's not at Waterbath.'

'Then where is he?' poor Fleda helplessly wailed. She caught herself up, however; she would do her best to be brave and clear. Before Mrs. Gereth could reply, with due obviousness, that this was a question for her not to ask but to answer, she found an air of assurance to say: 'You simplify far too much. You always did and you always will. The tangle of life is much more intricate than you've ever, I think, felt it to be. You slash into it,' cried Fleda finely, 'with a great pair of shears; you nip at it as if you were one of the Fates!⁴ If Owen's at Waterbath he's there to wind everything up.'

His mother shook her head with slow austerity. 'You don't believe a word you're saying. I've frightened you, as you've frightened me: you're whistling in the dark to keep up our courage. I do simplify, doubtless, if to simplify is to fail to comprehend the inanity of a passion that bewilders a young blockhead with bugaboo barriers, with hideous and monstrous sacrifices. I can only repeat that you're beyond me. Your perversity's a thing to howl over. However,' the poor woman continued with a break in her voice, a long hesitation and then the dry triumph of her will, 'I'll never mention it to you again! Owen I can just make out; for Owen *is* a blockhead. Owen's a blockhead,' she repeated with a quiet tragic finality, looking straight into Fleda's eyes. 'I don't know why you dress up so the fact that he's disgustingly weak.'

Fleda at last, before her companion's, lowered her look. 'Because I love him. It's because he's weak that he needs me,' she added.

'That was why his father, whom he exactly resembles, needed *me*. And I didn't fail his father,' said Mrs. Gereth. She gave her

186

visitor a moment to appreciate the remark; after which she pursued: 'Mona Brigstock isn't weak. She's stronger than you!'

'I never thought she was weak,' Fleda answered. She looked vaguely round the room with a new purpose: she had lost sight of her umbrella.

'I did tell you to let yourself go, but it's clear enough that you really haven't,' Mrs. Gereth declared. 'If Mona has got him –'

Fleda had accomplished her search; her hostess paused. 'If Mona has got him?' the girl panted, tightening the umbrella.

'Well,' said Mrs. Gereth profoundly, 'it will be clear enough that Mona *has*.'

'Has let herself go?'

'Has let herself go.' Mrs. Gereth spoke as if she meant it to the fullest extent of her cynicism and saw it in every detail.

Fleda felt the tone and finished her preparation; then she went and opened the door. 'We'll look for him together,' she said to her friend, who stood a moment taking in her face. 'They may know something about him at the Colonel's.'

'We'll go there.' Mrs. Gereth had picked up her gloves and her purse. 'But the first thing,' she went on, 'will be to wire to Poynton.'

'Why not to Waterbath at once?' Fleda asked.

Her companion wondered. 'In *your* name?'

'In my name. I noticed a place at the corner.'

While Fleda held the door open Mrs. Gereth drew on her gloves. 'Forgive me,' she presently said. 'Kiss me,' she added.

Fleda, on the threshold, kissed her. Then they both went out

XIX

※

IN the place at the corner, on the chance of its saving time, Fleda wrote her telegram – wrote it in silence under Mrs. Gereth's eye and then in silence handed it to her. 'I send this to Waterbath, on the possibility of your being there, to ask you to come to me.' Mrs. Gereth held it a moment, read it more than once; then keeping it, and with her eyes on her companion, seemed to consider. There was the dawn of a kindness in her look; Fleda measured in it, as the reward of complete submission, a slight relaxation of her rigour.

'Wouldn't it perhaps after all be better,' she asked, 'before doing this, to see if we can make his whereabouts certain?'

'Why so? It will be always so much done,' said Fleda. 'Though I'm poor,' she added with a smile, 'I don't mind the shilling'.'

'The shilling's *my* shilling,' said Mrs. Gereth.

Fleda stayed her hand. 'No, no – I'm superstitious. To succeed it must be all me!'

'Well, if that will make it succeed!' Mrs. Gereth took back her shilling, but she still kept the telegram. 'As he's most probably not there – '

'If he shouldn't be there,' Fleda interrupted, 'there will be no harm done.'

'If he "shouldn't be" there!' Mrs. Gereth ejaculated. 'Heaven help us, how you assume it!'

'I'm only prepared for the worst. The Brigstocks will simply send any telegram on.'

'Where will they send it?'

'Presumably to Poynton.'

'They'll read it first,' said Mrs. Gereth. 'Yes, Mona will. She'll open it under the pretext of having it repeated, and then will probably do nothing. She'll keep it as a proof of your immodesty.'

'What of that?' asked Fleda.

'You don't mind her seeing it?'

Rather musingly and absently she shook her head. 'I don't mind anything.'

'Well then, that's all right,' said Mrs. Gereth as wanting only to feel she had been irreproachably considerate. After this she was gentler still, yet had another point to clear up. 'Why have you given, for a reply, your sister's address?'

'Because if he does come to me he must come to me there. If that telegram goes,' said Fleda, 'I return to Maggie's to-night.'

Her friend seemed to wonder at this. 'You won't receive him here with me?'

'No, I won't receive him here with you. Only where I received him last – only there again.' As to this Fleda was firm.

But Mrs. Gereth had obviously now had some practice in following queer movements prompted by queer feelings. She resigned herself, though she fingered the paper a moment longer. She appeared to hesitate, then brought out: 'You couldn't then, if I release you, make your message a little stronger?'

Fleda gave her a faint smile. 'He'll come if he can.'

She met fully what this conveyed; with decision she pushed in the telegram. But she laid her hand quickly on another form and with still greater decision wrote another message. 'This from *me*,' she said to Fleda when she had finished: 'to catch him possibly at Poynton. Will you read it?'

Fleda turned away. 'Thank you.'

'It's stronger than yours.'

'I don't care' – and the girl moved to the door. Mrs. Gereth, having paid for the second missive, rejoined her, and they drove together to Owen's club, where the elder lady alone got out. Fleda, from the hansom, watched through the glass doors her brief conversation with the hall-porter and then met in silence her return with the news that he had not seen Owen for a fortnight and was keeping his letters till called for. These had been the last orders; there were a dozen letters lying there. He had no more information to give, but they would see what they could find at Colonel Gereth's. To any connexion with this inquiry, however, Fleda now roused herself to object, and her friend had indeed to recognise that on second thoughts it couldn't be quite to the taste of either of them to advertise in the remoter reaches of the family that they had forfeited the confidence of the master of Poynton.

The letters lying at the club proved effectively that he was not in London, and this was the question that immediately concerned them. Nothing could concern them further till the answers to their telegrams should have had time to arrive. Mrs. Gereth had got back into the cab, and, still at the door of the club, they sat staring at their need of patience. Fleda's eyes rested, in the great hard street, on passing figures that struck her as puppets pulled by strings. After a little the driver challenged them through the hole in the top. 'Anywhere in particular, ladies?'

Fleda decided. 'Drive to Euston², please.'

'You won't wait for what we may hear?' Mrs. Gereth asked.

'Whatever we hear I must go.' As the cab went on she added: 'But I needn't drag *you* to the station.'

Mrs. Gereth had a pause; then 'Nonsense!' she sharply replied.

In spite of this sharpness they were now almost equally and almost tremulously mild; though their mildness took mainly the form of an inevitable sense of nothing left to say. It was the unsaid that occupied them – the thing that for more than an hour they had been going round and round without naming it. Much too early for Fleda's train, they encountered at the station a long half-hour to wait. Fleda made no further allusion to Mrs. Gereth's leaving her; their dumbness, with the elapsing minutes, grew to be in itself a reconstituted bond. They slowly paced the great grey platform, and presently Mrs. Gereth took the girl's arm and leaned on it with a hard demand for support. It seemed to Fleda not difficult for each to know of what the other was thinking – to know indeed that they had in common two alternating visions, one of which at moments brought them as by a common impulse to a pause. This was the one that was fixed; the other filled at times the whole space and then was shouldered away. Owen and Mona glared together out of the gloom and disappeared, but the replenishment of Poynton made a shining steady light. The old splendour was there again, the old things were in their places. Our friends looked at them with an equal yearning; face to face on the platform, they counted them in each other's eyes. Fleda had come back to them by a road as strange as the road they themselves had followed. The wonder of their great journeys, the prodigy of this second one, was the question that made her occasionally stop. Several times she uttered it, asked how this and that difficulty had been met. Mrs. Gereth replied with pale lucidity – was naturally the person most familiar with the truth that what she undertook was always somehow achieved. To do it was to do it – she had more than one kind of magnificence. She confessed there, audaciously enough, to a sort of arrogance of energy, and Fleda, going on again, her appeal more than answered and her arm rendering service, flushed in her diminished identity with the sense that such a woman was great.

'You do mean literally everything, to the last little miniature on the last little screen?'

'I mean literally everything. Go over them with the catalogue!'

Fleda went over them while they walked again; she had no need of the catalogue. At last she spoke once more. 'Even the Maltese cross?'

'Even the Maltese cross. Why not that as well as everything else? – especially as I remembered how you like it.'

Finally, after an interval, the girl exclaimed: 'But the mere fatigue of it, the exhaustion of such a feat! I drag you to and fro here while you must be ready to drop.'

'I'm very, very tired.' Mrs. Gereth's slow headshake was tragic. 'I couldn't do it again.'

'I doubt if they'd bear it again!'

'That's another matter: they'd bear it if *I* could. There won't have been, this time either, a shake or a scratch. But I'm too tired – I very nearly don't care.'

'You must sit down then till I go,' said Fleda. 'We must find a bench.'

'No. I'm tired of *them*: I'm not tired of you. This is the way for you to feel most how much I rest on you.' Fleda had a compunction, wondering as they continued to stroll whether it was right after all to leave her. She believed, however, that if the flame might for the moment burn low it was far from dying out; an impression presently confirmed by the way Mrs. Gereth went on: 'But one's fatigue's nothing. The idea under which one worked kept one up. For you I *could* – I can still. Nothing will have mattered if *she's* not there.'

There was a question that this imposed, but Fleda at first found no voice to utter it: it was the thing that between them, since her arrival, had been so consciously and vividly unsaid. Finally she was able to breathe: 'And if she *is* there – if she's there already?'

Mrs. Gereth's rejoinder too hung back; then when it came – from sad eyes as well as from lips barely moved – it was unexpectedly merciful. 'It will be very hard.' That was all now, and it was poignantly simple. The train Fleda was to take had drawn up; the girl kissed her as if in farewell. Mrs. Gereth submitted, then after a little brought out: 'If we *have* lost – !'

'If we have lost?' Fleda repeated as she paused again.

'You'll all the same come abroad with me?'

'It will seem very strange to me if you want me. But whatever you ask, whatever you need, that I will now always do.'

'I shall need your company,' said Mrs. Gereth. Fleda wondered an instant if this were not practically a demand for penal submission – for a surrender that, in its complete humility, would be a long expiation. But there was none of the latent chill of the vindictive in the sequel. 'We can always, as time goes on, talk of them together.'

'Of the spoils – ?' Fleda had selected a third-class compartment: she stood a moment looking into it and at a fat woman with a basket who had already taken possession. 'Always?' she said, turning again to her friend. 'Never!' she exclaimed. She got into the carriage and two men with bags and boxes immediately followed, blocking up door and window so long that when she was able to look out again Mrs. Gereth had gone.

THERE came to her at her sister's no telegram in answer to her own: the rest of that day and the whole of the next elapsed without a word either from Owen or from his mother. She was free, however, to her infinite relief, from any direct dealing with suspense, and conscious, to her surprise, of nothing that could show her, or could show Maggie and her brother-in-law, that she was excited. Her excitement was composed of pulses as swift and fine as the revolutions of a spinning top: she supposed she was going round, but went round so fast that she couldn't even feel herself move. Her trouble occupied some quarter of her soul that had closed its doors for the day and shut out even her own sense of it; she might perhaps have heard something if she had pressed her ear to a partition. Instead of that she sat with her patience in a cold still chamber from which she could look out in quite another direction. This was to have achieved an equilibrium to which she couldn't have given a name: indifference, resignation, despair were the terms of a forgotten tongue. The time even seemed not long, for what were the stages of the journey but the very items of Mrs. Gereth's surrender? The detail of that performance, which filled the scene, was what Fleda had now before her eyes. The part of her loss that she could think of was the reconstituted splendour of Poynton. It was the beauty she was most touched by that, in tons, she had lost – the beauty that, charged upon big wagons, had safely crept to its home. But the loss was a gain to memory and love; it was to her too at last that, in condonation of her treachery, the spoils had crept back. She greeted them with open arms; she thought of them hour after hour; they made a company with which solitude was warm and a picture that, at this crisis, overlaid poor Maggie's scant mahogany. It was really her obliterated passion that had revived, and with it an immense assent to Mrs. Gereth's early judgement of her. She equally, she felt, was of the religion, and like any other of the passionately pious she could worship now even in the desert. Yes, it was all for *her*, far round as she had gone she had been strong enough: her love had gathered them in. She wanted indeed no catalogue to count them over; the array of them, miles away, was complete; each piece, in its turn, was perfect to her; she could have drawn up a catalogue from memory. Thus again she lived with them, and she thought of them without a question of any personal right. That they might have been, that they might still be hers, that they were perhaps already another's, were ideas that had too little to say to her. They were nobody's at all – too proud, unlike base animals and humans, to be reducible to anything so narrow. It was Poynton that was theirs; they had simply recovered their own. The joy of that for them was the source of the strange peace that had descended like a charm.

It was broken on the third day by a telegram from Mrs. Gereth. 'Shall be with you at 11.30 – don't meet me at station.' Fleda turned this over; she was sufficiently expert not to disobey the injunction. She had only an hour to take in its meaning, but that hour was longer than all the previous time. If Maggie had studied her convenience the day Owen came, Maggie was also at the present juncture a miracle of refinement. Increasingly and resentfully mystified, in spite of all reassurance, by the impression that Fleda suffered much more than she gained from the grandeur of the Gereths, she had it at heart to exemplify the perhaps truer distinction of nature that characterised the house of Vetch. She was not, like poor Fleda, at every one's beck, and the announced visitor was to see no more of her than what the arrangement of luncheon might tantalisingly show. Maggie described herself to her sister as intending for a just provocation even the agreement she had had with her husband that he also should keep away. Fleda accordingly awaited alone the subject of so many manoeuvres – a period that was slightly prolonged even after the drawing-room door, at 11.30, was thrown open. Mrs. Gereth stood there with a face that spoke plain, but no sound fell from her till the withdrawal of the maid, whose attention had immediately attached itself to the rearrangement of a window-blind and who seemed, while she bustled at it, to contribute to the pregnant silence; before the duration of which, however, she retreated with a sudden stare.

'He has done it,' said Mrs. Gereth, turning her eyes avoidingly but not unperceivingly about her and in spite of herself dropping an opinion upon the few objects in the room. Fleda, on her side, in her silence observed how characteristically she looked at Maggie's possessions before looking at Maggie's sister. The girl understood and at first had nothing to say; she was still dumb while their guest selected, after dryly balancing, a seat less distasteful than the one that happened to be nearest. On the sofa near the window the poor woman finally showed what the two last days had done for the age of her face. Her eyes at last met Fleda's. 'It's the end.'

'They're married?'

'They're married.'

Fleda came to the sofa in obedience to the impulse to sit down by her; then paused before her while Mrs. Gereth turned up a dead grey mask. A tired old woman sat there with empty hands in her lap. 'I've heard nothing,' said Fleda. 'No answer came.'

'That's the only answer. It's the answer to everything.' So Fleda saw; for a minute she looked over her companion's head and far away. 'He wasn't at Waterbath. Mrs. Brigstock must have read your telegram and kept it. But mine, the one to Poynton, brought something. "We are here – what do you want?" ' Mrs. Gereth stopped as if with a failure of voice; on which Fleda sank upon the sofa and made a movement to take her hand. It met no response; there could be no attenuation. Fleda waited; they sat facing each other like strangers. 'I wanted to go down,' Mrs. Gereth presently continued. 'Well, I went.'

All the girl's effort tended for the time to a single aim – that of taking the thing with outward detachment, speaking of it as having happened to Owen and to his mother and not in any degree to herself. Something at least of this was in the encouraging way she said: 'Yesterday morning?'

'Yesterday morning. I saw him.'

Fleda hesitated. 'Did you see *her*?'

'Thank God, no!'

Fleda laid on her arm a hand of vague comfort, of which Mrs. Gereth took no notice. 'You've been capable, just to tell me, of this wretched journey – of this consideration that I don't deserve?'

'We're together, we're together,' said Mrs. Gereth. She looked helpless as she sat there, her eyes, unseeingly enough now, on a tall Dutch clock, old but rather poor, that Maggie had had as a wedding-gift and that eked out the bareness of the room.

To Fleda, in the face of the event, it appeared that this was exactly what they were not: the last inch of common ground, the ground of their past intercourse, had fallen from under them. Yet what was still there was the grand style of her companion's treatment of her. Mrs. Gereth couldn't stand upon small questions, couldn't in conduct make small differences. 'You're magnificent!' her young friend exclaimed. 'There's an extraordinary greatness in your generosity.'

'We're together, we're together,' Mrs. Gereth lifelessly repeated. 'That's all we *are* now; it's all we have.' The words brought to Fleda a sudden vision of the empty little house at Ricks; such a vision might also have been what her companion found in the face of the stopped Dutch clock. Yet with this it was clear she would still show no bitterness: she had done with that, had given the last drop to those horrible hours in London. No passion even was left her, and her forbearance only added to the force with which she represented the final vanity of everything.

Fleda was so far from a wish to triumph that she was absolutely ashamed of having anything to say for herself; but there was one thing, all the same, that not to say was impossible. 'That he has done it, that he couldn't *not* do it, shows how right I was.' It settled for ever her attitude, and she spoke as if for her own mind; then after a little she added very gently, for Mrs. Gereth's: 'That's to say it shows he was bound to her by an obligation that, however much he may have wanted to, he couldn't in any sort of honour break.'

Blanched and bleak, Mrs. Gereth looked at her. 'What sort of an obligation do you call that?' No such obligation exists for an hour between any man and any woman who have hatred on one side. He had ended by hating her, and he hates her now more than ever.'

'Did he tell you so?' Fleda asked.

'No. He told me nothing but the great gawk of a fact. I saw him but for three minutes.' She was silent again, and Fleda, as before some lurid image of this interview, sat without speaking. 'Do you wish to appear as if you don't care?' Mrs. Gereth presently demanded.

'I'm trying not to think of myself.'

'Then if you're thinking of Owen how can you *bear* to think?'

Sadly and submissively Fleda shook her head; the slow tears had come into her eyes. 'I can't. I don't understand – I don't understand!' she broke out.

'*I* do then.' Mrs. Gereth looked hard at the floor. 'There was no obligation at the time you saw him last – when you sent him, hating her as he did, back to her.'

'If he went,' Fleda asked, 'doesn't that exactly prove that he recognised one?'

'He recognised rot! You know what *I* think of him.' Fleda knew; she had no wish to provoke a fresh statement. Mrs. Gereth made one – it was her sole faint flicker of passion – to the extent of declaring that he was too abjectly weak to deserve the name of a man. For all Fleda cared! – it was his weakness she loved in him. 'He took strange ways of pleasing you!' her friend went on. 'There was no obligation till suddenly, the other day, the situation changed.'

Fleda wondered. 'Suddenly – ?'

'It came to Mona's knowledge – I can't tell you how, but it came – that the things I was sending back had begun to arrive at Poynton. I had sent them for you, but it was *her* I touched.' Mrs. Gereth paused; Fleda was too absorbed in her explanation to do anything but take blankly the full cold breath of this. 'They were there, and that determined her.'

'Determined her to what?'

'To act, to take means.'

'To take means?' Fleda repeated.

'I can't tell you what they were, but they were powerful. She knew how,' said Mrs. Gereth.

Fleda received with the same stoicism the quiet immensity of this allusion to the person who had *not* known how. But it made her think a little, and the thought found utterance, with unconscious irony, in the simple interrogation: 'Mona?'

'Why not? She's a brute.'

'But if he knew that so well, what chance was there in it for her?'

'How can I tell you? How can I talk of such horrors? I can only give you, of the situation, what I see. He knew it, yes. But as she

197

couldn't make him forget it she tried to make him like it. She tried and she succeeded: that's what she did. She's after all so much less of a fool than he. And what *else* had he originally liked?' Mrs. Gereth shrugged her shoulders. 'She did what you wouldn't!' Fleda's face had grown dark with her wonder at the sense of this, but her friend's empty hands offered no balm to the pain in it. 'It was that if it was anything. Nothing else meets the misery of it. Then there was quick work. Before he could turn round he was married.'

Fleda, as if she had been holding her breath, gave the sigh of a listening child. 'At that place you spoke of in town?'

'At a Registry-office – like a pair of low atheists.'

The girl considered. 'What do people say of that? I mean the "world." '

'Nothing, because nobody knows. They're to be married on the seventeenth at Waterbath church. If anything else comes out everybody's a little prepared. It will pass for some stroke of diplomacy, some move in the game, some outwitting of *me*. It's known there has been a great row with me.'

Fleda was mystified. 'People surely know at Poynton,' she objected, 'if, as you say, she's there.'

'She was there, day before yesterday, only for a few hours. She met him in London and went down to see the things.'

Fleda remembered that she had seen them only once. 'Did *you* see them?' she then ventured to ask.

'Everything.'

'Are they right?'

'Quite right. There's nothing like them,' said Mrs. Gereth. At this her companion took up one of her hands again and kissed it as she had done in London. 'Mona went back that night; she was not there yesterday. Owen stayed on,' she added.

Fleda stared. 'Then she's not to live there?'

'Rather! But not till after the public marriage.' Mrs. Gereth seemed to muse; then she brought out: 'She'll live there alone.'

'Alone?'

'She'll have it to herself.'

'He won't live with her?'

'Never! But she's none the less his wife, and you're not,' said Mrs. Gereth, getting up. 'Our only chance is the chance she may die.'

198

Fleda appeared to measure it: she appreciated her visitor's magnanimous use of the plural. 'Mona won't die,' she replied.

'Well, *I* shall, thank God! Till then' – and with this, for the first time, Mrs. Gereth put out her hand – 'don't desert me.'

Fleda took her hand, clasping it for a renewal of engagements already taken. She said nothing, but her silence committed her as solemnly as the vow of a nun. The next moment something occurred to her. 'I mustn't put myself in your son's way, you know.'

Mrs. Gereth gave a laugh of bitterness. 'You're prodigious! But how shall you possibly be more out of it? Owen and I – ' She didn't finish her sentence.

'That's your great feeling about him,' Fleda said; 'but how, after what has happened, can it be his about you?'

Mrs. Gereth waited. 'How do you know what has happened? You don't know what I said to him.'

'Yesterday?'

'Yesterday.'

They looked at each other with a long deep gaze. Then, as Mrs. Gereth seemed again about to speak, the girl, closing her eyes, made a gesture of strong prohibition. 'Don't tell me!'

'Merciful powers, how you worship him!' Mrs. Gereth wonderingly moaned. It was for Fleda the shake that made the cup overflow. She had a pause, that of the child who takes time to know that he responds to an accident with pain; then, dropping again on the sofa, she broke into tears. They were beyond control, they came in long sobs, which for a moment her friend, almost with an air of indifference, stood hearing and watching. At last Mrs. Gereth too sank down again. Mrs. Gereth soundlessly wearily wept.

XXI

‘IT looks just like Waterbath; but, after all, we bore *that* together’: these words formed part of a letter in which, before the seventeenth, Mrs. Gereth, writing from disfigured Ricks, named to Fleda the day on which she would be expected to arrive there on a second visit. ‘I shan’t for a long time to come,’ the missive continued, ‘be able to receive any one who may *like* it, who would try to smooth it down, and me with it; but there are always things you and I can comfortably hate together, for you’re the only person who comfortably understands. You don’t understand quite everything, but of all my acquaintance you’re far away the least stupid. For action you’re no good at all; but action’s over, for me, for ever, and you’ll have the great merit of knowing when I’m brutally silent what I shall be thinking about. Without setting myself up for your equal I daresay I shall also know what are your own thoughts. Moreover, with nothing else but my four walls, you’ll at any rate be a bit of furniture. For that, a little, you know, I’ve always taken you – quite one of my best finds. So come if possible on the fifteenth.’

The position of a scrap of furniture was one that Fleda could conscientiously accept, and she by no means insisted on so high a place in the list. This communication made her easier, if only by its acknowledgment that her friend had something left: it still implied recognition of the principle of property. Something to hate, and to hate ‘comfortably,’ was at least not the utter destitution to which, after their last interview, she had helplessly seemed to see the ex-mistress of Poynton go forth. She remembered indeed that in the state in which they first saw it she herself had ‘liked’ the blest refuge of Ricks; and she now wondered if the tact for which she was commended had then operated to make her keep her kindness out of sight. She was at present ashamed of such obliquity and made up her mind that if this happy impression, quenched in the translated spoils, should revive on the spot, she would utter it to her companion without reserve. Yes, she was capable of as much 'action' as that: all the more that the spirit of her hostess seemed for the time at least wholly to have failed. The mother's three minutes with the son had been a blow to all talk of travel, and after her woeful hour at Maggie's she had, like some great moaning wounded bird, made her way with wings of anguish back to the nest she knew she should find empty. Fleda, on that dire day could neither keep her nor give her up; she had pressingly offered to return with her, but Mrs. Gereth, in spite of the theory that their common grief was a bond, had even declined all escort to the station, conscious apparently of something abject in her collapse and almost fiercely eager, as with a personal shame, to be unwatched. All she had said to Fleda was that she would go back to Ricks that night, and the girl had lived for days after with the dreadful image of her position and her misery there. She had had a vision of her now lying prone on some unmade bed, now pacing a bare floor as a lioness deprived of her cubs. There had been moments when her mind's ear was strained to listen for some sound of grief wild enough to be wafted from afar. But the first sound, at the end of a week, had been a note announcing, without reflexions, that the plan of going abroad had been abandoned. 'It has come to me indirectly, but with much appearance of truth, that *they* are going – for an indefinite time. That quite settles it; I shall stay where I am, and as soon as I've turned round again I shall look for you.' The second letter had come a week later, and on the fifteenth Fleda was on her way to Ricks.

Her arrival took the form of a surprise very nearly as violent as that of the other time. The elements were different, but the effect, like the other, arrested her on the threshold: she stood there stupefied and delighted at the magic of a passion of which such a picture represented the low-water mark. Wound up but sincere, and passing quickly from room to room, Fleda broke out before she even sat down. 'If you turn me out of the house for it, my dear, there isn't a woman in England for whom it wouldn't be a privilege to live here.' Mrs. Gereth was as honestly bewildered as she had of old been falsely calm. She looked about at the few sticks that, as she afterwards phrased it, she had gathered in, and then hard at her guest, as to protect herself against a joke all too cruel. The girl's heart gave a leap, for this stare was the sign of an opportunity. Mrs. Gereth was all unwitting; she didn't in the least know what she had done. Therefore as Fleda could tell her, Fleda suddenly became the one who knew most. That counted for the moment as a splendid position; it almost made all the difference. Yet what contradicted it was the vivid presence of the artist's idea. 'Where on earth did you put your hand on such beautiful things?'

'Beautiful things?' Mrs. Gereth turned again to the little worn bleached stuffs and the sweet spindle-legs. 'They're the wretched things that were here – that stupid starved old woman's.'

'The maiden-aunt's, the nicest, the dearest old woman that ever lived? I thought you had got rid of the maiden-aunt.'

'She was stored in an empty barn – stuck away for a sale; a matter that, fortunately, I've had neither time nor freedom of mind to arrange. I've simply, in my extremity, fished her out again.'

'You've simply, in your extremity, made a delight of her.' Fleda took the highest line and the upper hand, and as Mrs. Gereth, challenging her cheerfulness, turned again a lustreless eye over the contents of the place, she broke into a rapture that was unforced, yet that she was conscious of an advantage in being able to feel. She moved, as she had done on the previous occasion, from one piece to another, with looks of recognition and hands that lightly lingered, but she was as feverishly jubilant now as she had of old been anxious and mute. 'Ah the little melancholy tender tell-tale things: how can they *not* speak to you and find a way to your heart? It's not the great chorus of Poynton; but you're not, I'm sure, either so proud or so broken as to be reached by nothing but that. This is a voice so gentle, so human, so feminine – a faint far-away voice with the little quaver of a heart-break. You've listened to it unawares; for the arrangement and effect of everything – when I compare them with what we found the first day we came down – shows, even if mechanically and disdainfully exercised, your admirable, your infallible hand. It's your extraordinary genius; you make things "compose" in spite of yourself. You've only to be a day or two in a place with four sticks for something to come of it!'

'Then if anything has come of it here, it has come precisely of just four. That's literally, by the inventory, all there are!' said Mrs. Gereth.

'If there were more there would be too many to convey the impression in which half the beauty resides – the impression somehow of something dreamed and missed, something reduced, relinquished, resigned: the poetry, as it were, of something sensibly *gone*.' Fleda ingeniously and triumphantly worked it out. 'Ah, there's something here that will never be in the inventory!'

'Does it happen to be in your power to give it a name?' Mrs. Gereth's face showed the dim dawn of an amusement at finding herself seated at the feet of her pupil.

'I can give it a dozen. It's a kind of fourth dimension.[1] It's a presence, a perfume, a touch. It's a soul, a story, a life. There's ever so much more here than you and I. We're in fact just three!'

'Oh if you count the ghosts – !'

'Of course I count the ghosts, confound you! It seems to me ghosts count double – for what they were and for what they are. Somehow there were no ghosts at Poynton,' Fleda went on. 'That was the only fault.'

Mrs. Gereth, considering, appeared to fall in with this fine humour. 'Poynton was too splendidly happy.'

'Poynton was too splendidly happy,' Fleda promptly echoed.

'But it's cured of that now,' her companion added.

'Yes, henceforth there'll be a ghost or two.'

Mrs. Gereth thought again: she found her young friend suggestive.[2] 'Only *she* won't see them.'

'No, "she" won't see them.' Then Fleda said: 'What I mean is, for this dear one of ours, that if she had (as I *know* she did; it's in the very touch of the air!) a great accepted pain – '

She had paused an instant, and Mrs. Gereth took her up. 'Well, if she had?'

Fleda still hung fire. 'Why, it was worse than yours.'

Mrs. Gereth debated. 'Very likely.' Then she too hesitated. 'The question is if it was worse than yours.'

'Mine?' Fleda looked vague.

'Precisely. Yours.'

At this our young lady smiled. 'Yes, because it was a disappointment. She had been so sure.'

'I see. And you were never sure.'

'Never. Besides, I'm happy,' said Fleda.

Mrs. Gereth met her eyes a while. 'Goose!' she quietly remarked as she turned away. There was a curtness in it; nevertheless it represented a considerable part of the basis of their new life.

On the eighteenth *The Morning Post* had at last its clear message, a brief account of the marriage, from the residence of the bride's mother, of Mr. Owen Gereth of Poynton Park to Miss Mona Brigstock of Waterbath. There were two ecclesiastics and six bridesmaids and, as Mrs. Gereth subsequently said, a hundred frumps, as well as a special train from town: the scale of the affair sufficiently showed that the preparations had been in hand for some time back. The happy pair were described as having taken their departure for Mr. Gereth's own seat, famous for its unique collection of artistic curiosities. The newspaper and letters, the fruits of the first London post, had been brought to the mistress of Ricks in the garden; and she lingered there alone a long time after receiving them. Fleda kept at a distance; she knew what must have happened, for from one of the windows she saw her rigid in a chair, her eyes strange and fixed, the newspaper open on the ground and the letters untouched in her lap. Before the morning's end she had disappeared and the rest of that day remained in her room: it recalled to Fleda, who had picked up the newspaper, the day, months before, on which Owen had come down to Poynton to make his engagement known. The hush of the house at least was the same, and the girl's own waiting, her soft wandering, through the hours: there was a difference indeed sufficiently great and of which her companion's absence might in some degree have represented a considerate recognition. That was at any rate the meaning Fleda, devoutly glad to be alone, attached to her opportunity. Mrs. Gereth's sole allusion the next day to the subject of their thoughts has already been mentioned: it was a dazzled glance at the fact that Mona's quiet pace had really never slackened.

Fleda fully assented. 'I said of our disembodied friend here that she had suffered in proportion as she had been sure. But that's not always a source of suffering. It's Mona who must have been sure!'

'She was sure of *you*!' Mrs. Gereth returned. But this didn't diminish the satisfaction taken by Fleda in showing how serenely and lucidly she herself could talk.

XXII

✣

HER relation with her wonderful friend had however in becoming
a new one begun to shape itself almost wholly on breaches and
omissions. Something had dropped out altogether, and the question between them, which time would answer, was whether the
change had made them strangers or yokefellows. It was as if at
last, for better or worse, they were, in a clearer cruder air, really
to know each other. Fleda wondered how Mrs. Gereth had escaped
hating her: there were hours when it seemed that such a feat might
leave after all a scant margin for future accidents. The thing indeed
that now came out in its simplicity was that even in her shrunken
state the lady of Ricks was larger than her wrongs. As for the
girl herself, she had made up her mind that her feelings had no
connexion with the case. It was her claim that they had never yet
emerged from the seclusion into which, after her friend's visit to
her at her sister's, we saw them precipitately retire: if she should
suddenly meet them in straggling procession on the road it would
be time enough to deal with them. They were all bundled there
together, likes with dislikes and memories with fears; and she had
for not thinking of them the excellent reason that she was too
occupied with the actual. The actual was not that Owen Gereth
had seen his necessity where she had pointed it out; it was that his
mother's bare spaces demanded all the tapestry the recipient of her
bounty could furnish. There were moments during the month
that followed when Mrs. Gereth struck her as still older and feebler
and as likely to become quite easily amused.

At the end of it, one day, the London paper had another piece
of news: 'Mr. and Mrs. Owen Gereth, who arrived in town last
week, proceed this morning to Paris.' They exchanged no word
about it till the evening, and none indeed would then have been
uttered had not the mistress of Ricks irrelevantly broken out: 'I
daresay you wonder why I declared the other day with such assur-

ance that he wouldn't live with her. He apparently *is* living with her.'

'Surely it's the only proper thing for him to do.'

'They're beyond me – I give it up,' said Mrs. Gereth.

'I don't give it up – I never did,' Fleda returned.

'Then what do you make of his aversion to her?'

'Oh she has dispelled it.'

Mrs. Gereth said nothing for a minute. 'You're prodigious in your choice of terms!' she then simply ejaculated.

But Fleda went luminously on; she once more enjoyed her great command of her subject. 'I think that when you came to see me at Maggie's you saw too many things, you had too many ideas.'

'You had none at all,' said Mrs. Gereth. 'You were completely bewildered.'

'Yes, I didn't quite understand – but I think I understand now. The case is simple and logical enough. She's a person who's upset by failure and who blooms and expands with success. There was something she had set her heart upon, set her teeth about – the house exactly as she had seen it.'

'She never saw it at all, she never looked at it!' cried Mrs. Gereth.

'She doesn't look with her eyes; she looks with her ears. In her own way she had taken it in; she knew, she felt when it had been touched. That probably made her take an attitude that was extremely disagreeable. But the attitude lasted only while the reason for it lasted.'

'Go on – I can bear it now,' said Mrs. Gereth. Her companion had just perceptibly paused.

'I know you can, or I shouldn't dream of speaking. When the pressure was removed she came up again. From the moment the house was once more what it had to be her natural charm reasserted itself.'

'Her natural charm!' – Mrs. Gereth could barely articulate.

'It's very great; everybody thinks so; there must be something in it. It operated as it had operated before. There's no need of imagining anything very monstrous. Her restored good humour, her splendid beauty and Mr. Owen's impressibility and generosity sufficiently cover the ground. His great bright sun came out!'

'And his great bright passion for another person went in. Your explanation would doubtless be perfect if he didn't love you.'

Fleda was silent a little. 'What do you know about his "loving" me?'

'I know what Mrs. Brigstock herself told me.'

'You never in your life took her word for any other matter.'

'Then won't yours do?' Mrs. Gereth demanded. 'Haven't I had it from your own mouth that he cares for you?'

Fleda turned pale, but she faced her companion and smiled. 'You confound, Mrs. Gereth. You mix things up. You've only had it from my own mouth that I care for *him*!'

It was doubtless in contradictious allusion to this (which at the time had made her simply drop her head as in a strange vain reverie) that Mrs. Gereth said, a day or two later to her inmate: 'Don't think I shall be a bit affected if I'm here to see it when he comes again to make up to you.'

'He won't do that,' the girl replied. Then she added, smiling; 'But if he should be guilty of such bad taste it wouldn't be nice of you not to be disgusted.'

'I'm not talking of disgust; I'm talking of its opposite,' said Mrs. Gereth: 'of any reviving pleasure one might feel in such an exhibition. I shall feel none at all. You may personally take it as you like; but what conceivable good will it do?'

Fleda wondered. 'To me, do you mean?'

'Deuce take you, no! To what we don't, you know, by your wish, ever talk about.'

'The spoils?' Fleda considered again. 'It will do no good of any sort to anything or any one. That's another question I'd rather we shouldn't discuss, please,' she gently added.

Mrs. Gereth shrugged her shoulders. 'It certainly isn't worth it!'

Something in her manner prompted her companion, with a certain inconsequence, to speak again. 'That was partly why I came back to you, you know – that there should be the less possibility of anything painful.'

'Painful?' Mrs. Gereth stared. 'What pain can I ever feel again?'

'I meant painful to myself,' Fleda, with a slight impatience, explained.

'Oh I see.' Her friend was silent a minute. 'You use sometimes such odd expressions. Well, I shall last a little, but I shan't last for ever.'

'You'll last quite as long – ' But she suddenly dropped.

Mrs. Gereth took her up with a cold smile that seemed the warning of experience against hyperbole. 'As long as what, please?'

The girl thought an instant; then met the difficulty by adopting, as an amendment, the same tone. 'As any danger of the ridiculous.'

That did for the time, and she had moreover, as the months went on, the protection of suspended allusions. This protection was marked when, in the following November, she received a letter directed in a hand a quick glance at which sufficed to make her hesitate to open it. She said nothing then or afterwards; but she opened it, for reasons that had come to her, on the morrow. It consisted of a page and a half from Owen Gereth, dated from Florence, but with no other preliminary. She knew that during the summer he had returned to England with his wife and that after a couple of months they had again gone abroad. She also knew, without communication, that Mrs. Gereth, round whom Ricks had grown submissively and indescribably sweet, had her own view of her daughter-in-law's share in this second migration. It was a piece of calculated insolence – a stroke odiously directed at showing whom it might concern that now she had Poynton fast she was perfectly indifferent to living there. *The Morning Post*, at Ricks, had again been a resource: it was stated in that journal that Mr. and Mrs. Owen Gereth proposed spending the winter in India. There was a person to whom it was clear she led her wretched husband by the nose. Such was the light in which the contemporary scene was offered to Fleda until, in her own room, late at night, she broke the seal of her letter.

'I want you inexpressibly to have as a remembrance something of mine – something of real value. Something from Poynton is what I mean and what I should prefer. You know everything there, and far better than I what's best and what isn't. There are a lot of differences, but aren't some of the smaller things the most remarkable? I mean for judges, and for what they'd bring. What I want you to take from me, and to choose for yourself, is the thing in the whole house that's most beautiful and precious. I mean the "gem of the collection," don't you know? If it happens to be of such a sort that you can take immediate possession of it – carry it right away with you – so much the better. You're to have it on the spot, whatever it is. I humbly entreat of you to go down there and see. The people have complete instructions: they'll act for you in every possible way and put the whole place at your service. There's a thing mamma used to call the Maltese cross and that I think I've heard her say is very wonderful. Is *that* the gem of the collection? Perhaps you'd take it or anything equally convenient. Only I do want you awfully to let it be the very pick of the place. Let me feel that I can trust you for this. You won't refuse if you'll simply think a little what it must be that makes me ask.'

Fleda read that last sentence over more times even than the rest: she was baffled – she couldn't think at all of what in particular made him ask. This was indeed because it might be one of so many things. She returned for the present no answer; she merely, little by little, fashioned for herself the form that her answer should eventually wear. There was only one form that was possible – the form of doing, at her time, what he wished. She would go down to Poynton as a pilgrim might go to a shrine, and as to this she must look out for her chance. She lived with her letter, before any chance came, a month, and even after a month it had mysteries for her that she couldn't meet. What did it mean, what did it represent, to what did it correspond in his imagination or his soul? What was behind it, what was before it, what was, in the deepest depth, within it? She said to herself that with these questions she was under no obligation to deal. There was an answer to them that, for practical purposes, would do as well as another: he had found in his marriage a happiness so much greater than, in the distress of his dilemma, he had been able to take heart to believe, that he now felt he owed her a token of gratitude for having kept him in the straight path. That explanation, I say, she could throw off; but no explanation in the least mattered: what determined her was the simple strength of her impulse to respond. The passion for which what had happened had made no difference, the passion that had taken this into account before as well as after, found here an issue that there was nothing whatever to choke. It found even a relief to which her imagination immensely contributed. Would she act upon his offer? She would act with secret rapture. To have as her own something splendid that he had given her, of which the gift had been his signed desire, would be a greater joy than the greatest she had believed to be left her, and she felt that till the sense of this came home she had even herself not known what burned in her successful stillness. It was an hour to dream of and watch for; to be patient was to draw out the sweetness. She was capable of feeling it as an hour of triumph, the triumph of every-thing in her recent life that had not held up its head. She moved there in thought – in the great rooms she knew; she should be able to say to herself that, for once at least, her possession was as complete as that of either of the others whom it had filled only with bitterness. And a thousand times yes – her choice should know no scruple: the thing she should go down to take would be up to the height of her privilege. The whole place was in her eyes, and she spent for weeks her private hours in a luxury of comparison and debate. It should be one of the smallest things because it should be one she could have close to her; and it should be one of the finest because it was in the finest he saw his symbol. She said to herself that of what it would symbolise she was content to know nothing more than just what her having it would tell her. At bottom she inclined to the Maltese cross – with the added reason that he had named it. But she would look again and judge afresh; she would on the spot so handle and ponder that there shouldn't be the shade of a mistake. ·

Before Christmas she had a natural opportunity to go to London: there was her periodical call on her father to pay as well as a promise to Maggie to redeem. She spent her first night in West Kensington, with the idea of carrying out on the morrow the purpose that had most of a motive. Her father's affection was not inquisitive, but when she mentioned to him that she had busi-ness in the country that would oblige her to catch an early train he deprecated her excursion in view of the menace of the weather. It was spoiling for a storm: all the signs of a winter gale were in the air. She replied that she would see what the morning might bring; and it brought in fact what seemed in London an amendment. She was to go to Maggie the next day, and now that she started her eagerness had become suddenly a pain. She pictured her return that evening with her trophy under her cloak; so that after looking, from the doorstep, up and down the dark street, she decided with a new nervousness and sallied forth to the nearest place of access to the 'Underground.' The December dawn was dolorous, but there was neither rain nor snow; it was not even cold, and the atmosphere of West Kensington, purified by the wind, was like a dirty old coat that had been bettered by a dirty old brush. At the end of almost an hour, in the larger station,[2] she had taken her place in a third-class compartment; the prospect before her was the run of eighty minutes to Poynton. The train was a fast one, and she was familiar with the moderate measure of the walk to the park from the spot at which it would drop her.

Once in the country indeed she saw that her father was right: the breath of December was abroad with a force from which the London labyrinth had protected her. The green fields were black, the sky was all alive with the wind; she had, in her anxious sense of the elements, her wonder at what might happen, a reminder of the surmises, in the old days of going to the Continent, that used to worry her on the way, at night, to the horrid cheap crossings by long sea.[3] Something, in a dire degree at this last hour, had begun to press on her heart: it was the sudden imagination of a disaster, or at least of a check, before her errand was achieved. When she said to herself that something might happen she wanted to go faster than the train. But nothing could happen save a dismayed discovery that, by some altogether unlikely chance, the master and mistress of the house had already come back. In that case she must have had a warning, and the fear was but the excess of her hope. It was every one's being exactly where every one was that lent the quality to her visit. Beyond lands and seas and alienated for ever, they in their different ways gave her the impression to take as she had never taken it. At last it was already there, though the darkness of the day had deepened; they had whizzed past Chater – Chater which was the station before the right one. Off in that quarter was an air of wild rain, but there shimmered straight across it a brightness that was the colour of the great interior she had been haunting. That vision settled before her – in the house the house was all; and as the train drew up she rose, in her mean compartment, quite proudly erect with the thought that all for Fleda Vetch then the house was standing there.

But with the opening of the door she encountered a shock, though for an instant she couldn't have named it: the next moment she saw it was given her by the face of the man advancing to let her out, an old lame porter of the station who had been there in Mrs. Gereth's time and who now recognised her. He looked up at her so hard that she took an alarm and before alighting broke out to him: 'They've come back?' She had a confused absurd sense that even he would know that in this case she mustn't be there. He hesitated, and in a few seconds her alarm had completely changed its ground: it seemed to leap, with her quick jump from the carriage, to the ground that was that of his stare at her. 'Smoke?' She was on the platform with her frightened sniff; it had taken her a minute to become aware of an extraordinary smell. The air was full of it, and there were already heads at the windows of the train, looking out at something she couldn't see. Some one, the only other passenger, had got out of another carriage, and the old porter hobbled off to close his door. The smoke was in her eyes, but she saw the station-master, from the end of the platform, identify her too and come straight at her. He brought her a finer shade of surprise than the porter, and while he was coming she heard a voice at a window of the train say that something was 'a good bit off – a mile from the town.' That was just what Poynton was. Then her heart stood still at the white wonder in the station-master's face.

'You've come down to it, miss, already?'

At this she knew. 'Poynton's on fire?'

'Gone, miss – with this awful gale. You weren't wired? Look out!'[4] he cried in the next breath, seizing her; the train was going on, and she had given a lurch that almost made it catch her as it passed. When it had drawn away she became more conscious of the pervading smoke, which the wind seemed to hurl in her face.

'*Gone?*' She was in the man's hands; she clung to him.

'Burning still, miss. Ain't it quite too dreadful? Took early this morning – the whole place is up there.'

In her bewildered horror she tried to think. 'Have they come back?'

'Back? They'll be there all day!'

'Not Mr. Gereth, I mean – nor his wife?'

'Nor his mother, miss – not a soul of *them* back. A pack o' servants in charge – not the old lady's lot, eh? A nice job for caretakers! Some rotten chimley or one of them portable lamps set down in the wrong place. What has done it is this cruel, cruel night.' Then as a great wave of smoke half-choked them he drew

her with force to the little waiting-room. 'Awkward for you, miss
– I see!'

She felt sick; she sank upon a seat, staring up at him. 'Do you
mean that great house is *lost*?'

'It was near it, I was told, an hour ago – the fury of the flames
had got such a start. I was there myself at six, the very first I heard
of it. They were fighting it then, but you couldn't quite say they
had got it down.'

Fleda jerked herself up. 'Were they saving the things?'

'That's just where it was, miss – to get *at* the blessed things.
And the want of right help – it maddened me to stand and see 'em
muff it. This ain't a place, like, for anything organised. They don't
come up to a *reel* emergency.'

She passed out of the door that opened toward the village, and
met a great acrid gust. She heard a far-off windy roar which, in
her dismay, she took for that of flames a mile away, and which,
the first instant, acted upon her as a wild solicitation. 'I must go
there.' She had scarcely spoken before the same omen had changed
into an appalling check.

Her vivid friend, moreover, had got before her; he clearly suffered from the nature of the control he had to exercise. 'Don't do
that, miss – you won't care for it at all.' Then as she waveringly
stood her ground: 'It's not a place for a young lady, nor, if you'll
believe me, a sight for them as are in any way affected.'

Fleda by this time knew in what way she was affected: she
became limp and weak again; she felt herself give everything up.
Mixed with the horror, with the kindness of the station-master,
with the smell of cinders and the riot of sound was the raw bitterness of a hope that she might never again in life have to give up
so much at such short notice. She heard herself repeat mechanically, yet as if asking it for the first time: 'Poynton's *gone*?'

The man faltered. 'What can you call it, miss, if it ain't really
saved?'

A minute later she had returned with him to the waiting-room,
where, in the thick swim of things, she saw something like the
disc of a clock. 'Is there an up-train?'

'In seven minutes.'

She came out on the platform: everywhere she met the smoke.
She covered her face with her hands. 'I'll go back.'

APPENDIX

EXTRACTS FROM HENRY JAMES'S NOTEBOOKS CONCERNING *THE SPOILS OF POYNTON*

[Reprinted from *The Notebooks of Henry James*, edited by F. O. Matthiessen and Kenneth B. Murdock, Copyright 1947 Oxford University Press]

34 De Vere Gardens, W., December 24th, 1893.

Three little histories were lately mentioned to me which (2 of the 3 in particular) appear worth making a note of. One of these was related to me last night at dinner at Lady Lindsay's, by Mrs. Anstruther-Thompson. It is a small and ugly matter – but there is distinctly in it, I should judge, the subject of a little tale – a little social and psychological picture. It appears that the circumstance is about to come out in a process-at-law. Some young laird, in Scotland, inherited, by the death of his father, a large place filled with valuable things – pictures, old china, etc., etc. His mother was still living, and had always lived, in this rich old house, in which she took pride and delight. After the death of her husband she was at first left unmolested there by her son, though there was a small dower-house (an inferior and contracted habitation) attached to the property in another part of the country. But the son married – married promptly and young – and went down with his wife to take possession – possession *exclusive*, of course – according to English custom. On doing so he found that pictures and other treasures were absent – and had been removed by his mother. He enquired, protested, made a row; in answer to which the mother sent demanding still other things, which had formed valuable and interesting features of the house during the years she had spent there. The son and his wife refuse, resist; the mother denounces, and (through litigation or otherwise), there is a hideous public quarrel and scandal. It has ended, my informant told me, in the mother – passionate, rebellious against her fate, resentful of the young wife and of the loss of her dignity and her home – resorting to <the> tremendous argument (though of no real *value* to her) of declaring that the young man is not the son of his putative father. She has been willing to dishonour herself to put an affront upon *him*. It is all rather sordid and fearfully ugly, but there is surely a story in it. It presents a very fine case of the situation in which, in England, there has *always* seemed to me to be a story – the situation of the mother *deposed*, by the ugly English custom, turned out of the big house on the son's marriage and relegated. One can imagine the rebellion, in this case (the case I should build on the above hint), of a particular sort of proud woman – a woman who had *loved* her home, her husband's home and hers (with a knowledge and adoration of artistic beauty, the tastes, the habits of a collector). There would be circumstances, details, intensifications, deepening it and darkening it all. There would be the particular type and taste of the wife the son would have chosen – a wife out of a Philistine, a tasteless, a hideous house; the kind of house the very walls and furniture of which constitute a kind of *anguish* for such a woman as I suppose the mother to be. That kind of anguish occurred to me, precisely, as a subject, during the 2 days I spent at Fox Warren (I didn't mean to write the name), a month or so ago. I thought of the strange, the terrible experience of a nature with a love and passion for beauty, united by adverse circumstances to such a family and domiciled in such a house. I imagine the young wife coming, precisely, out of it. I imagine the mother having fixed on a girl after her own heart for the son to marry; a girl with the same exquisite tastes that *she* has and having grown up surrounded with lovely things. The son doesn't in the least take to this girl – he perversely and stupidly, from the mother's point of view, takes to a girl infatuated with hideousness. It is in this girl's people's house, before the marriage, that the story opens. The mother meets there the other girl – the one that pleases her: the one with whom she discovers a community of taste – of passion, of sensibility and suffering.

May 13th, 1895. I have just promised Scudder 3 short stories for the *Atlantic*. I have a number of things noted here to choose from; but wish, in general, to remind myself that, more and more, every thing of this kind I do must be a complete and perfect little drama. The little idea must resolve itself into a little action, and the little action into the *essential* drama aforesaid. *Voilà*. It is the way – it is perhaps the only way – to make some masterpieces. It is at any rate what I want to do.

There comes back to me the memory of a little idea I took up a year or two ago to the extent of writing a few pages – pages which I have just rummaged out of my desk: the idea suggested to me by one Mrs. Anstruther-Thompson, whom I sat next to at a Xmas dinner at Lady Lindsay's. She told me an anecdote that I noted at the time, in another book (than this) and have just hunted up. Reading over my little statement I find the case vividly enough, though very briefly, presented, and I can probably go on with my beginning. What is wanting is a full roundness for the action – the completeness of the drama–quality. I see the action up to a certain point, but what can be the solution, the denouement? The action is the mother's refusal to give up the house, or the things. But that is, in itself, no conclusion, no climax. What is it that follows on that? (*May 15th, 1895*.) I seem to see the thing in three chapters, like 3 little acts, the 1st of which terminates with the son's marriage to one – the dreaded one – of the Brigstocks. In this 1st act Mrs. Gereth takes the girl – her own girl (Muriel Veetch) – to her own house and adopts her there, as it were, shows her its beauty. Her initiation – their relation. A scene with Albert there, before the marriage. Mrs. Gereth's threat of rupture if it takes place. She must have had a scene with Nora Brigstock at Waterbath – the scene that determines her. All this splendidly foreshortened, as it were; as the whole thing must be. Then, Act II, the little drama of Mrs. Gereth's attitude, her preparations to leave the house – her going over it in farewell; then her collapse, her inability to *s'en arracher* and surrender her treasures. Of course in Act I all due prominence given to the element of Albert's 'want of taste' – his terrible, fatal *penchant* to ugliness, the thing that has made his mother precisely *want* so to redeem him, to safeguard, by a union with such a girl as Muriel Veetch – and makes her feel that the union with a Brigstock precisely loses him forever. All this crystal-line in Act I. It surely gives me plenty of material for that act. Each act is 50 pages of my MS. Well then, in II, I give her collapse, her

216

refusal to surrender. But I must carry the action on a step, a stride *beyond* that, to get the climax of my Chapter II. What can this climax be? May it be some act or step on the part of the son – some resolution, some violence of his? And then the denouement, the solution, the climax that Chapter III leads up to, may that be something done by Muriel Veetch? I have a dim sense that the denouement must be *through* her. One thing strikes me as certain, that she must really be in love with Albert. The battle between Albert and his mother must be arrayed – and she in some way intervenes. His 'taking up the glove' ends Act II. Muriel takes the field in Act III – she interposes, she achieves. I seem vaguely to disembroil something like THIS: That Mrs. Gereth's *démarche* in II, the circumstance of her deciding to fight, is that she determines to have all the most precious things removed to the dower-house. She not only determines it – she *does* it. The element of her resentment at the way 'the mother' is treated in England is an active force in this. Perhaps she has a sister married in France – a silhouette, a thumbnail sketch chalked in – who sharpens the contrast and eggs her on. She *despoils* Umberleigh, or whatever the name is – she *skims* it, she strips it. She has everything that is really precious and exquisite carted away to her own house. *She does it in Muriel's absence* – while Muriel is away on a family errand (her dying father or something of that sort). She does it too without telling Albert of what she intends. He comes and finds it done – comes back from his wedding-tour – or from some later absence. This discovery, on his part, is the 'climax' of Chapter II. The mother and son are face to face in a 'row.' He threatens to prosecute – his wife eggs him on. Muriel's intervention takes the form of trying to avert all this hideousness, getting Mrs. Gereth to make the terrible concession and restore what she has taken away. She secretly loves the young man – that is why. She prevails, Mrs. Gereth has the things restored. The horrible, the atrocious conflagration – which may at any rate, I think, serve as my working hypothesis for a denouement.

Osborne Hotel, Torquay, August 11th, 1895.
Voyons un peu où j'en suis in the little story of the situation between the mother and the son, in the little tale I have called the *House Beautiful* and of which I have hammered out some 70 pp. of MS.

It is a question of a concision – for the rest of my 150 pp. in all, my rigid limit, for the *Atlantic* – truly masterly. Mona Brigstock and her mother are down at Poynton, brought by Owen Gereth, who considers that Mona shows to great advantage there and is having a great success. This infatuated density, this singleness and stupidity of perception, so often characteristic of the young Englishman in regard to the inferior woman, is the note of his attitude throughout. It makes Fleda wonder, marvel – and marvel without jealousy – see clearly how much more *doué* he is for marital than for filial affection. He cares, comparatively, nothing for his mother – would sacrifice her any day to his virtuous, Philistine, instinctive attachment to Mona. It is only *for* Mrs. Gereth that Fleda is, as it were, jealous; she says, in the face of Mona: 'Good heavens, if she were *my* mother, how common and stupid she would make, in comparison and contrast, such a girl as that, appear!' What I should like to do, God willing, is to thresh out my little remainder, from this point, tabulate and clarify it, state or summarize it in such a way that I can go, very straight and sharp, to my climax, my denouement. What I feel more and more that I must arrive at, with these things, is the adequate and regular practice of some such economy of clear summarization as will *give* me from point to point, each of my steps, stages, tints, shades, every main joint and hinge, in its place, of my subject – give me, in a word, my clear order and expressed sequence. I can then *take* from the table, successively, each fitted or fitting piece of my little mosaic. When I ask myself what there may have been to show for my long tribulation, my wasted years and patiences and pangs, of theatrical experiment, the answer, as I have already noted here, comes up as just possibly *this*: what I have gathered from it will perhaps have been exactly some such mastery of fundamental statement – of the art and secret of it, of expression, of the sacred mystery of structure. Oh yes – the weary, woeful time has done something for me, has had in the depths of all its wasted piety and passion, an intense little lesson and direction. What that resultant is I must now actively show.

What then is it that the rest of my little 2d act, as I call it, of *The House Beautiful* must do? Its climax is in the removal – *must absolutely and utterly be: voilà* – from the house, by Mrs. Gereth, of her own treasures. What are the steps that lead to that? Well, these.

1st. Owen must have a morsel with Fleda in which he shows how happy he is with the result of their visit, and which she doesn't retail to his mother.

2d. Mrs. G., the morning they go (the Brigstocks), does take the alarm, though Owen doesn't give her the news himself. He hasn't got it yet – Mona doesn't speak till they get back to town. But Mrs. Brigstock has spoken more or less, and Owen has shown, does show, to Mrs. Gereth, how pleased he is. There must be a scene of some sort between the young man and his mother – and between Mrs. G. and Mona. Yet surely all this must be very, *very*, VERY brief and rapid – for it is after all preliminary, and the centre of gravity of the piece, which is that Owen marries Mona, is in danger of being thrust much too far forward, out of its place. As it is I've almost no room at all for my people to talk. What I think I want to make take place between Mrs. Gereth and Owen and Mona is the striking utterance on her part of some note of warning – some expression to them of her own ground, of what she expects, how she feels. It must take place before Fleda. Make it, *n'est-ce pas?*, that the pieces follow each other in this order.

(a) Owen shows himself to his mother *and* Fleda in the morning; and Fleda, after a vision of what is going on between them, goes out, leaves them together. She goes out into the grounds and finds Mona there; ten words about what passes between the 2 women. They come in again, and then it is that Fleda has the sense of what Mrs. G. has said to Owen – has probably, dreadfully said – about *her.*

(b) The scene, for Mrs. G., before Owen and Fleda, with Mona – the scene that as Fleda feels, practically settles and clinches Mona. (It is Owen's own indications that have, after the night when they went downstairs, alarmed Mrs. G.) They depart, the ladies and Owen, leaving Mrs. G. under the impression that she has frightened them away. *But Fleda knows better* – though she pretends to agree. It is then – after they are gone – that Mrs. Gereth lets her know or suspect, to her horror, what she has already seemed to divine, to apprehend – that she *did* speak (while F. was in the garden with M.) about her, F., being *her* ideal for a daughter-in-law. This it is that makes F. doubly sure that the engagement to

Mona will now be precipitated. Owen comes down alone in a few days, in fact, to announce it. What action does his mother then take? There must be the scene, *before* Fleda, about her surrender of the house – the scene of her, Mrs. G.'s, waiting for him to say, passionately, grievingly giving him a chance to say, that she may stay, that feeling as she does, he won't turn her out – or even that he'll give her up some of the things. But he doesn't say it.

Rather, indeed, why may he *not* say this last? Doesn't his mother have, there, her long-smothered outbreak – flash about upon him about Mona's barbarism and the horrors of Waterbath? It's a dreadful, fatal scene: Fleda sees it or knows it. *Then* it is she has the scene with Owen that is to come after her knowing what his mother has said to him about her. It leads to the fact that Owen *does* offer to let his mother keep some of the things. Fleda puts in her own plea for this and makes her own reflection. Owen tells his mother, before he leaves, what he'll do. Before the marriage, however, he retracts – he lets her know that his wife has refused to part with anything. It was as he showed her Poynton, that day, that she wants to have it. It was the sight of it that day, that settled her. Therefore he must keep faith with her – and after all isn't he within his absolute rights? The marriage takes place – all in Act III. Fleda isn't present at it – the young couple go to Italy. But after she is settled in her own house Fleda goes down to see Mrs. Gereth. The 1st thing she perceives in her house – her little dower-cottage – are the things Mrs. G. has removed from Poynton. *Voilà.* That was to have been the climax of my 2d act, as it were; but I don't see how it *can* be, with any feasible adjustment to my space, if I try to make my 2d act one with my second chapter or section – my little 'II.' My only issue, here, is in multiplying, throughout the whole, my divisions.

Osborne Hotel, Torquay, September 8th, 1895.
I am face to face with several little alternatives of work, and am in fact in something of a predicament with things promised and retarded. I must thresh out my solutions, must settle down to my jobs. It's idiotic, by the way, to waste time in writing such a remark as that! As if I didn't feel in all such matters infinitely more than I can ever utter!

My immediate necessity is to tackle again the question of one of the little stories that I have promised to do for Scudder: the question round which, in general, as I have found before this, such tragic little accidents are apt to cluster. By tragic little accidents, I mean the tragic accident of the waste of labour to which I have often found myself condemned in trying to do the short (the really, I mean, the very short) thing. I am just crawling out of one of them, in this particular connection: the attempt, in *The House Beautiful*, to meet Scudder on the basis of 10,000 words – an attempt that has ended, irremissibly, incurably, in almost 30,000 – leaving on my hands a production that *he* doesn't want and that I must try to make terms for in some other way, terms bad, terms sadd<en>ing, at the best. Ah, but let me not go, here, into the question of the reason for which this larger manner now imposes itself upon me – as it has every right and power to do: reasons with which my spirit is sufficiently saturated! Suffice it that I'm simply face to face with the little question: '*Can* I do the thing in 10,000 words or can I not?' The answer to it is surely that I'm not prepared to say I can't. The difficulty has been, I think, when I've failed, that I haven't tried *right*. I've lost sight too much of the necessary smallness, necessary singleness of the subject. I've been too proud to take the very simple thing. I've almost always taken the thing requiring developments. Now, when I embark on developments I'm lost, for they are my temptation and my joy. I'm too afraid to be *banal*. I needn't be afraid, for my danger is small. I must try now, to do the thing of 10,000 words (which there is *every* economic reason for my recovering and holding fast the trick of). I must try it, I say, on the basis of rigid limitation of subject. That is, I must take, and take only, the single incident. I know what I mean by the single incident. *The Real Thing*, *The Middle Years*, *Brooksmith*, even, *The Private Life*, *Owen Wingrave*, are what I call single incidents. Many others are essentially ideas requiring development. *Cherchons, piochons, patientons – tenons-nous-en* to the opposite kind. Try to make use, for the brief treatment, of nothing, absolutely *nothing*, that isn't ONE, as it were – that doesn't begin and end in its little self.

Osborne Hotel, Torquay, October 15th, '95.
My little story has grown upon my hands – I am speaking of *The*

House Beautiful – and will make a thing of 30,000 words. But though I have been scared at the dimensions it was taking – scared in view of the meagerness of the little subject – yet I think I see the way to make it fill out its skin and be very fairly solid and fine.

Fleda Vetch is down at Ricks – has come down to find Mrs. Gereth installed and in possession of most of the treasures of Poynton. I did what I could yesterday to handle her arrival, but I must thresh out finely every inch of the action from that point to the end. The sense of what her friend has done quite appals the girl, and what has now passed between her and Owen prepares her for a great stir of feeling in his favour – a resentment on his behalf and pitying sense of his spoliations. I am here dealing with very delicate elements, and I must make the operation, the presentation, of each thoroughly sharp and clear. If this climax of my little tale is confused and *embrouillé* it will be nothing; if it's as crystalline as possible it will be worth doing. I have, a little, to guard myself against the drawback of having, in the course of the story deter-mined on something that I had not intended – or had not expected – at the start. I had intended to make Fleda 'fall in love' with Owen, or, to express it *moins banalement*, to represent her as loving him. But I had not intended to represent a feeling of this kind on Owen's part. Now, however, I have done so; in my last little go at the thing (which I have been able to do only so interruptedly), it inevitably took that turn and I must accept the idea and work it out. What I felt to be necessary, as the turn in question came, was that what should happen between Fleda and Owen Gereth should be something of a certain intensity. My idea was that it should be, whatever it is, determining for *her*; and it didn't seem to me that I could make it sufficiently intense and sufficiently determining without making it come, as it were, *from* Owen. *Je m'entends.* – Fleda suddenly perceives that on the verge of his marriage to Mona – he is, well, what I have in fact, represented. My present question – not to waste words about it – is as to what takes place between them when he comes down to Ricks. For I seem to see it so – that he does come down to Ricks. Mrs. Gereth must have achieved her devastation by a *coup de main* – proceeded with extraordinary celerity: this is made clear as between her and Fleda: the way she proceeded – got off in a night, as it were – is made perfectly distinct. Definite questions and answers about this. Fleda's night, after this, in the 'lovely' room Mrs. Gereth had arranged for her – her suffering under it, hatred of it, hatred of profiting by such things at Owen's cost, as it were. What has happened makes her think only of Owen. His marriage hasn't as yet taken place, but it's near at hand – it's there. She expects nothing more from him – has a dread of its happening. She wants only, as she believes, or tries to believe, never to see him again. She surrenders him to Mona. She has a dread of his not doing his duty – backing out in any way. That would fill her with horror and dismay. But she has no real doubt that he'll go through with his marriage. In going down to Ricks she has only seemed to herself to be going further away from him. She has had no prevision – she *could* have none – that he would turn up there. All she has wanted is to hear of his marriage. Touch the note that it has seemed to her even unduly delayed – delayed in a way to act on her nerves. She has got no invitation, but she hasn't expected that. The light on Mrs. Gereth's action, however, that she encounters at Ricks, changes the whole situation; causes her to hold her breath – making her not know exactly WHAT may happen. Now, *voyons un peu, mon bon*: the whole idea of my thing is that Fleda becomes rather fine, DOES something, distinguishes herself (to the reader), and that this is really almost all that has made the little anecdote worth telling at all. It gives me a lift – an air – and I must make it give me as much of these things as it ever possibly can. But I am confronted with a little difficulty which requires my looking it as coolly and calmly as I can in the face and figuring it out. What I have seen Fleda do is operate successfully (to state it as broadly as possible), to the end that the things be mainly sent back to Poynton. Now there are 2 necessary facts in regard to this. One is that a certain event, or certain events, certain forces, *lead up* to it, with their irresistible pressure on the girl. The other resides in the particular way in which she responds to that pressure. She gets the things back. *How* does she get them back? My idea had been that she successfully persuades Mrs. Gereth to send them. That seemed possible and adequate so long as my thought was simply that she had a senti-ment for Owen: it seemed in the key of that little suppressed emotion. But now that the emotion is developed more and Owen himself is made, as it were, active, I feel as if I wanted something more – I don't know what to call it except *dramatic*. Let me make out first, however, exactly what precedes, and then I shall see my way a little more into what follows. Owen is brought down to Ricks by his discovery of the spoliation of Poynton. He has gone over, after his mother's departure, and taken in the scene. He has notified Mona, and Mona has then come over with him and seen for herself, and the upshot has been that – having had the matter out between them – he has come down to his mother to demand a surrender. I must *motiver* his coming – his coming in person. Mona has wanted him to communicate only through their solicitor. He won't do that – he will be more tender: but Fleda sees that he takes his own way first because Mona has been strenuous about hers. I must represent Owen as not coming down with a preoccupation about Fleda: he doesn't know she's there – he thinks she in fact isn't. He has come because he simply *has* to. The reason WHY he simply has to, comes out in what takes place between him and Fleda. His mother refuses to see him – he is over at the inn. She makes Fleda see him for her. This takes place the day after Fleda's arrival. The girl thinks of refusing – then she consents. She has tried to refuse – for the trouble and torment the thing inflicts upon her – and because she has made it her rule, now, not to meet him, not to 'encourage' him, not to let herself go to this 'lawless love.' It seems to me I have really here the elements of something rather fine. The fineness is the fineness of Fleda. Let me carry that as far as possible – be consistent and bold and high about it: allow it all its little touch of poetry. She is forced again, as it were, by Mrs. Gereth, to renew a relation that she has sought safety and honour, tried to be 'good,' in *not* keeping up. She is almost, as it were, thrown into Owen's arms. It is the same with the young man. He *too* has tried to be good. *He* has renounced the relation. He has determined to stick to Mona. He is thrust by his mother into danger again. Mrs. Gereth is operating with so much more inflammable material than she knows. The young people meet at first as if that scene in Kensington Gdns. hadn't occurred; and Fleda says to herself that he repents of it, is ashamed of it. But they get into deeper waters. He informs her of the *sommation* he bears to his mother. Then briefly, quickly, *de fil en aiguille*, they come to the question of his alternative – his alternative or contemplated course if Mrs. Gereth refuses. Owen lets her know – practically

224

what it is. It is Mona who now determines it. Mona has insisted on his *insisting* – and if he doesn't insist she will break off their marriage. She has made it a *condition* of their marriage. This is the climax of the 'scene' between the 2. It helps to constitute whatever beauty I may put into the thing. It is Fleda's opportunity – Fleda's temptation. If Mrs. Gereth doesn't surrender Mona will break, and if Mona breaks – *her* opening seems to lie there before her. Well – it's a part of what the girl does that she *resists*. She *sees* this, yet she does her best, heroically, to shut her eyes to it. She sees that Owen is ashamed of his disloyalty to Mona, and she has such a feeling about him that she doesn't want, she can't bear, to see him disloyal. That's about the gist of it. If I want *beauty* for her – beauty of action and poetry of effect, I can only, I think, find it just there; find it in making her heroic. To *be* heroic, to achieve beauty and poetry, she must conceal from him what she feels. I have it then that he shows, but that she doesn't. What's the matter with Owen is that he has never known a girl like her, and that it's a girl like her he wants. She reads it all for him and in him, and we see it as she sees it, without his telling, his coming out with it. It's all on *his* part inarticulate and clumsy; but we *see* – though she doesn't let him give Mona away. What does she do then? – how does she work, how does she achieve her heroism? She does it in the first and highest way by urging him on to his marriage – putting it before him that it must take place without a week's more delay. She settles this, as it were – she fixes it: she says *she'll* take care of the rest. It's the question of *how* she takes care of it that is the tight knot of my *donnée*. She sends Owen off, sends him back to Mona, answers to him for it that what they demand shall be done. At least, rather (for she can't of course really 'answer'), she gives him her word that she will do her utmost to bring the restitution about; and it's on this he leaves her, promising her, as it were, to get married immediately. That confronts me with the question of the action Fleda exercises on Mrs. Gereth and of how she exercises it. My old idea was that she worked, as it were, on her feelings. Well, eureka! I think I have found it – I think I see the little interesting turn and the little practicable form. How a little click of perception, of this sort, brings back to me all the strange sacred time of my thinkings-out, this way, pen in hand, of the stuff of my little theatrical trials. The old patiences and intensities

– the working of the old passion. The old problems and dimnesses – the old solutions and little findings of light. Is the beauty of all that effort – of all those unutterable hours – lost forever? Lost, lost, lost? It will take a greater patience than all the others to see! – My new little notion was to represent Fleda as committing – for drama's sake – some broad effective stroke of her own. But that now looks to me like a mistake: I've got hold, very possibly, of the tail of the right thing. Isn't the right thing to make Fleda simply work upon Mrs. Gereth, but work in an interesting way? She proceeds to the execution of Owen's commission *auprès de sa mère*, but she is conscious that she can proceed to it only by an appeal. *She* has no idea of there being anything else she can do. She appeals therefore, frankly, strongly – has the most strenuous and *equal* sort of scene with her friend that she has ever had. She places her behaviour in the light of honour, duty, etc. – of the failure of Owen's contract with Mona, which was to give her the house as Mona came down that day and saw it. She produces an impression – she shakes and influences Mrs. Gereth; but it isn't from the point of view of these special arguments that she uses. It's by the very fact of her urgency, the very accent of her earnestness, of her hidden passion. Mrs. Gereth guesses that hidden passion, and by this she's affected – she throws herself into the possibility. She pricks up her ears – she stares – she exclaims: she suddenly breaks out and charges the girl with the sentiment which is her motive, the sentiment that she has divined in her. Fleda, taken aback at first, upset, bewildered, sees in a moment the chance (towards her ideal end) that it will give her to admit to Mrs. Gereth the truth. She admits then – but admits nothing else; nothing of what has supremely passed between Owen and herself. There must be an absolute definiteness about what *has* passed: the promise, as it were, in exchange for *her* promise to act, that Owen has made her to go and get married. There must have been an opening here for the question of date, of postponement. Owen tells Fleda, in their interview, that Mona has postponed, so as to give him time to act and his mother time to restitute. (The *original* date of the marriage was otherwise close at hand.) Fleda makes Owen PROMISE to make Mona fix a day – make it by telling her that she (Fleda) undertakes for what Mrs. Gereth will do, and that she (Fleda) desires him to inform her to that effect. This constitutes a definite

226

transaction between him and Fleda. It is on this transaction that the girl, to Mrs. Gereth, observes a studied silence. (Fleda, by the way, has coerced Owen into this agreement, or transaction, as I call it, by being in possession – entering into possession – of his secret, as it were, without having surrendered to him her own. This secret of his change about Mona is *used* by her in her 'heroism.') She not only keeps Mrs. Gereth off the scent of finding out, of perceiving or inferring, Owen's condition, but she tells a virtuous, 'heroic' *lie* on the subject. 'Does he know?' 'Thank God, no!' Fleda can say that with truth; but when – at some turn of her investigation – Mrs. Gereth has a gleam of wonder sufficient to make her say: 'Can it be possible he doesn't feel as he did about Mona – that he likes *you*?,' Fleda emphatically denies this. But Mrs. Gereth insists. 'He has not said a word to you that could give colour to such a possibility?' 'He has not said a word to me.' *Reste* the question of the postponement. She learns, Mrs. G., that the wedding *is* postponed. It is really postponed to give her time to send back the furniture; but Fleda doesn't tell her this. She doesn't tell her of Mona's condition, as communicated by Owen; for in her appeal to her she has not put it on that ground – she has put <it> on the ground of Owen's honour, etc. But she *works*, as it were, the fact of the postponement – allows Mrs. Gereth to see a reason, an encouragement and hope in it. 'If he *should* break with her – *should* ask you to marry him, would you take him?'

'I'd take him,' says Fleda, profoundly. After this they *still* don't hear of the marriage. This determines Mrs. Gereth and she takes action in consequence. She sends back all but a few things – sends them all back and goes *abroad*.

From the point I have reached (Oct. 16th) it must all be an absolute and unmitigated *action*. I have in VII Fleda's impression of the situation at Ricks. This must go to p. 210 of MS. – to Owen's arrival and include what passes between the 2 women on the subject of it.

VIII–p. 211–240. The 'Scene' at Ricks between Fleda and Owen, including the latter's departure.

IX – p. 241–271; the whole business of the Restitution, between Mrs. Gereth and Fleda, including the former's decision.

February 13th, '96. I am pressingly face to face with the FINISH, for the *Atlantic*, of *The Old Things*, as the *House Beautiful* seems now destined, better, to be called. I must cipher out here, to the last fraction, my last chapters and pages. As usual I am crowded – my first two-thirds are too developed: my third third bursts my space or is well nigh squeezed and mutilated to death in it. But that is my problem. Let me state first, broadly, what I have now to show. The crude *essence* of what I have to show is this: that Mrs. Gereth sends back the things, that the marriage of Owen and Mona then takes place and that after the treasures are triumphantly relodged at Poynton the house takes fire and burns down before Fleda's eyes. Those are the bare facts. *Voyons un peu les détails.* Mrs. Gereth surrenders the things partly because she believes – has reason to – that Fleda will eventually come into them. But that calculation won't – doesn't – appear a sufficient motive: she must have another to strengthen it. She surrenders them therefore, furthermore, because she appears to see that the knowledge of their being back again at Poynton, as an incentive, a heritage, a reward, a future (settled there again immutably, this time), will operate to make Fleda do what she has so passionately appealed to her to do – get Mona away from Owen. She, Mrs. G., is seeing if Mona WON'T break. She does at first what the end of x shows her as doing – she keeps on the things as she threatens. XI must begin, I think, this way. It is that same evening.

> FLEDA: 'Well, then what answer am I to write Mr. Owen?'
> MRS. G.: 'Write him to come up to town to meet you there.'
> FLEDA: 'For what purpose?'
> MRS. GERETH: 'For any purpose you like!'

She sets the girl on him – cynically, almost, or indecently (making her feel AGAIN how little account – in the way of fine respect – she makes of her. Touch *that*, Mrs. G.'s unconscious brutality and immorality, briefly and finely). She presses Fleda – yes – upon him: would ALMOST like her, in London, to give herself up to him. She has a vision of a day with him there as 'fetching' him – IN SPITE of Fleda's fine fit about the young man's not caring for her. *She'll* see, Mrs. G. will, if he won't care. The very *essence* of this turn of the story is that the escape of the girl's 'secret,' the revelation to Mrs. G. that she loves Owen, completely alters (in a manner still for the better – as regards at least the mother's attitude) the relations of the two women. It develops them further – develops Mrs. Gereth's feeling *for* Fleda – though not Fleda's (with all her dimnesses and delicacies) for her pushing, urging, overwhelming, hinting, suggesting friend. It is on this basis of her 'love' that Mrs. G. now extravagantly handles her. She is free with her on it, bold, frank, urgent, humorous, cynical with her on it, beyond what Fleda's fineness enjoys. She alludes perpetually, wonderingly, *admiringly* to it – all the while – attributing to her a FIERCER kind of sentiment (judging by herself) than Fleda's sacrificial exaltation really *is* – making her wince and draw back in this flood of familiarity. At the same time I catch for her, here, in this connection – ADMIRABLY, I think – a prime element of my denouement. Fleda is left 'sick' at the end of x by her companion's threatened postponement of the surrender – but that only spurs her to renewed, to confirmed, action and endeavour. It is an *idée fixe* with her that she shall serve Owen – bring about the disgorgement. She becomes hereby capable of lending herself *in appearance* to Mrs. G.'s inflamed view of her possible effect on Owen and routing of Mona. The thing she still cherishes is Owen's secret (his shy, barely revealed feeling for her); everything else has been blown upon and she is willing to accept that condition of things and *use* it as far as she can. What I see is, here, that she MUST have one more personal meeting with Owen. It is the last time she sees him. She must go up to town – with a 'subtle' appearance of profiting by Mrs. Gereth's directions and injunctions and suggestions – she must go up to town and have, somehow and somewhere, an hour with him. Say at her father's in West Kensington. I just suggest to myself that. If I can from this point on only clarify this to the SCENIC intensity, brevity, beauty – make it march as straight as a pure little dramatic action – I shall, I think, really score. What Fleda writes to Owen after that opening bit of dialogue with Mrs. G. is that, 1st, he is to hold on, that it's difficult, but that she is helping him; and that 2d, she will come and meet him in town. It comes to me that her meeting with him in town must be *une scène de passion* – yes, I must give my readers that. Don't I get a glimpse, this way, of the real and innermost mechanism of my end? Fleda breaks down – lets Owen see she loves him. It is all *covert* – and delicate and exquisite: she adjures him to do his literal duty to Mona. They arrive at some definite and sincere agreement about this. That is the ground, the *fond*, the deep ground TONE of their scene. It must be for MONA to break – only for Mona. *He* mustn't – by all that's honourable – do it if she *doesn't*. He agrees to this – he sees it, feels it, understands it, gives her his word on it.

'But she WILL break if mamma doesn't send back the things. Therefore she mustn't NOW,' says Owen. Fleda's *aveu* has changed all.

'You mustn't say that – you mustn't. You so must do your part – impeccably. I've worked your mother up to it.'

'Very good – leave it so. But she won't – she WON'T!' says Owen jubilantly.

What I have my glimpse of as my *right* issue is that even while they are talking, as it were, Mrs. Gereth DOES. She does it because, 1st: she has a visit from Mrs. Brigstock in which she reads a virtual revelation that the marriage is off; and 2d: she does it to fetch Fleda. To make these things possible I must represent the meeting between Owen and Fleda as an incident of an ABSENCE that Fleda makes from Ricks. She goes up to town for a week – goes to her father, goes to escape Mrs. G.'s hounding on, AND to prove to Mrs. G. that she *will* go at Owen in the sense *she* (Mrs. G.) pleads for. So I have roughly something like this.

XI. The new situation at Ricks between the 2 women, on the basis of Fleda's *aveu*. Fleda's attitude on this new footing, and the letter she 1st writes to Owen. It tells him to hold on: she is serving him – it is difficult – he must be patient. She *1st declines* Mrs. G.'s suggestion about meeting him – then at last (after a *fortnight* [?]) she turns, changes, can't stand it at Ricks, pleads that she must go up to town. She goes with Mrs. G.'s high approbation. What Mrs. G. sees in it.

XII. Her meeting with Owen in town.

XIII. Her meeting, their meeting, with Mrs. B.

XIV. Her return to Ricks to find everything gone. The last have just left. Mrs. Gereth has ACTED. She shows WHY. Fleda is partly prepared. There has appeared that a.m. in the *Morning Post* an announcement that the marriage, etc., will not take place. Then she describes Mrs. B.'s visit – a stupid frightened visit – *to complain of Fleda*. For it comes to me that they must have had in London – Owen and Fleda – an encounter with Mrs. B. SHE COMES TO SEE

FLEDA – for news of Mrs. G.'s intentions and she finds Owen there. As an old acquaintance – her hostess, in Chap. I, at Waterbath, she knows her whereabouts or address. Yes – SHE COMES TO COMPLAIN. That encourages and determines Mrs. G. – she will, I have said, make it sure, 'fetch' Fleda and act on her. There she is – in the nudity of Ricks; but the news in the *Morning Post* rejoices her; and though Fleda, NOW THAT THE THINGS ARE GONE BACK, practically has her doubts and fears (*which she doesn't communicate*) the two women have together, an hour, a week of happiness and hope, *vis-à-vis* of the future. FLEDA MUST NOW HAVE LET OUT OWEN'S SECRET.

XV. The news that the marriage has taken place. This must (with other indispensable things) be a chapter by itself. They wait – the 2 women, first – for Owen to come down – almost immediately to propose for Fleda. The situation altered again – by a further shift – (I mean by Fleda's *aveu*, now, of Owen's 'caring for her') in a degree equivalent to that in which it has been altered *in x* by her *aveu* of her caring for him. They wait, they wait. Fleda tells Mrs. G. of Owen's offer to her of something from Poynton – anything: any small thing she can pick out. She rejoices: she says there is something at Ricks – the Maltese Cross. She will have THAT. (*It occurs to me that she had better not go back to Ricks – but that Mrs. G. comes up to town. The house is despoiled – the packers have been at it. Fleda has been on the* POINT *of going when she arrives. She learns from her that everything has gone – including the Maltese Cross. She arrives the evening of the day the M.P. gives the news of the rupture. She stays at an hotel. Owen is at Poynton.*) It is thus in London that the news comes to them together of the marriage HAVING taken place. It comes at the end of about 10 days. Mrs. G. then (her *state*, just Heaven, her condition) determines to go abroad. But she hears the young couple are going. LAST CHAPTER. – Fleda goes down to rescue the Maltese Cross and finds the house in flames – or already burnt down to the ground.

February 19th, 1896.
I shall push (*D. V.*) bravely through *The Old Things*; but I must, a little, look into the matter of Fleda's second meeting with Owen in London, and Mrs. Brigstock's finding them together. *Il me faut en tirer* everything – especially in the way of beauty – it can possibly

give. It *can* give, surely, some little *scène de passion*; but I want also, from this point on, the whole thing closely and admirably *mouvementé*. It must be unmitigatedly objective narration – unarrested drama. It must be in a word a close little march of cause and effect. Fleda is a week in London without anything happ<en>ing. Then Owen comes to West Kensington. He comes because his mother has let him know she is there. Fleda immediately challenges him – and he gives her that reason. His mother has written to him that Fleda has come up and has something to ask him on her behalf. He tells Fleda this. He has come to see *what* she has to ask him. She, painfully disconcerted, thinks Mrs. G. has been capable of meaning that she (Fleda) shall communicate to Owen *her* (Mrs. G.'s) idea. She is revolted – but Owen gives her a clue – in *his* having, as he shows, taken for granted what his mother *does* mean by Fleda's errand. Fleda actively CHALLENGES him on this – finds out instantly, before she lets him go further, as it were, what he has thus assumed – assures herself in other words that what she has *first* feared is NOT the case – that Mrs. Gereth has not put him up to the idea that she is in love with him. She actually cross-questions him about this; and his answers show – clearly enough – that Mrs. G. has *not* gone so far – that she has been still AFRAID to. Fleda *breathes*, at this – feels more free to receive him. Then *his* communicated vision of what his mother HAS *entendu* by her message gives her the cue for a basis to let him stay a little without her giving herself away by *emotion* of any sort. WHAT Owen has assumed is that his mother has commissioned her to ask him, for her, whether if she engages to send back the things he will break with Mona – on the basis that Mona's delay, Mona's WAITING, seems obviously to have suggested the reality of. Besides, nothing is more natural than that he should *rush* to Fleda for more news than her note and her silence have given, of *où ils en sont, tous*, in the interminable transactions – of *où il en est, lui*, as to what he may really hope. She has been 'working for him,' she has said: 'Well then, has nothing at all been done?' His mother's note has sent him to Fleda to hear what *has* been done. It is of the essence – or at least of the necessity – of this scene, that Fleda shall with real directness question him. She didn't talk of Mona before – she talks of her NOW. She questions him straight – as he questions her. He asks her what has happened, on her side, since their hour together at Ricks – she asks him what has happened on *his*. What does Owen tell her? – Her questions must DRAW OUT what he tells her. He must be categoric. So, on *her* side, to meet and satisfy *him*, HER information must be. What *has* he, then, to tell her? What has she to tell *him*? He has to tell her that they are still waiting – that Mona is – and he must speak of that young woman more plainly, as it were, than Fleda has let him do at Ricks. He must speak very plainly indeed. He must tell the extreme and, to him, humiliating tension of the things not coming. AT THE SAME TIME HE MUST let her know that if they DON'T come he is free, he is hers. He must tell her that he hasn't seen Mona for a fortnight – but that he has had to describe to her – *had* described to her fully his scene with Fleda at Ricks, every detail of that visit. Mona knows therefore that he is dealing with Fleda – that Fleda has absolute *charge* of their affairs. This knowledge is part of the tension – of his present trouble and embarrassment and worry. He *must* tell her all – he *tells* her all, every scrap. I mustn't interrupt it too much with elucidations or it will be interminable. IT MUST BE AS STRAIGHT AS A PLAY – that is the only way to do. Ah, *mon bon*, make *this*, *here*, justify, crown, in its little degree, the long years and pains, the acquired mastery of scenic presentation. What I am looking for is my joint, my hinge, for making the scene between them pass, at a given point, into passion, into pain, into their facing together the truth. Some point that it logically reaches must DETERMINE the passage. I want to give Fleda her little hour. She can only *get* it if Owen fully comes out. Owen can only fully come out if he sees what is really in her. He must offer to give up Mona for her – and she must utterly refuse that. What her response IS is that she will take him if Mona really breaks. Yes, here I get my evolution don't I? – an understanding between them dependent on the things not coming. The difference is now, with the other scene (at Ricks), that they are *really* – morally – face to face and that they *speak* of it all. But *voyons, voyons*, I must be utterly crystalline and complete, and my *charpente* must be of steel. What must be thrown up to the surface is the coming back, through Owen, of Mrs. Gereth's OFFER of Fleda at Poynton. Owen has understood it since – *lived* on it – and it all is *in* him now. Thus it is a prime necessity that Mrs. G.'s attitude shall be absolutely – NOW – recognized between them. Owen must KNOW, from Fleda

– must get it out of her, that his mother WILL absolutely surrender if he'll marry Fleda. Now it comes to me, in connection and accordance with this, that I must separate this London episode into 2 chapters, 2 occasions: making the 1st culminate in the arrival of Mrs. Brigstock at West Kensington. She then and there takes Owen away with her. She has come to get information and satisfaction from Fleda. She knows what Mona knows – that Fleda has charge of Owen's case *auprès de sa mère*. Owen, moreover, must have told Fleda that he has told Mona (by letter) of his having learned from Mrs. G. that she, Fleda, is in town. This is how Mrs. Brigstock knows it. She has more faith in the girl than her daughter has; and she comes to say: 'Do you realise this hideous deadlock?' Then she finds her daughter's worst suspicions and her jealousies confirmed, by what she seems to have surprised between the young couple upon whom she comes in. Owen must have told Fleda definitely that Mona is jealous. That is the prompt hinge or joint of his fuller frankness. But what I want to mark just here is the evolution of the second chapter of the pair. *This* is the chapter of passion – determined by Mrs. B.'s intervention. She has made him a scene of jealousy. By the chapter of 'passion' I mean the scene of Fleda's *aveux*. I don't see what it can do but take place the next day. Owen comes back to tell her what has happened between Mrs. Brigstock and himself. HE DOESN'T KNOW *she has made* up her mind to go straight down to Ricks. What overwhelms me, however, is the reflection that I have almost no space. FORTY PAGES of small (my smallest) penmanship (like this) must do it all. There can be almost no dialogue at all. This is an iron law. It is absolute. I can squeeze *what* I can into 40 pp.; but I can't have a line more. Therefore in XIII, at least, it must be pure, dense, summarized narration. How can I bring in Mrs. Brigstock, in the tiny space, if it isn't? But above all what I must fix is what is the basis of emotion on which the 2d meeting between Owen and Fleda takes place? They feel that the situation has altered by Mrs. B.'s intervention. MONA WILL BREAK. Fleda surrenders herself – she tells him that she will marry him if Mona does break. On this they get their little duet. It is their hour of illusion – it is their fool's paradise. But it is indispensable to make clear that Fleda won't listen to anything but freedom by Mona's rupture; and therefore to have made clear antecedently exactly what Mona's actual attitude IS – at the point the affair has reached. Mona – *voyons* – must have given an *ultimatum* – a date: if the things are not sent back by such and such a day she *will* break. This day is near at hand. Mrs. Brigstock has been ANGRY – therefore she will be angering Mona by the description of how she found the pair together in West Kensington. Fleda's *aveux* are all qualified – saddened and refined, and made *beautiful*, by the sense of the IMPOSSIBLE – the sense of the infinite improbability of Mona's not really hanging on – and by the perfectly firm and definite ground she takes on the absolute demand of Owen's honour that he shall go on with Mona if she DOESN'T break.

March 30th, 1896.
I am face to face now with my last part of *The Old Things*, and I must (*D. V.*) put it through with the aid of every drop that can be squeezed from it. It will take 10 days of real application – and then I shall have to get straight at the 65,000 for Clement Shorter.

What I have, here, is that, in XVIII, Fleda perceives what it is that Mrs. Gereth has done and why she has done it: the full proportions of the bribe, the bid, the pressure of her friend's confidence. I must do it all in 3 chapters of 35 pages each. In XVIII the impression on Fleda, the overwhelmedness, the sense that everything is lost, and her confession of everything to Mrs. Gereth – their complete intimacy and exchange of all emotion and explanation over the matter. I see the whole instalment as *between* them – but this chapter as especially between them. They have it out together as it were – they are more face to face than they have ever been. What they are together, face to face with, is the question of what Owen will have done – Fleda lets Mrs. Gereth see that *she* believes it's too late, believes that Mona holds him. Mrs. Gereth denounces him with passion – denounces him for a milksop and a muff, declares that he's less than a man and that she's horribly ashamed of him. Fleda defends him, and the chapter (18) which ought, after all, to be of 3000 words at most, terminates on their suspense. What I am asking myself is whether I bring back Owen at all. I am not well this a.m. and still shaky from a sick cold, a small assault of influenza; though convalescent, I'm not quite in my *assiette* and must puzzle my little problem out here with a mild patience and a considerable imperfection. But patience and courage – through endless small botherations and interruptions – will see me through – and I have only to *me cramponner* – and add word to word. *Se cramponner* and add word to word, is the endless and eternal receipt. *Owen is married* – that's what has happened; that is what I have to deal with in 19 and 20. HOW do I deal with it? How is the revelation made to the 2 women? It seems to me indispensable that OWEN should NOT come back. That's impossible – absolutely, and gives me ½ a dozen impossibilities and *gaucheries* of every kind. The whole thing *must* be between the two women, and the little problem of art is, finely, inspiringly, keeping it between them, to make it palpitate, make it close and dramatic and full to the very end. Little by little, as I press, as I ponder, it seems to come to me, the manner of my denouement – it seems to fall into its proportions and to *compose*. I see *4* little chapters, rather, of *25* pages each. I think, at any rate, I see Fleda return to Maggie's at the end of XVIII. There, after 2 or 3 days, Mrs. Gereth comes to her. Yes, Mrs. Gereth must *see* her there. This gives me the manner of my revelation to Fleda – it is Mrs. Gereth who makes it. Mrs. Gereth has had it herself from Owen: HE HAS COME TO HER IN TOWN TO THANK HER FOR WHAT SHE HAS DONE: he has been at Poynton and seen the things restored. Yes, that is it. That has clinched Mona, and they have been married at the registrar's on the spot. This scene of reproduction of these occurrences takes place between Mrs. G. and Fleda at Maggie's.

NOTES

PREFACE

1. p. 23 *the prick of some sharp point.* An excellent example of James's topicality. Louis Pasteur's successful vaccination of a child against hydrophobia in 1885 had revived medical interest in the technique: in 1889 there had been set up an English Royal Commission on vaccination, which reported regularly on its findings in a series of Blue Books.
2. p. 23 *the virus.* The existence of submicroscopic infectious agents had been demonstrated in 1892 by the Russian botanist Ivanovski.
3. p. 27 *Balzac.* Honoré de Balzac (1799–1850), the French realist novelist, who was admired, and sometimes imitated, by James.
4. p. 27 *two members of which had appeared.* James's memory seems to be playing him false here. According to Edel's *Bibliography*, his most recent publications in the *Atlantic Monthly* had been 'Glasses' (February 1896), 'The Private Life' (April 1892), 'The Chaperon' (November–December 1891), and 'The Marriages' (August 1891). Neither the chronology nor the subject-matter of these stories seems to fit this description of a trio.
5. p. 29 *the prize of battle.* Metaphorical allusions to warfare, of which of course the word 'spoils' itself is the most important, run throughout the novel.
6. p. 29 *brazen idols.* References to religious worship are also frequent in this novel (and, indeed, in other novels of James, for example *The Awkward Age* and *The Wings of the Dove*).
7. p. 29 *the muse of 'dialogue'.* In Greek mythology the nine muses were the patron goddesses of the arts.
8. p. 30 *Helen of Troy.* In Greek mythology, she was the most beautiful woman in the world, whose abduction by Paris initiated the Trojan War.

9. p. 31 *the surrounding tangle*. The theme of the tangle, the tapestry or the embroidery, also runs through the novel, and will find its culmination on p. 186, where Fleda accuses Mrs Gereth of slashing through the tangle of life 'with a great pair of shears'.

10. p. 32 *the full thick wash of the penumbra*. James, who had a talent for art criticism, liked to compare his technique to that of the painter or, as here, the water-colourist.

11. p. 33 *fine paste*. The 'paste' referred to here is that used in making porcelain. Note how the metaphors in this part of the Preface are connected with the 'things' themselves.

12. p. 33 *the web she seeks to weave*. The original Preface continues for another eight pages on the subject of the other two stories in the volume.

CHAPTER I

1. p. 35 *endimanchée*. Dressed in her Sunday best.

2. p. 36 *spells*. A hint that Mrs Gereth may be something of a wicked witch.

3. p. 36 *Vetches*. A vetch is a weak-stemmed plant which depends for its support – as Fleda does – on others.

CHAPTER II

1. p. 41 *Cadogan Place*. A square in the SW1 district. Interestingly, James tends to use genuine locations for the London homes of his well-to-do characters, and invented ones for those of the less prosperous. (See note to p. 137.)

2. p. 41 *Jacobean*. Belonging to the reign of James I (1603–25). The comparative political stability of the period and the general increase in wealth encouraged innovation in architecture, and the adoption of a modified Renaissance style. James I's mother was Mary Queen of Scots, whose execution in 1587 he seems to have accepted without protest for the sake of his own political advantage. There are parallels here with the relationship between Owen Gereth and his mother. See *The Portrait of a Lady* (1881) for a similar significance in the dating of the Touchett family home.

3. p. 42 *demons of Jews*. Mrs Gereth's anti-semitism may jar on the modern reader, but was probably taken for granted by James's contemporaries.

4. p. 42 *impressionist painter*. The late nineteenth-century French impressionist painters aroused much hostility from both public and critics, and were not really 'accepted' until the 1930s. Perhaps James is trying to hint that, although Fleda has a feeling for Mrs Gereth's old treasures, she is not as exclusively dedicated to the works of the past as her benefactress.

5. p. 45 *they would neglect them, ignore them, leave them to clumsy servants.* A premonition of the final disaster.

CHAPTER III

1. p. 48 *Louis Quinze*. The furniture of the reign of Louis XV of France (1710–74) is characterized by its delicacy and the rococo style of its decoration.

2. p. 48 *jolly*. James prided himself on his knowledge of contemporary idiom: this was definitely one of the vogue words of the period.

3. p. 49 *linen shrouds*. Although on one level this simply means the coverings which were commonly used to protect fine furniture in rooms not currently in use, there is nevertheless an air of foreboding in the use of the word 'shrouds'.

4. p. 49 *'Things' were of course the sum of the world.* James's irony here is obvious. His own attitude is more akin to that of Henry James Senior as expressed in 'Socialism and Civilisation': 'We degrade by owning and just in the degree of our owning . . . We degrade and disesteem every person we own absolutely, every person bound to us by any other tenure than his own spontaneous affection.'

5. p. 50 *keeping her mouth shut in a railway tunnel.* In the days of steam-driven coal-fired trains the effect of a train entering a tunnel was to fill the carriages with smoke. Usually, however, someone would have the presence of mind to close the window promptly.

6. p. 51 *a 'lady's magazine'*. This was the great heyday of women's magazine publishing: forty-eight new titles were launched between 1880 and 1900, so that it has not been possible to identify this particular one, though it *could* be *Madame* (1895).

7. p. 51 *antimacassars*. This was the age when men wore macassar oil as a hair dressing, and the oil tended to rub off on upholstery. Antimacassars – protective cloths, often embroidered

or decorated with drawn-thread work – are still sometimes draped over the backs of armchairs and sofas.

8. p. 51 *a silken thread*. This reminds us not only of the tangle/embroidery theme, but also of the story of Ariadne, in Greek mythology, who gave her lover Theseus a ball of thread, one end of which she kept hold of, so that he could find his way through the maze and kill the Minotaur. Ariadne was later abandoned by Theseus in favour of her sister Phaedra, as Fleda will be abandoned in favour of Mona.

9. p. 52 *shop*. In the slang of the period, this meant 'place'.

10. p. 54 *Don Quixote*. The hero of Cervantes' romance of the same name (1605), who misguidedly tries to behave like the great chivalrous knights of the past. In one episode he attacks a group of windmills, believing them to be giants.

CHAPTER IV

1. p. 56 *the 'Stores'*. The Army & Navy Stores in London (established 1871). Like many of the great department stores founded at this period, it catered primarily for the expanding middle and professional classes.

2. p. 56 *the underside of plates*. So that she could examine the manufacturer's marks.

3. p. 56 *'fetch' her*. Attract her. The expression is used again on p. 178.

4. p. 57 *n'en parlons plus*. Let's say no more about it.

5. p. 57 *had tossed the periodical*. This is reminiscent of the episode in Thackeray's *Vanity Fair* (1847–8), where Becky Sharp, on her last day at school, throws her leaving-prize, a dictionary, out of the carriage window as she drives away.

6. p. 60 *barbarian*. Originally, a Barbarian was one who lived outside the Roman empire: by extension, an uncivilized and uncultivated person. In Matthew Arnold's *Culture and Anarchy* (1869) the term is associated with the English upper classes and their preoccupation with athletic prowess.

CHAPTER V

1. p. 66 *a tenant on the property*. Large landed estates would consist not only of the great house and its surrounding gardens or parkland, but also of a number of farms which were let out to

tenant farmers. The rent from these would provide an income for the landowner and for the upkeep of the estate.

2. p. 67 *Liverpool Street*. One of several London railway stations mentioned in this novel. Liverpool Street serves the eastern part of England.

3. p. 67 *the single plate*. This is a sash window (as opposed to the older form of the casement window, which opened outwards), in widespread use in the late eighteenth and the nineteenth centuries. It is composed in fact of two plates, one sliding up and the other down.

4. p. 68 *a big square beam papered over in white*. The modern conservationist would probably shudder at this. We already know that there is no pasted paper at Poynton, which would account for Fleda's hesitation in praising it to Mrs Gereth.

CHAPTER VI

1. p. 72 *leather-legged*. Wearing leather leggings or leather boots.

2. p. 73 *West Kensington*. The area between Kensington and Hammersmith, which was not considered a fashionable place to live. Although only three or four miles from Marble Arch, on p. 131 it is described as a 'suburb', which may tell us something about the growth of London in the last eighty years, but is even more revealing as an indication of social attitudes.

3. p. 73 *profitable devotions*. Religious connotations again, though the 'devotions' in question are those that Fleda pays to people like Mrs Gereth, and which her father assumes are undertaken purely out of self-interest.

4. p. 73 *the Rubicon*. When, in 49 BC, Julius Caesar crossed this river, the boundary between Italy and Cisalpine Gaul, he realized that he was committing himself to a civil war with the Roman senators who opposed him.

5. p. 74 *old Worcester*. Worcester has been known for its porcelain since 1751: however, the designs prior to 1783 are generally held to be superior, hence Mrs Gereth's insistence on the 'old'.

6. p. 74 *a tucked-up frock*. The combination of the often-trailing dresses of the period, and the filth of the streets which, as well as the usual mud, were also full of horse dung, made it essential to hitch up one's skirt before crossing the road.

7. p. 74 *a hansom*. A two-wheeled vehicle for public hire, with room inside for two passengers.

8. p. 76 *the Marble Arch*. Until recently this monument formed the actual entrance to the north-east corner of Hyde Park, whereas now it is separated from it by traffic lanes.

9. p. 76 *the Park*. In James's novels lovers often stroll together in Hyde Park (for example, Kate and Densher in *The Wings of the Dove*, Millicent and Hyacinth in *The Princess Casamassima*).

10. p. 76 *a kind of pearl-diving plunge*. A suggestive metaphor to describe Fleda's sexual feelings for Owen. In a similar vein, sexual feelings in *The Portrait of a Lady* (1881) are conveyed in images of the flight of birds.

11. p. 77 *the great Gardens*. Kensington Gardens, at the western end of Hyde Park.

12. p. 77 *the old red palace*. Kensington Palace.

13. p. 78 *Kensington Road*. At the south-west end of the park.

14. p. 78 *four-wheeler*. A much larger vehicle than the two-wheeled hansom, with room for four passengers.

CHAPTER VII

1. p. 80 *saloon*. Another word for a drawing-room.

2. p. 80 *Atlas*. In Greek mythology, he was the Titan (descendant of the primeval gods) who supported the globe of the heavens on his shoulders. He is normally depicted bending beneath the strain.

3. p. 80 *under his globe?* The end of this sentence in the New York edition actually reads: 'even as she herself stared at the cabinet and hunching up the back of Atlas under his globe?' which does not make sense. We have therefore adopted the wording of the 1897 edition, which does.

4. p. 81 *morceaux de musée*. Museum pieces.

5. p. 82 *the Maltese cross*. Properly speaking, a Maltese cross has four equal arms with splayed and indented ends, like the German Iron Cross.

6. p. 82 *the great Spanish period*. Malta was only directly under Spanish (Aragonese, to be precise) rule for a comparatively short period, from the late fifteenth century to 1530, when dominion over the island was granted to the Knights of St John (subsequently known as the Knights of Malta) in flight from Rhodes. Malta, due

to its position in the Mediterranean, has always been of great strategic importance, and in the singling out of the Maltese cross for special mention here we can see the combining of the military and religious allusions which permeate this novel.

7. p. 83 *Tottenham Court Road*. Probably a reference to Maple's (founded 1841), which until comparatively recently was not only a furniture store, but also provided a removal service. At the turn of the century it was an enormous firm, employing about 3,000 people.

8. p. 84 *myrmidons*. In Greek mythology, a race of people renowned for their ferocity and ruthlessness, followers of Achilles in the war against Troy. (See note to p. 30.)

9. p. 85 *Louis Seize*. Louis XVI of France (1754–93). French furniture of the period showed a return to more classical lines, after the rococo exuberance of the period of Louis XV. The fact that Louis XVI was guillotined during the French Revolution may also be intended to occur to the reader, as a hint of the disaster which will ultimately strike Mrs Gereth.

10. p. 87 *the revolution*. Another premonition of disaster.

11. p. 88 *the muffled chorus of the kitchen*. The chorus in an ancient Greek play would comment on the action and even, on occasion, warn the protagonists. This, though, is the bathetic chorus of servants' gossip.

CHAPTER VIII

1. p. 90 *the flyman*. Driver of a one-horse hired carriage.

2. p. 100 *a swinging screen of green baize*. It was common in large Victorian houses to mark the entrance to the servants' quarters with a door like this. Presumably Mrs Gereth finds the green baize unaesthetic.

3. p. 100 *Brompton*. A fashionable district of London, south-west of Knightsbridge, with many handsome stucco houses – but of a period much later than Poynton, of course, and hence fit only for Mrs Gereth's scorn.

CHAPTER IX

1. p. 104 *pensioned*. In the sense that Fleda is a dependent of Mrs Gereth.

CHAPTER XII

1. p. 121 *'marks'*. Hallmarks on silver or gold, or manufacturers' marks on porcelain, for instance.

2. p. 122 *the explorer leaping upon the strand*. James is fond of images of exploration and discovery. See, in particular, *The Golden Bowl* (1904).

3. p. 127 *Universal Provider*. The title William Whiteley gave to his department store, which started in 1863 as a small draper's shop, but which by the 1880s had become a vast emporium.

4. p. 127 *The Morning Post*. This newspaper, first published in 1772, was amalgamated in 1937 with the *Daily Telegraph*.

CHAPTER XIII

1. p. 131 *the bitter tree of knowledge*. Literally, the tree of knowledge of good and evil, of which Adam and Eve ate the forbidden fruit. (See Genesis 3.)

2. p. 131 *penny bazaars*. Cheap shops, some of which were the origin of modern chain stores like Woolworths or Marks and Spencer.

3. p. 132 *the spoils*. This seems to be the first use of the title word in the actual body of the text.

4. p. 132 *Marie Antoinette in the Conciergerie*. Marie Antoinette, wife of Louis XVI of France (see note to p. 85), was, like her husband, guillotined during the French Revolution. Before her execution she, who had always loved luxury and gaiety, was kept in a particularly gloomy cell in the Conciergerie of Paris.

5. p. 132 *times were altered and good things impossibly dear*. Has there ever been a time when would-be collectors have *not* uttered this cry?

6. p. 133 *Buddhistic contemplation*. Tradition has it that the Buddha only attained enlightenment after a long period of utterly immobile meditation under a bo-tree.

7. p. 133 *accomplishments*. The usual 'accomplishments' of ladies of the period were drawing, painting in water-colour, embroidery, singing, and piano playing. The really adventurous could always go in for pokerwork or seagrass weaving.

8. p. 133 *a big, brave, flowery square of ancient unfinished 'work'*. What Victorian ladies called their 'work' was always a piece of

decorative needlework which they could take up in idle moments, for example between receiving callers. As readers of Elizabeth Gaskell's *Cranford* (1851–3) will recall, no lady with any social pretensions would have been seen doing useful sewing such as darning stockings or hemming sheets.

9. p. 134 *'afternoon'*. Servants were allowed one free afternoon a week.

CHAPTER XIV

1. p. 137 *Raphael Road*. This name seems to have been invented by James (see note to p. 41).

2. p. 138 *slavey*. A familiar name for the maid-of-all-work, the lowliest type of servant – presumably Mr Vetch can afford no other.

3. p. 143 *Ain't*. This form, still correct in the 1890s, has since been superseded by 'aren't'.

4. p. 143 *'perpetrated'*. A much more sophisticated word than we – or Fleda – would have thought him capable of.

CHAPTER XV

1. p. 148 *A year before*. In fact, it cannot be much more than six months.

2. p. 149 *boa*. A fur or feather stole, very fashionable at this period.

3. p. 153 *'As if I were one of those bad women in a play?'* Fleda is probably thinking of characters like Marguerite Gautier, the heroine of *La Dame aux Camélias* (1852) by Dumas *fils*. Marguerite is a reformed courtesan who is in love with Armand Duval: however, she gives up her lover at the request of his father, who claims that the association is damaging to the young man's reputation and to his sister's chance of making a good marriage. Shortly after her renunciation, Marguerite dies tragically of consumption. Verdi's opera *La Traviata* (1853) is based upon this play.

CHAPTER XVI

1. p. 156 *diving with her into smelly cottages*. It would be Maggie's duty as a curate's wife to visit her husband's parishioners, especially if they were poor or ill.

2. p. 156 *the scandalous drains*. Drains (once it was realized that defective ones could cause disease) were a recurring scandal in late nineteenth-century England. Enteric fever and typhoid outbreaks were still common, and not only among the lower classes.

CHAPTER XVIII

1. p. 180 *whose name she now made simple and sweet*. i.e. calling him Owen rather than Mr Gereth.

2. p. 181 *a dread*. A feeling akin to the 'sacred terror' which Van, in *The Awkward Age*, evokes in women.

3. p. 183 *the Registrar*. An Act of 1836 enabled marriage in a Registry Office as an alternative to a church ceremony. Originally designed to provide for religious dissenters, a ceremony before the Registrar was also popular with couples who wished to marry without the delay of publishing banns in church.

4. p. 186 *one of the Fates*. The three Fates, in Greek mythology, were depicted as controlling the span of man's life. One of them spun the thread of life, another measured it out, and the third, Atropos, snipped it off.

CHAPTER XIX

1. p. 188 *shilling*. For a shilling (five pence in decimal currency) one could send a telegram of twenty words, exclusive of the addresses of sender and recipient. It was a very popular means of communication at this time, when telephones were still comparatively rare.

2. p. 190 *Euston*. Railway lines from Euston Station served the Midlands and the North-western region.

CHAPTER XX

1. p. 198 *like a pair of low atheists*. See note to p. 183. Note that marriage in a Registry Office was what Mrs Gereth had actually advocated for Fleda and Owen; however, where Mona is concerned, it becomes a subject for scorn.

CHAPTER XXI

1. p. 203 *fourth dimension*. There was much speculation in the last quarter of the nineteenth century as to the existence and nature

of a fourth dimension. 'Suppose our (essentially three-dimensional) matter to be the mere skin or boundary of an Unseen whose matter has four dimensions.' (Stewart and Tait, *The Unseen Universe*, 1878, quoted in OED).

2. p. 203 *suggestive*. In the sense of appealing to the imagination.

CHAPTER XXII

1. p. 207 *I care for* him. Fleda is not being quite straight here. She has already told Mrs Gereth, quite explicitly: 'He's enough in love with me for anything!' (p. 182).

2. p. 211 *the larger station*. James seems to be being deliberately vague about the geographical location of Poynton. By Underground, from West Kensington, one could reach any one of the main-line stations in under an hour.

3. p. 211 *the horrid cheap crossings by long sea*. These included not only the Newhaven–Dieppe route, but also sailings from London Bridge.

4. p. 212 *Look out!* Readers of Tolstoy's *Anna Karenina* (1874–6) will recognize parallels between Anna's experiences on her last fateful train journey, and Fleda's at Poynton station. But whereas Anna ends by throwing herself under a train, Fleda is saved from a fatal accident by the intervention of the station-master.

FOR THE BEST IN PAPERBACKS, LOOK FOR THE 🐧

In every corner of the world, on every subject under the sun, Penguin represents quality and variety – the very best in publishing today.

For complete information about books available from Penguin – including Puffins, Penguin Classics and Arkana – and how to order them, write to us at the appropriate address below. Please note that for copyright reasons the selection of books varies from country to country.

In the United Kingdom: Please write to *Dept E.P., Penguin Books Ltd, Harmondsworth, Middlesex, UB7 0DA.*

If you have any difficulty in obtaining a title, please send your order with the correct money, plus ten per cent for postage and packaging, to *PO Box No 11, West Drayton, Middlesex*

In the United States: Please write to *Dept BA, Penguin, 299 Murray Hill Parkway, East Rutherford, New Jersey 07073*

In Canada: Please write to *Penguin Books Canada Ltd, 2801 John Street, Markham, Ontario L3R 1B4*

In Australia: Please write to the *Marketing Department, Penguin Books Australia Ltd, P.O. Box 257, Ringwood, Victoria 3134*

In New Zealand: Please write to the *Marketing Department, Penguin Books (NZ) Ltd, Private Bag, Takapuna, Auckland 9*

In India: Please write to *Penguin Overseas Ltd, 706 Eros Apartments, 56 Nehru Place, New Delhi, 110019*

In the Netherlands: Please write to *Penguin Books Nederland B.V., Postbus 195, NL–1380AD Weesp*

In West Germany: Please write to *Penguin Books Ltd, Friedrichstrasse 10–12, D–6000 Frankfurt/Main 1*

In Spain: Please write to *Longman Penguin España, Calle San Nicolas 15, E–28013 Madrid*

In Italy: Please write to *Penguin Italia s.r.l., Via Como 4, I-20096 Pioltello (Milano)*

In France: Please write to *Penguin Books Ltd, 39 Rue de Montmorency, F-75003 Paris*

In Japan: Please write to *Longman Penguin Japan Co Ltd, Yamaguchi Building, 2–12–9 Kanda Jimbocho, Chiyoda-Ku, Tokyo 101*